THE **WEIGHT** LOSS **CLUB**

DEVAPRIYA ROY has degrees in English literature and performance studies from Presidency College, Calcutta, and Jawaharlal Nehru University, New Delhi, where she is pursuing a PhD on the *Natyashastra* (at least, that is what she says when asked what she does). Once upon a time, she was the Keo Karpin girl. Her first novel, *The Vague Woman's Handbook*, was published in 2011. She is currently working on *The Heat and Dust Project*, the story of a quirky journey through India on an extreme budget, along with her husband, Saurav Jha.

THE **WEIGHT** LOSS **CLUB**

*The Curious Experiments
of Nancy Housing Cooperative*

Devapriya Roy

RUPA

Published by
Rupa Publications India Pvt. Ltd 2013
7/16, Ansari Road, Daryaganj
New Delhi 110002

Sales centres:
Allahabad Bengaluru Chennai
Hyderabad Jaipur Kathmandu
Kolkata Mumbai

Copyright © Devapriya Roy 2013

This is a work of fiction. Names, characters, places and incidents are either the product of the author's imagination or are used fictitiously, and any resemblance to any actual persons, living or dead, events or locales is entirely coincidental.

All rights reserved.
No part of this publication may be reproduced, transmitted, or stored in a retrieval system, in any form or by any means, electronic, mechanical, photocopying, recording or otherwise, without the prior permission of the publisher.

ISBN: 978-81-291-2425-8

10 9 8 7 6 5 4 3 2 1

The moral right of the author has been asserted.

Typeset by Jojy Philip, New Delhi.

Printed at Thomson Press India Ltd, Faridabad.

This book is sold subject to the condition that it shall not, by way of trade or otherwise, be lent, resold, hired out, or otherwise circulated, without the publisher's prior consent, in any form of binding or cover other than that in which it is published.

*In memory of my grandmothers,
Archana Roy and Geeta Mukherjee.*

PROLOGUE

It wouldn't have been called Nancy Housing Cooperative (Society) but for the government clerk's mistake.

The promoter, Bishwajit Nandy, had wished to immortalize his family name in brick and mortar. But the government clerk, in his rush to attend a distant aunt's funeral, had typed 'c' instead of 'd'—and the five-building colony ended up with a strange American teenage detective's name. *Nancy*.

The accident of naming had its own consequences. Though in other respects quite ordinary—the four-storey buildings were cream and beige, the hedges dark green and dusty—there was a strange quality about Nancy Housing Cooperative, a kind of X factor, that set it above its station. It was no different really from Basanti Housing to its left or Silver Wings to its right or Bengal MLF across the road, but *somehow* Nancy tended to give people ideas, made them vaguely dissatisfied with things as they were.

That is how The Weight Loss Club was born.

Or, perhaps, it wasn't like that at all. Perhaps the houses were as everyday as their neighbours until the lady with the portable garden arrived.

But that was afterwards.

BOOK 1
NANCY HOUSING

CHAPTER 1

1.1

September in Calcutta is a delicious time, Mrs Das realized as she stood in the balcony of her flat in Nancy Housing Cooperative (Building A-1). Subtly delicious, like creamy sandesh flavoured with cinnamon and dusted with pistachios.

Usually, Mrs Das had no time whatsoever to think about seasons. They went past unremarked in her head, except for sounding reminders to buy new raincoats for the boys or put the sweaters and blankets outside on the terrace. The sun would climb higher and higher March onwards and then, come October, evenings would begin to fall in a sudden hush, abruptly. But Mrs Das would only be concerned about the effects of 'season change' on the boys' health. Heaven forbid that they should fall ill and miss school.

It was half-past ten in the morning; the boys were in school. Mrs Das had already cooked lunch. She had polished the kitchen counter until it gleamed. She had watered the plants, finished her bath, done the puja, shaken out her long hair to dry after towelling it methodically, folded the clothes. A hint of the new peppermint-flavoured detergent clung to her hands even after the clothes were put away in their correct places. And still it was only morning. Mrs Das wandered from room to room, urgently looking for something that might need her attention, soothe her anxieties. But everything was in order.

She marched into the balcony, the starchy ends of her sari

crackling, and stood in the sunlight, looking intently at the square green patch in front of the building.

She rummaged through her mind, checking every nook and cranny. There *must* be important things to do—there always were. She turned vaguely in the direction of the boys' room and finally made up her mind. She would take out the books from the boys' bookshelves and dust them. They weren't due for dusting yet—that was what she did on Friday mornings. But the worry about the maths marks was ticking in her head like an annoyingly loud clock; it was better that she tackled the books. Why keep for later what one can do now? After dusting, she could make some snacks for the tuition teacher in the evening. Not that she really needed to make snacks for the balding middle-aged man with the butterfly moustache, a slightly sorry-looking creature. Just tea and biscuits would suffice. But she might as well. He would praise her home-made samosas effusively, and that was always something. He might, in gratitude, spend some more time with her boys, going over their algebra with a greater sense of patience.

Then, in a swooping rush, more errands came rushing to her aid. She would have to call her husband and remind him to pay the telephone bill; and while she was at it, they could quickly discuss the gift for the anniversary invitation next week. She could nip out to Gariahat Market for an hour or so this evening, her budget fixed at Rs 300. Plus a card and flowers, of course; those she would buy on the day from the corner shop. The flowers were a posh touch she had picked up from a former school friend whose father had been in the army. Though Das often complained about their uselessness, Mrs Das insisted on a bouquet and a card every single time.

Mrs Monalisa Das stood in the balcony, mulling over her list of errands. With every task her lungs expanded slightly. Any list of errands had that effect on her, as though the capacity in her lungs to draw in oxygen had magically expanded somehow. Sometimes, when she couldn't sleep at night, she would switch on the table lamp, pick up the little blue notebook she kept handy on the bedside table next to her and start scribbling a list of unfinished tasks. Das would not even stir.

This reverie about her precious lists was, however, rudely interrupted when a loud voice floated in from one of the neighbouring flats. Mrs Das was no curtain-twitcher; but if people were shouting in her earshot, she couldn't shut her ears now, could she?

1.2

'Bahu,' shouted Maaji Sahai. 'How many times do I have to ask for one thing? Will you *please* warm the oil for my massage and save my seven preceding generations from hellfire?'

'Yes,' replied Meera meekly. She did not point out that Maaji Sahai had not asked for the oil even once today; and naturally she did not point out that, if they were anything like Maaji Sahai, there was *no way* her seven preceding generations would ever evade hellfire. She left aside the khichdi she was making for Tara's lunch and silently proceeded to pour the golden mustard oil carefully into a ceramic bowl.

'Do it correctly. Tighten the lid properly after you're done with it,' the mother-in-law instructed. Could this girl do *anything* to satisfaction, she wondered.

Wordlessly, Meera did as asked. She added in the correct order the different herbs from the jars purchased last week from the Baba Ramdev Ashram, conscious of the hawk-eye monitoring her movements. Though the kitchen was a good ten feet from the divan in the drawing room, Maaji Sahai's eyes were up to the task.

'Warm it the *right* way, Bahu. Use your head. Boil water in the pan. Take it off the stove. Then lower the bowl in the water. Carefully, carefully, care-ful-ly. Don't let any water get in. Not a drop. The herbs will not work properly then.'

Each instruction was muttered unhappily in crisp Angika-infused Hindi as Meera's hands fumbled. What had she, Maaji Sahai thought with acute bitterness, done to deserve this? *She* had fulfilled her daughter-in-lawly duties with enthusiasm and imagination, including the regulation production of boys—two of them—and one daughter in addition. What was the point of bringing an educated rural girl for Suresh—the balance she had deemed right—if the girl neither brought the smartness or alacrity that her graduation degree certificate (high second class) was supposed to have infused into the housework, nor the expected rural charm and conviviality into her relations with the rest of the family? The old woman scratched her thinning scalp and sighed deeply; almost on cue, her younger granddaughter began to cry in her pram.

Maaji Sahai softened a bit. Theoretically, she had an ideological problem with this second granddaughter. There was no reason why the baby should not have been a boy. One girl, one boy—classic combination. But what was to be done? Couldn't quarrel with fate. 'Now, now, Bahu, why are you dawdling?' she said. 'Take Chhoti inside. She's had enough sunning. Any more, and it'll darken her complexion. Feed her, then give her a bath.'

'Yes, Maaji,' Meera replied as she approached the divan, the gold stud in her nose gleaming in a chance sunbeam that bounced off her forehead.

'Why haven't you worn a bindi?' her mother-in-law immediately demanded. 'Don't you know it will bring ill luck to my son? When will you learn these things?'

Meera touched her forehead fleetingly. As she picked up the crying baby from the crib, her pink pallu fluttering outward in the breeze like a flag, she mumbled: 'I think it has fallen off, Maaji. I had put on a bindi in the morning.'

As Meera walked towards her bedroom, Maaji Sahai voiced her latest obsession, activating the third person oblique she often assumed when she was going to be especially brutal: 'I *hope* she watches her weight. After Chhoti's birth, she has become a pumpkin. Exactly like that Bengali girl next door. Such a bad influence that Apu is! Nowadays, it is *very* important to retain one's figure. My son isn't some aira-gaira fellow, he's a software engineer. What was the point of bringing an educated girl if she will grow fat?'

Every night, Maaji Sahai watched hungrily the good daughters-in-law on telly, their gracious manners and glowing skin, the jewellery they had certainly brought from their maike, their gorgeous whip-like figures, their navels glistening lotus-like on flat, shapely tummies as deluge after deluge of suffering assailed their lives. Why couldn't she have got one of those?

Maaji Sahai dragged herself up from the divan and staggered towards the kitchen for her mustard oil, which the thoughtless girl had not, after all, brought to her. 'See. This is *exactly* what I mean!' she muttered to herself. 'Her mind is always elsewhere.'

Inside the misery of her bedroom, while Chhoti sucked on her sore purple nipple, Meera's eyes prickled. The tears began to flow, streaking her brown cheeks with kohl. Maaji was in savage form today and she could not remember if she had put the masalas in the sabji in the right order. Maaji could always tell. Meera *knew* she had become plump, but it wasn't her fault, was it? She had not wanted a Caesarean, but complications had arisen. Hadn't she given up eating breakfast though she felt lightheaded at times? Why was the diet not working?

Meera sobbed into Chhoti's soft head. She was always trying to do things right, but was it her fault if there was this strange tiredness about her limbs, unresolved clods of tiredness that slowed her down and made her cry at every small thing? Even Suresh had noticed! That must mean she was looking hideous.

Chhoti tugged on her swollen nipple, and Meera winced. For a second, she wanted to push the baby away, bang her down on the bed and howl in rage. It had been three months and, though it was not her first time, she still hadn't become used to the pain of breast-feeding. And nobody, nobody cared about her discomfort—she would be considered a terrible mother if she even complained about breastfeeding. Though her rage simmered, she quashed the terrible, unmotherly feelings. Sometimes, she was afraid that Maaji Sahai even read the thoughts in her head and plotted out punishments accordingly.

The doorbell rang. At the same moment, Meera located her round red bindi inside the fat little palm Chhoti was waving in her face—a little secret between the two of them. Meera's anger dissolved and she smiled wanly.

Maaji Sahai's voice sounded imperiously from the drawing room: 'Meera! Meera! Are you deaf? Come here this instant. Abeer wants to borrow some sugar.'

1.3

This was exactly the kind of thing that Abeer Mukherjee, for the most part a mild twenty-one-year-old, disliked fervently about his family, this family he was visiting at the moment (where the old witch would cross-examine him closely) and, of course, about the entire bloody colony. This was precisely what he detested, this extra-social tendency to lend or borrow sugar from time to time. Or milk for tea, onions for fish curry. On one occasion, he had been despatched from Mrs Sahai's to Mrs Das's to the old fogey Ananda Bose and, finally, to Treeza Matthew's—who never had anything in her fridge anyway—over some tomato puree. His mother had promised each time it was the last.

'Namaste, Bhabhi,' Abeer said politely to Meera, the one human being in the colony he knew was bullied far more than he was. 'Tara must be in school.'

Meera nodded, a shy smile on her face, and went into the kitchen to fetch a bowl of sugar.

'Somebody came suddenly?' asked Maaji Sahai. She had been waiting to quiz him.

'Yes,' Abeer replied. He would have not volunteered more information had he not known about the old witch's persistence. 'An aunt of my father's.'

'Which one?' Maaji's eyebrows crinkled in deep thought. 'The one from Keyatala? Or the one who lives in Kenya?'

Abeer had no idea. 'Yes, yes,' he vaguely mumbled and looked at the walls.

Meera returned with the sugar. Abeer grabbed the bowl with both hands and escaped.

The Mukherjees lived a floor above the Sahais. To begin with, both families had been deeply suspicious of the other when they had moved in a couple of years ago—until the two most prejudiced members of either household had found common ground. In broken Hindi and broken Bengali, Mamoni Mukherjee (Abeer's grandmother) and Maaji Sahai had discussed their respective daughters-in-law when they met in the community hall downstairs. That had led to thaw and neighbourliness.

Abeer returned home to find his father's aunt—from either Keyatala or Kenya—sitting majestically on the sofa, her feet tucked under her immense posterior, her crisp green cotton sari billowing slightly under the double attack of the ceiling fan and the table fan. It gave her the appearance of a starched balloon. Usually, nobody was allowed to put their feet up on the sofa in his mother's presence, so Abeer grasped the power equation instantly.

His mother snatched the bowl from Abeer's hands and rushed into the kitchen to ensure that the maid commenced the making of tea immediately. His grandmother fluttered about getting this and that—locally baked biscuits, savouries, roasted cashew, badam burfis, things that she carefully stowed away in the steel almirah in her bedroom.

Though he had withheld this crucial piece of information from Maaji Sahai, Abeer knew exactly why this fat aunt with the three warts on her face and a large faux bun concealed under a hairnet was being treated in such a queenly manner today. Within the extended family—and by God, in their case it constituted a small European town—she was known as a successful matchmaker. And the general opinion was that Abeer's sister Aparajita needed to be matched off. Urgently.

There were several problems, though. Apu was twenty-nine, 5'7", seventy-eight kilos and wheatish—points that counted entirely in her disfavour. The only saving grace was that she was doing her PhD in botany and taught part-time at a nearby college. If, however, she managed to get a government job, the game would apparently change. As of now, however, she had appeared unsuccessfully for eight interviews for a permanent position.

Before he could slink off, the aunt began to cross-examine Abeer. 'Engineering, huh? No? What is this BCA? Bachelor of Computer Applications? Oh, I see. But what is that? Why this BCA? Didn't you get through an engineering college? No matter, no matter, studying computers anywhere is very good these days...'

As the tea tinkled in with three different kinds of pakoras, Abeer made his escape. He entered his bedroom and put *The Best of Eagles* on loop. He strummed an imaginary guitar for a while, jumping up and down vigorously. Then, as the drumming of 'Hotel California' rose, he sat down on his bed, exhausted, analysing the annoying pimples that refused to stop sprouting on his chin. Then he played with his phone, attempting to systematically drown memories of a certain lovely face in the sheer ennui of the day.

There was a strike in college over placements: the last batch had hardly got jobs; there was an economic slowdown, apparently. 'Not for the IITs!' Abeer told himself darkly. He hated the IITs, with their smug sense of importance and the smug books written about them. As though no other institute was worthy of a book. The couple of boys from his school who had gone on to IIT-KGP made it a point to organize get-togethers at the South City food court every fucking time they were in town, talking about their oh-so-cool robotics clubs and the Spring Fest. 'Fuck off!' Abeer shouted angrily at the IIT boys. They went. But the lovely face was persistent—in spite of his pimples and job prospects, she continued to pop into his mind relentlessly, the girl with the grey eyes and a dimple on her left cheek.

Was there no peace for a guy?

Abeer scrolled through his list of contacts. It was a weekday, so his best friend Deep—who now studied medicine—was unavailable. Only his classmates would be free to talk now, and they would insist he come and join the dharna. He decided on Facebook as the only possible escape from the wretched boredom of the day.

He got about a quarter of an hour of solace. But when he checked out the latest photographs of grey-eyes-and-dimple (through another friend's profile; she was not friends with him), it only depressed him further. It appeared that she was surrounded, at various lunches and brunches, by either hot guys from her posh New Alipore para or super-successful IIT-KGP dorks (including one of his former school chums). Bloody phonies. And look at other girls commenting deliriously on the pictures of the IIT boys, even the ugly ones! Suck-ups.

Abeer immersed himself in Mafia Wars trade-offs. Naturally, his mother barged in: 'Get your didi on the phone. Ask her to come home as soon as classes get over. No need for her to go to the lab today.' She popped out of the room, then popped back in, her face glistening with sweat from slaving over the stove. 'There's no need to tell her that Moni Mashi is here. She'll get all tense and make a bad impression. Afterwards, go to Hindustan Sweets and get the mishti doi and sandesh.'

Abeer made a face and dialled the number.

1.4

Aparajita Mukherjee was already in a 'share' auto, on her way home, when her brother called. 'About ten minutes away,' she told him. He outsourced the task of picking up the sweets to her as he was busy. 'Busy Facebooking,' Apu muttered to herself and unhappily resumed the conversation with her co-passenger—she had met a neighbour at the auto-stand near Ballygunge Bridge. It was Ananda Bose, He Who Must Be Avoided.

He was rambling on, unhindered by the interruption of the phone call.

'The evening caregiver announced that she needed two cups of black coffee at night, and a cup of tea exactly at six-thirty. Our maid Madhobi was horrified and immediately refused. But you know how valuable these night nurses are. Ma has been without one three days in a row! I stepped in. Last night, I set the alarm and got up twice to make coffee for the nurse.'

Apu made polite commiserating noises, willing the auto to reach their neighbourhood quickly. The auto-wallah, a thuggish fellow with long, curly hair, was speeding on the bridge, overtaking much larger vehicles willy-nilly from the left. Cringing slightly at every breach of good sense and traffic rule, Bose pattered on: 'No wonder I was feeling very tired in college. Intense headache, you know? So I excused myself from the HOD and decided to go home.'

Ananda Bose was the colony bore—this was widely accepted knowledge. He lived with his once-imperious and now-bedridden mother, the still-imperious maid Madhobi and a couple of nurses (never the same two) at A-5. Nobody knew how old he really was, but he called himself 'a confirmed bachelor' and had an avuncular manner that seemed to suggest early forties. He taught philosophy at a local college, a government job that luckily allowed him to flit back and forth between home and work as the nurse situation demanded, and was obsessed with his mother. The colony people mostly avoided him if they could do so politely. But there was something about his unbrushed beard and poetic eyes, his unfailing politeness and interest in the doings of one's family members that would also cause them to stop every now and then. 'Last three times I avoided him, so this time it's hello,' they would reason to themselves and engage in conversation with him. (It was mostly about his mother's bedsores.)

As they neared Nancy, Apu excused herself and jumped off at the crossing, pushing some coins into his palm. 'You pay my fare at the stop too.' She smiled. 'I have to buy some sweets,' and disappeared.

For someone that hefty, Aparajita was quite nimble, thought Bose. Immediately, he felt stricken. He shamefacedly wiped that horrid, cruel, uncharitable thought from his head immediately and apologized to Apu mentally. Several times.

For all his oldish-man ways, Ananda Bose was actually only thirty-six, though he appeared older to people. Beneath his bushy eyebrows, his black eyes could sometimes twinkle merrily in humour. Sometimes, lines of Bengali love poems filled him with an intense feeling of loss. But he had been typecast, even by himself, in such a terrible and final fashion that it just seemed as if, for those moments, it was someone else. Not him.

It was nearly twelve by the time Ananda Bose reached A-5, which had a hibiscus tree beside it. Red flowers were strewn on the grass, filling the noon with a strange kind of beauty. His batik jhola dangling on his left shoulder, his white kurta flapping in the mild breeze, he climbed the stairs to his second-floor flat with the exaggerated gait of an old man. But the moment he got to the door, his steps quickened inexplicably.

Something was wrong.

It took him a second to realize what it was. The door was open and banging reluctantly against the frame. That was distinctly odd. His was one of the few flats in Nancy that had left intact the original padlock system that the builders had provided; almost everyone else had shifted to the more modern doorknob locks; that way, every family member had their own set of keys.

On other days, when Ananda Bose got home, it usually took the nurse and the maid about five or six minutes to address the door. They could not easily agree on who should perform the tedious tasks of having to walk up to the door, lifting a hand to reach the bolt and then actually opening it; they would debate who had done it the last time, dispute each other's figures, and only after several minutes would the door open with a flourish of annoyance in Ananda's face.

The drawing room was empty when Ananda rushed in; there was no one in the kitchen; the spare room which was nurses' central was unoccupied. 'Madhobi!' he shouted, and then tried to remember the current day nurse's name. 'Nurse!' he hollered as compromise.

There was no answer.

Ananda ran to his mother's room, his knees wobbling in worry. What had happened?

The door was ajar. Inside, he saw, the invalid was sleeping peacefully, under her pink mosquito net. On the armchair by the bed, Treeza Matthew from next door was stationed, dressed in a shabby cotton gown that ended at her knees. She looked lost as usual.

1.5

Treeza Matthew lived in the flat opposite Ananda Bose's. Her schoolteacher husband had been able to afford this place only on a thirty-year loan that took in his entire salary. After that, he knew he had committed himself to teaching three batches of annoying middle-school students English language and literature for six evenings a week. He was hardly home.

Treeza's morning had been usual. John had left for school at six-fifteen. He had worn his usual Wednesday uniform: the white half-shirt slightly frayed at the collars, old grey trousers which had retained their cut, wax-polished shoes that glistened. Amidst the terrible mess of Treeza's house—mountains of unwashed clothes, mounds of books that had yet to find shelves, sheets that lay piled in the drawing room gathering dust and clothes Treeza had forgotten to bring in from the balcony last week being leached in the sun—amidst the madness of this, John maintained his attire with deliberate dignity. Every day, without fail, he washed his clothes in the evening, put them out to dry and ironed them in the morning. Some evenings, once or twice a week, if Treeza's necessary clothes had amounted to a huge pile in the bathroom, he would wash them too. Next morning, he would wake up half an hour earlier, iron them and keep them ready for her.

Every morning at six, though she slept fretfully through the night, Treeza's eyes would open. Old habits die hard. In the past she used to be a secretary at a girls' school in Central Calcutta. That was how Treeza and John had met again as adults. At a church fair for students. Their families were from the same neighbourhood; they'd known each other marginally all their lives; but it was wonderful when they'd re-met, as grown-ups, at that fete, surrounded by tables laid out with cakes and cucumber sandwiches and fried chicken on paper plates. It hadn't taken them long to begin a sparkling conversation between the raffles and the darts. It had been easy to fall in love in the middle of noisy schoolchildren and parents reluctantly forking out money to please their offspring and their teachers.

But no longer was Treeza a secretary and, after John left, eating a breakfast of cereals and cold milk, she would go back to bed. Till nine o' clock she would be sunk in heavy stupor, somewhere between sleep and wakefulness, where unhappy dreams would assail her relentlessly. Finally, when the sounds in the kitchen had reached a crescendo, Treeza would haul herself out of bed. The day would have become hot and sticky, her limbs would ache, her hair stick to the nape of her neck in sweat.

When John had realized that Treeza forgot to eat something on most days, he had hired a maid; when the maid complained that Treeza frequently forgot to open the door to her, he had given her a key. So, when Anwara would see Treeza shuffling out of the bedroom, she would serve her a cup of tea with toast. Sometimes, Treeza would forget to drink the tea and it would remain under her bed for days.

On this morning, though, Treeza was having one of her better days.

She had woken up earlier than usual and decided to take her bath immediately. On most days, the bath became a chore that stressed her out beyond measure—the hours would pass, and she would find it more and more difficult to stand under the shower. Often, John would come back to see her unbathed, her hair unbrushed, sitting in front of the TV, weeping copious tears over a sentimental Hindi film. But today, she had taken a bath as soon as she had woken up. It had seemed a purposeful day.

She'd switched on the TV to a cookery show. The gorgeous Nigella Lawson was teaching people how to become a domestic goddess, how to bake a really divine chocolate cake. Dimly, Treeza had remembered her mother and sisters in the kitchen, the house heady with the aroma of a cake browning in the oven, and the sense of joy it evoked. She had rushed to John's study and grabbed paper and a pen and begun to shakily jot down the recipe. Anwara had been surprised at the sudden alacrity and brought in tea and biscuits with less grumbling.

The entire morning had gone by watching cookery shows. The tidiness of the studio kitchens had filled Treeza with faintly remembered happiness. It had been long, she had told herself. Long. She would turn over a new leaf. Today, she would bake a cake in the afternoon. Today, when John returned, she would ask him about his students and laugh with him like she used to. She would brush her hair and tie it with a blue ribbon. It was their special inside joke. A bunch of blue ribbons had been John's first-ever present to Treeza. The idea had struck him when, a week after meeting her at the school fete, he'd heard the little kids in his school singing:

> *Oh dear, what can the matter be*
> *Dear, dear, what can the matter be*
> *Oh dear, what can the matter be*
> *Johnny's so long at the fair*
> *He's promised to buy me a bunch of blue ribbons*
> *He's promised to buy me a bunch of blue ribbons*
> *To tie up my bonny brown hair*

Treeza had got the reference immediately—and enjoyed it no end. Ever since, she had tied her hair with a scrap of blue ribbon when she was sorry or happy or wanted something from New Market.

At about noon, Treeza heard loud voices in the foyer just outside their flat. The voices soon migrated downstairs, below her balcony. She seemed to recognize familiar inflections. Was it Anwara? And who else? Soon, though, she was absorbed in a Bengali cookery show and the voices had gone further and further away. And then she heard a faint cry.

Something strange stirred in her head and, for the first time in days, Treeza slid on a pair of slippers—John's—and stepped out into the corridor, the TV filling her flat with the sounds of normalcy. In her faded blue cotton nightdress and her partly dry hair clinging to her earlobes, Treeza Matthew had gone next door to inspect. For the first time in months, she had remained focused on a matter long enough to inspect it.

The flat opposite theirs belonged to Ananda Bose and his mother. Treeza liked Ananda Bose: he always smiled shyly and then quickly looked away, he never asked questions. Treeza had never met his mother. But, following the noise, she had made her way into the Bose household.

All the flats in Nancy were designed on the same template. A drawing room with a tiny study on the right and a long corridor leading into two bedrooms inside. There seemed to be no one around today. Sunlight had sneaked in and drawn patterns on the dust in the bare drawing room. A slam outside had indicated to Treeza that the door to her flat had shut in the wind. She had remembered then that she had no keys. In fact, where had she kept her keys? She hadn't used them in a while.

There had been a mild moaning from one of the rooms. Treeza had ventured in and found an old lady under a pink mosquito net on a four-poster bed. 'Who's there?' the lady had snapped, punctuating her moans. 'Nurse?'

'No,' Treeza had replied in her accented Bengali, speaking to an outsider after almost a month. 'I live next door. Nobody is there in the house. I thought I heard you asking for something. So I came to ask.'

'Oh,' the lady had said. 'Good. Now get me some cold water. I'm dying of thirst. There is a blue bottle in the fridge that has my water in it. Boiled for twenty minutes, then cooled. Bring it.'

Half an hour later, when Ananda Bose returned, he found Treeza Matthew in the armchair, looking out of the window. His mother was sleeping.

After the immense relief that his mother was fine and the house still unrobbed, Ananda suddenly blushed, his fair features turning a delicate shade of burnt crimson. Treeza's blue cotton nightie ended well above her dimpled knees. That was far more female anatomy than he was accustomed to viewing in person.

Sandhya

Summertown, Oxfordshire.
Sandhya was in the garden when the postman slipped the packet through the door.

She had woken up earlier than usual that morning, with a strange pinch of anxiety she attributed to the impending journey. She had washed up, the warm water silky and comforting against her eyes, rubbed a pinch of sesame oil into her temples and walked down to the garden, where it was not yet light. The cold might still her scattered thoughts.

She was all packed for tomorrow. Sheila would come in and take charge of the ashram later today. There was hardly anything to worry about, this was a yearly affair; yet the sense of unease remained.

Sandhya walked among the shrubs, the distinctive smells of her beloved herbs mingling into a characteristic scent. Autumn brought with it that languor—apples and pears lying in abandon below trees, the elderberry clusters clinging tenaciously still.

When she would return from Rishikesh five months later, there would be an entirely different combination of fragrances to welcome her. Lavender blossoms would colour the eastern corner of the garden a delicate mauve. It was lucky that Sheila shared her love of gardening, tending to the plants with the same care she lavished on their students.

Sandhya seated herself on the platform that stood in the middle of the garden, folding her legs in padmasana, slipping into meditation with the ease with which the exhausted embrace sleep. Within a minute or so, a soft, warm swirl began to flow inside her and the chattering within quietened; the sharp cold air did not bother her any more.

After half an hour, as light fell gently, like honey thinned with milk, on the house and its surrounding greens, she allowed herself to arise from her meditation. The morning sounds of Summertown streamed into her ears. The earliest buses rumbled past; birds chirped; a few students who belonged to bicycling clubs zoomed down their route for the day, braving the cold with the smugness of those committed to fitness. The young staff of the café next door had started reporting to duty—one by one they came and rang the bell; blueberry muffins would be baked by the batch, coffee would be brewed in large cafetiéres for morning walkers who stopped for an early breakfast.

Sandhya opened her eyes, quickly regaining alertness as she discerned the shuffle of mail. She arose, stretched and went into the hall to look. Perhaps there was a bill or two she'd forgotten about?

The biggest envelope at the bottom immediately caught her attention—it was, in fact, a large brown packet. She often received books in post, but this was soft and saggy—a thick sheaf of paper, perhaps? She absently traced its outlines and then looked closely at the squiggles above the stamps.

The envelope was postmarked Calcutta.

CHAPTER 2

2.1

By the time Apu reached their building, a little breathless, beads of sweat had appeared on her brow and dotted her upper lip. Her mother was waiting downstairs, a large canvas bag dangling from her shoulder, wringing the end of her sari agitatedly.

The instant Abeer informed Mrs Mukherjee that Apu was already on the way home and was bringing the sweets herself, she had pounced on a plan. Now she stood, just outside their building in the shade of the laburnum tree, ready to ambush Apu the moment she arrived. She had even managed to buy some kachauris from the neighbourhood shop.

'What happened? Is everything all right?' Apu asked her mother.

'Nothing, nothing,' she replied and hustled Apu upstairs—to the Sahais' apartment—and rang the bell.

Meera came out in an excited fashion—it was most unlike her—and rushed Apu to her bedroom, while Mrs Mukherjee followed in their wake.

Chhoti was asleep in her crib. Apu's best blue chiffon was laid out on Meera's bed, and Meera, it seemed, had been rifling through her small collection of jewellery. Twinkly bits and bobs were scattered on the bedspread. Apu was confounded.

Mrs Mukherjee turned to Apu and finally addressed the mystery. 'You remember Moni Mashi? From Keyatala? The cousin of your father's maami? Arre baba, the one who made the match between Meelu's daughter and that Microsoft boy in California. We went to that wedding last year, mone nei? She knows that you are of marriageable age now—she has come to talk about possibilities. So I want you to enter the house looking nice. Meera will help you dress.'

Apu was so astounded—and so annoyed—that for a few seconds she was speechless. By then Meera, was flashing a couple of silver jhumkas in her face: 'Apu, the blue meena work will match nicely with the sari. Hain na, Mausi?' Mrs Mukherjee nodded happily. At least somebody was giving the matter the importance it deserved.

'What is all this nonsense, Ma?' Apu finally found her voice. 'Are you insane? And why do I have to impress Moni Mashi? *She's* not marrying me! Plus, I am returning from college. It's idiotic to be dressed up like this.'

'Humph,' Mrs Mukherjee retorted. 'Shut up and listen to what I am saying. No, no, no, don't even *try* to argue. Returning from college indeed! Keep all your logic elsewhere, Apu. I want you to make a very good impression when you enter the house. Period. Moni Mashi has a notebook in her head. With long lists of eligible bachelors. Meelu Di has told me she has a very mystical process of working. The moment she sees the girl in question, she uses her instincts to zero down on *three* eligible boys from that notebook. Mostly, it's with the first of the three that the match is finalized. So her first impression of you today is *very* critical. If you go wearing this horrible yellow salwar kurta, only bank clerks will come to her mind!'

'Oof, Ma,' Apu snapped, 'stop being so dramatic. Who cares about Moni Mashi and her precious list?'

'What do you know of these matters? Just listen to what I am saying. Get dressed, come home as though from college. Be very nice to her. Say you can cook if she asks. Okay?'

Meera nudged Apu in the exact manner she would use while prompting Tara to answer politely when strangers asked her her name. (Though Meera was almost four years younger, she was more like an elder sister to Apu—the reversal of roles was something both enjoyed.) Apu glowered, but said yes with ill grace.

Mrs Mukherjee looked at Meera beseechingly. 'You try to talk some sense into her.'

'Yes, yes, Mausi. I'll get her ready. You go home.' This was the most fun Meera had had in weeks. Her wretched day had lit up when Mrs Mukherjee had popped in, confiding the plan to her and Maaji.

Mrs Mukherjee snatched the sweets, savouries and mishti doi Apu was still clutching unhappily in her hands and made her way out.

'I told the lady I was going to get sweets,' she was heard elaborating as she left. Maaji Sahai twittered understandingly. In matrimonial matters of any sort, Maaji Sahai's cooperation could be enlisted very easily.

2.2

Meera looked at Apu and smiled. 'Abhi to bas shuruyat hai. And you're already getting agitated! Do you want a cup of tea?'

'Yes, please.' Apu sat down on the bed with a thud. 'I just can't believe the lengths to which Ma will go to get rid of me!'

Meera handed her a tube of face wash in response. 'Try this. It's lovely. Like ice-cream.' Maaji Sahai did not approve of Meera spending much on cosmetics—or any of the things she had labelled dainty-but-useless. 'Why face wash when you can use soap?' she had said to Meera. 'Even Deepika Padukone uses soap. She endorses it on TV, doesn't she?'

Meera hardly had any shopping expeditions of her own either— Maaji would tag along anytime Suresh took her and Tara to the mall. That meant they'd have to take the baby too. Maaji would eat her fill at the food court and then, in a drawn-out affair, trawl through several shops, exclaim loudly at the price tags, especially of fancy lingerie ('Thousand rupees for this bitty piece of lace?

Such lace lavished on underwear? Chhi!'), which belonged in the dainty-but-evil category. She had expressly forbidden them from buying *anything* at the mall. Even on sale. Though most of the stuff comprised things Meera wouldn't wear anyway: dresses, trousers, luscious skirts and shoes with six-inch heels. But, sometimes, a jewelled watch would catch her eye, or a bag—like the other day, when she had seen a large tote in soft red leather, which would have matched perfectly with the sari she had got on Holi—or little silver slippers with kitten heels (dainty-but-dangerous). Then there was the vast floor of goodies for the home—fine bedsheets and silk cushions, scented candles and beaded curtains (dainty-but-waste-of-money), hand blenders and sets of knives. Meera wasn't allowed to buy anything. Ever. Often, on these excursions, she felt like stabbing Maaji—the aforementioned knives would be nifty—or tripping her down the escalator.

It was only rarely that she managed to sneak out to the medicine shop nearby on her own, when Maaji wanted Crocin or Enteroquinol, and then she might smuggle in some bewitching cosmetic stuff discreetly. The strawberry face wash that she had handed Apu, with its companion fruit-peel face pack, was acquired on one such trip.

Apu sniffed the tube curiously and went to wash her face. At least she had shampooed yesterday.

In the kitchen, Meera chucked some tulsi leaves into the saucepan; then she grated in a dab of ginger. Apu was her most favourite person in the colony—in Calcutta, for that matter. Somewhat like a sister. Though her own sisters, back in their large small-town houses, led, at Apu's age, vastly different lives: sunning pickles, rolling papads and bringing up three children each, with great gusto. They were adepts at domestic life—effortlessly essaying things Meera had no energy at all to do and Apu, busy with her classes and her PhD, would not dream of doing.

A cloud of envy hovered around Meera, unsure of where to settle. Apu was her most favourite person in Calcutta, she repeated to herself. And it was not anything about *Apu* that she was jealous of anyway. Just that she would give anything, *anything*, to have all this excitement around her. Dressing up, being fussed at by her mother, meeting a few eligible boys, falling in love with one of them, maybe—and then, ah, then there would be a *wedding*. A honeymoon. In Meera's opinion, Bengali weddings were the *most* fun, though Punjabi celebrations were always being showcased on TV. In her case, none of these things had happened properly—not the romance of a courtship period, not the careful shopping over months and months from shops specializing in weddings, certainly not a honeymoon, tauba! 'A room is a room,' Meera had overheard Maaji muttering to a distant relative, 'whether in Shimla or at home. So what is the need to spend money and go to Shimla? Does money grow on trees or what? *I* never had a honeymoon!' As it is, after Meera's father had passed away—a month after her graduation results—her brother's wife had been desperate to get her married off in a hurry. Her father had harboured hopes for Meera, that she would do an MA, a BEd after that, become a teacher. But it had taken the brother exactly a month to find Suresh (what *great* good fortune!), and her sister-in-law exactly a day to assign Meera's childhood room in the attic to her two nephews. Now, every sign of her having occupied it once—her books, her postcards of Hrithik and Ameesha stuck on the walls, her college clothes and one or two antakshari prizes—were all gone.

Meera stirred the sugar, thinking how Apu had the luxury of being churlish about something she would do anything to borrow—the sparkly promise of new that was about to come. Her own life seemed to have finished all the fun part in a speedy trailer and had now settled into a deathly dull exposition. She sighed and looked at the plate of biscuits iced pink. Though meant for Tara, she had become addicted to them. Apu loved them too. She opened the tin, took out a few more and guiltily piled them on the plate. Thankfully, Maaji was sunning her toes and oiling her scalp; she wouldn't notice. She prepared to take the tray into her bedroom.

While Meera fussed in the kitchen, battling minor jealousies, Apu stood uncomfortably across from the dressing table. She had washed her face twice, drawn her mass of curly hair back carefully, though one or two tendrils escaped, and applied the fruit-peel face pack. She looked at her face, now stretched tight in the ghastly pink mask, critically. She impartially observed her round cheeks (too plump), her forehead (decently shaped but *always* oily!) and her nose (a very ordinary, very average, very mediocre nose—even a tad too slim for her face). Her eyes were nice, she decided, large and brown and warm. And Meera was always complimenting her eyebrows, shapely and naturally arched. But overall, Apu decided glumly, *even* if she lost weight, she would be plain. Homely. *And* with small breasts. This depressed her immediately. She usually never thought of her looks. She happily spent her days teaching, studying, laughing, pottering around, reading this and that, her desires blurry and unfocused. But the minute matrimonial matters came up, she became conscious of her looks and her weight and her bust. She looked away from her face and concentrated on the reflection of the room in the mirror.

In Apu's eyes, there was this grown-up quality about Meera's bedroom, a sense of intimacy that faintly embarrassed her. Her blouses and ample bras piled casually over her husband's shirts and undershirts, their toiletries heaped together in the bathroom, the sweet, milky smell of their new baby. To Apu, this was all slightly erotic. Things she did not know much about, things she was almost afraid of ever acquiring. The fertile ease of Meera's manner, a *mother*. She always felt a little shy about her lack of worldly knowledge—and by that she knew she meant sex, but even in her head, Apu was restrained in her choice of words— compared to Meera.

Apu willed the face pack to dry quickly. She was feeling hungry now, and impatient. She was also feeling a little drowsy. She just wanted to wash her face, wipe it dry, climb into the large bed next to Chhoti's bassinet and go to sleep, both of them watched over by Meera. She did not want to go home and participate in all the drama. It was sure to be ugly.

This was not the first time Apu's mother had tried to arrange a match for her, not by a long shot. The last four years had been a string of humiliations. Some funny episodes, but mostly humiliating.

She closed her eyes and her face disappeared from the mirror in a flash.

Moments later, Meera swished the curtains apart and entered with the tea.

2.3

'I have no words to thank you, Mrs Matthew,' Ananda Bose said again.

Treeza was now sitting on the lone grey worn-out sofa in Bose's drawing room while Bose moved around vaguely, from the fridge which stood in one corner of the room to a triangular table at the other end, straightening a magnet here or a calendar there. Then, rather formally, he went to the kitchen and got her a tall glass of water, spilling a little on the tray.

'Call me Treeza,' she said, observing everything with a slight smile. 'Mrs Matthew is so formal. You know me for more than a year now, Anand. No?'

Ananda Bose blushed slightly. There was something stirring in the way Treeza, with her expressive eyes and full pink lips (and those long fair legs), said *Anand*. His name sounded smarter somehow, as though it belonged to somebody else. Somebody smarter, more polished, perhaps a laptop-wielding, globe-trotting, *modern* academic. He unconsciously drew himself up to his full height and straightened his kurta.

Treeza, to her own great surprise, found herself sliding into her old self. Cute. That was how people would describe her usually. Pert. She had a way about her that men found charming. She would flirt good-naturedly with them, especially if they were older and Bengali, thus liable to be just a little wrong-footed. She was also kind. She knew instinctively—or at least used to know instinctively—how, through one or two swift easy steps, one could make a stranger feel more confident, surer of themselves, even slightly happier. People would linger around her office outside the principal's room just to chat with her for a moment or two. Durwans, teachers, ayahs, parents, even the students. Everyone used to adore Treeza.

But all that was in the past. In the last nine months or so, after she had resigned, she had descended into a place where Treeza was no longer Treeza, where life had changed into something else. A long, blank interlude edged with wispy trails of smoke.

In the presence of Bose, however, in these odd circumstances, she found she could slip back into her forgotten self. *He* would not judge her. So she could actually relax. Something she could not do these days in the company of most people, even her own mother and sisters. Only with John, or characters on TV.

In any case, Bose's was a chaotic household. Not one that would immediately fill her with guilt about the state of her own house. Bose was single, slightly awkward. There was no way he would make her feel small. She could afford to be herself. She could be kind to him.

Treeza drank the cold water as though it were something to be relished. Thanked him. Pushed her hair away from her forehead.

Ananda Bose settled into a plastic chair he had dragged in from another room. He attempted to make conversation.

'Treezaji,' he opened, 'I see your husband leaving very early in the mornings. His school probably starts at seven?'

'School starts at eight,' Treeza replied. 'But John has always been a morning person. He takes the six-fifteen bus, the 3C/2, from the bus stop here. It's almost empty early in the morning, and he likes to sit and flip through a book. He's in school by six-forty. Then he can catch up on his reading for the classes. He's a total workaholic,' she added fondly.

For the last many months, John had not read a book on these

bus rides. He just sat with his eyes closed, a dull pain throbbing at his temples. Wondering, before the hectic activity of the school day absorbed him fully, exactly what had gone wrong. When? Did the spirit of sorrow creep in through the window some careless night, while they were happy and snug in their warm bed, and then take over the whole house? Marking every inch with its stamp? Had they tempted fate by buying this house when, really, everybody knew they couldn't afford it?

But Treeza did not know this. Treeza, like the best of us in pain, had been obsessed with her own sorrows so much so that she could hardly see the changes that had come over John these last few months. But right now, in any case, Treeza was playing at normal families. Treeza was Mrs Matthew of A-5. Vivacious, funny, kind. John would have been delighted at her progress this morning.

'I was never a morning person, alas!' Bose replied reflectively. 'I hate waking up in the morning, you know? But what to do? These nurses have made my life miserable. I have to make coffee for the night nurse every morning at the crack of dawn.'

'Why can't she make it herself?'

'Our maid won't let her enter the kitchen. They don't get on. *She* will also not make the coffee. She has to catch up on her sleep. I have an old-fashioned hotpot in my room. I use that.'

'Hmm,' Treeza said, surprised at the feeling which welled up in her heart. One day, she decided, after she had cleaned up the house, she and John would invite Anand over for dinner. He needed a little company.

'But where *is* the nurse? And your maid?' Treeza asked.

'No idea.' Ananda Bose was mournful and resigned. 'When they turn up I shall definitely fire one of them.'

He didn't seem very threatening to Treeza.

'So Treezaji,' he continued, 'what shall we do about your house? You can stay here until Mr John returns, no problem…'

Treeza couldn't imagine doing that. John would return well after eight in the evening. And suddenly, in a quick, robust stroke, that familiar feeling of blankness began to dim her mind. It advanced in leaps and bounds and she sank deeper into the sofa.

'Do you want to call Mr John?'

Yes, yes, that was right, she should call John. He would know what should be done. Treeza tried to dispel the blankness. But she could not for the life of her remember John's number. 9830... she thought, no, no, 9038...? It was saved on her phone. She mumbled something about not wanting to bother John.

Ananada Bose was extremely solicitous. 'Does anybody else have a set of spare keys? I could go and get them for you then. Or, if you like, I can take a taxi to Mr John's school and...'

'No, no,' Treeza said. 'You are very kind.'

It came like a fever, this sweeping dullness of the mind. Suddenly, Treeza felt flushed under the skin, her palms and feet becoming hot, beginning to sweat. It was impossible for her to address anything. In any case, she knew there was no point, her mind and body would let her down sooner rather than later.

If Anand Bose noticed anything, he did not say. He excused himself for a moment, in his shy, awkward way, to go and check on his mother.

When he returned, Treeza was sitting up a little straighter. 'My maid,' she said, 'my maid Anwara...*she* has spare keys to the house.'

It was a breakthrough moment for Treeza—she had managed to separate this strand of useful information from the jangled mass of confusion raging through her. But she was now pale and biting the corners of her nails.

'Do you have her number?'

Treeza shook her head.

It was all in the phone. The phone was in her flat.

2.4

It was going to be a late lunch at the Mukherjee house. But Moni Mashi had been stuffing her face relentlessly ever since she arrived, so she was happy to sit back and simply catch up on gossip. The first round of tea was served with three kinds of pakoras: onion, mashed potato-and-chilly, and prawn. When Apu's mother said she was going to get sweets and mishti doi, Moni Mashi did mumble something to the tune of 'Don't bother with all these formalities…' but she had been pleased. On Mrs Mukherjee's return, the second round of tea had come, accompanying freshly fried kachauris and a homemade tamarind relish.

By quarter to two, it was almost time for Apu to return, and the whole house was filled with the delicious aroma of onions frying and cinnamon sputtering in oil. Moni Mashi was satisfied. Apu's mother had repeated several times that if only Moni Mashi had arrived with a day's warning, mutton korma would have been on the menu, along with her famous dhokar dalna. All she could manage at such short notice, she had reported apologetically, was chicken do-pyaza and pulao, with spicy fried fish on the side, thank God they had some pomfret slices at home. Moni Mashi had purred and arched her back, and the conversation had become more expansive.

'Arre baba, let your mutton korma be. Now, am I a guest? A stranger, that you are cooking up such a storm? Haan? It is the job of pishis and mashis to find out at what stage matrimonial matters are. It is, in fact, a tradition. My mother was also a renowned matchmaker before me. She only made successful marriages, mind you.'

'Of course, of course.' The grandmother nodded in agreement. Everybody knew about Moni's redoubtable mother, Chhobi.

Mrs Mukherjee, between the tempering and the stirring, stood behind her mother-in-law, tremulous with hope, ladle in hand, listening carefully to every word that issued from Moni Mashi's red-lipsticked mouth.

'Nowadays, one keeps hearing about Internet marriages.' The word Internet was uttered at a lower pitch, smoky with disgust.

'Yes, yes,' Mrs Mukherjee said, 'Abeer was also telling me—'

'I know,' Moni Mashi interjected, annoyed. 'All these young boys and girls like Abeer, always on the Internet, always on Facebook, always clicking and clacking. Nonsense! They think they know everything. Arre baba, are successful marriages so easy? Ask me. My own niece Lily's daughter joined shaadi.com with great fanfare. All this traditional matchmaking was apparently too downmarket for her—she had done an MBA, was earning a big salary. What happened? Two whole years on shaadi.com, then she got married to some Hindustani chap who was earning 16 lakhs a year at Reliance apparently, and after one year...' Moni Masi lowered her voice, and the Mukherjee women and their eavesdropping maid drew closer; Abeer, who was hovering around the door and dipping into the conversation without wanting to, was, in spite of himself, intrigued. 'Die-vorced!' Moni Mashi finished. 'God knows what happened. And they had spent so much on the wedding! Total die-vorce.'

Mrs Mukherjee drew back. Solicitous about the pain of others—poor Lily Di, what misfortunes!—she kept quiet. At least for now.

Moni Mashi continued: 'All this Internet business is highly risky. When a match comes through somebody known, say, me, you know that I have only your best interests at heart. No? Who is there to give guarantee for all these Internet grooms?' All three women nodded vigorously. 'Big risk all this Internet business is, very big risk.'

Abeer, nauseated, pretended to retch into the potted money plant on the windowsill and slunk back into his room. When the fuck would they serve lunch? These annoying retrograde women, always gossiping. Abeer had respect only for the modern sort of girl. Grey eyes—that was modern.

Before the hapless daughter-of-Lily was further discussed though, Apu made her grand be-sari-ed, bejewelled entrance. Mrs Mukherjee, however, would have been much happier if she had been smiling more radiantly. But at least, thanks to her quick thinking and Meera's dexterity, Apu was not wearing that ugly shade of yellow. The blue was becoming, as were the earrings and the glass bangles. Meera had even brushed her hair and spread it artfully over her shoulders, covering her slightly chubby arms. Mrs Mukherjee began to have a good feeling about things.

Sandhya

Summertown, Oxfordshire.
The house looked forlorn that morning.

Dr Sheila entered the hallway with her set of keys, and was immediately struck by this. The house felt forlorn. It was nothing new, though. Sheila would begin to feel the spirit of the house drooping, dimming, dwindling, degree by degree, the day Sandhya started packing for the annual journey to India. And on the day she came to formally take charge, the house would somehow feel drier, barer, slightly awkward, as though the walls and furniture had been stretched out, pulled apart, and then assembled all wrong. It was eerie. She only hoped that someday she would live in a place that reflected her soul as clearly as this house reflected Sandhya's.

Dr Sheila was very tall, with broad shoulders and waves of blonde hair flying about. Perhaps her general air made her seem a little bumbling, all hands and legs. She wasn't bumbling, really—she was a superb surgeon—but she liked being boisterous and free with her limbs. She consciously remembered her childhood and tried to approximate the unselfconsciousness of that time.

She entered the parlour, dumped her bags on the sofa and quickly re-crossed the hall to the breakfast room on the other side.

A few of the students chose to stay back every year to say goodbye to Sandhya. Many would clamour to take her to Heathrow, but Sandhya would have none of that. She would take the coach from Oxford, insisting on travelling alone. In the days she lived in London, Sheila would come to meet her at the airport on her return in March, but during the onward journey, Sandhya liked to be alone.

The breakfast room hummed with the voices of the five students who'd stayed back, though the season of classes was over. After their morning meditation sessions, they were alert and bright-eyed, and often hungry. Though most of them maintained the rule of silence while eating, after they'd finished, they'd drink their tea together and exchange notes. The room would hum with their voices.

Sandhya encouraged this camaraderie. Frequently, she joined them in the buttercream-yellow breakfast room with its white curtains and rustic furniture, and the morning conversations would stretch till noon. In summer, the large windows would be left open and sunlight would stream in, bouncing off the Cotswold stone, mingling with the glow of their voices. Sandhya was an unorthodox teacher. Come afternoon, though, each student would have to put in three hours for the communal work of the ashram—in the garden, assisting the gardener, in the kitchen, and then there was the unenviable job of cleaning.

'Hello, Dr Sheila,' they all chimed, their different voices merging pleasantly when they saw Sheila.

'Hello, hello,' She replied, pouring herself a glass of freshly squeezed orange juice from the jug. 'Where is…?'

'We haven't seen Mataji all morning,' Chloe said immediately.

Sheila was surprised. That was almost never the case. She checked in the garden, the conservatory, the orangerie, the library. Then she went upstairs to Sandhya's quarters, a modest suite of rooms separated from the rest of the house by a door and a passage.

Sandhya's door was almost never latched, but it was an unwritten rule that nobody would disturb her unless it was something urgent. Sheila pushed open the door and entered the passage on soft feet. Almost immediately, she could see the white of Sandhya's sari by the window in her study. She paused.

Sandhya stood silent, looking at the cherry tree in the corner of the garden. It seemed she were in a painting that the artist had left incomplete. She was still, her entire body wrapped in a tight ball of silence. Sheila drew back, wondering if she should interrupt at all.

CHAPTER 3

3.1

Mrs Monalisa Das was the mother of two boys, the twin-light of her eyes, the double-staff of her (future) blind old-age. They were good boys, Class 9 and Class 7, solid. Not the best, of course, but they could be. It was simply because they did not try hard enough, they did not think about the future enough.

Mrs Das would be thinking of them, and their futures, and trying, on their behalf and hers, all the time. While she was doing her chores, while she was brushing her hair, while she was sleeping at night, next to Das. She would be conspiring to see if she could motivate them to greater heights. Or, failing that, cajole, push, punish, pray to her myriad gods.

Sometimes, all the plotting exhausted her; less frequently, it made her feel guilty. They were good boys, they plodded along in their fashion. How much could one do as a parent anyway? How much could *she* do? The times had become difficult—so much competition, so much Nepotism-by-the-Rich. Mrs Das would find herself sighing. No chance at all for the ones of average merit, like her boys. But then the proportion of merit was not their fault, per se. Overcome with guilt, for a week or so she would cook her heart out, feed them their favourite dishes, and console herself in a tired way for producing them the way they were. It was all destined, she would inform herself bitterly. Of course Bablu would do badly in his physics exam; naturally Gublu's grammar was eccentric—her husband was not an extraordinary man, after all.

Soon afterwards, though, would come an occasion for her to go to their school. Fees or something. And then she would meet the school-gate moms. The cycle would start all over again.

The school-gate moms were a particular breed of mutant momzillas. In America these were recognized as a social category: the soccer moms. Bengal had not come up with any specific term, but that was perhaps because one didn't need a name for a group as large as eighty per cent of all Bengali moms. In their cotton saris and dusty flat chappals, the school-gate moms spent the greater parts of their day outside the school gate, assembled in little groups in the high-ceilinged waiting room the school administration had kindly provided, or, in the pleasant winter months, on the grounds of Presidency College close by. Every other day, they might nip out for errands, finish a bout of grocery shopping or visit a tailor nearby for some blouses and kurtas. But errands notwithstanding, the women essentially spent their day waiting together for the school-day to get over. They chatted, gossiped, forged rivalries. Over the years, they had organized their lives in such a fashion that everything revolved around the school. It was a famous government school, an old school. Every year it produced state toppers, every year it produced joint-entrance rank-holders. It was such good fortune that their boys studied there.

Most of the school-gate moms lived far away, some in the suburban small towns surrounding the city and connected by suburban trains that were desperately crowded in the mornings and evenings when the mothers-and-sons alighted. The mothers would wake up around five (as did Mrs Das), cook breakfast, tiffin, lunch, and then accompany boys—even boys in their late teens who were old enough to travel alone—to school. They managed their lives to suit the regimen of academic polishing that was inflicted on their sons. It was their day job and their hobby. It was often their religion. Their husbands were left to fend for themselves. The husbands probably did not mind.

The school-gate moms were also very cliquey. They managed the best tuition teachers and the best 'suggestions' for board exams through an elaborate network governed by grapevine and jealousy. It was all very complex.

The moment the last bell rang, signalling the end of school, these mothers would experience a collective frisson. In a few moments the boys would arrive; immediately, the mothers would begin examining their bags, pulling out notebooks and answer scripts if they'd been returned, books where new chapters had been underlined, tiffin boxes to check if everything had been eaten. They marked each day with little reminders: today the history marks will be announced; Mrs Bose will complete the Bengali syllabus today and give suggestions; today is the physical geography exam: the blank maps of the world must be located with cities correctly. Paris, London, Berlin, New York—the mothers learnt their positions with the sons. One day, their boys would be heroes in these grand old cities, they would be heroic engineers and doctors.

It was a fine art, this remembering and agonizing, this sort of love.

Over packed lunch, the boys would have to go over their performances and those of others. Most notably, they had to recite the honours that had been bestowed upon the First Boy and the Second Boy, the minor gods in each form. Sometimes, other fights were brought up, and mothers would eagerly take custody of cudgels, bury or cherish hatchets depending on their hormones and ambitions. Naturally, there were mothers who were best friends, especially if their boys were not in competition in the same class. These best friends would also take sides. It was intense and it was fun.

Then, as afternoon waned, mothers-and-sons would leave the school premises and board buses to different tuitions. Durjoti Dutta was the last word in chemistry for higher secondary; B. Bagchi could predict half the maths question paper in the board exams. From Baguiati to Sinthir More, these mothers-and-sons would brave the rains and the Calcutta traffic that congealed quickly on hot, tarred streets. In the buses, the mothers would hastily find seats for the boys. They would stand, but the boys must sit. A healthy snack would be handed, and a book. They were to read and eat. The mothers would look satisfactorily at the arrangement, wiping the sweat on their brow with square pieces of towels they carried instead of handkerchiefs—the journey was long, they would get a seat eventually.

Every single time Mrs Das went to school and encountered the school-gate moms—as she had done the morning before—all her fears cascaded into an exquisitely drawn-out panic. She gave in to her obsessions with great relief. She began to plot and plan and work hard at the boys' future, against the grain of destiny or merit or any of that nonsense. Hard work is destiny, she would tell her boys. What was that English saying? Merit is one per cent inspiration and ninty-nine per cent perspiration. Was it merit or success? Never mind, she would tell them it was merit—and that was that.

3.2

Between two and three o'clock in the afternoon, Mrs Das was in a state of pleasurable agitation, getting everything in order for the rest of the day to progress smoothly. The table was set. The food was neatly apportioned in microwave-safe glass bowls with matching covers. While the boys would shower, Mrs Das would heat up everything. The microwave had revolutionized her life. There was a jug of sweet lemonade spiked gently with salt cooling in the fridge. The boys would come home by quarter to three if the traffic was manageable, and after lunch and thirty minutes of TV (during which time she would constantly interrupt with questions, as she went through their bags) the tuition teacher would arrive.

But it was early yet.

Anwara, the maid, was in the kitchen, doing the dishes. Unlike her very uncertain relationship with Treeza Memsaab, Anwara got along very well with Monalisa Das.

Mrs Das's house was perfectly kept; her boys were brought up well; her husband may not be priority number one in the scheme of things, but his needs were tended to perfectly. Anwara approved. Mrs Das's homemade samosas were crisp and golden. Mrs Das's bathrooms were clean and fragrant, her drawing room cosy with red curtains and matching rugs. This was how one was supposed to live when God had been kind and given one a nice house. Not like Treeza Memsaab, tauba tauba! Was that any way to carry on? Anwara admired Mrs Das's style and copied her decorations in her tiny house, which too was spotless and curtained. Mrs Das was generous in some ways; she would give away old bedsheets and spare lengths of curtain cloth, old notebooks for Anwara's school-going kids, and clothes the boys had outgrown.

To allay her tension—Bablu's maths marks were due—Mrs Das got Anwara to make some tea. It was not the time for tea, but her nerves were on the edge. Yesterday, Mrs Ghoshal, ringleader of the school-gate moms, had announced that unless one did well in maths consistently, right from Class 9, the school would not consider giving them science in Class 11 and 12. Higher Secondary maths was so tough, the school could not have boys failing. And, of course, without science, one's career was as good as finished. It was all right for Mrs Ghoshal. Her son took tuitions from the school maths teacher, who was, as luck would have it, their tenant—it was well-known in that circle, though Mrs Ghoshal would neither admit to it nor share the contact details.

Mrs Das downed three samosas one after the other. Bablu was very scared of maths.

Anwara, sitting on the floor and drinking her glass of tea, was grateful for the samosas. She had had a long day and was feeling lightheaded. The fight with the nurse had rattled her, but Madhobi was an old friend. She was the one who had introduced Anwara to the colony. She would have had to take her side and shout alongside.

Anwara took little bites from the golden triangle, the pastry melting in her mouth, and chattered.

'Bechara Bose Babu. These ayahs and nurses will rob him blind but he will neither notice anything nor believe Madhobi Didi when she reports. His mother's room is like a treasure chest, full of nice things. Blue-and-white cups and plates from Vilayat, hand-embroidered bedsheets and tablecloths in fine cotton, even jewellery. Madhobi Didi keeps an eye on everything. As she well should—she's practically a family member. These ayahs are always on the lookout for things to steal. Half the cupboard is empty now...'

Mrs Das sipped her tea, one eye on the clock. 'Achha, is that so?' she asked, grateful for the distraction. Poor Ananda Bose. Everybody was acquainted with the bare bones of his problems.

'If Madhobi Didi tries to report all this stealing, Bose Babu will either just wave her away or get furious and say that she is doing politics, conspiring to get rid of the ayahs. He will accuse her of trying to drive him crazy. Poor Madhobi Didi. Today, she decided ispaar ya uspaar. She knew the ayah had stolen the sky-blue teapot—she had herself kept it outside last night—and followed her outside the flat and demanded she open the bag. What drama!'

'So did they find anything in the bag?'

'Not the sky-blue teapot—God know where she's hidden it, for it's sure as hell not in the old lady's room—but a small silver photo frame. The ayah tried to claim it was hers, but luckily there was a photo of Bose Babu as a baby in it. So, finally, after all that she had to suffer, Madhobi Didi was vindicated.'

Mrs Das finished the tea in one long slurp. 'Have lunch here today,' she told Anwara. 'In the afternoon you can help me clean the kitchen.'

Anwara agreed with alacrity. She loved opportunities to keep away in the afternoon from the nagging of her mean mother-in-law and earn a little extra. Half the extra cash would have to go to the mother-in-law for watching the kids. But even so.

3.3

The Mukherjees were lunching with their honoured guest, although Mrs Mukherjee, in spite of Moni Mashi's admonitions, had refused to join them and was busy supervising. The fish had to be fried just before serving for it to be deliciously crisp.

Moni Mashi was talking expansively about her success rate in matrimonial affairs and dropping broad hints about the eligible boys she could command at the click of her fingers.

Apu was most uncomfortable. And it was not just the tactless talk. Sweating profusely inside her blouse—damn the georgette—with hairpins digging into her scalp, she concentrated on her plate. She was so hungry she could eat a house. The tea and biscuits had merely whetted her appetite, breakfast had been half a day ago. In any case, stress made her awfully hungry.

Abeer, sitting next to Apu, could not believe the quality of conversation. Joining the dharna would have been far better. He would have liked to take his chicken and pulao and escape to the bedroom, where he could eat in peace while watching a movie or episodes of *Dexter*, but no. His mother insisted he sit at the table and answer dumb and positively prying questions politely. Anyway, he had already made a plan with Deep—he'd escape to Deep's college in the afternoon, and then a bunch of them would go and catch a movie somewhere. Perhaps a slightly wicked one at Roxy. Abeer out, he told himself. Matter of moments.

'When do you finish your PhD?' Moni Mashi asked Apu, after listing the virtues of some boy or the other. She was not supplying any specifics as yet.

'Another couple of years,' Apu replied. 'I'm running experiments and analysing the data at the moment. No results yet.' She smiled.

'Hmmm,' said Moni Mashi, 'let's see about that. If the boy is abroad, shona, then the PhD will have to go. There is a nice boy I know. Very good family…'

Mrs Mukherjee felt a whoop of joy. Finally, details!

Apu's eyes widened. There was no way she would let the PhD go down the drain. She began to say something, but her mother, realizing the drift, immediately swooped in.

'Have some more of the do-pyaza, Moni Di. Do you not like it? Another slice of fish? There. What about you Apu? Some pulao?'

Forced into a corner, Apu acceded to the pulao. She asked for a piece of chicken.

But immediately Moni Mashi stretched out a hand atop Apu's plate. In a grave voice she commanded: 'No more pulao. No chicken. No, NO.' She looked at Apu and said sternly, 'Shona, for the boy in Chicago, you *must* lose ten kilos. At least eight. And it has to start from today, from now. It is a matter of my prestige. I have given my word to your grandmother. I cannot bring an ordinary match. I have also given my word to the boy's grandmother. But extraordinary boys—especially a tall one who will be matching with you—have extraordinary standards. How many tall boys in our Bengal? No? The clock has begun ticking. He will come from Chicago in March, and you have to meet him then. Eight kilos at least. And it's a done deal. If all goes well, there can be an engagement in March itself.'

Even the grandmother was slightly stricken at this speech—there was something obscene about it. A silence descended on the table, though Moni Mashi continued to pick out flecks of flesh tidily from the bones. She finished the pulao, relishing each mouthful, satisfied at the apparent tough love she has doled out.

Apu's face was crimson. Her brother hoped to heaven it was fury and not embarrassment.

'Moni Di, you are absolutely right. I have been telling Apu to join a gym or something for the last six months. To at least go for walks. Our colony has a nice pathway around it, perfect for morning and evening walks. Now look here, Apu, listen to what your mashi is saying. You *must* listen to her. She has only your best interests at heart. I am so happy you have spoken your mind Moni Di, that is what one's own must do. No hiding behind sweet words, truth is best. Come, come, Moni Di, this way. Wash your hands. We'll have dessert afterwards. The doi and mishti of our para is, even if I say so myself, extremely good.'

The chirping somewhat diffused the stuffiness that had gathered in the room. The grandmother poured some cold water for Moni Mashi, who pushed back her chair with a loud screech and complained good-naturedly that she had eaten so much that she would have to be lifted by a crane. She followed Mrs Mukherjee to the washroom.

Abeer observed tears rolling down his sister's eyes. He was a little embarrassed himself. He shuffled out feeling awful.

3.4

It was a quarter to two. Monalisa Das was pacing in the drawing room when she heard footsteps outside. She opened the door, her heart pounding. She really hoped Bablu's maths marks were good. Eighty per cent at least. Otherwise it was all over. Everything.

But at the door was Ananda Bose. Mrs Das blinked. What was the man doing here?

Bose beamed. He was very polite really. And quite tall. He seemed to be towering over Mrs Das like a benign giant.

'Namashkar, Mrs Das. How are you? I'm so very sorry to disturb you at this odd hour. But I believe you have a maid called Anwara? The security guards informed me, though they were not entirely sure. Could you give me her phone number?'

Mrs Das was gobsmacked at this speech. For a rare nanosecond, she lost sight of Bablu's future.

Anwara had been eavesdropping from the kitchen and bounded out. 'This is Anwara,' Mrs Das muttered. 'Is there a problem?'

'Bose Babu,' Anwara began to speak at a loud pitch without any prompting, 'Madhobi Didi is absolutely right. She has been right all along. The nurse was actually truly…'

Ananda Bose seemed not to follow or even hear any of that. 'Do you work at Treezaji's house?' he asked.

'Yes, yes,' Anwara replied, stopping her story, unsure about this line of questioning.

Bose began to explain the entire matter of Treeza's door, her kindness and his subsequent gratitude in a long-winded way. Mrs Das invited him inside. He promised to come another time. Anwara in tow, he left for their building. Since Anwara carried Treeza's duplicate key tied at the corner of her dupatta, the matter was resolved quite simply, though Ananda Bose was of the opinion that something about all this had made Treeza quite ill. He had settled her on the sofa as he came in search of Anwara. He wondered if she might need any medicine. Thank God he'd found Anwara—she could take care of Treeza. He had had enough drama for a month!

Amidst the melee, quiet as mice, the two boys entered their home. Bablu's face seemed ashen, his mother immediately noted. Her face lost colour rapidly too.

Sandhya

Summertown, Oxfordshire.

'Sheila darling,' Sandhya said, turning from the window, 'Sometimes I wish I had not given up drinking.'

Dr Sheila was slightly relieved. If Sandhya could joke about it, the drink-worthy thing could not be very serious. Had they miscalculated their taxes? This year they'd done it themselves. The ashram couldn't really afford an accountant if they were to run the yoga schools in the Cotswold villages.

She was not surprised, of course, how quickly Sandhya had sensed her presence ('Mataji really has eyes behind her head,' Mike and Maya had been discussing the other day); Sheila was no longer taken aback by these things. She'd known Sandhya's spooky insights for a long time. She took these as a matter of course, much as Dr Watson with Holmes. Funnily enough, this comment never failed to elicit a full-belly laugh from Sandhya. Holmes! She had told Sheila about long afternoons on their Caribbean island, when she would read Sir Arthur Conan Doyle's books in a gloomy library, rain pelting on the sloping roofs.

'So, in the absence of stiff Scotch, we'll have to sit with a cup of tea I guess.' Sandhya smiled, pulling up a chair. 'Lame though it sounds, it'll work. The kettle is on. Will you do the honours? I have much to tell you.'

'You haven't been down this morning at all?' Sheila asked, tinkering with the tea things that were kept on a small table in a corner of the room.

'Oh, no. I'd been down in the garden at dawn, and then there was a bit of a surprise in the post. After that, I've been up here. Contemplating. I fixed myself some breakfast.'

Sheila handed Sandhya a mug. 'I'm peckish,' she said, nibbling on an almond square left on a plate along with the tea things. Sheila doused her lavender drink with honey and sat down on the other side of the table.

Sandhya slid a thick sheaf of papers across the table.

'What is all this?' Sheila fumbled for her glasses; they were slung around her neck as usual. 'Looks like something from a bank.'

'Close enough. It's from a lawyer's office. In Calcutta. The letter on top sort of summarizes everything.'

Sheila read it in silence, looking more and more surprised as her eyes crept downward. 'I don't understand this,' she said finally. 'Who are these people?'

'Long story,' said Sandhya.

BOOK 2
TWO WEEKS LATER

CHAPTER 4

MONDAY

4.1

The city was overcast. Late-monsoon turbulences had originated in the Bay of Bengal a couple of days ago. Ever since, the sky seemed to be sporting a woolly grey uniform and bouts of torrential rain flooded the streets. Sheet lightning flashed now and then. Abeer sat in class glumly and looked out of the window.

Their college was an ugly specimen of global modern architecture. All steel and glass and concrete and marble. Its tiled courtyard was bordered by a manicured hedge—that was about the only shot of green. The look was supposed to be impressive, but Abeer found it clinical. Pointless. A pathetic attempt to mask the institute's lack of pedigree with a glamorous newness. He'd much rather take the desultory unkempt feel of Jadavpur University—*far* cooler—or the old-world charm of Presidency College, with its clock tower and cavernous corridors. Instead, he was stuck with the high points of a glossy brochure: air-conditioned classrooms (that were either mind-numbingly cold or just warm and airless like a breadbox), a snazzy conference room (which, nevertheless, failed to attract very many companies on placement day) and a digital notice board (that was far more annoying than a regular notice board, as one would have to wait moronically in front of it for a quarter of an hour every day, only to check if anything relevant to them was flashed upon it).

Abeer was feeling rather bitter. Ever since he found out earlier today that Mandakini Mandal, the girl with the grey eyes and chin dimple, would probably not be coming in to college today. Being in love was tough. Especially if you had no real connection to the one you loved, no source of authentic news, no bridges to her windows, as it were, and had to depend upon the general grapevine. It was a very difficult sensation to live with, like a constant stomach ache. Except it was more in the chest area. The word heartache was, however, not quite accurate. It was more like a lung dysfunction—you just didn't breathe right. Couldn't breathe right.

Classes had resumed last week after the dharna petered out. The principal had issued a circular (on the digital notice board) that all protesting students would be suspended forthwith—and therefore fail the semester—if they did not resume classes immediately. It had the desired effect.

Abeer sat in a corner at the back of the classroom. Next to his pal Aditya Jaiswal, or AJ, who was busy reading a comic.

The professor pattered on about psychology in the workplace. It was one of those insanely boring courses that nobody took seriously but which one would have to eventually pass. On a regular day, Abeer wouldn't have attended it for a thousand bucks. But rumour had it that attendance at *all* lectures would now be monitored strictly, even in these dumb pass courses. You wouldn't be allowed to take the finals if you didn't have seventy-five per cent attendance.

'See, AJ, this is exactly what happens when you do a dharna without any real agenda,' Abeer had remarked to Aditya earlier. 'You don't achieve anything concrete. And then, suddenly, because of your over-smartness, out of nowhere *attendance* becomes an issue. The administration has to get back at us one way or the other. So now people can't bunk idiotic lectures any more. What a waste of time!'

'It sucks,' AJ had agreed sadly. Then he'd asked, 'Gum?' When Abeer said no, annoyed that his friend did not pay more attention to his theory, AJ returned to his comic.

Abeer was in a bad mood a lot these days. For one, things at home were in high-drama mode. On the best of days, home could be intensely trying. And now, given how stressful the situation was, with his mother and sister locked in an ugly war, his life was *way* miserable. For another, there was the bout of flu affecting Calcutta. Unless she came to college, there was naught that he could do.

The psychology lab was on the fifth floor. (Another instance of the pretentiousness of their institute: there were no classrooms, only *labs*. They even had a literature lab. Lame.) From where he sat in the corner, he could see well beyond the compound wall. There were rows of old houses on either side—genteel single-storeyed and occasional double-storeyed buildings in matching minuscule plots and faded greens and pinks and yellows, houses that somehow gave the impression they had been designed by the same architect and now occupied a strange spot in the space-time continuum, as though they had been clean forgotten. As though nobody had come to visit their inhabitants in yonks. That was Abeer's second quibble with their institute's architecture. The whole steel-and-glass look *might* have worked if they were in the techno-hub of Sector V in Salt Lake or Rajarhat, or even if they were in the central business district of the city. Instead, here they were, in the middle of what was a former refugee colony in Tollygunge (where the average age of residents was seventy), sporting this monstrous sore-thumb look.

It was raining in a vague, haphazard fashion; the wind blew the raindrops first this way then that, spotting the windows on the eastern wing as a prelude and then dotting the asphalt on the street. People rambled past with colourful umbrellas—lucky sods who could actually smell the rain breeze and hear the thunder. Abeer and the classroom full of poor shmucks were cushioned from the heady weather by the tall glass windows and the faint stale hum of the AC. Outside, rickshaw-wallahs cycled at great speed, their heads covered with polythene packets, a sheet of blue plastic wrapped around their shoulders as a ballast against the weather. Abeer looked longingly at the tiny shop, on the other side of the street, which sold chicken rolls, cauliflower samosas and egg chowmein. It was doing brisk business. Various umbrella-less souls were trooping in. He could imagine them huddled around the formica tables inside, drinking steaming cups of Nescafe. He wondered what the day's specials were. A plate of momos might be good. Or, better still, hot thukpa. God, he was hungry.

Abeer had hoped fervently that the rain would taper off this morning, but nada. According to the Met office, the depressing weather was to continue. Heaven knew when Mandakini Mandal would resume college. Last week he'd heard she had come down with flu. There was no chance she'd return to class if this pissing weather continued. *Just* as he'd managed to get within sniffing distance of Mandy Mandal, the flu epidemic overtook Calcutta. The gods were *never* on his side.

After a great deal of politicking and plotting, after buying seniors more cigarettes and fish fingers than he had ever consumed himself (he was currently deep in debt at the momo shop), Abeer had successfully manoeuvred himself into the music committee of their annual fest. Mandy Mandal was one of the volunteers who'd been picked by seniors at the outset. Not only that, she'd been made artist coordinator, an unimaginable honour for a second-year student. But then, her grey eyes, and the red light on her dad's car, were known to open rare doors. Abeer, though a third-year student, was not picked for music at all. He was assigned to day events, the most boring lot of them all. Quiz and debate. Where you would only get to meet the dorkiest characters in the college circuit. Ooh, I'm so smart and special! Ooh, I'm vocal about issues! Ooh, I know the capital of Swaziland! Bloody nerds. And this was just the guys. The girls were all of the above *and* smug like nobody's business. As though they were so superior.

However, Abeer had continued to follow events in the music committee. When his classmate Partho Goswami flunked a paper and his father forbade him to participate in any extra-curricular activities whatsoever, his place, luckily also as an artist coordinator, fell vacant. Abeer swooped in, bribed the fourth-years with shop-bought chilli chicken and homemade chocolate sandesh while holding forth on his knowledge of classic rock and raaga darshana. After a week's worth of sycophancy, he managed to worm his way in. But, unfortunately, his inception into the committee had coincided with Mandy's flu. Fuck.

Abeer decided to focus on the silver lining. The fest was in February. There was a lot of time to woo her. In any case, Mandy was bound to get better soon. Come to think of it, his pimples might be gone by the time she rejoined the committee. Abeer's mood improved somewhat. Mandy Mandal, he doodled on his notebook. Mad Mandy, Mad Mandy, Madly L. Mandy.

The professor started distributing printouts busily and Abeer was forced to concentrate a little on the affairs in the classroom. Finally, after a good hour or so, the buzzer rang. (Instead of a regular bell they had a modern buzzer—that was how poncy they were). A sense of liberation instantly infected the air.

AJ put away his comic and gushed: 'Chal yaar, aaj cinema jayenge. Matinee show. You can't imagine the super-hot posters I saw this morning.' In fact, they were so super-hot that he'd had to hide his hard-on in the metro with his comic. But no need to divulge all that.

'Pagal hai?' Abeer said seriously. 'Don't you remember? I have the music committee meeting this afternoon.' He noted, hopefully, that the drizzling had tapered off. Maybe Mandy would come after all. She lived fairly close by and had a car at her beck and call.

AJ's face darkened briefly. He had become seriously addicted to the semi-porn B-grade English films that ran in Chaplin and Moonlight. He was always on the lookout for company to catch one of those. (He had a mysterious source of pocket money too.) But he hated going alone. That was just too lame. True, he didn't have a girlfriend. True, these films were the highlight of his life. However, he drew the line at going to these alone. But he knew how much effort Abeer had put into currying favour with the music committee—he'd had to lend him money several times last month. He'd joked that it might have been cheaper for Abeer to fight elections and win. 'Can we at least go tomorrow?' he asked Abeer hopefully. 'You know these films don't stay on for too many days. This one seems very good, G.'

In their circle, sometimes Abeer was called G. Mukherjee to Jee to G.

'We'll see about tomorrow,' Abeer replied. 'But after my meeting today we can go over to Deep's college. He always has interesting stuff going on.'

'Okay,' AJ replied. Better hanging out with the future doctors than returning home. He'd ring his mother with a story about group study. He could even stay over at Abeer's house tonight. If he was ever spotted at home before dinner, his father would insist that he go and sit in their shop next door. All his male cousins had helped out while they were in college. 'They were only studying BCom pass course, Papa,' AJ felt like saying to his father, 'not BCA.' But such talk would not be tolerated.

AJ lived in a higgledy-piggledy family house in a narrow lane in north Calcutta. There were some twenty-five rooms in it, most of them added to the original eight or ten as the family had grown, with no particular eye for symmetry. Abeer loved it. AJ could not wait to escape it. All the men in the Jaiswal joint family were associated with the family cast iron business. Their neighbourhood was called Lohapatti. AJ claimed it was the most soul-deadening area in Calcutta. Abeer would hotly dispute this and point out that Nancy was, by far, the most boring and soul-deadening area. At least AJ was only three stops away from New Market by the metro. Five stops to Park Street. AJ, the first in the family to refuse doing a BCom, would be compelled to agree, after detailed analysis, that his was a slightly better geographic location. But he would promptly add that Abeer's quality of life at home was definitely better than his. Far fewer people, no threat of being sucked into a family business—a soul-deadening one—looming overhead. On top of that, Abeer got to eat non-vegetarian food almost every day. He had a point about the food, Abeer had to agree, though ever since Moni Mashi's visit his mother had put everyone on diet. But what about the fact that AJ's cousins were not averse to slipping him 500-rupee notes to cover their tracks every now and then?

'Do you want to grab a bite before your meeting?' AJ asked.

'Oh, absolutely. I am going to eat two double chicken rolls right away. I've been imagining that first bite for the last half hour. That's what got me through this class. In fact, I'll buy both chicken rolls—'

'Double chicken rolls,' AJ interjected.

'*Double* chicken rolls at once and take one bite from each.'

AJ burst out laughing. He knew Abeer would do exactly that, and it would become a major talking point in the eatery. In fact, he'd probably do the same. It was a neat idea, come to think of it.

They gathered their bags and walked out of the classroom together. Abeer tried to calculate the probability of Mandakini making a surprise appearance at the meeting (fifty per cent) and the exact words with which he would introduce himself ('The name is Bond. Abeer Bond.'). AJ wondered how he should fill the hours of Abeer's meeting. Perhaps he could download a movie secretly in the computer lab? That way he'd have his cake and eat it too.

4.2

It was six-thirty when the guys finally left the institute. It was dark, but the weather was particularly fine, all breezy and cool. Not at all muggy like the last few evenings had been, purple hours sandwiched between bursts of rain.

All the way in the auto to Deep's college, AJ had to hear Abeer's sorry saga. It was a little difficult for him to concentrate on the details, and Abeer could really blather on in excruciating detail about Mandy matters. AJ's mind was still submerged in the blue fug of the film he'd just caught. Turned out, right under the noses of the computer lab professors, certain seniors (certain geniuses would be a more accurate description) had created a hidden database labelled 'Erotic Films worth Watching or Whatever'. They used the institute's super-fast server to download movies in the blink of an eye and used complex codes to create a virtual Fort Knox where these were stored. Hundreds and thousands of films. A hundred-thousand films perhaps. French films, Polish films, even—hold your breath—Pakistani ones. Various levels of erotica. AJ had stumbled on it entirely by accident and was paranoid that he might not be able to access it again the next day. The geniuses who had created such a virtual Fort Knox probably kept changing the complex codes every night. But even if he couldn't find it right away, at least he would have a cause. For the rest of his college life, he would keep looking for the codes to this blue heaven.

But one thing was final. If he managed to locate it again tomorrow, this would revolutionize their lives. At least, his and Abeer's. He had decided there was no need to tell others in their class. This was obvious: you kept the route to heaven a secret. Others would too.

'AJ.' Abeer poked him from the side. 'You are not listening to me, yaar.'

'No, dude, I am totally listening to you. So you were sitting in the committee room and listening…'

'I was sitting in the committee room and listening to everyone's ideas about Rock Night.'

'Sorry, when exactly is Rock Night?'

'You *weren't* listening. Let me do a quick recap. The first day of Jashn—yeah, that's the name of the fest, we decided today—that is, on 12 February, is quiz-and-elocution in the afternoon, and eastern music at night. We are trying to get Rashid Khan for the evening. On 13 February, we have debate and antakshari, and at night we have scheduled the Bangla band performance. Our people are talking to both Bhoomi and Chandrabindu.'

AJ smirked at the 'our people'. Who did they think they were? The CIA?

Abeer continued at great speed, desperate to come to the Mandy part of the story. 'Dude, did you know these Bangla bands charge a bomb? Anyway, we are looking into sponsorships. But the third and final night is the real deal. Rock. Night. We are thinking of...' Abeer turned to look at their co-passengers (two schoolgirls in pigtails and their harried mother) and then lowered his voice as though revealing a state secret: 'Indian...wait for it...Ocean. Indian Ocean. You know what that means, right? It's going to be *legendary*!'

In addition to Indian Ocean, Abeer was also a fan of Barney Stinson. Though he did not have a smidgen of the latter's luck with girls.

'Umm, okay.' AJ failed to understand the insane obsession these convent-educated Bengalis had with rock music. He preferred Bollywood, thank you very much. And no, he wasn't in the least embarrassed about it. Wasn't Bollywood music taking over the world? He had begged Abeer to consider inviting Sonu Nigam or Alka Yagnik for the final night, or at least Kailash Kher, but Abeer had shushed him and said that would be preposterous. Well. AJ turned to his friend: 'But what is the tragedy, yaar? Why are you sporting a long face?'

'Because at the exact moment we decided on Indian Ocean, Mandy entered. With Rocky. They were all smiles and cuteness, like a couple. And I heard later that the reason Mandy was not in college all day was not because of her flu but because Rocky had taken her to Flury's.'

AJ whistled.

'To propose.' Abeer spat out the words in agony.

'Whaaat?' AJ was thrilled. He was extremely sorry for his friend, but this was thrilling news. Much more excitement than he had ever experienced.

'Apparently Mandy hasn't said yes. She needs time to think. But she's also very flattered and very *into* Rocky at the moment.' Abeer mimicked the simpering girl in Mandy's class who had narrated all this to him.

The auto swerved dangerously and Abeer nearly crashed out.

They were dangling from the front seat of the auto, perched on either side of the driver. AJ gulped and clutched Abeer's bag to pull him in. Rocky, or Rotnobeer Hajra (though nobody called him that), was a final-year student and head of the music committee. He was a star student. Everybody knew he was stuck in this college and not dazzling professors at IIT-KGP with an invention a day because he had had a bad bout of chicken pox around the time of the IIT entrance exam. He was tall and muscly and had a shock of curly hair. His face was pleasant, though not quite handsome; his sense of humour was wicked; his prospects nearly as good as those of the IIT boys. Though nobody knew his GRE score, it was rumoured to be Ivy-League worthy. He was the founder of the college band and its lead guitarist. To be brutally honest, if Rocky had his eyes on Mandy, Abeer's probability to score was less than one per cent. AJ thought fleetingly of the money they'd invested into this bad business. But obviously he couldn't comment on it. This was not a time to dwell on monetary affairs. 'He will go to America next year, yaar,' he told Abeer comfortingly. 'But she will be in college.'

Before Abeer could reply, their auto skidded to a halt. '8B, 8B,' the auto-wallah screamed. AJ handed him a twenty and carefully counted the change that was returned.

'At least she hasn't said yes to him yet. That means there is hope,' Abeer said morosely.

4.3

Deep studied at a private medical college right next to Jadavpur University. His girlfriend Shriya's cousin, Molly, had been Mandy's classmate in school (a very posh convent); thus Shriya, through Molly, had a lot of information on Mandy. Sometimes Shriya would invite Molly to their evening addas—those were bonus nights for Abeer.

Molly studied literature at Jadavpur University (JU English, it was called in the right circles) and was the epitome of cool. She smoked pot, read Neruda and Cavafy, and sometimes came to class in a pair of tiny denim shorts paired with an oversized white T-shirt, her hair pulled back in a severe bun. On one such memorable day, when she'd added hot pink calf-length socks to the ensemble, along with a pair of floaters, she had joined the medical students, plus AJ and Abeer, for what had been planned as an evening of entertainment. They had taken a cab to the river-front and AJ had nearly had a cardiac arrest when Molly nonchalantly scrambled onto his lap to fit in. The cab was very crowded. Usually, only people's girlfriends sat on their laps, that too with great protestations of coyness; Molly hadn't known AJ from Adam. She'd chatted with him very amiably, though AJ could hardly bring himself to reply intelligently. Halfway through the taxi ride, she'd brought out a couple of Cubans from the depths of her hot pink jhola and handed one to AJ.

Molly was something else.

Deep's girlfriend, Shriya, though very fond of Molly, was as different from her as chalk from cheese or, as Abeer said, chocolate from cigarette. Shriya was wonderful. You could take her home to your mother, she'd be a best friend to your sister, and she'd love you through thick and thin. But she was no Molly. Molly would, most probably, do none of the above properly. Or she might do all of the above with great aplomb. For about three months. And then run away to live in a tree. It all depended. Shriya was like Lily. And Shriya and Deep were the Lily and Marshall—quasi-parental figures—to the rest of the group. (AJ secretly wished he could be Barney but it was not bloody likely—his luck with girls was just as bad as Abeer's.) However, perhaps because they were so different from each other, Shriya and Molly were very close. And Molly, though she was a bit flaky, was essentially a kind-hearted sort. On some days, she would take pity on Abeer and try to find out the state of Mandy Mandal's affections through a flurry of phone calls or texts. On some other days, though, she might not know Abeer from Adam.

Today, when AJ and Abeer entered the canteen, they found the entire gang in attendance. Abeer had texted Deep, and he had assembled everybody he could find for an SOS evening. Luckily, the canteen was deserted. Semester exams were around the corner and most of the students were busy swotting at home. Shriya gave Abeer a hug, dealt out a few comforting phrases and promptly went behind the counter to get beer cans stashed in the fridge (they pooled in and rented half a rack from the canteen owner). Their other friends, Rahul (who was always high) and Shabnam (the class topper), were wrapped around two benches, reading paperbacks. They uncurled themselves to greet Abeer and AJ with appropriately sorrowful expressions. AJ's heart lurched a little as Molly appeared from somewhere. Today, Molly was in a blue cotton sari and looked rather like a strict schoolteacher. Only, smoking hot.

Over the drinks, Abeer went over the entire episode again. In some places he enacted out various bits. AJ rolled his eyes once or twice. He was also distracted once or twice by Molly's spectacularly oversized spectacles, the sight of which led inexorably to a contemplation of the unique cut of her white sleeveless blouse. But it did not seem right to try to talk to Molly on the side while all this drama was underway. He also began to doubt if Molly remembered him at all.

Finally, Abeer wound down. 'So this is how matters stand, as of today. She hasn't said yes to Rocky yet, but he's clearly in the lead. Does anyone have any ideas as to what my strategy should be? *Any* ideas?'

The boys were silent. The girls clamoured to speak.

Shriya said, 'Okay, so there's another guy in the picture. Makes it more challenging, right?'

Shabnam added thoughtfully, 'I think the strategy to adopt is obvious, G. You should become a friend. A really good friend. Someone she can trust. You'll be spending many hours working together. That's the way to go. You'll be goofy and funny and always there for her. You'll be the safe space. When the cookie crumbles regarding this stupid Rocky, as it's sure to—I'm sure he'll get a blonde in America, he seems the type—you'll be there. Tada!'

'You're a genius Shabnam,' said Abeer gratefully. 'This does seem a good way to go about things.'

There was much cheering and congratulating of Shabnam. With an idea like this, the war was almost won.

Molly thumped on the table and shouted, 'Order, order.' She took out her phone, looked meaningfully at Abeer and said, 'Let Operation Befriend Mandy begin. AJ, get me another beer.'

AJ trotted to the fridge obediently. When he returned with the beer, he found Molly had placed her phone at the centre of the table. It was on speaker mode, every ring rending the air. The others were silently shushing each other.

'Hello?' Mandy answered finally. Her voice was sweet and kind of smoky. A-1, Rahul gestured to Abeer.

'Hi, Mandy, Molly here. This is my new number. I lost the old phone, blah blah blah. It was too much trouble trying to get the old number back. You know me.'

'Oh, hi. That's great, Molly. Thanks for letting me know. I'll save it right away.'

'So, how are you, girl? How is Dozey?'

Dozey was Mandy's dog. This subject lasted for a while until Abeer sharply rapped Molly on the knuckles.

'So, Mandy, a little birdie told me that a certain rockstar is paying a lot of attention to you. Is it true?'

'Mo-lly!'

Mandy sounded all twinkly and shy. Her voice was full of smiles. Abeer looked crushed.

'Molly, I don't know where you get all your news! Well, I don't know. I like him a lot. But you know how I have so much going on. My semester, the music committee, rehearsals for the play at the para puja pandal. I don't know if this is the right time for me to be in a relationship. You know?'

'Uh-hm, uh-hm,' said Molly.

'But he's so hot, Molly! And so grown-up,' continued Mandy. 'He likes wine. In fact, he knows his wine. He knows how to tip properly. He's so different from all the other boys I meet. Let's see how it goes…'

There were meaningful giggles at both ends. Molly winked at the others to indicate she was merely play-acting. She would never giggle genuinely at Rocky-the-enemy's charms. 'What about you, Molz? Seeing anyone yet?'

Molly laughed. 'Single and loving it, Mandy. You know me. Oh, meant to ask—have you met my friend Abeer? He's in your music committee too. Great guy. Lovely to hang out with. Goofy, funny, reliable. You should totally work with him. Otherwise, these committees can really get boring. No?'

'Abeer? Which one is that?'

'Oh, he's one of my best friends. He's just joined the music committee. He was single-handedly managing all the intellectual events, quiz and debate and stuff. But then someone dropped out or something and he was brought in as a specialist. He's quite an expert in rock music. I think today was his first meeting.'

'Oh, I get it. You mean the friendly-looking fat guy? Okay, sure, I'll tell him you're our mutual friend. Rocky is so busy with his internship and the band and his other commitments, it'll be nice to have a pal. Especially someone who knows his rock. I'm more of a pop girl. Anyway, gotta go. See you soon, Molz.'

'See you soon, Mandy.'

'Bye.'

'B-bye.'

Molly hung up embarrassedly. The speaker had turned out to be a very bad idea. The word fat hung over the room like a toxic bubble.

'She finds you friendly, Abeer. And you can teach her all about rock music. Cheer up!'

'Shut up AJ,' Abeer snapped. 'She said fat. Didn't you hear? F-A-T. It's a lost cause.'

The others wondered what to say.

'She sounded a bit bitchy,' Rahul began tentatively.

'And a little self-important,' Shabnam added.

'No, Rahul, she's not bitchy at all. Neither is she self-important. She's very, very nice,' Abeer protested hotly. 'It's just that she's way out of my league. And what she said is true. I am fat. Hideously fat.' His voice shook slightly both times he said fat.

'You're not fat, Abeer,' Molly consoled. 'Just big. In America, you'd be the mainstream. Here you stick out a bit among these lanky-panky Bengalis.'

Abeer stood abruptly. The chair banged against the floor. 'I have to be home, guys. You all have your exams to prepare for, right? Thanks for everything,' he said in a dignified manner and marched to the door.

AJ got up too. 'I'll come with you.'

They walked out of the canteen to find it was raining cats and dogs. But Abeer did not want to wait in the shade for even a moment. He surged ahead into the rain, mud squelching grimly under his feet. In an instant he was drenched.

The lights of the city were dimmed by the curtains of water that sluiced down. AJ sighed and rolled up his trousers and followed in the direction of Abeer's large outline. It would be a miracle if they found an auto in this weather.

SANDHYA

Tuesday.
Sandhya's hotel in the city, just off Park Street, was an old-fashioned one. Once upon a time, it had been quite famous. But nowadays, with young professionals favouring modern places with flat screen televisions and tuna melts at midnight—never mind the small, shiny, homogenous rooms—it had become, like many other Calcutta institutions, a sleepy reminder of a more refined past. A pleasant memory, but irrelevant. The hotel did not have a name. Just an address: 15 Middleton Row. Nor did they believe in any sort of advertisement or gimmicky offers. Mostly people called ahead to reserve rooms based on word of mouth

recommendations. The room rates were quite reasonable. And it was usually full.

The hotel was set back inside a walled compound with a wrought-iron gate: a tiny lawn in front, a courtyard at the back, and a fine two-storey house with a pillared portico. There were only about ten rooms for guests and a couple of suites. The rest of the house was occupied by the family and the staff. Both floors had largish parlours where guests could entertain visitors (though not after 10 p.m.). There was a dining hall downstairs where prefixed meals were served at stipulated hours, each meal serving at least one traditional Armenian dish. It was quite charming, really, if one had no quarrel with the cluttered decor favoured by British housewives at the turn of the last century, all footstools and doilies and slipcovers and silver photo frames with pictures of beloved dogs. If you looked closely, all of it was old and faded. At some places, hidden artfully by paintings, the walls had damp spots. The carpets had frayed patches. But however closely you looked, it was not likely you'd find a speck of dust.

The place was owned and run by an old Armenian lady, the redoubtable Irene Arrathoon, one of the cornerstones of the rapidly dwindling Armenian community in Calcutta. Most of her family had immigrated to Canada, but one grandson and his Goan wife had stayed back, with their kids. They supervised the day-to-day running of affairs. But Mrs Arrathoon, possibly ninety now, was still the undisputed mistress. It was she who led the war against dust, and she could often be spotted around the house, wielding a feather duster. The staff too were quite ancient. Sandhya, who had turned sixty this summer, felt positively guilty asking 'housekeeping' for a jug of water or an electric kettle from the kitchen—everyone in housekeeping was seventy-five at the very least, and a little rheumatic.

Dr Sheila had recommended the hotel highly; she often came to the city to lecture on gynaecology at the Medical College. The ashram at Rishikesh had made the arrangements on Sandhya's behalf. Someone had called the week before to book a room for her. A simple room had been requisitioned.

The simplest room had thus been assigned to Sandhya.

It was on the second floor and had *only* a large four-poster bed (piled with paisley-patterned bedclothes), an armoire, a couch with a tweedy dustcover, an armchair, a large dresser by the window and a quaint little bureau in the corner. All of the furniture was old, and polished till it gleamed. There was a mantelpiece by the wall, stuffed with knick-knacks.

It was an airy room with a high ceiling. Since Sandhya did not use air conditioners (the only mod con the hotel provided, though the ACs were the huge old-fashioned models that had been introduced in Calcutta some twenty-five years ago), the windows were open this morning, flooding the room with a spun-gold light. It had rained all night and the roads were full of puddles. There was a wet, ripe smell in the air, a faint whiff of rotting perhaps, but the sky was a fresh washed-out-and-tumble-dried blue, a gorgeous blue. It was a lovely day.

Sandhya had landed in Calcutta early last evening, her flight from Delhi having been delayed. Owing to the weather, the traffic had been awful and it had taken her more than two hours to get from Dum Dum to the hotel. Mrs Arrathoon had immediately taken her under her wing. But Sandhya had been too exhausted for conversation. She'd just had some fruit for dinner and retired.

It was at dawn today that she'd flung open the windows and meditated peacefully as light shot through the dark sky, bathing it a milky rose. When the chirping of birds reached a crescendo, she'd gone downstairs for a walk.

At seven, Mrs Arrathoon came to the upstairs parlour and saw Sandhya leafing through the old books. 'Good morning Sandhyaji,' she said, in her quavering musical voice. 'Slept well?'

'Thank you,' Sandhya replied to the bird-like old lady, her white hair coiffed elegantly. 'I slept very well.'

'Your friend Dr Sheila always stays with us when she visits. She is a kind woman, Dr Sheila is. She indulges an old lady and has long conversations with me.' Mrs Arrathoon settled into the sofa opposite Sandhya. 'She has told me much about you. I am so glad to be able to host you here.'

'Thank you, Mrs Arrathoon.' Sandhya smiled. The old lady had a warm, crinkly smile. Her face was a web of fine wrinkles. Sandhya had not noticed it last night, but her eyes were little pools of blue—she was enchanted. 'You have a lovely place,' she said.

'It is difficult to maintain the house now, you know. My grandson always badgers me about it. We have to smarten the place up. We have to install TVs. Split ACs and whatnot. He's after my life. I've told him he better wait for me to snuff it, then he can do whatever he likes.' But Mrs Arrathoon smiled when she said all this and the blue eyes twinkled. '"What is your problem?" I ask him. "As long as we can make ends meet?" You see, Sandhyaji, I look at the books myself. I know what is going out and what is coming in. But then, my grandson says that now I should turn my mind to spiritual matters, not worry about the business!'

Sandhya laughed.

'Now, to important things. Do you have to go anywhere? There is a taxi strike today, so it might be difficult to find one outside. Would you like to borrow the car? It'll bring you back here after you're all done. We'll add the tab to your bill.'

'That would be great, Mrs Arrathoon,' Sandhya said. 'I do have an appointment this afternoon. I had no idea about the strike. It would be convenient if I could have the car.'

Mrs Arrathoon looked at her guest curiously. 'You are a strange kind of holy person,' she told Sandhya finally. 'You are not surrounded by people claiming to be intermediaries and students and managers and whatnot! I have seen holy people in my time, my dear. You don't seem quite like them.'

'But I am not a holy woman, Mrs Arrathoon. I am just a teacher. And I've come to Calcutta on a strange errand, not to lecture or hold workshops. But it is just as well. It is exhausting being a guru these days—one has to keep up with global trends. I am quite looking forward to being completely on my own, stripped of all the titles, and the duties too.'

'Lucky for me.' Mrs Arrathoon twinkled. 'You can be my teacher. The Hindus say you need a teacher to help you turn to spiritual matters. I have you now,' she declared.

Sandhya extended her hand and grasped the old lady's. Mrs Arrathoon's palm was both soft and calloused. Moisturizer had been creamed into skin cracked and edged with age. The smell was a familiar sweet one—Vaseline and time. In that instant, a series of faces, and the sharp memory of Caribbean rain flitted across Sandhya's mindscape. She squeezed Mrs Arrathoon's hand and said, 'You're the wise old woman, Mrs A, you don't need a guru. We can learn from you.'

CHAPTER 5

TUESDAY, NOON

5.1

At a quarter to one, Apu entered the staff room, flung down the files she was carrying onto her desk and finally breathed a sigh of relief. It had been a busy morning. She'd had back-to-back classes at the crack of dawn, and then there was the annoying task of overseeing lab work. The chief problem of being a lecturer on contract was that the permanent staff dumped the most boring subjects on one, and long, long hours of laboratory supervision. Apu was exhausted. Theirs was a morning college and the first class was held at the unearthly hour of 6 a.m. Since the permanent staff also tended to hog the more earthly hours, the first two lectures, six to seven and seven to eight, were invariably allotted to the contractees.

The staff room was deserted. Most of the teachers had left already. The routine was drawn up by one of the older professors and the last period was also allotted to the lesser mortals as a matter of course. In the case of botany, Apu's department, it was almost always lab work at the end of the day. Apu dropped herself into her chair. Then, tsking at her own absentmindedness, she hauled herself up again, walked to the small red refrigerator kept in the corner of the room and glugged some cold water directly from the bottle. She took the bottle to the sink at the corner of the room and splashed some of the icy water on her face. It felt good. A shriek sounded outside, followed quickly by another. It must be yet another birthday. Or yet another rat scare. 'Oof, these silly girls!' Apu muttered primly.

It was an all-girls' college, though not one of the posher ones. And after one o'clock, it became a bit of a school. Laughter and loud conversation mingled with feverish plotting and planning. God knows what it was they plotted, Apu thought. Movies? Love affairs? Elopements? She had studied for her BA at Scottish Church and missed what she thought of as the far more balanced energies of a co-ed college. There was this *implosive* quality she sensed in each of the all-girls' colleges she'd taught in. And there had been a few. Until she got a permanent job, it seemed this cycle was to go on—one semester at one college, another semester somewhere else. But she'd been teaching here for nearly eight months now and, at the risk of jinxing it, she had to admit to she liked it well enough.

For instance, she knew—and looked forward to—the hush that was coming. Around half past two, in a swoop, the college building would suddenly become still, as though all the giggling and conspiring had been swallowed by the walls. The girls would have left the premises, taking their laughter and anxiety into the cluttered canvas of Gariahat Market. But the hush on the stairways and common rooms would quickly spread to lecture halls and laboratories and the courtyard at the back. Sitting in her corner of the staff room, Apu would look at the flame trees outside the windows and think her thoughts in peace. Far better than going home.

'Don't you feel scared?' Meera had asked her the other day. 'Sitting all by yourself in the empty college building?' On the contrary, Apu told her, she felt safe. 'One day, I'm going to take you there, Meera,' she'd said. 'You'll see. You can just sit by the window for hours and watch the squirrels chasing shadows in the garden. You can just let your mind be blank. It's a nice, free feeling.' Meera had moped and said that it was not bloody likely that the old witch would undertake to look after the girls for an afternoon and let her go to Apu's college. But if that ever happened, could they also eat biryani somewhere? 'Of course,' Apu had said happily, 'My treat!'

Not that Apu had the luxury of soaking in silence every afternoon. Almost every other day, she had to go and meet her supervisor at Ballygunge Science College or to the National Library in Alipore. She also had to run a few errands for her mother downtown. Even for her supervisor. But at least once a week, she made it a point to stay back until the cleaning ladies shooed her out at five. She'd sit in the staff room and read.

Apu took out her lunch box and propped up the Bengali novel she was currently reading on the table. She was famished. But her mood soured instantly when she opened her tiffin. *This* was what her mother had packed for her to eat after such a long morning of being on her feet and listening to nyaka girls asking nyaka questions? Two tiny rotis (that would fit into her palm) without any butter or ghee? Just a greenish blob of sabzi, a bowl of unsweetened curd, a salad without any dressing?

It was not that this food was particularly bad—this was what her mother had been packing for her for the last two weeks. Apparently, most people in north India had this sort of a lunch every day, except many more rotis, Mrs Mukherjee had told her a hundred times in the last fortnight. But somehow, today, with her feet aching and her stomach rumbling, the food became a metaphor for Apu's life. Dry, inspid, and going from bad to worse. She was on the verge of bursting into tears when Sadia entered the staff room.

'Hi,' Sadia announced cheerfully, heaving in large bags.

5.2

While Apu contemplated her lunch tearfully, Mrs Monalisa Das, who was also in the vicinity, in Gariahat, was vaguely drifting from shop to shop. It was a quarter to two and she had some time to kill before her friend arrived. She'd left Anwara to hold fort in the meantime.

The general confusion that characterized Gariahat Market on usual days was far heightened in the rain. Under overcast skies and the looming threat of rain, the buying and selling and haggling was enacted with a far sharper edge of hysteria. Mrs Das felt right at home.

Hundreds of people were walking past—in a single file, since there were hawkers displaying a dazzling array of stuff on either side, monopolizing the pavement. Plastic sheets covered the makeshift shops, darkening the pavement even more. There were a few people who'd clearly begun their puja shopping already, though the real mad burst of pre-puja shopaholism would commence in October, when wise males and agoraphobics would be wary of steeping even one toe into that bubbling cauldron of oestrogen and annual bonuses. Mrs Das joined the early-bird shoppers, hogging whatever little was available of the pavement and demanding discounts bossily.

The footpath, as the pavement was popularly called, was almost entirely taken over by hawkers. The 'right to hawk' was one of the fundamental rights in Bengal, and even though the semi-permanent bamboo-and-tarpaulin structures were illegal, they were tolerated. Even encouraged. Once a year, a few of these were demolished half-heartedly by the corporation, and the women of Calcutta would rise up in arms at the unfairness of it all. Gariahat was an epic existence in Bengal folklore, right between Tagore's family home in Jorasanko and Tiger Hill in Darjeeling. What would Gariahat Market be without its hawkers? Just a row of pricey shops. It was the hawkers who kept the prices in the fancy shops in check, Mrs Das often suggested. They were a precaution against inflation, as it were.

'Nonsense,' Das would reply. 'They are part of a giant network of thugs.'

'Hawkers are poor people!' Mrs Das would fume, over breakfast, every time the corporation claimed its pavements.

'Do you know how many accidents happen because the footpaths are taken over? And the chaos in traffic every day?' Das would say. Usually, he went along with Monalisa's opinions on most matters. But hawkers were his pet peeve.

'Please!' Mrs Das would exclaim.

'Do you know many of these hawkers earn more in a week than I do in a month? The entire business has been estimated at Rs 15,000 crores, only in Calcutta! And they don't even have to pay any taxes.' Das could be a little grumbly about taxes.

'Hawkers are poor people,' Monalisa would reiterate. 'Don't forget that they have to pay hafta to the political gundas.'

'They *are* the political gundas!'

'Please. As good Hindus we cannot snatch away their livelihood.' Mrs Das would be firm. Finally, she would say, 'Even Didi supports hawkers.'

These days, Monalisa Das had taken to ending many of her pronouncements with this ultimate flourish. Didi supports concentrating on maths, she told her sons. Didi supports punctuality, she instructed Anwara. Didi supports cotton saris, she told her mother-in-law in Durgapur, 'I will buy you a really good cotton dhonekhali this puja. Georgette is over-rated.' Mrs Das adored Didi.

Mrs Das drifted from shop to shop. The sun had come out after a three-day hiatus and there were glittering puddles everywhere. She checked the prices of bedsheets and wall-hangings, cutlery and underwear, comparing it all with what had been quoted last week. She was alarmed that almost on all counts prices seem to have risen. 'Have you gone out of your mind?' she admonished the plastic-flower-wallah who wanted Rs 100 for a bunch of fake white roses that had pearly fake raindrops stuck on them. 'What is the point of Chinese things flooding our market if you will ask American prices for it?' she screamed at the guy.

Mrs De called Mrs Das when she'd almost reached Golpark in her quest for lifelike plastic flowers for their bathroom. In Golpark, where the market finally petered out, the owners of second-hand book stalls were sunning their books vigorously. Their business suffered the most during rains. 'Sorry, Monalisa, I had great trouble finding a taxi,' Mrs De panted. 'Where are you?'

'Golpark, Boudi.'

'Oh that's great. Wait outside Ramakrishna Mission. I'll be there in five minutes.'

5.3

It is an unwritten survival strategy of our times that every woman must have at least one close friend who's fatter than her. In Apu's case, this was Sadia.

Sadia Siddiqui, like Apu, was a lecturer on contract. She worked in the English department and was quite popular with the girls.

'I thought you'd left,' Apu said. 'Shouldn't your class have ended at twelve?'

'Today I was screening a movie actually. In my post-colonialism lecture. You know?' Sadia had done a PhD from JNU. She was always trying to introduce cool teaching techniques, much to the shock of the older members of the faculty.

'Which movie?' Apu asked as Sadia drew a chair to her desk and settled down. They usually ate together.

'*Lagaan*. Half of it. We'll see the second half tomorrow. It's a really long film. Is this your lunch?'

'Yeah,' Apu said mournfully. 'You know how my mother is cracking the whip these days.'

'Oh, yes. The Chicago boy. I'm really going to miss you, Apu, when you go off to Amrika.'

Sadia was from Ranchi. Only about three or four years older than Apu. She had come to Calcutta after her marriage and finished her PhD while travelling between Delhi, Calcutta (where the in-laws lived), Ranchi (during both her confinements) and wherever Ali was posted. Her husband, Ali, was in the army and currently in Draas, which was a non-family station. So Sadia and her boys stayed with the in-laws, in their large house on a really noisy lane off Rafi Ahmed Kidwai Road in central Calcutta.

The house was full of people. Sadia's husband had three brothers and all of them worked in the government. She had three sisters-in-law who happily took turns looking after her boys all day. After all, Sadia's evenings were spent overseeing the convent education of *all* the children (all four siblings had, uniformly, two children each). The family was very proud of the daughter-in-law with the doctorate, the first woman in the entire khandaan to sport a PhD. The sisters-in-law were content and placid and round and good-natured; it appeared that the plump, cherubic look was favoured by the Siddiquis. So Sadia was one of the most secure people Apu had ever met.

However, Sadia did not have many friends in Calcutta. Though her in-laws were as Bihari as her own family, they had been in Bengal for several generations. So the sisters-in-law were all from that very superior community—the Bengali Muslims—who, like the rest of Bengal, were slightly contemptuous of Biharis. The sisters-in-law spoke to each other in rapid Bengali. This was not a problem as everybody else in the house was pretty conversant with Bengali too, especially the men. But it meant that Sadia, the youngest and most celebrated, was not included in this charmed circle. In her husband's absence, while Sadia's relationship with everyone at home was very good (in a polite and functional and grown-up way), it could hardly be called intimate. Sadia's colleagues, on the contrary, were her friends. She had collected a nice bunch from all the institutions she'd worked in. They were far more ready to talk to her in their peculiar Hindi and English, and to correct her pidgin Bengali.

'Sadia!' Apu cried. 'You're speaking as though matters have all been finalized and the wedding cards are being printed.'

'But they will be. Soon enough. He's coming in February, na?'

'Yes. I'm supposed to lose weight by then and become Barbie.' Apu crunched her salad moodily. 'Meera and I were trying to inspire each other to go for these daily walks. But you know how her mother-in-law is. She'll keep calling her fat. But the moment we go for a walk, she'll call on the cell and summon her upstairs. It's a terrible power game.'

'Poor Meera,' Sadia commiserated.

Sadia had never met Meera, but given that they both hailed from Jharkhand—and they shared Apu—they were familiar with each other's stories and bound by empathetic ties. 'That sounds exactly like Nusrat's mother-in-law. In fact, hers is worse. Nusrat just has to sit down, and the mother-in-law will start hollering. "Nusrat, come and give me a glass of water. Nusrat, where are my spectacles? Nusrat, your wicked son must have hid the remote, come and find it." Nusrat reads the newspaper in the bathroom before her bath!'

Nusrat was Sadia's elder sister.

'I haven't brought any lunch today, Apu.' Sadia sighed. 'Our maid didn't come this morning. I sent the kids to school with potato chips in their tiffin boxes.'

Apu pushed her lunch box towards Sadia.

Both of them looked morosely at the food.

'Do you...' Sadia began tentatively, 'want to go to My Club? I'll buy? But I know you're on a diet, I shouldn't tempt you. In fact, forget I said anything...'

Apu was already on her feet and bundling the sad rotis back into the tiffin box. She chucked her novel into her bag. 'Please,' she said plaintively. The whiff of shrimp fried rice and spicy fish had begun to waft in her direction from afar.

'Are you sure?' mumbled Sadia guiltily.

But Apu was already outside.

5.4

Mrs De was thin as a reed and walked very fast. Her speed on roads, however, paled before her verbal velocity.

Mrs Das huffed and puffed to keep up with her. But then, Mrs De was her guru. She had, over the years of following Mrs De around, developed great dexterity in keeping up with her pronouncements. Thus, Monalisa Das neatly caught each pearl that Mrs De flung over her shoulders as she threaded her way through dense traffic and anarchic pedestrians, Mrs Das close on her heels. They walked through lanes and by-lanes; Mrs Das tried to memorize each turn and crossing.

'Where I'm taking you Monalisa,' Mrs De said, 'it is a temple. A temple of learning. If there is one person in Calcutta who can sort out Bablu's maths problems, it is him. He is a god.'

Mrs Das felt a grateful jolt in her heart. It could have been happiness, but it was slightly marred by streaks of anxiety. 'But will he take Bablu? It is the middle of the session, after all.'

Baraha Bagchee, a.k.a. God of Maths, a.k.a. Khadoos Chukandar (owing to his unfortunate beetroot-shaped face), a.k.a. Bor Da, had retired as head of the department from a reputed high school in south Calcutta. But his chief fame was as a renowned tuition teacher. His maths lessons drove the ghosts of algebra and calculus haunting homes of hapless parents to a place far, far away. He had nurtured many IITians, many scientists (now mostly employed by the military-industrial complex in America), many corporate high-fliers in their tender years. Several records had been achieved under his tutelage—records of the 'highest marks in board exams' persuasion. Mrs De had brought Monalisa Das up to speed on the glorious career of Bor Da by the time they reached his house.

It was an old-fashioned house with a concrete plinth in front. Traditionally, this was called a rauk; and, traditionally, its purpose was to provide a convivial spot in the neighbourhood for evening adda as the hot summer sun waned. Endless cups of tea would come from the kitchen and the host would join a bunch of neighbours and friends for a hectic debate on football records or Soviet policies. It was a great and classless institution. In Bor Da's house, these days, the rauk was a convenient spot for students to gather and conduct romances or rivalries speedily, before one batch trooped out and another slunk in. Mornings and evenings, there were thirty pairs of shoes lined up on the rauk.

At half-past-one, however, the house seemed like a regular one.

Mrs De rang the bell. The door was opened by a short, dumpy woman with a dour face. The room she ushered them into was dark and dominated entirely by a gigantic blackboard at one end. The woman, presumably Mrs God, pointed silently to a couple of chairs and disappeared inside. 'Wife is a schizophrenic,' Mrs De whispered to Mrs Das.

Mrs Das digested this information.

In a few moments, God entered. He was tall and bald and fair, with a long, thin beard. 'How are you, Mrs De?' he asked expansively. 'Sit, sit.' He pulled up a stool for himself.

Mrs De came to the point immediately. 'This is Monalisa Das, Bor Da. An old friend. We lived in Baranagar together. She's more than my sister, really. You have to take her son under your wing.'

Bor Da smiled enigmatically. There were only two coordinates he was ever interested in: 'School? Class?'

Mrs Das gave him all the details, and then, with moist eyes, added, 'Mastermoshai, you know these cruel times. Cut-throat competition everywhere. How will my boy survive if he doesn't do well in maths? I cannot understand what the problem is. He's a good boy, sits with maths every day...' Naturally, she didn't mention the other teacher. 'Please save me, Bor Da. I am at your mercy.'

'Hmm. See, Mrs Das, let me tell you, I am very choosy about who I take on in my classes. I take only thirty students in each batch. And they are the best thirty. The brightest. The stars of tomorrow. Every year, I take a test in April and pick the thirty best from that group. Many mothers come and cry in this room, Mrs Das, but I cannot help them.'

Mrs Das's face became redder and redder. Why had she not known about this great man's methods? Why hadn't she been more proactive? Why hadn't she got Bablu to take this test? In fact, why hadn't she even heard of this test? It was final. Bablu's life would be a string of failures. And it was all her fault.

'However,' Bor Da said—and Mrs Das looked up in agitation and joy—'however, whatever my rules might be for the general public, if Mrs De brings me a friend, a sister, then I cannot say no.'

Mrs Das's eyes widened. Really?

Bor Da ran two batches for Class 9 (higher secondary board): median and advanced. Bablu could be the thirty-first student in the median batch. Four hours on Sunday mornings. Mrs Das accepted gratefully. She couldn't help wondering though, privately, what the advanced class would be like. Did it lead straight to the hallowed gates of IIT Kharagpur or BITS Pilani? Naturally, given Bablu's 23/100 score in the last exam, she couldn't beg for him to be put in the advanced class. She took what she got. Next year.

It was decided that Bablu would start his classes next Sunday.

As they began to take their leave, Bor Da said, 'It is important that you know this, Mrs Das, and convey it to your son. The reason I can never refuse Kumkum De is not because she and I are bound by one great success story. That we are. But it is because she and I are bound by one great failure.'

Mrs Das knew what he meant. The reference was to Mrs De's son Riju.

Mrs De shook her head sadly, as she did every time she met someone who'd known her only son Riju in the glorious days.

Riju had been pronounced brilliant by all his teachers and Mrs De was envied intensely by both relatives and parents whose offspring he outshone in class. But alas, before his Class 10 exams, Riju had had a nervous breakdown. It took him four years after that to finish school, and five to complete college. Mrs De had been able to withstand this agony only because Riju's sister had fulfilled her brother's share of the promise—as well as her own. She was a doctor in America (AIIMS and Johns Hopkins) and married to a young American surgeon. She was the success Bor Da had groomed to rewrite the narrative of Riju. (Riju was now a local real estate broker and lived at home with his parents.)

Mrs Das realized in that poignant instant that her son, her Bablu, too had been taken on by Bor Da to ameliorate the wound Riju had unwittingly left on his soul. What a teacher! She felt tears gathering in the corners of her eyes.

A gentle rain was falling now, and outside Bor da's door the two friends brought out their umbrellas.

Mrs Das said to Mrs De, 'Boudi, how can I ever repay you for this?'

Sandhya

Tuesday, late afternoon.
The lawyer's office was on Amherst Street in north Calcutta. At one time, this had been the heart of the city; now, it was just the old, congested, decaying half, comparing unfavourably to the far posher south of the city.

As the car wound its way through narrow lanes with faded once-imposing mansions on either side, Sandhya was struck by the strange shimmering beauty of north Calcutta. She had come to the city once before, about twenty-five years ago. But given her history—how she had almost made the city her own before it all came crashing down—she had been in a tearing hurry to move on. So Calcutta had been merely a port to Dakshineshwar, where she'd spent several days, before travelling on to Puri. The only place she'd been keen to visit in the city was the Kali temple at Kalighat. At that time, she'd still been young, somewhat foreign, new yet to her spiritual heritage, so she'd hungrily tried to soak up as much as she could. And yet, she'd been wary every single moment in Calcutta. From some angle or the other, the faces of strangers would suddenly seem familiar. It would fill her with waves of sweet dread for a moment or two, and then she would suddenly see she was wrong. She didn't know them at all.

Her windows rolled down, Sandhya gazed outside. It was true that there was much chaos and some garbage on the streets, that the roads were broken in some parts and impossible to navigate at others, but the masterful character of the city was captured in every inch of its canvas—grey skies; old buildings that had been built in a unique fusion of colonial and Indian impulses, their paint peeling off; tram lines glistening in the soft, silent rain; book stalls and hardware stores; men selling gramophone records; auto-rickshaw stands; men selling pirated CDs by the thousands; large buses jam-packed with people desperate to get somewhere; sweetmeat shops with mounds of kachauris on the counters; groups of men whiling away their time looking at the rivers of traffic. Every frame of the city was memorable. No wonder the city produced so many poets, Sandhya thought.

On one street, where the traffic inched along very, very slowly, she observed a long row of fancy jewellery stores, one after another, their storefronts glittering with lavish ornaments. But curiously, in front of these shops, vegetable sellers had taken over most of the pavement and flooded the concrete with vegetables—robust cauliflowers, bright red tomatoes and fresh green bell-peppers.

'What is this place?' she asked the driver.

'Bowbazaar Street,' the driver replied.

Sandhya chuckled to herself. Bond Street ought to do the same. Remind its customers that there were things more valuable than their just-purchased jewellery. Like the humble, knobbly radish. She smiled again at the thought, and then reminded herself quickly: 'Hippie alert!'

Dr Sheila and Sandhya had come up with the 'Hippie alert!' and subsequently the 'Commie alert!' as a comment on their own work when it tended to sound preachy or self-righteous. It was a bit of a joke. In almost all the talks they would hold in the early days, in women's institutes and village council halls in the seventies, on healing lives through food sadhana and yoga, in the days when they were very earnest and extremely serious and, perhaps, Sandhya realized now, a bit annoying, some or other group of men in the audience would invariably call out 'Fuck these hippies!' and leave. Eventually, things changed. Britain changed. And Sandhya and Dr Sheila learnt to employ jokes and anecdotes, especially when speaking to large audiences. It worked far better. But even now, they would sometimes scribble 'Hippie alert' in the margins of each other's articles or the galleys of their books.

The appointment with the law firm was at four. But they reached Amherst Street much earlier. The driver was as ancient as the rest of Mrs Arrathoon's staff, and as efficient. Within minutes, he had found the right building. He dropped her there, gave her his phone number, took her number—when Sandhya was in India she was compelled to use a mobile phone—and then went off to park somewhere.

The lawyer's chambers were on the ground floor of a large mansion painted in the traditional burnt-brick colour. Sandhya admired its symmetry, the pleasing proportions of the gracious marble columns in front, the clear lines. Unlike many other buildings of its vintage, this one had been restored well and maintained afterwards. The lawyers were certainly in business.

Three steps led up to a black door. Praful Sen and Pranoy Sen, Solicitors. The names were printed in discreet bronze lettering on the black door. Slightly unsure of herself, Sandhya rang the bell.

A young girl in a smart grey skirt suit opened the door. When Sandhya gave her name, the girl said, 'Oh, hello, Madam. Advocate Sen has asked me to take you to his room if that's all right.'

The girl's heels clicked on the smooth red-stone floor as she made her way through the hall, her hair streaked red and sashaying, past several waiting rooms, to Praful Sen's office. It was a large well-appointed room with floor-to-ceiling wooden bookshelves stashed with law volumes and a large mahogany table in the middle. Sandhya sat on one of the chairs.

'Would you like some tea or coffee?' the girl asked her.

'Just a glass of water please.' Sandhya's throat felt scratchy.

'Sure.' The girl disappeared and then returned with a bottle of water and a glass.

Sandhya closed her eyes and attempted to still her heart. It was beating like a twenty-year-old's. She stored this up in her mind to tell Dr Sheila.

'I am sixty years old, Sheila, and have spent a large part of the last thirty years of my life in meditation. In the lawyer's office, following up on that letter, I am a girl again. Heart fluttering, throat dry—the whole deal.'

'What *is* it with lawyers?' She could hear Sheila joking.

'Oh, no!' Sandhya imagined herself saying in response. 'What is it with old lovers?'

CHAPTER 6

TUESDAY, EVENING

6.1

Dark clouds had bunched together in the northwestern corner of the sky. It was only about five, but a pall of gloom was gathering quickly over the city. Treeza said sweetly, 'Johnny, how can we possibly go in this weather? They know we don't have a car. They'll understand. We can drop by to wish them happy anniversary some other time.'

John had been prepared for this. 'Russi is sending us his car, Treeze. It'll come around six.'

Rustam Mody was John's friend and colleague. A bachelor with family money, his job at the school, as the music teacher, only served to amuse him mildly. His raison d'être was his involvement in the lives of his friends.

Treeza bit her lip.

'It's going to be fine, honey,' John said, coming close and pushing back her hair from her face. 'There are going to be no strangers. It's just the family.'

'I'd have preferred strangers,' Treeza replied. She turned and wandered into the kitchen.

John was caught off-guard by the strong morning-after odour that reeked from Treeza. Had she forgotten to brush this morning? Had she not eaten anything all day?

A spring of fury released in him. He had taken the evening off to be able to go with her tonight. It was her sister's anniversary. Russi, the only one privy to his troubles, had gone on and on the last few months, saying that going out more was just the thing for Treeza. He was always offering the use of his car, his club, his cousin's hotel in Darjeeling. But what was the bloody point if Treeza refused to make any effort?

Taking the evening off for John meant having to juggle his entire schedule—fit in two batches on other days. As it was, getting a consensus from the students on when they could have the rescheduled class would be excruciatingly difficult. It was not their fault really; the poor sods had every single one of the weekdays blocked, with piano lessons and swimming classes and science tuitions and Carnatic music. But neither could the class just be cancelled—there was the pressure of both syllabi and parents. And what was all this trouble for? John's anger now spiralled upwards rapidly. His nostrils flared, the vein on his forehead began to pop. *Why* was Treeze behaving like this? She was not the only woman in the world who—

'Have some tea, darling,' Treeza said softly.

John opened his eyes and saw her setting a tray on the divan. Two cups of tea. Two bourbons each. Treeza was looking at him intently, her lower lip trembling slightly. He forced himself to smile. In the gloom, her eyes were a reddish brown. The colour of honey congealed in a jar. They could become a warm golden when she laughed, like honey spooned over pancakes on late-Sunday mornings. His stomach dropped. Much of the tea had slopped into the saucer and the bourbons were wet. As suddenly as it had come, John's anger subsided.

It was going to be all right, he told himself. *He* would make a mammoth effort and make it all right. He would resume lighting candles at the shrine of Mary and Baby Jesus. He would borrow Russi's car more often. He'd plan a holiday somewhere. They would get through this together.

Someday they would look back at this year, this annus horribilis, and forgive these versions of themselves.

6.2

In Meera Sahai's house, there were suitcases everywhere. Usually, every year in September, Suresh and his siblings gathered their families in the ancestral home near Patna for an annual puja in memory of their father. This year, Suresh had no leave, so the others had decided to visit Calcutta instead. They hadn't met Maaji Sahai in a while. The memorial service could be held in Calcutta this time.

Meera was not consulted in the tendering of the invitation. Even if she had been consulted, she would have had to say yes.

Suresh's elder brother Ramesh was a bank officer, now posted in Siwan. He was in his late thirties, a solid sort of chap in many respects. He was kind enough and patient enough, but two things must be said of him: he was a person who had fixed ideas about most things, and he was inordinately proud of his software engineer brother. He felt that it was *his* efforts that had facilitated Suresh's rise—and this premise was not unfounded. After the death of their father, Ramesh, at twenty-five, had automatically become the head of the family; he was the one who had overseen the education of his siblings and, in a few instances, even funded their fancies: Suresh's LML Vespa while in college, their sister Lovely's expensive dance lessons. He'd married them off too. He'd been a good elder brother. His wife, Nalini, a reed-thin woman who always covered her head with the end of her pallu, was a thrifty housekeeper. She was so organized that Meera guessed (correctly) that if quizzed she would be able to reel off the exact location of *each* item that she had packed for the fortnight into the four medium-sized suitcases the family had brought along, their two and their boys' two. Ramesh and Nalini had two sons, fifteen and fourteen, and they mostly kept to themselves. They went to a boarding school in Netarhat and were unfailingly polite, if aloof, in any domestic space.

Suresh had gone to Howrah station early in the morning. Fortunately, Danapur Express had arrived on time. He'd dropped everyone home, gulped down some breakfast and left for office pretty much on time. He'd been prepared to take a half-day off in case the train was late, but was very glad that he managed without. Suresh hated missing office. It was one of his quirks. He had been like that in school too, and college. Hundred per cent attendance throughout. Luckily for him, his daughters had been most gracious and chosen to be born at midnight; he hadn't had to miss office on either day.

Meera sighed in the kitchen as she made tea. The entire day could be enumerated through the chores: sending Tara to school, tending to Chhoti, tea and breakfast for everyone, tending to Chhoti, mid-morning tea, tending to Chhoti, making and serving lunch, tending to Chhoti, picking Tara up from the bus stop, clearing the table, and now, tea again. Damn the clouds, Meera thought, looking mournfully out of the kitchen window: Maaji wanted pakoras.

She had woken up very early this morning and, in the afternoon, with her sister-in-law sharing her bed and chatting about their many relatives, she'd had no rest at all. Her head pounded. Little electric rays seemed to be needling her eyeballs and darting through her skull. Her left shoulder was frozen from carrying the baby around while doing a hundred things; Chhoti, like all babies, was taking the arrival of guests rather badly. She was snivelling, constantly demanding her mother and generally being difficult. Meera's throat was dry. Nothing seemed to quench her thirst—not cold water, not warm water, not orange juice. She craved tea, but she knew it would leave her mouth bitter and thirstier.

Midway through making the tea, Meera realized she couldn't remember where the besan was. How could she make pakoras without besan? The onions and cauliflowers remained half-cut on the counter; Meera began to rummage around for the besan. She was sure that half-a-packet had been stashed somewhere. But where?

She began to take all the containers out of the shelves, one by one, and then, in a mad rush, two by two. Hysterically she checked each dabba: corn-flour, sattu, saboot masala, chawal ka atta, chane ki daal, rajma, badaam, sugar-free sachets hoarded from Café Coffee Day by Maaji in case she had diabetes someday—but there was no besan. Meera's hands began to tremble.

'Arre, Meera, kya ho gaya?' Nalini entered the kitchen. Meera stood on a stool, searching for the half-packet of besan in the corners of the kitchen, in shelves where more remote things were stowed—basmati rice for pulao or silver vark for sweet dishes or her prized La Opala dinner set. She was far away from the gas. The water for the tea was boiling over. Nalini quickly switched the gas off. 'Meera, Chhoti is bawling her eyes out. Didn't you hear?'

'No,' Meera replied, filled with great rapid rage. 'No, I didn't hear anything.' Why couldn't Chhoti leave her alone for a minute? What sort of a monster child was this? Was she also joining the rest of the clan in tormenting Meera?

'She must be hungry, poor thing, as it is she's thin as a stick,' Nalini said. 'What are you searching for?'

'Bhabhi, besan,' Meera mumbled. She decided not to take umbrage at the thin-as-a-stick comment. Besan. To make pakoras for our darling mother-in-law—or didn't you know that?

'Koi baat nahin,' Nalini said. 'If there is no besan, we can make fried bread. There's bread in the fridge. No?'

Meera's anger simmered. 'No, Bhabhi, Maaji doesn't like bread in the evenings.' To elaborate, she added: 'Digestion.'

'Oh-ho. Acchha, why don't you go and tend to the baby? I will make the tea for Himself and Maaji and send the boys to the shops to buy some besan. They can take Tara with them too. Meanwhile, I'll finish chopping the vegetables. And then maybe you can make your tulsi-ginger tea later, to go with the pakoras?'

Nalini switched on the light in the kitchen. The sudden illumination dazed Meera for a second, as though a severe wave had come and punched her in the stomach. She suddenly wanted to vomit. How foolish it had been of her! She was scrambling about in the dark when all that had been needed was the switch. As Nalini busied herself with the tea, feeling even more annoyed with herself, Meera went into her bedroom and locked the door.

6.3

They stopped briefly at Russi's father's shop on Russell Street in order to buy appropriate presents. It was a charming, old-fashioned shop that Treeza had adored at one time; she would spend hours trawling inside and planning with Russi's dad what curtains she would buy when they shifted to the new house, what table mats, what bedclothes. But today, five minutes before reaching the store, she insisted that she wanted to browse in the bookstore on Park Street instead. Could John pick her up from there once he was done?

John was extremely annoyed. How did she expect him to pick presents for Yasmeen's anniversary on his own? How was he to know what would be apt for her sister? But Treeza had already marched on, her orange-and-green scarf a distant peg in the sunset. John knew the emotional minefield she could present any moment, so he decided to let her be. He entered Mody Emporium alone, smarting. What if Russi's dad were there? Wouldn't it appear frightfully rude to use their car, their discounts, but not bother to come to the shop and say hello? Treeza should stop behaving as though she lived in a bubble. She was beginning to embarrass him now.

Luckily, the old man was not in the shop. But, as always, he had left standing instructions with the staff that John be treated like royalty. He had also told the accountant that they were to charge wholesale prices only. Coffee was brought in the instant he entered and, as he walked around and sipped the comforting caffeine, one by one the staff came by to say hello. They seemed disappointed not to see Treeza, but they were trained to ask no questions. Eventually, John settled on a white hand-embroidered bedspread with matching pillow-cases and was allowed to pay Rs 500 for it, which was about one-third the marked price.

Usually, John was not so magnanimous when it came to buying presents for the extended family—Yasmeen and co. had, for example, given them two coffee mugs last Christmas—but today was different. They had managed to evade family dos in the last many months and, somehow, this evening, he was also eager to impress, to put forward a sparkling face on their behalf. That they were doing fine. They just lived far away now, they were busy, but otherwise they were doing great. At least Treeza understood that part of the bargain. She had even made some effort with her appearance. It was her family, after all, and they were always full of drama. Though John had known them forever, he was still a little afraid of Treeza's sisters. In their presence, he invariably became the neighbourhood chhokra who had shown the temerity to date their baby sister and then marry her.

At seven, when they reached Yasmeen's house on Eliot Road, one block away from where John and Treeza had lived until recently, the party was in full swing. The door was open.

Treeza's eldest sister, Maria, was the first to spot them. In her long red dress, she made for a powerful gorgon. 'Do we know you?' She accosted them at the door. 'You seem jana-pehchana, but I don't think we've met before.' Her voice was essentially singsong, and that somewhat softened her annoyance. Maria was a mother hen, and she hated to be rebuffed in her excessive clucking. Treeza and John had evaded her well-meaning, affectionate interference for a while now, and she was justifiably miffed. John smiled and gave her a hug. Treeza kissed her lightly on her cheeks and inhaled the familiar talcum powder and rouge, a scent of the simultaneous love and hate that in childhood stood between the sisters and the world. Relenting slightly, Maria moved away from the doorway and shouted to the roomful of guests: 'Look who's here. It's the English teacher and his wife. I thought he had killed her and run off with the insurance money, you know!'

Maria's husband, Bertie, a short, tubby man who was always compensating for his wife's histrionics, now came forward and took over.

'You watch too many murder serials, Maria. Too much of that *CID* shit. Our Johnny boy do away with his wife? Isn't she the apple of his eye? So big loan he took to buy her a dream home, man. I'd be more worried about him. You three sisters are perfectly capable of murdering innocent menfolk like us and burying us somewhere far away, I tell you.'

Treeza giggled and hugged her favourite brother-in-law. 'I tell you, Bertie, it is not that we have *not* discussed this idea.'

Yasmeen emerged from somewhere. She was wearing a fuchsia skirt with black tights. Most unbecoming as usual, but loud and pink was her style and her husband humoured her, showering her with compliments. She teetered towards them on very high heels. The exact pink of her skirt and hair band. 'Hai, hai, it is our Treeza jaan! Where is that teacher husband of yours, haan? Now come inside and let me look at you properly. At least this green suits you. It's a very pale green, but it does look nice since you're fair. Though I don't know why your skin is looking so dull. That part of town doesn't seem to suit you, haan? If you came wearing black or navy blue, I swear to God I would have forced you to wear one of my dresses. You can't dress for mourning all your life, girl. Mama was saying you don't return her calls these days? As for Maria and me—well, we are dead to you, aren't we?'

'Stop it, Yasmeen. Don't talk such rot all the time. Now see if you like your present. Johnny has chosen it. If you hate it, you blame him.'

John had already threaded his way to the other end of the room, smiling and nodding to everyone. Treeza's relatives, their old friends, his sister Poppy, his uncle Mike. That was the joy of belonging to the same neighbourhood—they really were one large family. Damn. It was impossible to escape these people.

Uncle Mike called out to Treeza: 'Treeza, my girl, when will you two have a housewarming, haan? It's been months that you two shifted to your new house at the back of beyond. Are you going to ever invite us old folks or what? So busy, you are, with each other? Honeymooning?'

Treeza grabbed the excuse to escape from her sisters. She gave Uncle Mike a hug and from her bag took out a little red packet. 'Hello, Chachu,' she said, 'I picked up a paperback for you. I know you like reading these.'

Mike smiled, mollified. John's parents had been dead many years and Mike had been good to John and his brother in the past. Now Poppy lived with him and his wife and it was rumoured that she would inherit their wealth. But John did not mind. God knew, Poppy needed a break.

'We'll have you all over very soon,' Treeza announced to the rest of the room, kissing Poppy on both cheeks in the French style. 'You know how it is, na? With this Mount Everest loan to pay off, Johnny is working so hard, it's insane. I never get to see him. It's like we live in different countries.'

The relatives made agreeable noises. Johnny's loan had assumed mythic proportions in their circles. Everyone was interested in how it was working out.

At the makeshift bar by the balcony Yasmeen's husband was handing out drinks. 'Hello, Johnny boy, what you want? Whisky?'

'Happy anniversary, Terry.' John replied. 'Give us a hug. Give us also a really stiff whisky, will you?'

Terry gave him his drink, a quick hug, and then bustled off somewhere else. Apparently, the caterers had just arrived and were unloading the food. At any party that Terry threw, two things were certain: his wife would be dressed ludicrously, the food would be amazing.

John shut the door gently and stood alone in the balcony. Terry's family had lived in this fifth-floor flat for some forty years now. Terry's brother Bo had been his classmate at Calcutta Boys' School. His best friend. The two of them would sleep in this balcony on summer nights. Hundreds of thousands of summer nights.

John looked at the sea of traffic below, through the jumble of electric wires glistening in the rain, round full drops sliding along and dripping from the ends. The dark here was familiar to John, more familiar than any other dark, anywhere else in the world. It was broken by a million pin-pricks of lights glimmering around, warm, happy lights in other people's windows. The air here was more familiar too. The red buses and the yellow cabs; the smell of rain on the asphalt; the whorls of noise radiating from below, from that solid ball of big-city noise that engulfed Eliot Road till the wee hours of morning; the whiff of other people's dinners; the strains of other people's guitar practice.

Bo and John had both done literature in college. At St Xavier's, they had joined the same clubs, taken the same pass courses, doubledated sets of best friends. After graduation, Bo, on a strange whim, joined the army. John went on to do his masters. On finishing his training with flying colours, Bo, in his captain's uniform, proposed to Poppy, and then went off to his first posting, while John joined a research programme at university. The plan had decided by Bo: John would go to England for research; the captain and his wife would go to visit him for their honeymoon. John had tried telling them once or twice that even on a scholarship he would have to slum it out. But Bo had said that was fine, he was a soldier, remember? Barracks weren't exactly fancy hotels. One year later, Bo was dead. He was given a hero's send-off.

John had dropped out of the MPhil and gone back to their old school as a teacher. In every classroom, he confronted the memories of Bo. That was his lot to bear, maudlin and sentimental though it sounded. He embraced it.

If it wasn't for Bo, John would insist that he and Treeza move back to this neighbourhood, to their old haunts. He would shake her shoulders and seize her hand and promise that even they could be happy here. Again. But after Bo... And now the universe held no record that a boy called Bo had made elaborate plans on summer nights in this balcony, except for him, a flawed incomplete friend, and his sister, Poppy, who had become a prissy old marm. After Bo, John was sure of one thing. No corner of the universe was exempt from sorrow. Especially not for him.

'Johnny…' Treeza pushed open the balcony door open and snuck her head around it. 'Come! Everyone's looking for you. They are going to cut the cake.' On second thought, she entered and stood next to him, her elbows on the railing, mirroring his pose, inhaling the familiar dark, like him. 'Yasmeen loved the present.' She touched his sleeve. 'You know she can't wait till after the party to open presents.'

There was something open about Treeza just now, something in the way she leant over the railing. John wanted to say: 'You want one of these embroidered sheets too? For us?' But instead he said, 'Sure, let's go in.'

He said that but made no move. Treeza smiled a half-smile.

'Treeze,' John said impulsively, 'why didn't you come to the shop with me?'

In response, Treeza turned to go. For an instant, as she turned, her body froze at an angle, and John could guess her eyes darkened and the warmth and openness in her limbs solidified quickly. But her voice was unchanged when she replied, her back turned to him. Her voice was light like the lightest of silk scarves, pale like the sky in the morning.

'I went to get the book for Uncle Mike, John. Now come. They're waiting.'

SANDHYA

Wednesday.
From: sandhya_shantiashram@gmail.com
To: sheilagibson@yahoo.co.uk
Dear Sheila,

I am writing to you from the Armenian hotel which has now

become my favourite. The bureau in the room reminds me of the one my father had back at home, and the weather too, strangely, has been wet and glitteringly sunny in turns. Much like the Carib.

The letter from the lawyer's office had tipped the scale. And now it is as though the cosmos is turning things in its way, indubitably, to unleash these forces that will change everything. And then again, after winter, it will come together again. In some form.

I am trying to distance myself from all the noise and yet reach the centre.

Yesterday, I went to the lawyers. It was all a big surprise. I shall tell you the details when we speak. In any case, the entire picture is not quite clear yet.

To cut a long story short, Sheila, I find suddenly that I have to stay back in Calcutta.

I have written to the ashram in Rishikesh to make alternate arrangements for the rest of this year and, perhaps, for the remainder of my trip. It was a difficult letter to write and I can only imagine the consequent trouble for you. But if you ask my honest opinion, it will be good for Swamiji to be the head this year. It is a timely reminder for me too. I must not get too used to the ashram, nor they to me. Since I have turned sixty, I increasingly feel the time is nigh for me to take more time off. There is too much glamour these days in being a saadhvi, it seems. It has become too difficult to get away.

I shall be shifting out of the hotel to a more permanent home in the city soon, I think, though I shall miss having Mrs Arrathoon clucking over me. I will let you know of the move as soon as I have an address. The lawyer's office, in the interim, has attached a young intern to assist me.

Meanwhile, hope all is well with you and Mark. How are the girls?

Give my love to all at Summertown.

Sandhya

CHAPTER 7

SATURDAY
7.1

Ananda Bose had become a creature of habit. One was likely to think the opposite of him—and, in all honesty, such an opinion was not unfounded. The air he gave off was one of distinct unattachment to routine. In his youth, in his student days, he would mostly do as he pleased: though a philosophy major, he often attended lectures with students of Bengali literature; rain or shine, as the need arose, it was always he who kept vigil beside the sickbeds of friends, and later, after university, parents of friends; sometimes, he awoke early and went for morning walks; at other times, he would read late into the night or cultivate new hobbies; he might vanish for days at a stretch and eventually return with great knowledge of Baul music or Madhubani art.

Even now, though the rhythm of his life had been completely transformed since his mother's illness, his colleagues would tell him at the start of each weekend: 'Lucky man, Bose. No wife to please. No children to teach maths to. No Big Bazaar to shop at. How I envy you, free-bird-Bose. Do as you please, guru, do what you like. I have to visit my in-laws in the suburbs while you watch Paoli Dam in the bloody cinema hall! My wife won't even hear of it.' Each of the men said something on these lines, every week. (The women rushed into the weekend headlong, no time for chitchat.) Bose would smile as usual and linger in the staff room on Friday afternoons. He visited the library to see if there were any new books he could borrow, but the librarian, still a new bride, was in a hurry to close up and leave. He never did confess to anyone how ordered his weekends had become, how predictable. He also never let on that he had no idea who Paoli Dam was. And, in any case, his colleagues, for all their assumptions about his free-bird lifestyle, never really bothered to ask him on Monday mornings what he'd been up to. They were eager to report stories of their outings in Big Bazaar and the suburbs, and the clever, often mean things their wives and children had said.

On Saturday morning, Ananda Bose looked out of the window of his bedroom. The skies were overcast again. The hibiscus tree was full of flowers and framed picturesquely against the backdrop of A-1, Mrs Das's building, and the gloomy sky was roiling. Bose sighed. The last few days had possibly seen the worst weather in Calcutta this year. Muggy, airless mornings, so humid that one broke out in a sweat even in the bath, sunny in short bursts but not enough to dry the clothes that lay slowly reeking in everybody's verandas. Long, still evenings when rarely a leaf fluttered. It was desperate weather, intense enough to make a lonely man lose his mind. It seemed the grey streak was to continue.

Ananda Bose sipped his tea and nibbled his toast and wondered what he could do. The museum? A play? One of the art galleries? Maybe he should try the zoo today. It would probably be empty but for the animals. And that led him to the thought: did the animals in Alipore Zoo have any shelter against the rain? The giraffes, for instance?

He would have to leave in the next two hours. Things were running smoothly at home, touch wood. After their very public spat, in a strange U-turn, Madhobi and the nurse had returned home together, three hours later, the best of friends. Both fell at his feet and apologized profusely for having left the patient alone. Bose, stunned by their truce, had not probed further. There had been no drama in the interim.

Every Saturday, exactly at ten, Ananda Bose's sister, ten years his senior, would come down from New Alipore to spend time with their mother. Sometimes, she would be accompanied by her children; rarely, when matters were serious, her husband might put in an appearance. On most days, Bose would spend a quarter of an hour with his sister, after which she would rapidly descend from mildly annoying to completely intolerable. That would be his cue to leave, ostensibly on errands or seminars, or to libraries. He would return home at half-past-five, drink tea with his sister, digest her theories on everything. In the evenings, she was marginally better; perhaps the whole day with their mother sobered her a tad bit. She would also be in a hurry to leave. Her husband would pick her up and together they would go grocery shopping.

The physician would come by at half past six. Bose would discuss his mother's health in great detail with him, and often suggest medication changes. Eventually, the doctor would leave, exhausted, and Bose would relax, having got the house back to himself. He would play some music in his room, take a shower and sit down with a drink. It was usually a double malt.

In the morning, when he looked out of the window and gazed at the clouds, the only decision Bose had to take was whether it would be the Gorky Sadan Library today or the Academy of Fine Arts. The formula for the rest of the day would remain untweaked. For a free bird, it was all hopelessly banal. But he was not particularly perturbed this morning; he had trained himself to be happy with his lot.

He had trained himself to forget what it felt to be awaited somewhere.

7.2

At the ungodly hour of eight-thirty, Abeer was hauled from bed and ordered to the milk booth near the colony. He tried suggesting that he'd been studying late at night, but his sister, who was home for some unhelpful reason, pointed out that since he had been hogging the WiFi, it was likely he was watching a movie. Apparently, her research had been interrupted. Why couldn't she go, Abeer thought. Ever since the diet had been enforced, their mother was trying to spoil her *without* the help of food.

Was eight-forty any time for a self-respecting human to step outside home on a Saturday? But there was a long queue at the milk booth, which he reluctantly joined, and fresh-faced, freshly bathed Bengalis were going about their business, discussing news, chasing buses, trampling through mud and, in general, being annoying busybodies. Mrs Monalisa Das stood ahead of him, her chin determined as usual. Wondering how her sons could tolerate her rigorous regime, Abeer stretched and turned around. And immediately wished he hadn't. Behind him, rushing to join the line, *The Telegraph* tucked under his arm, was Ananda Bose. Oh fish! Fish, fish, fish.

Last week, a bunch of them had decided that they were swearing far too much. It was leading to embarrassing episodes, with four-letter words being used in front of professors a lot or, more importantly, in front of the girls they were trying to impress—apparently, the new thing trending (other than the word trending) was that girls didn't like four-letter words any more. So it was a pact. They'd say fish instead of fuck, and shoot instead of shit (or saala, in the case of AJ).

'Hello, Abeer,' Bose said, and his face lit up.

It really lit up, became radiant, Abeer observed. It made him a little guilty. 'Hello, Ananda Da.'

'How are you, Abeer?'

'I'm fine, just busy with exams, you know,' Abeer replied.

'Ah, yes. You're studying something technological, aren't you?' Bose said.

Abeer did not go into details. Integrated BCA-MCA, not BTech, blah blah blah. People always thought it was a great talking point.

'So what courses are you taking this year?' Bose asked, genuine interest in his eyes. Details didn't matter, but ideas did. And what were courses but histories of ideas?

Abeer began to recite his courses mechanically. When he came to 'The Basics of Philosophy' (the most boring course of the lot, in his opinion, even worse than 'Psychology in the Workplace') Bose went into raptures.

'I am very happy to hear that, Abeer, very happy indeed. I didn't know that you techies had any courses on philosophy! But what is a human being without philosophical frameworks? In fact, each human being is a philosopher, in his or her own way.'

Most techies *didn't* have courses on philosophy in the third year. They were lucky. But since their principal's daughter taught at a radical college in the US, where one could study engineering and semiotics simultaneously, he had inflicted this course on them.

Ananda Bose and Abeer walked back to Nancy together. Bose had asked about the philosophy seminar in detail (Abeer wasn't sure of it but fudged around) and promised all help whatsoever in what he assumed was Abeer's philosophical quest. Did Abeer need any books? He could even give Abeer one or two extremely interesting articles from contemporary journals. If he was interested, of course.

Abeer murmured thanks several times. He wondered if he could go home, eat breakfast and then go back to bed. Mmm. But if he ate, that would certainly ruin the remnants of sleep in his eyes, he wouldn't be able to recall quite the same texture of sleep again. It was tough, but he would have to choose: breakfast or bed? Perhaps breakfast. A nice double-egg omelette with cheddar stuffed inside, a stack of toast with butter. Maybe a blob of strawberry jam on the last toast. Aah! Some mixed fruit juice, maybe. Absentmindedly, he kept walking with Bose, agreeing with him, dreaming about the breakfast—and then, naturally, he came across Mandy Mandal in his thoughts and got even more distracted—until he realized what Bose was saying.

'I am so glad, Abeer, that you evinced interest. This has, in fact, made my weekend. I do understand that as a future leader of technology you will naturally be more interested in those areas of research. But that is why the beauty of logic will also appeal to you so much. The elegance of it. Ah!' Bose rang the bell. 'Come in, come in!'

Abeer realized with a start that he had agreed to something—what?—rashly, and was now about to enter Bose's flat. Fish, fish, fish!

'We can have tea together and discuss. Thank you for coming,' Bose said.

Abeer was trapped. 'But my mother will be expecting me,' he managed to say. 'The milk, actually, for tea, and my grandmother's shabur khichuri.'

Bose entered the house and said, slightly disappointed, 'Okay, perhaps you can take the books on logic, then? And while I look for these you can at least have a cup of tea. Or Madhobi can reach the milk to your—Didi? You're early today.'

Abeer Mukherjee was gobsmacked. Sitting on Ananda Bose's sofa, in a pair of slim white trousers, was Mandy Mandal.

Abeer closed his eyes and opened them again.

It was her. In a pink T-shirt.

Mandy Mandal was playing with her iPhone. A large woman in a starched green sari stood imperiously behind her.

Abeer looked at Bose, whose face had turned puce.

'Didi, this is Abeer Mukherjee, very bright young boy. A neighbour.'

Meanwhile, Mandy had looked up from her phone. 'Hello, Mamu,' she mumbled, and then looked at Abeer. 'Hi,' she said tentatively.

Abeer's mouth opened and closed but no sound emerged.

'Abeer, this is my niece Mandakini,' Bose said. 'She is also a student of technology.'

'Integrated BCA-MCA, Babu,' the large woman corrected.

'In fact,' Mandy said, smiling, 'Abeer is my senior, actually. We're in the same college. Aren't you in my music committee too?'

Abeer was not sure if any words might come out of his mouth. So he smiled. Or attempted a smile. He was half-certain that the result was a clownish grimace. He tried to smoothe his clothes and hair simultaneously and dropped the milk packet with a plop at his feet. He tried to pick it up discreetly, without flashing his giant butt in anybody's face.

Bose said, 'Come, come, great stuff. Now that we know you are friends already, even more reason you should stay on. Have some tea.'

The large woman, who was obviously Mandy's mother, said, 'I have brought some excellent shingaras from our para. Pedigree-wala shingaras, Abeer. I am sorry to say, Babu, no shop in this newbie area makes good shingaras. I think you will like them, Abeer. Sit, sit.'

'I'll ferret out the journals,' Bose said. 'Didi, Abeer is very interested in philosophy.'

'Wow,' said Mandy.

Abeer finally found some presence of mind. 'Ananda Da, Mandy, Mashima,' he said, 'I shall come back in a trice. I'll drop off the milk and tell my mother I'm here. I'll only be a second.'

7.3

The madness in Meera Sahai's house had reached a new high. More suitcases had been added. The sister-in-law, the positively prying, perfectly evil younger sister of Ramesh and Suresh, Lovely—the lovely one with the bitter-gourd tongue—had reached Calcutta yesterday morning. Meera and Nalini, and to a lesser extent the brothers and the nephews, were already reeling from her stinging words. The badly kept house. The ill-designed kitchen. The small rooms. The lack of air conditioners in the small rooms (Lovely's husband distributed air conditioners to hotels in Gaya, Bhagalpur, Arra, Chhapra and Munger; their house even had an AC fitted in the store room, it seemed.) No flat screen TV. Then there was the general taste of Meera's cooking. The bad temper of the baby. The awkward limbs of the boys. The distance between their flat and any place of interest, such as New Market. Nothing had escaped her comprehensive gaze.

Meera was affected most of all. Not only was she mistress of the above-critiqued house but also the lack of proper sleep and rest had already set her teeth at edge.

When Nalini spotted Meera sobbing in the bedroom, after Lovely laughed at the shapes of her pooris, she tried to take matters in her hands. She was far more adept at housework. Her pallu didn't slip from her head, her pooris were perfectly round. She tried to take over.

It didn't help. For one, Meera felt even worse, as though her position in her own house was being threatened; she began to react even more sharply to everything that was said. For another, there was Lovely.

Lovely Srivastav, formerly Sahai, had not come to the quasi-parental house for a vacation after three whole years to sing paeans in praise of the sisters-in-law. She had to do enough of that in her own sasural. She had come to get some rest. She wanted her son off her hands, she wanted to gossip in peace with her mother and have tea and snacks brought to her, she wanted her hair oiled in the morning and, yes, in the evening, she wanted to be taken out to the malls and shopping arcades that she had heard Suresh and his darling wife frequented.

On Saturday morning, Meera and Nalini were feverishly scrubbing utensils in the kitchen when Apu dropped in for a visit. Apu's mother had come the evening before, with piles of extra pillows, bedclothes and mattresses (which Abeer had lugged in, glowering). But Mrs Mukherjee had done the right thing. With Ramesh's family, the house was already bursting to the seams. Meera wondered where Lovely and her entourage—she had brought a nanny for her little boy, a young tribal girl from Jharkhand—would fit. But eventually it had been managed. Lovely and her entourage were settled in Maaji Sahai's room, with a bed on the floor for the nanny. Ramesh and his sons were in the little study, between the couch and the floor. And Suresh slept on the divan in the drawing room; that way, he could get ready and leave for office early in the morning without disturbing the whole family. Meera and Nalini and the girls got to stay in her bedroom. Lovely was not happy about this at all since Meera's bedroom had a balcony; she wanted to swap. But Maaji Sahai demonstrated the superiority of her own mattress to Meera's and the fact that the balcony might be dangerous for her naughty little boy, so that was that. The extra bedclothes had helped enormously. It was exactly the sort of thoughtfulness Mrs Mukherjee was known for.

Apu spent a few minutes with Maaji Sahai and admired Lovely's jewellery and her little boy. Luckily, the child demanded chips and Maaji remembered her puja, so Apu could slip out to the kitchen for a while. Nalini was happy to see her and chatted amiably, even as her hands were busy cleaning. But Meera glared at Apu from the corner and began to bang the clean utensils on the counter with far greater force than necessary. Apu took the hint. She excused herself from Nalini and went to Meera's bedroom to play with the baby. In a few minutes, Meera came in and locked the door behind her. She strode in angrily, stood in front of Apu, crossed her arms and said, 'Apu, hear me once and for all, you are not going to talk to these chudails. *Any* of them. Why are you giving them so much importance, haan? Or do you also find them more interesting than me?'

If Apu was a little disturbed by Meera's excessive reaction she didn't show it. She offered the baby to her. Meera declined.

Apu tickled Chhoti's cheeks and said, 'Meera, don't be stupid. You are my best friend. The only reason I am being nice to these chudails is so that they don't give you a hard time about this too. Exactly how many minutes we waste talking and laughing. How many chapatis could have been rolled in that time. Maaji could have been a statistician, you know. Listen, seriously, if that old crone is a little happy with a few false words of praise for that dumb daughter and that spoilt little boy, I am happy to play along.'

Meera said, finally, in a grudging voice, 'I know. I just wanted to shout at someone a little.' She sat down on the bed and sighed. 'Sorry,' she said.

'I know, I know,' Apu said. 'It's fine. You want to hear bad news? After all this dieting and starving, not only have I *not* lost any weight but I've also put on two kilos. Can you believe it?'

Meera looked at Apu.

'We really have to start going on those walks again. Meera?'

Meera had a round face. Her eyes were black like coal, deep rather than bright. She had long hair that was now drawn behind tightly into an untidy bun. There were dark circles under her eyes, plunging the rest of her face in shadow.

Suddenly, Apu was very worried for her friend. Used to asking Meera for advice rather than tendering any, she mumbled, 'But enough of my sorry saga. I haven't seen you all week so I had to tell you this.' She extended one hand to Meera's shoulder. 'How are you, Meera?'

The question began to buzz around Meera like a bee. The bed seemed to rock with the question. The clouds outside began to advance inside. The light in the room dimmed. Meera's legs were frozen. She had no answer to Apu's question.

The baby started to cry; the phone on the dresser began to ring; Nalini knocked on the bedroom door and called urgently: 'Meera, Meera, Suresh is calling you.' And Lovely's voice could be heard loudly in the next room, regaling her brothers: 'Meera Bhabhi is busy talking to the next-door girl, Bhaiya. But don't you know you have to be MSc-PhD to be her friend? That is why she has no time for the likes of us. Me, BA incomplete!'

Apu flushed.

The phone continued to ring; Chhoti kept crying; Nalini knocked again. Meera kept sitting on the bed.

'Meera,' Nalini called again. The phone stopped ringing.

Eventually, Apu got up, pushed the bawling baby into Meera's lap and went to open the door.

7.4

On Saturdays, John returned home in the late afternoon. While he was walking home from the bus stop, and it began to drizzle, he realized he had left his umbrella somewhere. In the bus? Or was he lucky and hadn't brought it out of the chamber at all?

His chamber. Treeza had started calling his sad little classroom his chamber, and him the doctor of grammar. When he first started teaching, and requests began pouring in for extra classes, John had rented a room on the ground floor of an old house on S. N. Banerjee Road, fairly close to school, where he could teach his English language and literature classes. It had been very convenient when they lived in Eliot Road. If the weather was fine, he would simply walk to and fro.

In the early days after their wedding, Treeza would drop in unannounced and bring a swirl of laughter and colour into the drab room with its discoloured walls, the twenty chairs and one old blackboard. His students would remain distracted for the rest of the class, long after she left. When they shifted to this new part of town, he'd debated if he should shift the whole affair closer home. But then his existing students would not move, their syllabus was not yet complete, the housing colony might not even allow it. So he left the arrangement as it was. On hindsight, it was a wise decision. He couldn't imagine having to teach in such close proximity to Treeza's breakdowns.

As he walked inside the gates of Nancy, exchanging a few words with the two guards who sat there, a car followed him inside. It was a white sedan. After a bit, the driver came abreast of him and a young girl with flyaway hair leant out and asked if he knew where A-5 was. John said, yes, of course he did. As it happened, he lived there. It was straight down, only about fifty feet ahead and the first house to the right. Next to the hibiscus tree. 'Why don't you come in?' the girl said.

John noticed her hair had bright red streaks. 'No, that's all right,' he replied. 'It'll take me a minute to get there anyway. I'm afraid you'll have to park near the main gate, though.'

The driver went ahead as directed. By the time John reached, the passengers had alighted. The girl with the red flyaway hair was accompanying a distinguished-looking lady in a white sari. They all trooped into the foyer, where all the letter boxes were lined up, to avoid the fat raindrops now falling in a flurry. John could not be sure how old the lady was, but the girl was in her early twenties. The lady folded her hands in a namaskar and said hello. The girl said to the old lady, 'We have to go to the second floor.'

'Oh? I'm on the first,' John said. 'No elevator, unfortunately. Are you moving in?'

Almost at the same time, the girl and the old lady replied. 'Not quite sure…' the girl said noncommittally. 'I think so,' said the old lady. The girl looked at her, surprised and caught off-guard. The old lady smiled.

John had reached his flat. In a burst of spontaneity, he said, 'I am John. My wife Treeza and I live here. Perhaps you'd like to come in later for tea? And, of course, if you need any help…'

'Thank you,' said the old lady. 'Very nice to meet you, John.'

John observed that though her English was almost completely flat, there were traces of a British accent. Very slight.

They began to ascend the stairs, the red-haired girl bringing a bunch of keys out of her bag. John remained standing outside his door. Each floor in Nancy had two flats; there were two doors facing each other. At one end, the stairs went up. The other end jutted out like a balcony, affording a pleasant view. The sort of a view that a housing colony which was part of the dense urban sprawl encircling Calcutta could afford. It was pleasant enough in its way. One saw other box-like houses that people had paid for dearly and filled with pretty things, well-kept patches of green, a few trees, a few colourful curtains. Wind chimes people had hung by their windows sent out tinny sounds on the breeze.

John looked at three huge bundles of bamboo piled outside.

The pujas were near. And just like that, almost as the moment dimmed into nothing, as his eyes flitted idly from the bamboos to the branches now bent low in the wind and back to the rain-swept pathway in front, it became clear to him.

Clean and sharp, like the movement of a scalpel, clarity came as darkness dropped outside from the skies and the strange old lady went upstairs, and the girl with red hair. John realized, with the ease of clouds breaking and leaves receiving rain, why Treeza had not entered Russi's shop. There was no reason why he remembered this little nugget of information now, as the rain pounded on the gravel chips outside their building and the sky grew so dark that lights were switched on, one by one, in people's windows.

Ever since the evening of Yasmeen's party, in his mind he had searched continuously for something, through the shelves of books and drawers stuffed with memories and notes, in his head, in boxes and boxes of images. He had rifled and hunted, even as he taught Shakespeare to Class 11 or punctuation to the middle school bunch. The torrents made little pools that then eddied and whirled below, finally running into the ditches where at night frogs would appear.

He now knew the answer, and it was obvious. So obvious that he was surprised he had missed it himself. Treeza did not want to enter Russi's emporium. For, when you entered the shop, on the right, you would see rows and rows of soft, hand-embroidered beautiful little clothes for children. They were displayed by the counter, they came from near and far, they were pure cotton and, in some cases, pure silk. They were clothes around which women clustered, and one or two men. Parents, mostly.

SANDHYA

From: sheilagibson@yahoo.co.uk
To: sandhya_shantiashram@gmail.com
Sandhya,

I'll have you know that my inbox is bombarded with mails from around the world. Mataji is considered absconding! I am having to reassure hundreds of people—often by eschewing the truth—and it would be all right, I suppose, if I wasn't so worried about you myself. Our phone conversations are so short and you are being so cryptic, I am quite at sea. But if you are indeed serious that you shall stay on in Calcutta, then I will have to formally let people know that you are taking a year off to do deeper sadhana or something like that. In a way, this is in character: people perhaps expect you to do such things. It is *me* that they expect to sort out the practical mess. Oh, dear! Anyway, as you said, Swamiji can head the ashram in Rishikesh for now. Let me see if I can actually take that sabbatical I've been threatening my dean with all these years, and convert your workshops into mine instead of cancelling them completely.

All else okay.

Sheila x

BOOK 3
OCTOBER

CHAPTER 8

SANDHYA

From 'Instead of an Introduction', Solstice (1994).
I am Sandhya; I am a brahmacharini.

Though not a writer by any account, I have *authored a few books before this one. On yoga, ayurveda for women, Indian philosophy, a thesis on mantra and music (music being my old passion, my old career), and one or two on comparative religion. The book-writing, though, was somewhat accidental.*

After my initiation into the monastic order, I began to progress slowly on the learning curve of my new subjects. At this time, I would often hunt around for specific books. When I didn't find these in English, my guru would order me to study the subjects in the traditional way—with traditional teachers and traditional texts—and then write *the books I had been looking for. But I am afraid these have all been serious volumes.*

I have also written a few books for children, a far more pleasurable activity. They mostly came about when my grandnieces and nephews, and the children of some of my students, demanded stories on cold evenings. (These young ones would have been compelled to accompany their parents and spend long months at either of my ashrams, humouring the adults all around.) I am happy to report these books, at least, are not serious.

But until now I have not found in myself the courage to write my own story—to trace the circuitous journey that brought me to my calling. Even though I speak of it freely, there is something about the act of writing one's memoirs, spiritual though they might be, that requires one to confront the past again and again, to sift through old fears and old sorrows mixed indiscriminately with joys and portions of guilt; the writing of it makes it real again, if only for an hour or a week, and we live in its shadow.

That said, I think I am old enough to feel a fondness for all of it now—the whole bag of memory and longing; old enough to feel a fondness for even the excruciating agony of disease and the stench of disinfectant in hospital corridors. After all, I have been granted three extra decades by fate, when there was a time in my youth I would have been grateful for three months.

You see, at twenty-three, cancer had coursed through my body and pronounced on me its sentence. At twenty-seven, I was doomed to die.

This is my story.

8.1

October brought blue skies.

Calcuttans heaved a sigh of relief as the pall of grey dissipated. They commenced with alacrity their ritual shopping and planning and dipping into holiday neuroses.

October brought honey-dipped dawns that by noon hour deepened into a rich hot day, the sun stinging the skin ever so slightly.

Women began ticking off items on elaborate lists—clothes to buy for family and staff, lunches and dinners to be hosted for friends. Each had made long lists, from which a few names, depending on insider information, were eventually scratched out. (If, for instance, you bought an expensive sari for a sister-in-law who had bought none for you that year, it would be sticky now, wouldn't it?)

Men began complaining severely about accelerating acidity and depleted bank balance over the excesses of spouse and children.

The air in Calcutta was festive, bordering on hysterical. Houses were already being festooned with strings of lights; it would be another week, though, before they began to be lit up in the evenings, little red and blue and yellow dots of light glittering like jewels, each teeny bulb surrounded by an orb of dust. But the arrival of Durga, on a palanquin this year, on the sixth day of the month of Ashwin, shasthi, was still a fortnight away. Things would calm down and then burst into electric jolts, only to calm down again, several times before that.

Nancy Housing Cooperative was equal to its responsibilities in the festive season.

The modest park that stood in the middle of the colony, with a pair of swings and a small slide meant for young children, was the venue for Nancy's annual puja. Every housing colony worth its salt in Calcutta had its own Durga puja, and, of course, every neighbourhood had several.

There were forty flats in Nancy, eight in each of the five buildings. Only about thirty-two of these flat were occupied—Sandhya made it thirty-three—and so the total funds collected from the residents did not add up to a very grand sum. Nancy was essentially a middle-class colony. Even on paper, it was categorized as MIG: (home to the) Middle Income Group. But the bankers and lecturers and executive officers and senior government clerks and mid-level journalists who lived in Nancy, and were enthusiastic about the puja (though not that all of them were religious), galvanized their contacts and gathered sponsorships zealously.

It was morning. The light seemed yet unused, the air sweet and fresh still. Sandhya paused by the park, and then took a few steps inside. The green grass was moist under her thin slippers. She had been out buying vegetables from the neighbourhood market, and now she rested her cotton jhola, bursting with fresh produce—a bunch of lettuce, half-a-kilo of peas, cherry tomatoes, carrots, and a medium-sized pumpkin—on a bench. She silently observed the men who were building the pandal.

The more fancy pandals in Calcutta, the ones which won awards and attracted hundreds of thousands of visitors each day, were replicas of internationally recognized monuments or, even better, internationally imagined ones. For example, Hogwarts (though somebody had sued somebody and the thing ended badly, the execution, by popular consent, had been grand). The fanciest of pandals were fascinating interpretations of folk art or, these days, of recycling. (Last puja, a neighbourhood had won critical acclaim with a pandal made entirely of discarded plastic water bottles). Nancy, in comparison, had modest aspirations. This year, they were to have a simple, elegant structure, modelled on a Roman ruin marked by a row of prominent Corinthian pillars in front. Mrs Das had picked it out from her younger son's history textbook, and since Mr Das headed the puja committee this year, it had been selected.

But Sandhya didn't know any of this background; she knew about the scale of the Durga Puja in Calcutta, of course, and was glad, since she herself worshipped the devi; but she had no experience of the puja here. And she was yet to know any of the residents of Nancy personally.

Sandhya savoured the stillness of the moment—the sense of how every second stretched and exploded, enveloping the precise and relentless histrionics of the men as they scaled the bamboo scaffolding, tossed around ropes, shouted to each other, handled hammers and nails. They built a house for the goddess from scratch with smiling ease. Their thin brown bodies glistened with sweat, though the day had not become warm yet. The leader of the men was a pious Muslim who broke every working day thrice to do his namaaz. Sandhya had noted this from her bedroom window. One of the younger boys would join him on some days. On other days, he would use the break to smoke a bidi.

Sandhya had moved into Nancy the previous weekend, even as the late monsoon rains almost brought the city to a halt. Mrs Arrathoon had been wont to let her go; Sheila had been doubtful; and the young intern the lawyer's office had attached to her, the girl with the red hair, had been surprised.

The lawyers, the estimable Pranoy Sen and his father, the

octogenarian Praful Sen, both formerly of Inner Temple, had been prepared to offer alternatives to their celebrity client. They kept suggesting 'furnished flats' in 'posh' localities, suitable for 'expats'. But Sandhya was not interested—for one, she did not want to cheat even a little bit. For another, unlike other men and women of her vocation, who made a song and dance about grandeur, she had no interest in being driven around or installed in luxurious rooms or be made much of. As it is, she had begun to call herself a *retired* brahmacharini now, so the norms ought to be stricter than before. A small place where she could cook for herself would be enough, she had told the advocates.

Then there was the entirely subjective slant. Even before she had visited Nancy, when she had gone through the letters that had been left to her, she had almost made up her mind. And after she went to the colony, something about the twilit hour—and perhaps the dimensions of Nancy's ordinariness, its solidness—had made her immediately certain about moving there. The energy of the building, the way the rain came in from the east, the young neighbour with the smouldering core of regret and longing—all of these nudged her along to a decision.

'We old women believe in signs and things, my dear.' Sandhya had consoled the red-haired girl on the way back. 'Maybe you'd like to help me buy some plants?'

'But you haven't even seen the Ballygunge flat yet, Mataji,' the girl had said.

Sandhya had patted her comfortingly on the shoulder. The girl lived in a large airy flat on Gurusaday Road herself, with her doctor-parents and dogs and several household staff. She couldn't imagine how or why anybody, especially someone who had disciples ranging from heads of state and ministers to musicians, writers and even a few minor Hollywood actors, could think of staying in a small residential colony in one of the newer developments of the city, a boring part of town, really, where the road leading to the block of houses were lined on either side by vegetable vendors and hawkers selling rubber slippers, Rexine bags and sparkly clothes. The girl had hoped to have Sandhya installed close by and show her off to her friends. 'Do you know *who* I am with?' she had already whispered into her phone several times that day.

The firm of lawyers had come to be well-acquainted with Sandhya's fame. Through the ministrations of the young PR-savvy administrators of the Rishikesh ashram, several articles on Sandhya published abroad and a few influential reviews of her most important books had been faxed to Messrs Sen and Sen before the appointment. This had all been done without Sandhya's knowledge. After reading these, the girl with the red streaks in her hair had been very excited about following Sandhya around, hoping for wisdom and transformation between the car rides and the legal stock-taking. As it were, she had loved the bestselling *Autumn in the Ashram: A Woman's Spiritual Quest in Three Continents* by the American author Betsy Goldberg. The book was now being made into a film by Ang Lee, no less. Betsy Goldberg was a student of Sandhya's—one of the articles reported it—and it was at Sandhya's request that the name and location of the ashram had been changed in the book. But, basically, *Autumn in the Ashram* was set around Sandhya. The girl was gobsmacked. Imagine that!

But, fortunately for Sandhya, nobody at Nancy seemed to know of these articles or books, let alone of these heads of state or actors. The Sens were, true to form, extremely discreet.

Sandhya was only too happy to start this new still phase of her life, almost incognito, away from her homes and worlds—which had of late become too full, too busy perhaps—and make one final peace with the past.

8.2

Ananda Bose had just set out for college. He adjusted his watch strap and walked past the park in his starched white kurta and faded blue jeans. A light beard had sprung on his face; he hadn't had time to shave this morning before setting out. He had no classes today, so he would go to college only in the second half. He was on his way to the Medical College, to meet his mother's chief oncologist, and ask if there were any alternative ways of relieving her pain. It was now getting to be too much—even the nurses were beginning to feel the strain. But then he saw the lady in white standing in the park, his new neighbour, and after hesitating a moment or two he walked towards her.

'Good morning, madam,' he said. His voice was friendly, the timbre rich and warm. His students often joked that he could have been a news reader on AIR—he had that firm, unhurried quality of speech.

As Sandhya turned towards Bose, the sunlight behind threw her face in darkness for a moment. Then she moved and he followed, and when he caught her eyes, he was immediately arrested by her brown face and its noble features. There was something about her presence, he noted immediately. A sort of *centredness* within her, as though she was still inside, quietly drawing everything around towards her core. In contrast, it seemed to him that his inner self—he did not usually use such vague phrases; but whatever was inside him—was always streaking this way and that. He beamed at her.

Sandhya had seen him often from her window, walking up to their common entrance below or leaving the house in a rush, clutching a mass of papers, the ubiquitous *Telegraph* tucked under his arm. A tall man with a slight stoop and a fair face that had now begun to show a bit of weight below the chin and around the neck, a layer here and there, blunting his essentially sharp features, moulding them to a rounded benign-ness—a kind man but lonely, was Sandhya's first thought; a young man, really, his eyes gave away his age; a young-old man grappling with the nearness of death.

'Good morning,' Sandhya said, smiling and folding her hands as he had done. 'Lovely weather.'

Almost as soon as the words had left her lips, she realized she was being hopelessly British. But the man seemed to think about her comment seriously. He reflected for a moment or two and said, 'It is fine weather, certainly. But it tends to get a little too intense at noon. By October it ought to have mellowed more, you know. It usually does. I suppose by the time the pujas are here it will be spectacular weather.'

'Is that right?' Sandhya replied gamely. 'Of course, it is my first time in the city in decades, so I wouldn't know. But it's very nice to meet you, Mr—'

'Bose. I am Ananda Bose. I'd be glad if you just called me Ananda.'

'So glad to finally meet you, Ananda. I've seen you around. I think it's just us in A-5, and Mr and Mrs John?'

Bose nodded. 'That's right, madam. I live with my mother and our housekeeper. Unlike the other buildings, A-5 is mostly unoccupied.'

'Oh, sorry.' Sandhya remembered herself. 'I'm being very rude, Ananda. I haven't introduced myself yet—I'm Sandhya.'

'Indeed, madam,' Ananda Bose replied with a big grin. 'But I have recognized you.'

8.3

'AJ, AJ, A-effing-J,' Abeer summoned urgently. 'Please wake up, yaar. We're going to be horribly late. You think you can keep Bhoomi waiting?'

AJ was sprawled on his stomach on Abeer's bed. His feet were sticking out in an ungainly manner, but at 6'3" he didn't fit into Abeer's regular Bengali-sized bed. He made no sign he'd heard.

Abeer bustled out of his room to check on breakfast. Aloo parathas had been promised this morning, but there didn't seem to be any progress on that count either. By now the house should have been wafting in that trademark smell. Today was such an important day. The foolish people around him didn't seem to care a whit. 'Ma, Ma!' Abeer shouted in annoyance in the general direction of the corridor that led to the other rooms from the drawing space. 'We have to leave soon.'

His sister came out of her room scowling. 'Stop shrieking. Ma has gone for a puja committee meeting. If it is breakfast you want, Ma has left elaborate instructions. Ask Didi in the kitchen. Don't bring the house down.'

Apu was in a foul mood. Their maid had been instructed to serve only toast to Apu. Aloo parathas were not for her.

Abeer took a quick peek into the kitchen. Didi was still kneading the atta. Before he opened his mouth, she grumbled: 'Now, you wait. Won't I serve breakfast to your grandmother or your father or your sister, hyan? Other days I don't see his face before nine o'clock, the breakfast gets cold on the table, but today he wants breakfast at eight! Go, wake your friend. I will see what I can do.'

Abeer hopped around some more, tried to point out that it was way past eight, but to no avail. He returned to his room and found AJ still sleeping on his stomach. He collapsed on his bean bag at the foot of the bed, deepened his voice to copy AJ's dad, and shouted: 'Adi! Adi!'

'Haanji, Papa?' AJ was up like a shot. He took a few seconds to process his surroundings. Abeer was laughing. AJ promptly rolled back on to his stomach, muttering: 'Saale, G. Main tujhe dekh loonga. Bas mujhe uthne de.'

Abeer kicked his dangling feet and shouted, 'AJ, enough! Wake up now. You know what an important day it is. Mandy will be coming around any moment. You want her to see you in this state?'

Since Abeer kept on aiming small, precise kicks at AJ's feet, he was compelled to leave the bed. He meandered into the tiny toilet that was attached to the room and banged the door shut.

Abeer checked his phone. It was eight-twenty already. Mandy must be on her way.

8.4

Ananda Bose rummaged in his bag desperately. After registering an initial tremor of tiredness, Sandhya's face had resumed its calm. The workers walked past towards the gate of the colony in a single file.

They'd been working since seven this morning and would now take a short tea-and-muri break.

Bose finally brought a small book out from his bag. It was carefully covered in newspaper. 'Madam,' he said, 'it is such a coincidence. Last evening I was looking through my bookshelf and I found this book, *your* book.' He handed Sandhya the slim volume. 'I started reading it again. Your face in the photograph looked familiar. It took me a minute or two to place you. In fact, it doesn't seem as though you have aged at all, though this book is many years old. I must tell you, madam, this book has been a favourite of mine, ever since I first read it. I'd bought it at the book fair.'

Sandhya turned the pages of the book. It was *Solstice,* a sort of spiritual memoir that she'd written in the early nineties. The book had been her biggest mainstream success, in Britain and the US and, strangely, in New Zealand, though it had never been published in India. Parts of it had even been included in anthologies chronicling Caribbean voices—now these were taught in university courses; her use of memory, myth and legend had provided a unique alternative perspective, critics said. The royalties had helped fund the Summertown ashram, the extension of the Rishikesh ashram, even the ayurvedic hospital.

'I was deeply moved by this book, madam, though I must confess I am not a believer. My father was a Communist. But unlike many other Communists of that generation, he was very respectful of other epistemologies. I have taken after him. I hunted for more books by you but found only one. A comparative study of the various schools of Indian philosophy, from the perspective of yoga.'

'Ah, yes.' Sandhya smiled. 'My most academic book. I was younger then, Ananda, and was always getting into discourses with philosophy scholars. I live in Oxford, so it is a logistical hazard. Too many of them would extol Indian philosophy as deep, profound wisdom one moment, and then, in the very next breath, reject its validity as a subject to be studied in the modern way. So

I embarked on a massive project, rephrasing the questions our ancient philosophers asked in the jargon preferred by my modern colleagues. But worry not, I am far more relaxed these days. Not so keen to convince people any more. You are a man of philosophy too, I think?'

'Guilty as charged, madam,' Ananda said. 'Though, man of philosophy sounds too grand for what I do. I teach at a local college.'

They conversed for a while on the obscure and the vague. Crows and mynahs hopped around them on the grass, peaceably picking out this and that. One or two squirrels blazed along the grass at lightning speed, their bushy tails aloft. The sun grew hotter.

Sandhya picked up her jhola and began to walk slowly out of the park, Ananda Bose in step next to her.

'Madam, the last few days, a question has been circling in my mind. Continuously. That is actually why I stopped and disturbed you. Also, I am not in a great hurry this morning. The doctor I am going to meet—for my mother—will not come before 11 30…' Bose checked himself. 'Sorry, sorry, I tend to go off-topic a little…'

Sandhya gestured that it was fine.

'I mean, when I saw you, madam, I thought I should ask, if you do not mind that is. The question that is circling in my mind: what is the difference between Dwaita-Dwaita and Vishishta Dwaita?'

But before Sandhya could answer—and even before the question could remind her of her youth, and the sort of questions her Bengali friend always asked at the most improbable of places—their attention was diverted by a car speeding along noisily. Ananda Bose recognized a glimpse of his niece at the window. The car then stopped a few furlongs ahead. It was indeed his sister's car, though Bose never remembered pointless things like make and model. Three young people trooped out; his niece leading two boys as though on leash. One of the boys was, of course, Abeer; he sported an appropriate hangdog expression. Bose was happy to see him, though Abeer, like his other bright students, had disappointed him of late. (After showing a few sparks of interest in philosophy, they all drifted off to greener pastures, usually in feminine company.) The other boy was thin and towered over them. He looked world-weary.

'Hello, Mamu,' Mandy said. 'I have dropped Ma off at your place. We are going on some important work for the college fest. I'll be back in the evening to pick her up.'

'Ananda Da,' Abeer said, slightly apologetically, 'this is my friend AJ.'

'Hello,' Bose said, bobbing his head, and elaborately introduced Sandhya to the youngsters.

In a minute or two they left, leaving in their wake a sticky wave of cologne and perfume and charged hormones lingering limply.

Ananda Bose ran his fingers through his hair and gesticulated awkwardly, as though pushing these scents away. He looked at Sandhya and repeated his question.

Sandhya

From Solstice.
United nominally by their proximity to the Caribbean Sea, a polymorphous group of islands and mainland territories form that multilingual, multiracial, multireligious region called the Caribbean. The Caribs are most renowned for their beauty, their sportsmen and, chiefly, for their spirit of enjoyment. Thousands of tourists come each year.

Perhaps you too have visited the islands at the time of the carnivals? When all is awhirl in colour, rhythm and aroma? Or you may have come on a cruise in search of sun and sea, and rum—these Caribbean cruises were very popular when I was a girl; still are, I think. And rightly so, for how scenic are the views and vistas from the beachfront hotels? The sea grey and blue and green, depending on the hour and the season, white froth running through your feet like molten pearls.

Yet, the histories of these lands—together and apart—are

complicated webs of cruelty, of segregation, of desire, exile and guilt. A history written in blood. You are surprised, I see. You thought it was the ideal place to visit when you were battered by life?

Originally peopled by Amerindians, the island where I was born was one of the first to be 'discovered' by Christopher Columbus as he voyaged into the New World, looking for territory and trade routes. It was fought over by the Dutch, French, Spanish and, of course, the British, who finally prevailed. African slaves were brought in to work on the plantations after the original inhabitants were defeated and enslaved, and the lands were taken over. Over several hundred years, the religions and ways of the Africans were completely broken, along with their spirits. The only traces that remained of their indigenous cultures were coded in music and food; slave food, a delicious cuisine built around leftovers and bits and bobs, salt fish, pig tails and a handful of okra.

But then the wheel of time took a few turns.

In 1833-34, after slavery was abolished across the British Empire, it grew difficult to find people to work in the huge sugar and tobacco plantations that had brought unimaginable wealth to several enterprising white colonists. Emancipated slaves refused to work in such conditions. To address this labour shortage, a new idea was devised. In the autumn of 1844, the British Indian Government legalized emigration of Indian labour to Jamaica, Trinidad and Guyana.

Soon after, agents began to roam around in India, tempting wretchedly poor people with stories of great wealth that was for the asking in these faraway islands. Those who agreed to go were mostly men, but also women and couples, whose livelihoods had been lost in British India when the decimation of indigenous handicrafts had led to a huge increase in the ranks of landless labour. With nothing much to look forward to in their lives, these people agreed to overcome an age-old taboo and cross the seven seas.

These wretchedly poor were then rounded up and taken to the ports of Calcutta or Madras, and loaded into ships like chattel. (Not all instances of recruitment were voluntary, of course—there were several incidents of coercion and kidnappings.) During the journey across the kala paani, as they would leave behind their land and its ties, these people would routinely become subjects of rape and disease. Often the dead and the very ill would have to be left behind on pit-stops or thrown overboard. This terrible ordeal would brand the jahajis and jahajins for life.

After three or four months on choppy waters, they would finally find themselves in a new world.

As each man landed and was given a contract of indenture—a piece of paper with his thumb imprint on it—his new life as a Calcutta coolie would begin. In the little rooms couples shared in the modest barracks, babies were born; in the common courtyard where food was cooked, friendships were struck for life.

The black incumbents whose salaries these Calcutta coolies had undercut gave these small brown men and women, the lowest in the hierarchies of these parts, an appropriate epithet: they were the 'new slaves'. In time, these new slaves made the new world their home too, although there was always something provisional about this adoption. There were also issues between the old slaves and the new which were carried forth into the future—a tragedy of spirit that hindered the flourishing of the island.

In 1874, my great-grandfather Gobin Misir arrived in our island, along with three hundred men and women, and was indentured to Mansfield Lodge, to work on its massive sugar plantations. 'Chinitat,' he had been told, was the name of the island. This was where I was born, though the wheel of time had turned a few times before that.

In my later years, when I returned to the history of my people, I immersed myself into the archives of oral history and searched with the eyes of one chastened by pain herself. I realized how the women who had been violated on the journeys would have shuttered themselves into a silence within, their grief passed on through their wombs to their children; their men, often blaming themselves for the 'disgrace', would have turned on them in violence and rage. This would be a recurrent cycle—the more the men felt powerless, with greater force would they turn on the women and even the children. The East Indians were marked by this shadow. It is this shadow that many, like me, had been desperate to escape.

From the time I was fourteen, I wanted to become someone else in a new place, start over. London would make me new, I would think, feverishly hoping and dreaming. London, the mothership.

I did become new. The cancer which nearly killed me eventually made me new. But, before that, it made examine closely the very history I had set out to forget.

For, you see, we hold in our bones the histories of our past, and the sorrows of our ancestors. Forgetting is not enough. The only way to deal with past grief is to live through it, work through it, and heal from within.

CHAPTER 9

9.1

When Mrs Das was angry—really furious, nostrils flaring, eyes darting, hair charged with static—Mr Das was seized with fear. A peculiar brand of fear.

In their youth, when this was less of a common occurrence, he would find it all very arousing. The memory of her thighs flashing through the thin cotton maxi she had started wearing around the house—those days she was slim and athletic (and he still had a head full of hair)—the image of her striding around powerfully, agitated and loud, would come back to him again and again the next day and distract him while he tallied figures in the bank. Even in those early days, he was in awe of Monalisa.

But if he tried to lead matters in a more erotic direction while she was in one of her fits, it never worked. And now, of course, these days, it was out of the question. For a moment, Das considered the possibility of a romp in the bedroom; every now and then he did, desire clouding his eyes. But she would not allow it—had not allowed it properly, like in their youth, the last few years. She was a woman with a mission now, she didn't care about sex. She was always wired, always plotting and planning and obsessing. Apparently, other wives were the same, he had gathered. Many of his colleagues at least complimented him on the delicious packed lunches Monalisa sent every day, alongside sweetened curd and salad in separate bowls, a little piece of cake if she had been baking;

they complimented him on the well-organized Bijoya parties she threw in their neat little flat with its colour coordinated furnishings. There were other wives—so wrapped up in the children that they didn't bother to send any tiffin or throw any parties at all. Das was lucky that way, several colleagues had confirmed. As long as she allowed him to watch TV in their bedroom (softly, so the boys next door were not disturbed while they mugged up history), Das had no complaints.

If there was one thing Das had learnt in these fifteen years, though, it was this: when Monalisa was angry, it was best to cower and remain silent until the storm passed.

In no way could this storm be anticipated or stemmed, and this morning, Das found himself in a tight corner as Monalisa swished papers and magazines loudly, clattered utensils, banged the refrigerator door, polished the microwave with a vengeance and issued orders to Anwara, all the while raging and ranting, her large breasts heaving as though she were coming down with an attack. He had taken an RH that day—Monalisa had nagged him to—so that they could complete their puja shopping. The boys had too many tuitions and things over the weekend and needed to be ferried back and forth, so a weekday shopping expedition had seemed a good idea. But now her mood was completely soured.

'I cannot *be-lieve* that he would even *suggest* such a thing!' she huffed.

The person who had suggested the unthinkable was their elder son.

'Not even a month has passed since he came home with twenty-three out of hundred in maths.' Her hands polishing the dining table stilled for a moment and she turned to look at her husband. '*Twen-ty-three* on hundred!' Her voice rose in a shrill falsetto, as though still disbelieving it. Her hands danced in the air. '*Fail* marks. You know what the highest was? Ninety-three. Moni Chatterjee's son got ninety-three. But then they say he is a genius.' Her hands returned to the glass-topped dining table that Das had paid a heart-stopping eighteen thousand to buy from Homeshop. He had felt sick for two days. *Eighteen thousand* for a table? She angrily squirted the cleaning fluid on the glass surface. It was a peaceful blue-coloured liquid that smelt citrussy and synthetic. 'Bablu cried and cried after that. I believed him when he said that it was the tuition teacher's fault. He said Pal Babu is an old-fashioned teacher, good enough only for Gublu and so on. I did not tell him anything. I was extremely understanding, like a modern-day friend-mother and all that! I thought night and day how I could help him, I didn't sleep, I lost my appetite. After all, without maths there is no future. I begged Boudi, and Boudi begged Bor Da. Through so much trouble we managed to get him into this coaching class. Every other boy prepared for months to get accepted into this class, and he got in simply on request! How lucky is he? And now he tells me this?'

Monalisa quivered to a hurt silence.

Das thought he might escape to the bedroom. He had no interest in finding out what abominable thing his elder son had suggested. He wanted to slink away and watch the news. Perhaps he could sleep for half an hour?

'Anwara!' Monalisa thundered. Das froze in his spot. 'Can't you see Dada Babu has finished his tea? Take the cup away.'

Anwara scurried forth like a rabbit and bore the cup away.

Monalisa wearily pulled out a chair and sat down in front of him. 'He told me this morning that some of his class friends were planning to go to Kalimpong for a week after the pujas. He says he wants to go with them. Listen to the boy!'

Over many years of being married to her, Das had learnt a valuable lesson. Things that seemed simple to the naked eye—a boy wanting to go on a holiday with friends, for example—were not so simple. Ever. He desisted from making any comment.

'He knows very well that through the fortnight after puja Bor Da has scheduled classes on alternate days for the whole batch. That way they will finish the Class 9 syllabus before the puja holidays end. After that they will start the Class 10 syllabus and do practice problems for the final exams for the rest of the year. Knowing this full well, how can he suggest going to that rich boy's grandfather's house that week? Hyan? My blood pressure has shot up.'

Monalisa got up again and gathered her cleaning arsenal. She now attacked the low coffee table in the seating area. She squirted more fluid and started moving the sponge in a circular motion. 'No shame, no sense of responsibility. Nothing. I am appalled! After all the effort I put in, this immaturity? Of course he's not going to go—has a mad dog bitten me or what? But that at fifteen, when he knows the second-most important exam of his life is at sixteen, he can suggest such a preposterous thing is what has made me so mad. Holiday! Have I been on a holiday these last three years? Every single day I'm doing their duty, your duty. When your mother visits, I do her duty too.' A speck of spit wavered on her lower lip.

Das sighed and shut his eyes. He tried to remember his elder son's face but found nothing. He was a good father. But Bablu belonged all to Monalisa now.

9.2

Mandy ordered Darjeeling tea and chocolate cake for herself, while the boys agonized over their decision. Finally, almost as an anticlimax, they settled for chicken sandwiches. The aloo parathas that had been packed for them had long disappeared in the madness of the busy morning. The trio had settled by a window in the far corner. Mandy was a regular and bestowed gracious smiles all around. It was around eleven. Flury's was relatively empty: the lunch crowd hadn't come in yet and the breakfast brigade had left a while ago, having devoured cheese omelettes and beans on toast in great volumes. The waiters were enjoying the lull, straightening a tablecloth here or laying fresh cutlery there.

AJ gazed sleepily at the flow of traffic on Park Street. The bookseller outside the window tried to entice passers-by with pirated copies of *Fifty Shades of Grey*. While the other two gadded on about their fest, AJ considered buying a copy. He was not much of a reader, but after all the hullaballoo in the media he had popped into their college library and asked if they had a copy he could borrow. The librarian had first glared and then ignored him. Later he'd heard there were, indeed, two copies, but the faculty were monopolizing them; he might as well invest in a copy himself.

Unlike AJ, who wore his morning stubble and still looked tired, Abeer and Mandy were bright and beaming. Not only had they managed to book Bhoomi but had also hung out for a bit with the band members earlier today while they jammed. It was all so cool. The only thorn in Abeer's happiness, that Rocky bastard, was due to join them in a while. AJ had suggested that they leave Mandy to wait for Rocky in Flury's. He could think of far better things for them to do. For instance, they could hang out at Oly Pub. Or catch a movie. The appointment for the sponsorship meeting was only at three; they could join Mandy and Rocky then. But Abeer would have none of that. They'd argued about it interminably last night, when Abeer analysed and dissected the schedule Mandy had texted—she was very organized, one had to agree, though AJ was of the opinion that the organized girls were also bossy. Abeer was adamant. 'This is our best chance to get to know Rocky, AJ,' he had said. 'It is good to have information on the enemy. It will be a wise move.' AJ thought that as far as moves went it was pathetic and loserly, but he kept this view to himself.

When the food arrived, Mandy poured the tea delicately and asked for a spare cup. Since AJ was not particularly interested (and since he saw that Abeer was dying to share Mandy's tea), Abeer was rewarded with a perfectly brewed cup of chai, with a light dash of milk. Unlike other times when the food would have disappeared in no time, Abeer took small tidy bites of his sandwich.

'What is the play about?' Abeer asked Mandy.

'Oh, it's a sex comedy of sorts. I have a minor part. It's actually a girl-with-a-dog, so Dozey is in it too. Isn't that cute? But all the other actors are very serious, you know. They insist on a full-cast rehearsal every evening. Our director is pretty famous. Nalanda Dutta? He has directed several important one-act plays last season.'

'Oh, yes yes, I think I've heard of him,' Abeer claimed. 'So this is going to be staged on Ashtami?'

'No, Nabami night.'

'Well, we'll drop by if we are free, though that seems unlikely. AJ and I have an invite to the Nabami night party at Tolly. In case we don't enjoy that so much—it sounds quite lame, actually—we'll come to your para and catch the play. Triangular Park, right?'

AJ rolled his eyes.

Mandy nodded.

Abeer then began telling her about a trip he and AJ had taken to Ghatshila last year and how AJ had nearly adopted a kid—a baby goat, he quickly clarified, a little black-and-white thing on the way back, until the owner rushed to them and accused them of stealing the kid to eat. AJ was horrified at the insinuation and told the owner he was a pukka Jaiswal, fully pure-veg. 'Except on Mondays through Fridays, and when he stays over at my house!' Abeer laughed.

It wasn't quite like that, of course, but AJ didn't want to say anything. Abeer was telling the story pretty well and Mandy was giggling happily as she nibbled at her chocolate cake. The kid was damn cute all right, AJ remembered. Molly would have liked it too.

The blissful idyll was interrupted half an hour later, when Rocky, in a plain white T-shirt and a pair of distressed jeans and Ray-Bans, appeared at the doorway. Instead of coming straight to their table, he stopped and chatted at a couple of other table, where, it seemed, he had two discrete sets of pals. And then he sauntered towards them lazily. AJ saw the instant curdling of Abeer's happiness; he also saw the rosy blush that coloured Mandy's cheeks almost at the same moment.

9.3

'Hello, Bhaiya?

'How are you all? Bhabhi? The boys?

'Oh, that's good. Yes, we are all right here. Maaji is with us, her health is fine, yes. Lovely has come visiting with her son too. Jethji is here with Bhabhiji and the boys. They are doing well too. Bhaiya, Babuji's puja will be done in Calcutta this year.

'Oh? I'm sorry to hear that.

'Bhaiya, it's something else, I just wanted to ask you—will it be possible for you to come and take me for a few days?

'No, no, nothing is the matter. I'm not crying. Really.

'Nothing has happened. Just that I have not been home in a long time. You people have not seen Chhoti either. No, no, all is well. I am not crying.

'Okay, yes, I understand. I will ask her. I don't want to impose or anything. No, no, don't talk to Suresh about this. It's fine. Yes, yes. December is okay. Or January.

'No, I am not crying, Bhaiya. Okay, I will call you again later. I have to go now.

'Bye.'

Sandhya

From Solstice.

Unlike my other ancestors, none of whom had managed to escape the narrative of desperation that was the lot of the new slaves, Gobin Misir, my great-grandfather on the paternal side, was lucky. He did not have to toil long at Mansfield Lodge. When the sirdar of the coolies discovered he was a Brahmin, with sufficient knowledge of mantras and rituals to impress the poor coolies, his job description was quickly altered. He was made the resident pujari of the makeshift temple that the Indians had recreated in a shed near their barracks; the other labourers chipped in to maintain him. He soon began to earn his keep—blessing and counselling people, doing pujas, keeping fasts, smoothing ruffled feathers and making peace. When he was twenty-seven, the sirdar married his young daughter to Gobin and settled on them a plot of land and a small house.

It seems to me now that even if he had *started out as a young man happy to take a short cut out of the crushing grind of plantation life to be a career priest (whether a Brahmin or not), in a few years Gobin Misir really did grow into his role as a repository of traditional knowledge, particularly of ritual, myth and legend from the old country. Over time, his amateur astrology won him several admirers, including among the Africans. While he continued to remain aloof from monetary matters and consider his role in the community his chief vocation, his clever wife Dropatie began to run a small shop on their premises. Whether it was because locals were genuinely fond of Misirji or whether his wife dropped hints that buying from her would help them curry favour with the astrologer himself, one cannot say, but the shop began to do brisk business.*

My grandfather too followed in his father's footsteps, remaining a well-loved priest, although his brothers became successful traders. The East Indians, by now, had several temples; the Misirs had several shops.

My father, however, was a modern man, trained in English (in addition to compulsory morning lessons in Sanskrit—the Indians on our island were notorious for pushing their children), with equal curiosity in his youth about trends in Continental philosophy and the Rastafari movement closer home. It was only after he got married that he settled down somewhat into a trade; he became a doctor's assistant, and studied history, religion, botany and literature hungrily in his free time. Books were expensive, time was limited; yet, he persevered, keeping elaborate notes in longhand in lined notebooks. As though he were preparing for university exams. These notebooks, which I have inherited, never fail to move me to tears.

By the time my three brothers were born, my father had acquired several (useless) degrees from open universities across the world; these were paid for by his grandmother Dropatie, quite a landlady by then and rather fond of this slightly unworldly grandson. My brothers were all good students, but none of them quite understood my father's zeal to pursue knowledge for its own sake. In time, all three of them would turn out be practical men, astute in business.

As the youngest—I came ten years after my third brother—and the only girl, I was the apple of my father's eye.

The estrangement that was to come would, in some ways, refashion us both.

CHAPTER 10

10.1

Treeza was alone at home when the call came. She was, in her pale blue nightie, sitting in front of the TV, flipping channels. She'd had a cup of tea with a biscuit earlier, but in all likelihood she would skip the rice and dal that had been made for lunch. Anwara had left. Usually the phone would ring and ring and then fall silent; nobody would answer. Today, on a whim, Treeza picked it up.

After Yasmeen's anniversary party, Treeza had had two consecutive good days. She began to clean out the closet and arrange her books. But something upset her. It could have the magazines with celebrity babies, the books with a phrase here or an image there, her own closet might have overwhelmed her with memories. Fact was, she had quickly tired of the effort and left both tasks midway.

Much to John's despair, she was back to square one. She still had difficulty taking simple decisions. Should she take a bath? Should she leave the bed? She was exhausted all day. She cried copiously in front of the TV. She still had nothing to say to him in the evenings and, at night, she drew far away from him and pretended to be asleep under a cotton sheet wrapped like a shroud, though he often heard stifled sobs through his disturbed, patchy sleep.

Rila rang around mid-morning.

In the beginning, Treeza didn't even recognize her voice—they hadn't spoken in three months. Rila began on her usual tack, wrong-footing Treeza immediately, spinning her usual spiel about the children asking after their aunt…how could Treeze and John forgotten them this way? Were they not their closest kin of all, save the sisters, of course, and Treeza's mum?

Treeza sat down on the sofa as she twirled the cord. But she felt nothing. None of the usual annoyance flooded through her.

'Why didn't you come to Yasmeen's party, Rila?' Treeza asked her sister-in-law. She had no other talking point, nothing to say when Rila demanded how everybody was, if they were planning a holiday. 'It was a good party. Everyone came. Poppy was there.'

'Oh, but we were in Singapore that time, Treeze, didn't Yasmeen say? The kids and I spent three weeks in Pune after that. Mummy was most insistent that I visit her. I told her I can't stay away from Calcutta during the pujas, never have in the last ten years! So I returned yesterday. Jeff is back on his boat now. As usual!' Rila sighed theatrically.

Her husband Jeff, John's elder brother, was in the merchant navy. A pleasant man, if slightly fond of his drink, Jeff was away at sea most of the time. That left Rila free to spend his hefty salary imaginatively and do pretty much what she pleased. Shopping, mostly. Beauty parlours. The club and women's committees. Changing the furniture around in their lovely flat in South City. Joining fancier and fancier gyms. Taking the kids to expensive dance classes.

There'd been a time when they'd lived in the same house on Eliot Road, all of them.

It was an old house, a lane away from Yasmeen and Terry, with high ceilings and skylights where sparrows nested all year. The hum of traffic would swirl inside the large rooms all day long, the sun filtering in through the windows and drawing strange patterns on the excessive Victorian furniture that came with the house—the huge beds, the large rickety armchairs that could fit two at a time, the monstrous wooden armoires.

Jeff would be away most of the year; Rila would be flitting around town in his silver Esteem, leaving her little boy to spend all his afternoons with Treeza, who would return from school by two and slip into bed with a book. Charlie, as he grew up, would escape from his nanny and curl up next to her, demanding stories, one after another. He grew to become a piece of Treeza's soul. When his sister was born, he took to spending the nights too with John and Treeza, in their bed. On some nights, they would transfer his sleeping body to his mother's room. On other nights, he stayed, occupying the warmest, most loving spot between the two of them. It was after Jeff and Rila shifted, after Charlie was gone, that Treeza had begun to plan a family, *her* family.

'How is Auntie?' Treeza asked about Rila's mum, a right old witch, just to be polite.

'Oh, she's fine. Busy as ever. The bakery's doing very well now, she doesn't have a minute to sit down and talk. They've extended it to the patio, put in some tables and chairs. It's completely transformed. It's a café now. Young people are in and out all day. Business is good. How Pune has changed, Treeze, you can't imagine!'

'That's great.'

'It's Tasha's birthday I'm calling you about, Treeze, next month. She wants a full princess extravaganza. I am going to need your help to plan it all out. You see, the thing is…' Rila's voice dipped to a secret-sharing softness. 'I'm pregnant again. That's why we went to Singapore, to celebrate. After we decided we'll go ahead with it!' she trilled 'Now we're ready to tell everyone.'

'Congratulations,' Treeza trilled too, on auto-pilot. 'Great news.'

'It was an accident, as you can imagine. I was very undecided when I realized I was knocked up. I was extremely annoyed with Jeff, you know, he's so careless about protection. *Three* kids! How am I going to manage? I was just thinking of looking for a job or starting a business, now that Tasha's in school all day. But Jeff was adamant about keeping this baby. Now everybody's teasing me about my sailor husband and how he can't keep his hands off me. You know? Fact is, there are two ways of looking at it. One is, of course, all the trouble for me. But the other, it's funny, but I'm feeling quite young again, Treeze, and sexy, haw haw haw, though my doctor asked me to be very careful the first three months. We didn't want to tell anyone, thirty-six is no age to have kids. Anyway, back to business. I need your help with the birthday party.'

'Sure,' Treeza said, her voice light, rising like a fairy cake. 'Let me know what you want me to do.'

'Thanks a ton, darling. I will. See if you can come up with any ideas. It's a princess party, everyone has to wear pink. And I want to go all out because she's very jealous about the new baby. We've had to tell her!'

'I'll do that, sure. Say hi to Charlie from me. And a big kiss to Tasha.'

'Will do. Bye, girlie.'

'Bye.'

After Treeza hung up she wandered to the balcony, her breathing still even. There was no one outside, except a few pigeons hopping around in the grass in front and the workers building the pandal. There was no one out there, anywhere, that she could talk to, nobody who would understand the language of her agony. No one. The sun was hot and she ducked back in after a moment or two.

She switched off the TV. She went into the kitchen and dragged out a huge box from one corner where it had been stowed. She began to peel off the several layers of dust-covered brown tape that sealed the top. The box had remained in the dark corner of the kitchen ever since they'd moved in.

10.2

'I hate him,' Abeer said moodily, the fifty-sixth time in the last two hours. AJ had kept count.

'He's a bloody fucking bastard, no doubt,' AJ agreed, for the fifty-sixth time, though he'd tried to mix it up with insults. Hindi, Bengali, Tamil, Spanish—there were colourful phrases for Rocky (and his parents) in many languages.

The boys were sitting in a tram, heading towards College Street. It was two o'clock. They would eat a Mughlai paratha each at Coffee House and then go to that sponsorship meeting on Prafulla Sarkar Street.

Rocky had made it clear the moment he arrived at Flury's that Abeer and AJ were absolute expendables as far as he was concerned—but he'd insinuated it very subtly.

Rocky kissed Mandy lightly on the cheek as he came to their table and sat down next to her. Then he shook hands with the boys. She'd blushed, the rouge persisting on her cheeks long after Rocky's stubble had brushed past her chin, slightly embarrassed at his—this smart grown-up *man's*—attentions. Rocky put his arm around her lazily as he ordered. His fingers played on her bare shoulder the whole time, at her delicate clavicle, where the thin straps of her sleeveless top ended. He chatted pleasantly with the boys as though they were young, pointless (and sexless) cousins, as though they were fans of his or something. Who knows, perhaps that's the picture Mandy had given him? He paid for their food and their Coffee Sprugli (that he absolutely insisted they order). It was the Flury's special, he'd pointed out.

'I know,' Abeer had replied combatively, though he didn't stop Rocky when he ordered it for all of them, except Mandy, who stuck to Darjeeling tea.

An hour later, he'd asked for the check and told the boys, 'I think there's no need for four people to go for one sponsorship meeting. You two can easily deal with it on your own.'

'But, but,' Abeer had blabbered, 'AJ is not part of the music committee. Plus, it's Mandy's contact.'

AJ had nodded vigorously.

'That doesn't matter,' Rocky had said in that lazy drawl that had now begun to get on Abeer's nerves. 'AJ can easily go with you. Meanwhile, I have a lead on Indian Ocean. Mandy and I will follow it up.'

'Manju Di will be happy to meet the two of you, no problem.

I'll text her. You can use my car,' Mandy said eagerly. 'It needs to go to Nancy anyway. I'll tell my driver. Rocky will drop me home afterwards.'

AJ had, in spite of himself, grinned at her choice of words. Sure he will. *Afterwards.*

Rocky and Mandy had both relaxed perceptibly at AJ's smile; they were friends after all, they were supposed to understand.

Abeer had to say, finally, just to keep matters unsuspicious: 'No, no, that's okay, we don't need the car. We'll manage. You two enjoy!'

AJ remembered that Rocky had winked at them as Mandy called her driver.

'He really is hateful, isn't he?' Abeer persisted. 'The pompous, vain, foppish bastard, with his iPhone and his accent. Who the fuck does he think he is? That gaa…'

They'd reached their stop. AJ jumped off the tram lightly and crossed the road on nimble feet. The signal was red. Two other people cut in from the side, after AJ, a rotund couple who took their own sweet time. Abeer followed them, jumping down with a thump, still muttering under his breath. In the interim, though, the signal had changed. Traffic lunged at him, and he was transfixed. An auto nearly banged into him, the driver stopping only just in time. Abeer stumbled from the impact and fell down.

'Stop, stop!' A couple of shop assistants from the book stalls that lined College Street started shouting, immediately jumping onto the road. 'Student, student, shabdhan, shabdhan,' they urged, waving their hands dramatically. All traffic halted.

The auto-wallah who'd nearly run over Abeer demanded bossily: 'Nyaka naki? Have your eyes gone or what?' A balding passenger stuck his head out from the backseat of the auto: 'Where is your brain? Who gets off a tram in this fashion, without looking left or right? Think of the way he had to brake to save you! I think my hipbone has got dislocated. All these boys, nonsense!'

By the time AJ negotiated the maze and returned, Abeer was

back on his feet and dusting himself vigorously. Hanging his head, he crossed the road in silence.

The autowallah called out, 'Saala, first blind, now dumb also? Bokachoda!'

10.3

Sandhya was washing utensils after lunch when the first crash came.

Afternoons were quiet in Nancy. The noise outside that filtered in through the colony walls was only a distant hum, a mere shadow of its robust reality. Only after three, when the school-going children returned in little groups, would their chatter fill the air with intermittent bursts of life. The sound, sudden like a gunshot, solid like a meteor, rose upwards from below Sandhya's kitchen, followed by the smoky tail of shattering.

A vase perhaps? A wicked breeze sometimes did the rounds in the late afternoon.

Sandhya was rinsing the final item in her sink, a glass, when the second crash sounded. Whatever broke was smaller in size than the first. That much was evident.

She turned away from the wash basin, brows furrowed. She was wiping her hands on the kitchen towel when the third blow struck. A heavy-bottomed glass item this time. Big. It was quickly followed by a fourth, a smaller thing which did not break but simply rolled away. Metal?

Whatever it was, it could no longer be considered accidental. Sandhya shut her eyes for a few seconds and concentrated, her back ramrod straight.

It was not clear what she saw, but she made up her mind.

By the time she reached her door and slid on a pair of slippers—she was usually barefoot inside—two other crashes had sounded. Glass hitting the mosaic with a sharp crack, then the full ringing of shattering. A thousand hollow, tinny sounds issued simultaneously all around. It was heart-breaking in its finality.

Sandhya pulled her door shut and went downstairs.

Sandhya

***From* Solstice.**

Life in our village in the island was not very easy, especially as the sixties heralded a time of new racial unrest. Democracy had inaugurated a chapter of struggles.

I had always been a bright student, and my father personally supervised my education, spending long hours with me as I worked on math, history and English. His dream for me and my brothers was to help us escape the limitations—not so much a material poverty, though that too was true since my father's job brought in only a modest salary, but a poverty of imagination and opportunity that he sensed, a sinking feeling of marginality—which had clipped his own dreams.

It was my mother who provided a different current in the household, simpler and perhaps more fatalistic. Ever since my teenage years, as she tried to mould me in her ways, I rebelled. I am ashamed to confess, I even began to disregard her, look down on the simplicity, blind to its essential elegance. The only thing I took from her was the singing; I had a good voice, like her.

My mother. Sitala.

She was from a rustic family of peasant cane cutters still mired in poverty. She was never obsessed with escape. It was true that her eyes held within the sorrows of her migrant mothers and grandmothers; yet, in her kitchen, she concocted magic, sometimes from a nearly empty larder. Her dals and curries and her potions and stews filled our house with the smell of nourishment. It was only later that I learnt the value of one's mother's kitchen—and the possibilities of healing it holds.

I woke up every morning to her melodious voice singing, in languages unknown yet so terribly familiar, of the love of gods and people. She would sing as she swept and cleaned, her voice dipping and curling as smoke rose from the old-fashioned stove and chickens crowed in the backyard.

After my bath, and before I sat down to eat, I was taught by her to fold my hands before the gods and goddesses of the household altar and offer a song. As I grew older, the tempo of the song increased greatly, finishing it in two minutes flat. My mother would laugh at my hurry. 'The lord will have you sing for hours, girl,' she joked. 'Just you wait.'

In a couple of hours, though, as morning became day, I would be almost unrecognizable. In my white shirt and navy skirt and black shoes, I was ready for my English-medium education, the one that would help me escape.

It would be afternoon when I returned from school. The rhythm of my schizophrenic existence brought me back to a quiet stillness after the noisy world outside. I read English romances on the mat outside the kitchen, where my mother pounded masalas, shucked grain, snipped spinach or conserved fruit. The sounds of the kitchen mingled with the cry of the wind and the waves and were recorded in my brain as the mnemonic, not for comfort or love or joy, but a unique mix of all three, unmarked by the fear of loss. Perhaps it was peace.

As my world expanded bookishly, I began to feel claustrophobic, as though everything that constituted home was merely a perch from which I ought to fly out as soon as I could. Ever since I was fourteen, I had come to know I would leave this home as soon as I could—that I must leave if I was to breathe. Seize my own destiny, take life by the scruff of its neck. I always imagined that what I would invent would be a glamorous, independent life in London. London, the glorious metropolis, the centre of the world, which would rinse out of me my provincial childhood.

London would make me new.

CHAPTER 11

11.1

On the first floor landing of A-5, it became quickly clear that it was the Matthews' flat which was the site of the storm. The door of the facing apartment—Ananda Bose's—was open, the maid peeping out curiously. At Sandhya's appearance she fled inside.

Sandhya rang the bell. Once, twice, thrice.

A minor, half-hearted crash sounded in between.

Eventually, after the fourth ring, the door opened.

Treeza, whom Sandhya had never seen before, stood before her, diminutive in a pale blue nightie, her fair face red and wet with tears, framed by a mass of curls. She held a bone china quarter plate in one hand.

Sandhya entered the girl's hallway and firmly shut the door. Treeza was too shocked to react or resist.

'Don't mind me,' Sandhya said softly, walking gingerly to a sofa in the corner, avoiding the shards and the chunks of white china. 'Finish what you are doing. We can talk afterwards.'

The floor was littered with wreckage; the larger part of a dinner set had been demolished in the last few minutes. In the middle of the room sat a box, now half-empty, advertising its contents: a thirty-six piece La Opala dinner set.

Treeza hesitated by the door. Then she came and sat down on the sofa, though not too close to Sandhya. She carefully set down the plate on the floor, her hands shaking slightly.

Sandhya extended her hand and touched her shoulder. Drawing closer, she pushed Treeza's hair from her forehead with a firm but kind hand.

The old lady's hair was peppered with grey, though her face was smooth and brown, firm and kind, like her hand. Her palm was cool and almost seemed to singe Treeza's hot flushed skin. But, after a second, the palm seemed to relax her nerves somewhat.

'Anger is good sometimes, my dear,' Sandhya said. 'Don't stop on my account. In fact, I can help you finish that box if you like.'

Treeza managed a shaky smile. 'Who are you?'

'I'm Sandhya. I moved in upstairs some time ago. Your husband had invited me to come over.'

Treeza nodded, slightly blank still.

'I think it was because he sensed that you and I could be friends. You see, I am new in the city, new in this colony. I have no friends here.' Sandhya picked up the plate and handed it to Treeza. 'Go for it.'

And suddenly, as quickly as it had ebbed, energy coursed through Treeza's thin frame. The memory of her rage throbbed and ballooned inside her. Treeza forgot her hesitation, her embarrassment, the unwelcome guest. She stood up and hurled. The plate hit the opposite wall and crashed on the floor, smithereens scattering all around. Little bits of white china with pink flecks. It was followed by pudding ramekins, then a gravy boat, a large serving plate.

'They have used up all our happiness.' Treeza spoke with bitter hatred. 'It's not like they didn't have enough of their own; they did. But they still used up John and my share. And now, you won't believe what they've done now. She has even stolen my baby. She is having *my* baby now.'

Treeza sat down next to Sandhya, her body shaking with sobs now, unresolved sorrow making her burble like a little child who was hurt, issuing that deep, searing cry that went straight to the heavens and scared mothers witless, that primeval cry which went on and on and on.

'Hush, darling,' said Sandhya.

The familiar words made Treeza look up for a second, then she began to weep. Tears ran down her cheeks like sooty rivulets. Half-uttered broken words issued from her lips.

Sandhya felt her eyes moisten too. It was old grief, one of the oldest in the world. For it was not just a mother losing her young but the loss of the promise that had appeared to transform her. Sandhya knew the colours of this grief. 'Come here, silly girl. Nobody can use up your happiness, I promise you. Come.'

Treeza buried her face in Sandhya's lap. For a moment, even as she wept, she detached herself from that bottomless well of grief and thought it was the strangest thing to have happened—this kind hand on her forehead, this kind lap. Was this lady really a neighbour? Treeza watched many crime serials on TV—that was what she watched mostly, unable to tolerate the love stories of others—so she could not help wondering, just a teeny bit, even as she wept bitterly on this strange lady's lap. Was this lady an axe murderer?

But she needed someone to talk to. Lord knew she did. Besides, at least the axe murderer was kind enough to push her way into Treeza's unravelling life, the way no one else had pushed in, not her sisters, not even John.

11.2

As the diet progressed (badly), Apu dreamt of food. When she woke up in the morning, she dreamt, without fail, of aloo parathas or cauliflower samosas. Either. Never both. What sort of a moron would mix the two in the same meal? You eat the cauliflower samosa with sharp tamarind chutney. The aloo paratha you pair with your mother's homemade tomato sauce (never was red so beautiful as in the thick, pulpy homemade sweet-and-sour tomato sauce) or with the mango pickle Meera made in summer.

Come winter, Apu would eat kachoris stuffed with a spicy filling of peas, and stuffed potatoes. When Apu was younger, their clan would go for a picnic every New Year, proper picnics where they would cook outdoors, by the side of a stream which tinkled through a meadow or on a mango orchard somewhere. Every year, they would have peas kachoris, the circle of aunts rolling them out with effortless ease. And the keema stuffed potatoes her grandmother made, so sweet, so savoury, such a fugue of flavours in the mouth. The comfort that the humble potato can give, the fullness of a potato cooked on a slow fire… Apu could write a tribute to the humble potato, if only she could write.

Two hours later, when she left home in her salwar-kurta (size L), the colourful odhni fluttering, her hair tied behind in a messy knot, Apu dreamt of moong daal ka halwa. Moong dal halwa *dripping* in ghee. Meera loved it too. Oh, Meera, Meera! The more Apu worried about her friend, who had not washed her hair in six days now, who was always angry, who cried for an hour every morning, the more she craved the moong dal halwa. When would all those wretched Sahais leave? Let Nalini stay, though—perhaps she could make the halwa at home—but let the old witch go!

In the lab sometimes, as she supervised the annoying girls, their skirts getting shorter and shorter, their kurtas plunging deeper and deeper, Apu thought of the fish batter fry. Oily, tender, the batter deep-fried to golden. Apu could cram one into her mouth and hold that moment still.

Apu was so hungry. So intensely hungry.

11.3

John rang the bell at Sandhya's around five past nine, clutching the note she had left him downstairs in slightly sweaty palms: 'John, come upstairs to my flat for dinner. Treeza is with me. Hope to see you soon. Sandhya, A-5/4.' He had rushed upstairs without even changing his shirt.

'Hello.' Sandhya greeted him warmly. 'Sit, John. Make yourself comfortable.'

The room was a mirror image of John's drawing room downstairs, and yet it was completely different. The walls were bare and white, and the corners of the room scrupulously clean. It was illuminated by a couple of wooden stand lamps. At one end were two elegant wooden settees arranged artfully; at the other was a hand-spun mat on the floor, lined with several cushions covered in bright Indian prints. Jasmine incense burned in a corner, though the music which played was Mozart. There were no whatnots or dust gatherers cluttering any of the surfaces; it was remarkably spare. John looked around, slightly intrigued by the quality of sound that surrounded him and discovered that it was an old-fashioned record player. A Phillips one, as it happened, the same as his, with identical boxy brown speakers.

John sat down and rubbed his head tiredly.

Sandhya gave him a glass of water.

'I am going to be plain with you, John. Since I have been an interfering busybody, poking my nose into your affairs shamelessly, I might as well be plain.' She told him all that had happened.

John was quiet for a few minutes. He was not surprised, he finally said, though this was the first time Treeza had broken stuff. It could have been dangerous, of course, with so much glass around. He was grateful Sandhya had intervened. He buried his head in his hands. Though his heart was racing, his body felt like lead.

'But anger is a good sign, John, a step up from pure grief.'

He hadn't known that.

Sandhya had brought Treeza upstairs. ('After she decided I was not an axe murderer after all, she was as trusting as a lamb.') Then she had given Treeza a sesame-oil head massage (which she had not minded) and insisted she take a hot bath (which she had minded, but Sandhya had not listened to her on this). After that, she sat in a fresh set of clothes in the last two hours of the sun, her hair drying. She had cried in spurts again but not spoken much. Sandhya had given her a bowl of hot vegetable soup with butter. She had had a few spoonfuls and then, since her eyes were heavy with sleep, Sandhya had put her to bed. She had been sleeping ever since.

John popped into the bedroom. It was as bare as the drawing room, with just a bed in the middle and a dresser by the window. Treeza's body was hidden by the cotton duvet, her still-damp hair hanging from the edge of the bed. She had been crying out in her sleep, twice her face was wet with tears and needed to be sponged, Sandhya said.

Suddenly, in an alien bed, Treeza looked much like a strange princess he needed to rescue. But John was out of ideas. He came back to his seat and drank his water.

'I am an old woman, my dear,' Sandhya said. 'My methods are tried and tested. I hope you are not offended.'

'Sandhyaji,' replied John, 'this is India. Friends and neighbours become family. There is no question of any offence. You have been very kind.' His voice choked with emotion. 'She has had a very tough time. If you can help her…' He could not finish the sentence. Guilt rose in him like fire. All through the bus ride home, he had been ranting against Treeze in his mind, against her selfishness, her insensitivity to his pain, the wall she had erected around herself. 'I am very tired,' John said finally.

'Before I interfere further in your affairs, John, I must tell you about myself. Come, while you have dinner, I shall spin my story. You must forgive me—I have already eaten. I usually eat by eight. This way.'

Sandhya led John into the little room adjoining the drawing room, where there was a table, big enough for two, laid for one person.

11.4

When darkness fell, Apu craved a medium cheese patty, each layer of flaky pastry emphasized by the sharpness of cheddar. But not only that. A perfect meal must be lugubrious. Each bite ought to be alternated with a mouthful of something sweet, something moist. An Oreo cheesecake perhaps, the soft cream cheese a perfect foil to the patty. Or a chocolate hazelnut tart with a hint of orange somewhere. Apu walked to the bus-stop and contemplated the fuzzy outline of evening that the city wore. Her contract at the college was coming up for renewal; her supervisor was insisting she present her PhD dissertation in front of the external committee soon; her mother was counting calories day and night, looking at Apu from every angle, calibrated judgement in her eyes. The boy in Chicago, all said and done, had a nice name: Abhiroop.

At night, when she stood on the balcony, adjoining the room she shared with her grandmother—the two of them in matching twin beds—Apu dreamt of Nizam's Hyderabadi biryani, the nuts and raisins dotting the subtly flavoured rice and meat generously. And of course, the potato. That heavenly potato, spiced with such perfection, cooked in such flavoured smoke. The Chicago boy's mother had spoken to Mrs Mukherjee. The parents would meet around the puja, though Apu would see them only when the boy was in town. Mrs Mukherjee was counting on these three months heavily—they would transform Apu into someone else, slim and elegant and fashionable.

Apu stood in the balcony by the mango tree silvery in moonlight, ravenous, her stomach growling on most days, wondering idly at the probability of Abhiroop Lahiri being her soulmate.

11.5

After the simple but delicious dinner, John washed his hands and ducked into Treeza's room for a minute. Sandhya's spare bedroom had already become Treeza's room in his mind, as though Treeza had, in this new foreign space, become a girl again. As though by casting aside that complicated marriage bed—a beautiful bed that they had bought off their old landlord before shifting to this new house—she had left behind all their problems. He was a little jealous already. He wanted to get in beside her, on this warm, clean bed with the fine cotton sheets smelling of lavender, in this clean white room with nothing else but the moonlight rushing in through sheer curtains.

'John?' Sandhya called softly.

He followed her to the drawing room again. Sandhya's story—that strange story told to him in such a crystal-clear manner—had moved him to hope again. Dimly. She had found a bottle of wine, Sandhya said, and was pouring him a glass. He sat on one of the settees, actually looking forward to the red wine.

'I don't drink any more, but you must help yourself,' Sandhya said, placing the glass and the bottle beside him on the single low table. 'Now tell me everything.'

John began the story with Charlie. And Treeza's love for Charlie.

'Treeza was very attached to him. I knew she would be a great mum one day. Then, suddenly, Rila announced that their house was ready—we hadn't known until then that they'd bought a flat of their own, but that was them, all drumrolls and big announcements—and that they would be shifting in a month. It was suddenly as though everything was changing too fast. Treeze cried each night until they left, after which she became sad and annoyed all at once, not eating properly, missing school. She complained that Rila hadn't invited her properly to the South City place. I said, what nonsense, family members don't invite each other. I took her over one evening. Charlie was thrilled to see her—as was Natasha, the little one—but even I felt it immediately, it was a little different, slightly awkward. All the jokes that had fit effortlessly into our fourth-floor Eliot Road house with its peeling walls and shadows and long lines of ants, seemed from a different world. Suddenly, in a week or so, the texture of everything had become formal and ill-fitting. It was not particularly any of us, not Rila nor my brother, to be fair. I think it was just the time.

'Treeze didn't speak to me all night and through the next day. Then she announced it was time for us to have a baby, our baby. Our very own made-to-order, perfect little creature. I was eager enough, madam, since to me the time had always been right.

'You're not going to believe it, but she fell pregnant almost instantly. We were so thrilled we told everyone, though my mother-in-law had said that one must wait and not tempt fate. But we were too happy to wait; our doctor, a modern, scientific lady, was equally sensible about matters of fate. She said it was all shipshape. Treeze was already planning every little detail, buying second-hand books about baby names and baby food, you know, those books for parents?

'It was the last week of the first trimester when a sudden pain arose in her back. I remember every detail clearly. It was Saturday morning. December. Christmas was around the corner. We'd had a late breakfast, muffins and milk for Treeze—she had very specific cravings. At ten-thirty, the pain was a vibrating ball. By eleven, it was streaking across her abdomen. At eleven-fifteen, she was bleeding and crying like mad. By the time we went to the nursing home, it was over.'

John had never recounted this story before. Sandhya sat far away from him, on the mat. Her face was in darkness. It helped. John allowed himself a pause.

'Our young doctor and her senior colleagues were equally mystified, since everything had been perfectly in order. "It happens," they assured us, again and again, in Hindi, in Bengali, in English. "It doesn't mean anything. We have seen so many couples face this first heartbreak, but then they've gone on to have healthy babies. Several babies. You just have to be optimistic," they said.

'But Treeze was in a completely different mode. After the tears had subsided—it took about a fortnight—she got rid of all the books she had. She got rid of all the knick-knacks she'd bought. Every single thing that could have reminded her of this episode. It was as though this baby had not happened. She avoided her family. We never spoke of it. She sat down with a notebook and went through every day in detail. Jotting down points. From the day she thought she'd fallen pregnant, the first missed period. Every day. Had she felt anything? Had something disturbed her? Ah, yes, it was Poppy. It had to be. My sister. Unhappy Poppy, jealous Poppy,

Poppy who was bitter and single. Was it the sesame toast she ate with Rila one afternoon? It was absolutely harrowing, madam, but I went through it with her, holding her hand. For days she pored over the entries in the notebook. Finally, she told me that she would quit. It was the job that had tired her out. And then she said, hugging me close since this was a big thing to even speak out loud, we should see if we could move.

'My friend Rustam had heard about this flat. The promoter is known to him. We got a good deal on it. There was no way we could have afforded this. Bank managers hardly give out loans to schoolteachers, you know. They've even made a Bollywood film on this, I was reading somewhere! But with all our savings, we could manage to give the down payment. Four lakhs. And the promoter, he is a very capable man. He got us a loan from a cooperative bank that gave a good rate of interest. My entire salary would go, of course. But I had my tuitions. And Treeze assured me, once our baby was a little older, we could take paying guests or something—decent college-going girls. That would bring in more than her salary anyway! The study has an independent bath, it would be perfect. Two girls. Once again, we were on a high.

'You're not going to believe it, madam, the night before we were to move here, Treeze told me she was pregnant. All the fear I had about money dissolved in an instant. New house, new baby.

'Treeze did not unpack for fear of upsetting the little one. She lay on the divan all day, reading magazines and munching nuts and oranges. She ate healthy meals. No one knew about it, not friends nor relatives, not even her mother. We were not going to tempt fate one bit. She noted down everything she ate, spoke to the doctor every weekend. I borrowed my friend Rustam's car every time we went to the doctor's, though I never told him where we were going or why. We would park the car in front of a restaurant and walk the ten steps to the back entrance of the clinic, we were that secretive.'

John had finished his wine. He refilled the glass with water and drank it all at once.

'Nothing helped. We lost our baby again. On the eighty-third day. This time it was more serious. She needed to be kept in the nursing home for a few days. I had to inform her mother and sisters. But the doctors found no abnormality. Once more, they assured us, again and again, in Hindi, Bengali and English, that it was part of life. These things happen.'

Sandhya

From Solstice.

The mid-sixties saw a severe heightening of racial tensions, though matters never really came to a head. After I completed my O-levels, at sixteen, my father began to wonder seriously how he might be able to send me off to England where I would continue my studies. He had great dreams for me: I would be a lawyer, perhaps? A scholar, most certainly. I would do him proud.

My father's nephew, my cousin R, lived in London. He was persuaded by my father to take me in for a year, as my guardian, while I completed my final year of school in England. That way I would have a far better chance of getting into college on a scholarship. On the island, there was only one scholarship offered to Oxford or Cambridge after the completion of A-levels—it was intensely competitive. One of my brothers had won that scholarship, but the other two had been wrecked by the attempt. My father did not want to take that risk with me.

My cousin R was married to an English girl. Their marriage had been a matter of great controversy in the extended family, but only my father had approved of and blessed the union. Thus, through the complex karma that defines large families, R was compelled to take me in, even though my father could hardly send much money every month. R arranged for me to study in a local comprehensive, which accepted me on the basis of my high O-level scores. I would stay in their house on the outskirts of London and appear for my A-levels from my new school.

In 1966, at the age of sixteen, I boarded the ship Empire Windrush, which would take me to the Tilbury docks. I still remember what I wore: a long grey woollen skirt, a white shirt with a lace collar, a grey coat that matched the skirt (though they were acquired separately, from two different second-hand shops) and patent leather shoes. My friends in the island had gifted me a colourful scarf that I'd tied around my wrist. My folks would see the scarf from a distance, even when the ship was a dot in the horizon, the girls had said.

My mother had had no say in this decision to send me off to England so early on, though she began making preparations diligently. She made new clothes for me since we could not afford to buy new ones; she packed food that I might crave. I remember her crying in silence for days before I was scheduled to leave, even as her fingers mended my shawls or adjusted the hemlines of my skirts, making them longer. Though I comforted her dutifully, I was caught up in excitement; it seems cruel now in retrospect, my thoughtless excitement. But there it was—I was finally leaving.

It was only in my little cabin in the Windrush, *with my father stowing in the suitcase underneath the bunk, my mother wiping her eyes surreptitiously, that I realized the enormity of what lay ahead. It was then that I cried, in the narrow bunk, cried bitterly and long. My father did not allow himself to cry.*

It was summer in London when I reached. Perhaps the most beautiful summer I have seen in the city in all my thirty-five years there—Meg joked the city had brought out its A-game to welcome me. That was Meg, my cousin R's wife, with a round open face and a pronounced Yorkshire accent, though I wouldn't know the kind of accent it was then. I didn't know either that a face as brown as mine, among the shiny suits and bowler hats sported by the emigrating blacks who disembarked from Empire Windrush *looking just as lost as me, was hardly that welcome to London any more. After several instances of race riots in the UK, particularly in parts of London, in 1962 the Immigration Control Act had been passed, through which Commonwealth citizens had been denied the right to move automatically to the UK. My travel too had required a lot of paperwork. But Meg, known in our family as Meg-who-stole-R, was kind and cheerful and smiled broadly, revealing a chipped tooth. I took to her immediately. Her smile and the London summer defined my arrival.*

There was no rain that afternoon. The sun was shining, the skies were gentle, a powder-blue. The trees of London were in bloom. Over the next few days, Meg taught me the names of flowers I had never seen before: mauve foxgloves, bluebells, buttercups and white ox-eye daisies; and then there were the climbing jasmine, the honeysuckle, rambling roses and wisteria, all in bloom. Meg and R's house was tiny, with thin walls; their street was narrow, dirty and listless; the landlady was very annoyed that another brown face had been imported; and Meg and R rowed often. But I had come prepared to fall in love, and so I did. However, even I was not prepared for the passion with which I would cling to the big city so soon after my arrival.

I did not look back then on what I had left behind.

CHAPTER 12

12.1

October progressed. The pujas were but a week away. Little by little, the gold of the day deepened into richer fuller afternoons, temperatures dropping a degree or two to facilitate harried daytime shopping. Dusk came sooner. But even before evening fell in glorious purple swathes, millions of 'toony bulbs'—the tiny now-entirely-China-manufactured lights in red, gold, green, pink and blue—began to glitter in the city, strung on long loops and hung on building facades. It didn't matter if the house was a four-storeyed work of art designed by a hip young architect or a glorified shack patched up with other people's leftovers; it didn't matter who lived inside. In Bengal, lights were distributed equitably in the season of the goddess. The really spectacular lighting arrangements surrounding the pandals, the elaborately designed and mounted scenes—politics, international affairs, myths and legends, all depicted entirely through the play of lights—would come alive only a day or two before Shashthi.

The electricity bill of every household would double that month. It was common knowledge that the neighbourhood puja would tap into overhead wires; people didn't really mind.

Mrs Monalisa Das and Mrs Chhanda Mukherjee were not particular friends. The only reason they were thrown together every October was this: both ladies were meticulous (bordering on obsessive) about the puja part of the holidays. While the younger women of the colony were busy planning out each ensemble carefully, beginning with Shashthi evening, when they would favour Western casual to Dashami evening, with sindoor khela performed in the traditional red-and-white saris, Monalisa Das and Chhanda Mukherjee would be drawing up elaborate lists—who would cook the bhog on which day (mostly it came down to the two them and old Mrs Pal of A-2), who would cut vegetables, who would ensure that all samagris had been delivered the night before, who would help the pandit and his assistant at every stage, who would administer the queues for Anjali. They would go from house to house, recruiting volunteers.

This morning, Mrs Das and Mrs Mukherjee were sitting in the community hall of the colony, taking out all the brass utensils that were reserved for use during the pujas. Last year, they'd put these away themselves, carefully matching each item with a numbered list. Ha, how the prices of brass had gone up in the last six years, when they'd bought all these to initiate the puja at Nancy! Both women were highly efficient, and they mostly worked in silence; though their hands would sort and shelve steadily, they would essentially be wrapped in their own worlds.

Birds chirped, a baby bawled somewhere, the two guards chatted by the gate. Mrs Mukherjee and Mrs Das were in a chatty mood today; they were guardedly discussing the new neighbour, Sandhyaji, whose fame had by now spread through Nancy, though in every household it had morphed into a unique cloud of information. The Pals, who were very into Art of Living, said after making enquiries that she checked out, even Sri Sri was her friend. The Sens, whose daughters lived abroad, denounced her as a fake. The Qureishis reported on her Hollywood links—Mr Qureishi was a journalist—but most people didn't really believe these. The octogenarian Chanakya Chaudhary, scholar and noted contributor to 'Letters to the Editor' in *Ananda Bazaar Patrika*, was convinced she was CIA.

'It seems she is a very famous yoga teacher in America?' Mrs Mukherjee asked.

'Maybe she is famous in America. But I heard she lives in the UK. Oxford, near the university, they are saying.' Thanks to Bablu's syllabi, Mrs Das's geography was not vague at all. 'Though I hear she has a big ashram in Rishikesh too. Even bigger than Baba Ramdev's ashram by way of acreage.'

'Oh.' Mrs Mukherjee digested this. 'Why is she here?'

'All that I don't know. But I hear she is very kind and friendly and all that. I was thinking that we might want to involve her in the puja preparations, Boudi. What do you say? We need people. This year Meera Sahai will have to drop out, I think.'

'Oh, yes. Poor thing. She is not well at all,' Mrs Mukherjee mumbled. What to do about Meera? But she persisted with her enquiries, even as she checked the kosha-kushi for the numbered stamp at the back. 'So, she is Indian? This lady?'

'That also I don't know, Boudi. My information is from my maid. Anwara has become her big fan suddenly. Ever since the old lady took that crazy Mrs Matthew under her wing, she is full of her tales. She was dying to get a job at this house-ashram or whatever, and now finally this Sandhya lady has hired her. Anwara is becoming too smart, Boudi, too smart for her own good. She didn't tell me what salary the old lady is giving her. That is the problem with NRIs. They come and inflate the heads of these servants with the big salaries they give, and the rest of us have to suffer. Anyway, apparently her Hindi is accented. But if she speaks Hindi, one way or another, she must be Indian.'

'We should go and welcome her, Monalisa, on behalf of the puja committee. Let's go today.'

'Yes, sure. But don't you want to speak to the flower-wallah first? Remember how last year he failed to supply the 108 blue lotuses for the Sandhi puja? God, what a mad scramble that was!'

'I'll call that rascal right away. Thank God you knew that family who ran a nursery. We must invite them for the Nabami lunch this year, no?'

'That's a good idea. I'll reserve a couple of coupons and call them tonight.'

On the four days of the Durga puja, communal meals were organized by the cooperative. Caterers provided a morning repast where people broke their fast after the anjali—the numbers were dwindling each year as the young people kept late hours these days and never woke up in time for the morning anjali—and then a somewhat traditional lunch was served: chhanar dalna on Saptami, khichuri on Ashtami and mutton-curry-and-rice on Nabami. Every family was allotted four coupons for each meal. Extras would have to be bought separately. Dinner, though, was not organized in Nancy. People ate out a lot during the pujas.

As the head of the puja committee, Mr Das was de facto head of the food department. Naturally, it meant that Mrs Das had an important role in the selection of menus.

She said now, 'In fact, Boudi, we can also explain the whole chanda system to this yoga lady. How she has to pay Rs 2,500 and will be entitled to four coupons.'

Mrs Mukherjee nodded briskly in agreement. 'Let's go after I speak to the flower-wallah.' She had an idea herself; she was quite keen to make friends with the yoga lady.

12.2

In this one week or so, Sandhya, Treeza and John had fallen into a rough pattern that almost made them into an odd sort of a family.

Treeza had effectively moved in upstairs with Sandhya, quickly assuming the role of a schoolgirl niece on holiday. She had not returned to their flat even once since that fateful afternoon. John had been very surprised when he'd returned home the first day after the demolition of the dinner set. Treeza was not home. He'd gone upstairs and found her in Sandhya's guest bedroom, sleeping soundly under the cotton duvet smelling of lavender. He'd had dinner as before, and discussed with Sandhya a possible course of action. They couldn't just be mooching off her this way, now could they?

'Oh, no, John, you mustn't think that way at all,' Sandhya had said. 'I must have some karma with the two of you—no, don't laugh!' She'd smiled herself. 'An old woman like me is allowed to be mystical and hippie and have these views. Perhaps in my last life you'd given me a home when I had need of it? Or food when I was hungry. Or support when I was broken. Who knows?' John had laughed again, his burden suddenly made light.

'I am a brahmacharini, John. Anywhere I live is an ashram for me. And, in an ashram, all who require a home are welcome. Your Treeze needs to get away from everything that is familiar to her in order to be able to return to it of her own will, healed. Give her time.'

John had humbly accepted Sandhya's direction and hospitality.

Treeza was not worried about appearances. There was something about Sandhya and her hermitage that had provided her a sliver of promise, and she clasped it now with the force of one drowning. She took for granted Sandhya's guest room, the bed with the fragrant cotton sheets, the dresser by the window and the white curtains that filtered golden light inside. She took for granted the head massage Sandhya gave her every day, after which she would sit in the sun.

Sandhya did not mind her presence at all, though in keeping with the assumed roles, she allowed herself to be strict about a few rules: after the first two days of sleeping at all hours, Treeza now had to wake up by seven; she had to eat; she had to take a hot bath; she had to help with household chores; she had to have her hair oiled. There was no TV, of course, and Treeze had no patience these days with books.

John minded his wife's disappearance from their house, a little—as though it were his failure—but he went along with it. He had managed to locate Sandhya's books on Flipkart and had even ordered one on yoga. Ananda Bose had, in the meanwhile, lent him *Solstice*.

Since she had no cooking to do for the Matthews, Anwara had taken over the washing of clothes; she would even iron Treeza's stuff and deliver these upstairs, dimpling and flowering in the presence of Sandhya. So eager was she to be a part of Sandhya's unorthodox ashram that on the fifth day she secured a job. She would be in charge of cleaning. It was fine if she came in the afternoons.

Every night, after returning home, John would come up to Sandhya's flat, in a fresh shirt, almost like a young beau bearing a little present. Flowers sometimes for Sandhya's table; red oleanders or hibiscus from the school garden on another day for her altar; a bottle of fresh cow's milk from a shop Rustam had recommended; ghee from the same shop; papayas and musambi and pomegranate in a bag; a lemon grass plant since Sandhya had mentioned it. He would find Treeze moving lightly around the house, barefoot, speaking occasionally from shadows and corners. But she would be in clean clothes, her hair tied behind neatly like a girl's, her skin clear and bright. She would open the door when John came in, and smile shyly and disappear. While John and Sandhya chatted, about his students and hers mostly, and also about England—had she been to the Lake District, to Edinburgh, to Stratford-upon-Avon?—Treeza would sit on the mat, half-listening, playing with the cushions. At dinner time, she would recite what it was she'd done to help: she'd shelled peas or peeled potatoes, chopped onions and carrots, learnt to make pumpkin soup.

John would do the dishes and leave by ten. By that time, Treeze would have sneaked into *her* room. She never peeped out when he left, though every evening he hoped she might slide on a pair of slippers and sheepishly join him as he went home, to *their* home, the house he had broken his back to buy for her. She stayed back.

Every morning, as he left for school, John would see Sandhya walking around the colony. She would tell him that things would yet become all right, he just had to be patient. She would tell him that Treeze had not opened up about anything as yet, she had neither asked about Sandhya nor spoken of herself. She would spend the day following Sandhya around, yet keep a distance. But at night she no longer cried out or sobbed loudly, though sometimes when Sandhya went to wake her up in the mornings tears would have left large splotches on the pillow cases. He would have to be patient, Sandhya said, her voice kind. 'How are you, John?' she would ask him every morning and be genuinely interested to know. John would mumble something in reply.

He had no option but to trust her.

12.3

Mrs Das and Mrs Mukherjee rang the bell at Sandhya's around eleven-thirty, prepared to be surprised, and they were. Sandhya opened the door in her white khadi sari and blouse, a ladle in hand. Her face was brown, unlined and framed by a crop of short hair. They introduced themselves. She welcomed them inside warmly, gestured to the settees and returned to the kitchen to stir the soup. Treeza Matthew was there, sitting quietly on the mat. Neither Mrs Das nor Mrs Mukherjee had seen Treeza Matthew more than once or twice, though everybody knew her pleasant and polite husband. He was the one who responded to all notices, made all payments to the cooperative, even corrected the English of the notices and memos.

Mrs Das, of course, knew Anwara's version of Treeza—there was not much that Mrs Das did not know about the colony—but she was smart enough not to let on all that. Instead, she allowed Mrs Mukherjee to do the talking while she gaped hungrily at the simplicity of the house. The elegance of the few items of furniture, the clean lines and tasteful colours, the complete absence of clutter. Monalisa Das was a little stumped. She had never believed in the power of such silence in décor; perhaps she had never met anyone like Sandhya.

Sandhya, meanwhile, had brought in four bowls of soup on a tray.

Half an hour and two helpings of soup later, several things were established: Treeza Matthew and Sandhya would help in the Puja preparations; Sandhya, unfortunately, did not quite favour astrology herself but she might be able to recommend some memory-strengthening tonic for Mrs Das's boys; she would certainly share the recipe for the soup; she would be happy to meet Mrs Mukherjee's PhD-scholar-daughter Aparajita Mukherjee and teach her yoga, though weight loss was a complex matter, and it was health which was important—one must focus on the health part, the weight part would follow.

'My guru used to say that since we have to climb up the slippery pole of karma all by ourselves and carry our own weight, it helps if we don't carry extra baggage. But that baggage is often mental. Our body is always trying to tell us about our health, but we are too busy to listen. Why we eat what we eat, why we crave what we crave. Being too heavy or too light is just a metaphor the body uses to tell us about its state. I'd be happy to teach Aparajita yoga, Mrs Mukherjee. But it will be for health, really. The weight loss part would be incidental.'

Mrs Mukherjee thanked Sandhya profusely. She would send her daughter ('difficult girl, though essentially very good girl, would definitely learn yoga seriously and be a committed student') to meet Sandhya.

Mrs Das would come by another time with a detailed breakup of duties.

After the two ladies left, Treeza, who was feeling a little left out, immediately asked Sandhya if she might learn yoga too.

12.4

AJ was practically living in Nancy these days, Apu realized. The thought annoyed her. As though one pesky fest-planner was not enough, they now had two in that limited space. Twice the number of phone calls and smelly socks and WiFi monopolizers. There was only one thing to recommend AJ: he was quite affectionate. Well, another: he was definitely smarter than her stupid brother. Much more worldly-wise. And that damned fest they were supposedly planning was months and months away! Basically, it was all an excuse to not study.

Apu was walking towards Sandhya's building, grumbling in her head. Strings of lights glittered on the four-storey buildings of Nancy. But the festive season only made Apu more depressed; everything seemed to have gone wrong this year. To begin with, her mother had instructed her not to shop now but three months later, when she had become slimmer and that Abhiroop Lahiri of Chicago was about to come. Then, there was Meera. Her mother would probably not suspend the diet even during the pujas, though, of course it was possible to cheat since her mother was always busybodying around, managing this and that.

This evening, her mother had ordered her to meet Sandhya as soon as she came back from college. Apu had not been keen at all, but then she'd Googled her and found loads of very interesting links. In general, Apu was not at all keen on celebrities, but this Sandhya lady's Wikipedia page was quite fascinating. However, why on earth was she here, in their godforsaken little colony? Anyway, at least learning yoga would be good. Apu watched yoga shows on TV sometimes, lithe girls doing impossible feats in sexy black leotards—very depressing. One learnt nothing from them. 'Ask her what she will charge, okay?' her mother had said as she'd given Apu a cup of tea and two digestive biscuits. 'In any case, whatever it is, it will be a valuable investment. I don't think she will overcharge. Why, she has taken in that Treeza girl for free! Mrs Das was saying she has taught yoga to even Hollywood actresses.' Apu had set the cup aside in disgust.

Apu reached A-5, second floor. She rang Sandhya's bell—the flat opposite was locked. Her mood soured further, when she saw that Sandhya—who looked exactly like her pictures, broad smile, brown eyes twinkling in genuine kindness—had another guest. It was Ananda Bose.

As though that were not irritating enough, Bose jumped up and greeted Apu enthusiastically. He began to introduce her to Sandhya in very flattering terms. Then, after a bit, he calmed down and Apu and Sandhya chatted vaguely. Apu did not want to mention the yoga classes in front of Bose at all. She agreed to have tea instead.

A young girl drifted in from somewhere and shyly sat next to Apu. Ananda Bose immediately introduced Apu to the girl—Treeza Matthew—using florid (although very flattering descriptions) for both, but this time it seemed to help somewhat. Apu and Treeza smiled at each other guardedly, waving aside Bose's descriptions. (Apu was a genius; Treeza's kindness was legendary.) Apu was mollified slightly.

A marvellous aroma of cinnamon toasting wafted out of Sandhya's kitchen. Apu's stomach rumbled. She tried to distract everyone by asking Bose the first question that popped into her head.

'Mr Bose, how are things in your college?'

'The usual,' Bose replied modestly, not mentioning that he had published a paper in the Edinburgh-based *Review of Applied Ethics*, edited by the legendary Isabel Dalhousie. 'But I meant to tell you, Ms Mukherjee, that vacancies have been advertised in our college. There are two permanent positions in botany. The HOD is a dear friend of mine—he is very into plant psychology, you know? It's a new area of research, completely nascent, but I am very keen on it. If you like, I can get you an application form. Also, if you drop in at my college one of these days, I am sure Prof. Jha would be happy to meet you.'

'Thank you,' Apu was forced to say. 'That would be very kind of you.' Oof, she did need a permanent job. Even if it meant taking the help of Ananda Bose.

'Maybe I should look for a job too,' Treeza Matthew murmured to herself.

From a distance in the kitchen, Sandhya observed her guests, soon to be her friends. Sandhya wondered if the grace of guru might touch their lives.

She had been a teacher long enough to take nothing for granted, and to not get too fond of her pupils. But Treeza had already broken that barrier; and now, even Ananda Bose. That afternoon, Ananda Bose had invited Sandhya to his house to meet his mother. Was there any relief she could suggest? The old lady's body had shrunk to a bird-like state, light and small, though she had once been tall like her son. Ananda Bose had lifted her tenderly, fed her medicine with loving reprimand. She had a powerful voice still and, like an opinionated child, had resisted her son. Sandhya had worked with thousands of cancer patients; yet the smell of decay within would hit her like a sock in the stomach. Sandhya had closed her eyes and prayed by the bed. But it was clear that the end was nigh. The praana had begun to leave her body. It would not be long before the old lady was freed from pain. But what would happen to young-old Ananda Bose when the mother—now the child—left his life?

Treeza and Apu sat quietly while Bose chattered on. Sandhya had been drawn to Apu immediately. She could be a great strength to people in her life; she had the quality of steadiness, of character, which does not draw attention to itself and is essentially unassuming. But what was that hunger streaking through her?

And Treeza—what was that secret boxed inside? With Treeza, Sandhya could not be sure. Outwardly, she seemed to have improved. But then hot baths and going to bed on time could reverse niggling problems easily. But Treeza was one of those—if she did not heal from within, even after spending a month or two with Sandhya, when she appeared to have conquered her all ghosts, she could revert in one day to the exact contours of life before, with all the guilt and depression and no food and feelings of rejection running riot. But what was it that was eating her from within?

Unknown to themselves, this little group, nudging and prodding each other over space, was already adjusting itself around Sandhya, a still point in the turning tides of time.

Calcutta too had now become her karma bhoomi, though she was uninhibited by reputation or form. Perhaps this is what all of it had been about. The exhaustion of unresolved karma. The new breath of freedom from the traditional guru's role.

There would be one or two more in their ranks, Sandhya could see. Though their auras were yet uncertain.

But that was still a few days away.

Sandhya

From Solstice.

The Swinging Sixties. They were heady times—many argue that it was the only *period that the city of London was cooler and hipper than New York and Paris! The Beatles had arrived, neatly cleaving London history into pre-Beatles and post-Beatles; the more conservative among the British middle class were denouncing them as evil.*

My school was about ten minutes away from Chelsea, the London borough that in the sixties had become the bohemian quarter of the city, the nerve centre of Swinging London. Meg worked as a shop assistant in an avante garde boutique, The Sweet Shop, on King's Street, run by the legendary designer Laura Jamieson. A few doors away, Mary Quant would invent the mini skirt.

We would leave home together in the morning, chattering all the way. Though she was nearly twenty-eight to my sixteen, Meg and I got along well. I was like a sponge, absorbing everything she said about fitting in, copying her phrases ('Chop, chop!', 'Guv'nor', 'Old thing') and never ever slipping into West Indian patois, even with my cousin. I helped out at home, doing the dishes scrupulously, never complaining about the food that was not to my taste. After school, I would pop into Chelsea and spend a couple of hours wandering around. Sometimes I would just help Meg out in The Sweet Shop in the afternoons. Supermodels and singers and hippies and wannabes all sat on the floor-to-floor carpet, leaning against sequinned velvet cushions and listening to Dylan songs playing on a gramophone. It was all very atmospheric.

I sent blue aerogrammes home every week; I received aerogrammes in return every week. Since each letter took weeks to arrive, news arrived on a time lag. My eldest brother and his wife were going to have another baby. My mother was suffering from anaemia. And my father (His letters were the most demanding, the most difficult for me to process: How was I doing? Was I studying hard enough? Was I visiting the museum regularly?) I loved my father so much, but all the new things that I was learning every day, the new words and the new mores, whirled around me loudly, constructing transparent walls, separating me from him, from my family. It was difficult to tell them the colours and sounds of the world I'd discovered, to recreate my experiences in those small blue squares. They would disapprove of my afternoons in The Sweet Shop instead of in a library. ('You're spending time in a tailoring store! Is that why you're in London?') I slipped into the bad habit of repeating platitudes, even as my inner life broke away from their wellspring: I am fine, I would write every week, though the weather is damp and cold; Meg is very kind; my grades are good; I have fitted in quite well; the girls in school like me well enough and the masters are impressed. In truth, the girls—except a few—found me provincial and too dark; the masters were indifferent. My mother sent a lovingly designed grey woollen skirt for Meg in the post.

But it was true that in school I found it was easy for me to cope. I was fairly ahead in math, history and geography, and good enough in literature and language. I began to get involved in extra-curricular activities, really coming into my own in the music club. Though I had never been formally trained in classical music, I had always accompanied my mother in songs, and my lilting voice, more sweet and husky than powerful, seemed to captivate the others. There were two other girls of Caribbean descent in the music club. Marie and Nella. Both coloured. They had grown up in London and, compared to me, were positively adult and refined. Marie took me under her wing, and Nella, beautiful Nella, the London-born daughter of janitors from Jamaica, introduced me to other singers in the school, mostly white girls pining intensely for a dark voice.

It was a time when eclectic was in, and my repertoire of Indian songs—whether they were the bhakti songs my mother hummed all day or the wedding songs my sisters-in-law danced to—were pronounced 'great material' by the girls in the club; we would play around with the rhythms, building up the tempo and mixing it up with other styles, chiefly Calypso, my clear high-pitched voice complimented by their timbred choruses. Chutney music had already become big in the Caribbean, and Marie and Nella thought we could try out some experimentations of our own. In the meantime, I was also being re-educated in music. I was introduced to jazz and psychedelic rock. And, of course, to the Beatles.

When it was time for me to pick out a college after my A-levels—in which I did well but not spectacularly, much to the disappointment of my father—instead of honouring the wishes of the family and opting for something stolid and respectable, something that might help me support the family back home, I picked theatre. My music club friends and I had discussed that voice training would be good for me: we were already planning to do great things in music in the future, world-conquering things. I could not take up music, of course, since the only sort of music taught in college was Western classical, and I was not brave enough to take up acting! Marie joined English literature and Nella decided against going to college altogether.

We all got part-time jobs on King's Street and Carnaby Street, where fashion rules were being rewritten, in order to be able to afford LPs and gramophone records. We had begun to follow music from around the world, buying Indian records from the India Store on Oxford Street, my only links then with the ancestral land. We moved into cheap digs in the back lanes of Chelsea, with Marie's guitar and Nella's keyboards. In those parts, every other house boasted of a poor singer with matted hair who would be The Next Big thing. To be fair, Bob Marley and Eric Clapton, both Chelsea residents those days, did go on to become Big Things.

The aerogrammes became more difficult to write, the ones that came in a flurry of reprimand (Theatre? What on earth was I to do with theatre?) became too difficult to open.

And then, almost to simplify matters for me, Meg and R decided to get a divorce. That made it easy, in a sense. It was inevitable that I inherited Meg, and with our estrangement from R, my guilt and my father's rage could solidify into a wall.

Four years later, I completed my college degree with a median second class. My Indian streak of caution had remained: I was the only one in our group to have completed my studies, even though it meant I had to work extremely hard, juggling classes with music rehearsals. The chutney sensation in the Caribbean had now reached the cool quarters of the British Isles. The time seemed propitious. We launched Chutney, our four-member band (Marie, Nella and I had acquired an Oxford don's blue-eyed flaxen-haired guitar-playing daughter who sang the blues), formally, and began to perform what we called chutney-fusion. It was a fresh new sound where Indian and African impulses were blended into a quirky character, woven with bluesy lyrics. West Indian grammar and patois made great lyrics, fused with Hindi and Bhojpuri. In those days, experimental bands were dime-a-dozen, and yet, in a few months, Chutney began to get some press coverage. We even landed several gigs. By the time the first anniversary of Chutney came, we had acquired a manager and there was talk of a proper tour.

I was twenty-one. My gamble had paid off. I could smell a whiff of success. What did it matter that the only news I got of home comprised pointless little snippets through distant relatives and other East Indians—all singularly boring provincials who did not understand my intense musical quest? When I was a bigger success, I told myself, a true East Indian self-made success story, I would visit home. My father would forgive me. My father would be proud of me.

It was going to be soon.

CHAPTER 13

13.1

The Weight Loss Club. It was the lovely Mandy Mandal who, on Saptami morning, coined the clever catchphrase to denote Sandhya's three chelas. Her uncle, Ananda Bose; Abeer's sister, Apu; and the wispy girl with the massive curly mop of hair. All three seemed to be following Sandhya around, though the wispy girl, of course, didn't need to *lose* weight—the opposite, if anything. Mandy had seen it all last evening, at the puja in Nancy. Abeer had given her the general background too, though AJ felt he was being a bit disloyal to his sister and Ananda Bose in his quest to sound funny. But Mandy had only meant to be clever and quippy, not rude. She was, in fact, interested in Sandhya—especially in the Ang Lee angle— though she did not know *what* she should say to her. She couldn't quite ask if it was *interesting* being Sandhya, which, really, was what she wanted to know. As a beautiful girl with a trophy boyfriend, a play and a bunch of friends who worshipped her, Mandy didn't have that much time at hand to be interested in weight loss clubs. She was perfectly proportioned. She could have been a model.

'My mother should also join The Weight Loss Club, you know, guys. All this yoga and stuff would be good for her.' That is the context in which Mandy had used the name. But it stuck. Abeer and AJ gave it popular currency.

When it reached Apu's ears eventually, she admonished: 'You idiots, it really *is* a weight-loss club; but it's *mental* baggage we are

talking about. Not that you fools would understand such subtleties.'
But Apu said this much later; in any case, it was beside the point.

Mandy, AJ, and Abeer were in Rocky's house when she came up with the name. They had spent the better part of Saptami morning at Rocky's, waiting for the music committee meeting to start. At least, Abeer and AJ were waiting for the meeting to start. Mandy was happy to flit around from room to room, basking in her ownership of everything. From here, they would go to Nancy for lunch. Abeer was waiting patiently for this car ride in Mandy's vehicle—assuming, of course, that Rocky wasn't coming too. After a late lunch at Nancy, Mandy and her mother would go home so Mandy could rehearse for her play two nights later. AJ was sure that they would *have* to go to Triangular Park to watch that play with Mandy and her dog, though Abeer was still pretending they had a party at Tolly Club on Nabami night. This Rocky bastard would also no doubt be around.

He was *so* intolerable! All morning AJ and Abeer had made mental notes.

Rocky lived in a beautiful bungalow in Salt Lake. As if that weren't bad enough, he had an entire floor to himself since his parents apparently wanted him to be able to jam in peace. Mandy had provided the commentary. On Rocky's floor, there was a small book-lined drawing room, a guest room and a music studio—a gigantic room with wall-to-wall carpeting, cushions on the floor, a huge music system, and at least a thousand CDs. Then there was Rocky's bedroom. Grey wallpaper and white furniture and bedclothes.

Abeer was nauseated. Rocky should at least wait for a six-figure salary to be offered to him and *then* be all metrosexual—this was plain obnoxious. AJ was a bit impressed by the grand scale of Rocky's lifestyle. He had even started praising everything like a fan boy—until Abeer glared at him and pinched his arm.

The rest of Rocky's band—four or five long-haired dudes with stoned eyes—were currently holed up in the studio, mixing cocktails and rolling joints. Rocky was extremely matey with them; with the music committee members, he was offhand and superior—he ignored them except when he was throwing open his father's substantial bar with great panache and urging them to drink freely.

According to Abeer, this was all in very bad taste. But Mandy was busy being the queen bee, without realizing the extent of bad taste on display. Finally, around twelve-thirty, the meeting was held. A large number of people were too drunk on the free liquor by then to even follow proceedings.

'Right, so we have everybody worthwhile here. Those who haven't been able to make it to this meeting obviously are too lame to have been included in the committee in the first place.'

Several kinds of laughter ensued: whinnying, guffawing, cackling, throaty, scratchy. Rocky came into his element even more.

'Rashid Khan has been booked. Bhoomi has been locked. And Indian Ocean have been loaded.'

There was huge cheering.

'We have raised, thanks to our brilliant networking and my lovely Mandy's Manju Didi, a total of seven lakhs, in cash. Liquid gold, man, liquid gold. There is also newsprint space, magazine placement and radio time too. In other words, we have exceeded our own expectations. That means we will not only entertain everyone as they've never ever been entertained in their lives but we will also leave a legacy.'

'Woohoo!' Rocky's lead singer crooned.

'Hear, hear!' shouted Mandy.

'We will use the extra money to upgrade the existing instruments of the music committee. What say?'

There was wild cheering by the drunk and the drunker.

Abeer, who had not wanted to touch either salt or sugar at Rocky the Bastard's house, was stunned into a shocked silence at this unilateral announcement. If there was extra money, shouldn't the finance committee of the fest be consulted before the music club spent it on instruments? Other departments might need cash. Food, for instance. He tried to get AJ to protest—Mandy would mind if he said anything—but AJ was at the bar again, mixing red and white wine. Crap, thought Abeer. He turned to where Rocky had been standing and immediately gagged.

Rocky and Mandy weren't exactly making out. But he was drunkenly playing with her hair.

Abeer decided to leave.

Then, there was the disgusting sound of retching. Somebody vomited. Abeer turned to his right again and saw it was AJ. Fucking bastard!

The others looked away and pointedly walked past. Why did AJ have to get drunk at *Rocky's*? Abeer pulled the glassy-eyed AJ away from the pool of vomit.

'Take him to the washroom, man,' said Rocky. 'Don't worry. My people will clean it up. Not the first time it's happened at my party. Some people can't handle free drink.'

Everyone, except Mandy, laughed. She tried to come towards them, her face reflecting concern, but Rocky pulled her arm and took her somewhere else.

AJ followed Abeer like a lamb into the guest bathroom.

13.2

On Ashtami day too, Meera failed to make an appearance. Maaji Sahai, Lovely and son, and Nalini's two boys came down for breakfast as usual, bestowing smiles all around. Lovely was one of the most enthusiastic people in Nancy this year. She had even been recruited to help in a minor capacity—along with a couple of young, overdressed brides, she was deputed to distribute prasad to all the houses. The moment Apu spied them, she alerted her mother. Mrs Mukherjee and her mother-in-law, Mamoni Mukherjee, immediately descended on the Sahais and began chattering loudly. What a lovely sari Lovely was wearing, where did she do her shopping?

Sandhya in tow, Apu quickly went to their building and rang the bell at the Sahais'. Nalini opened.

'Oh, Apu! I am so happy to see you,' Nalini said, opening the door with the baby at her hip. 'I need your help. You can't imagine *what* I am saddled with!'

'I know, Bhabhi, I know,' Apu said. 'Don't worry. I've got Sandhyaji. She can fix everything.' Before Sandhya had time to contradict this grand statement, Apu asked, 'Where is Meera?'

'I can't even begin to describe what strange stuff is going on, Apu. Meera has gone mad. Absolutely mad.'

While Apu shook her head in disbelief, and even a touch of arrogance—oof, this judgemental housewife from Bihar—Sandhya's eyes registered genuine confusion and fear in Nalini.

'I think of Meera as my own sister, Apu, that is how I am managing everything alone. God knows what has happened in the last two weeks. She doesn't want to pick up her child, she doesn't want to feed her child, she can't even hear the child crying. I am not exaggerating one bit. She can't hear anything. As though her brain has frozen. And now I'm scared to even leave the child around her. See for yourself—' Nalini pulled Chhoti's hand outward. The little plump pink arm, perfect in every way, had a clear bite mark on it: a row of adult teeth had left its mark.

Apu gasped. 'Impossible!' she hissed. Absolutely impossible. It must be that Lovely bitch.

'No, Apu,' Nalini said sombrely. 'It happened the day Lovely, Maaji, the boys and I had gone out. I give Chhoti her bath these days. I am sure it wasn't there before. I went out only *one* day. After Himself left for Patna. Nobody was at home except Meera and Chhoti. Tara was out with us. We came back to find Meera lying in the bed, her back turned to Chhoti, and Chhoti was lying in a pool of shit. I couldn't tell anyone about this bite. I'm extremely scared. Is it a spirit or what? Mataji?'

Sandhya had been looking outside. In the balcony there was a tulsi plant. It looked a bit dry. 'I know what has happened,' she said, her fingers tapping Nalini's shoulder urgently. 'We need to speak. Where is the husband?'

13.3

As per tradition, Sandhi puja was offered in the darkest hour of night, at the cross-section between Ashtami and Nabami. The last twenty-four minutes of Ashtami and the first twenty-four minutes of Nabami together form that powerful slice of potent night when Devi as Chamunda destroys evil, her beauty more terrifying than ever. Sandhya, along with the few other Devi-inclined residents of Nancy, sat in the community hall in front of the idol. Durga was resplendent in the traditional daaker saaj, silver and white foil used creatively to fashion her clothes and ornaments. Her face was golden and her three eyes drawn exquisitely. The priest performed the rituals, his face shining in the firelight. Sandhya sat behind everybody else, her face in darkness. Eyes closed, she meditated upon Chamunda.

Perhaps four or five minutes before the forty-eight minutes of Sandhikkhhan were up, she felt herself slipping deeper and deeper into a void. She welcomed the feeling without getting exhilarated— that would have interrupted her flight. She would merely have to be ready to receive; often one could have visions in such a state. Never literal, they came from the depths of the unconscious, elucidating the past or the future. Sandhya never touted the prescience of these visions. But then there was nothing strange about them either. If the mind is sufficiently calm and the cosmos draws back, if only for a moment, the seed of the present can show the tree that had borne it and the tree it will bear. If only one can be sufficiently quiet.

It was a forest. There was the sun, a large orange sun, slung in the horizon. A woman wandered around with a child. Sandhya did not see her face. She sat down under a tree. The woman, a mother really, began to feed the baby, cradling it to her chest. The baby cried. Still the mother tried to feed it. The baby cried louder and louder until the forest became dim with its sorrow. The mother forced the child to the other breast, her face still in the dark. Yet, though Sandhya could not see her features, she felt the mother's rage course through her. A hush came in the forest, like an icy wind. The baby became silent.

Suddenly, gasping in fear, Sandhya came back to herself, breaking out in cold sweat.

When she opened her eyes, she found she was sitting in the park, in straight view of the Roman ruin. Only Mrs Mukherjee and old Mrs Pal were still there, hovering around the priest, helping him pack up.

Mrs Mukherjee came up to Sandhya. 'You were meditating very deeply, Ma. Even when all the bells and cymbals rang, you didn't move. People left noisily. But you didn't hear anything?'

Sandhya wiped her forehead and arose.

'Shall I walk you home?' Chhanda Mukherjee asked again.

'No, no, Chhanda, that's fine,' Sandhya said urgently. 'Is your daughter in bed? I need to speak to Apu right now.'

13.4

Nalini kept vigil all night. On Nabami day, Apu and Treeza watched Chhoti and Tara in Sandhya's house through the day, spoiling the girls to bits, while Nalini tried to snatch some rest. Meera's days were spent in her bed; she got up only to go to the bathroom. It was as though she had become deaf. She didn't hear anything. Not the drumbeats outside her window every morning, the dhaakis dancing rhythmically, not the clang of cymbals and bells, not the chant of the mantras in the morning, not the cries of the children as they ran round and round and fired little toy pistols. Meera heard nothing.

Mrs Mukherjee had sent Maaji Sahai, Lovely and her entourage and the boys to the neighbouring colony, Bengal MLF, where Aamir Khan films were being screened all day. AJ and company were camped there and promised to help out the Sahais in case they needed anything. Suresh was still away on his trip to Bangalore. He would only return on Dashami evening, after which, it had been decided, Sandhya would speak to him.

Sandhya remained in the puja area, with its fragrance of crushed petals and earthen lamps and camphor. She was exhausted. She had spent many hours praying, last night as well as this morning, but no other visions had come. No directions. Sandhya felt for the first time that perhaps she ought not to have come this way, staked out on her own, given into the pull of maya yet again. She should have listened to Sheila. Given power of attorney to the Sens and allowed them to sort it all out. But now it was too late, now she was stuck. Sandhya sat quietly and observed what was going on.

It was four in the afternoon. The last batch had only just finished lunch. It included John, Mr Das, Pal Babu and two or three other gentlemen. They were now sitting with the caterers and deciding the menu for tomorrow night. Dinner was usually not included in the package, but since there was enough cash left over, perhaps a simple dinner might be provided? Biriyani and raita, perhaps, John suggested.

Mrs Das came towards Sandhya, accompanied by a thin woman in a bright blue starched cotton sari. 'Namaskar, Ma,' Mrs Das said, smiling. 'This is my friend Kumkum De. Dearer than my own sister. She lives in Sinthir More, where we used to live before.'

Kumkum De's Hindi was pidgin like Monalisa's. She touched Sandhya's feet before Sandhya could protest. 'Thank you for the brain tonic formula, Ma. I have dictated it to my daughter in America. For her children. They are still small. But very intelligent. I told her about you—to read that book about you on which cinema is being made? She is a doctor, you know.'

'You're welcome,' said Sandhya. Mrs De had thinning hair and dry nails. She was definitely vata prakriti, extremely vata. But if she didn't ask for a tonic for herself, Sandhya could only smile politely.

'I know, Ma, you don't approve of astrologers. But Mrs De had invited the most brilliant astrologer ever to her house yesterday. Baba Akaalananda. I took the boys there, Ma. He was uncanny. He could predict all past and future, you know? Down to the last mark in the last exams. He has told Bablu to take maths very seriously.' As Mrs De excused herself and walked towards the idols of Durga and her children, hands folded, Monalisa Das sat down on the floor in front of Sandhya, her back to the door. 'I'm so tired, Ma, I can't tell you how tired! These last few days have been such hard work. And there are the boys and their thousand things.'

Behind Monalisa, the open doorway framed a perfect rectangle of blue sky. Voices floated in from outside—John, the caterer, Mr Das. The afternoon was on its last stretch, lazy and long. People had gone indoors to snooze. The final night, Nabami, was the night of revelry. The hum of traffic far away seemed to float in, or perhaps it was her imagination. Monalisa arched her back and stretched her hands. Behind her, in the sky framed by the open door, an orange orb of a sun, a very bright familiar sun, slipped in. It was as though the sun was floating between Monalisa's arms.

Instantly, Sandhya stood up.

'Monalisa, can you please take me to your house? Right now?'

Monalisa was stunned. 'What, Ma?'

Sandhya rushed out. 'Mr Das,' she told the balding gentleman with the placid face, 'I must go to your house right now. John, come with me,' she ordered.

By this time, Sandhya had acquired a basic geography of Nancy. She ran towards A-1, John in her wake. Mr and Mrs Das followed, dumb-founded. Gublu had been playing cricket within the garage of A-1; he ran behind them, hopping and skipping, bouncing a rubber ball.

'Open the door,' Sandhya told Mrs Das.

Mrs Das produced her keys and tried them. But the door didn't respond. 'It's latched,' she said, looking at her husband in confusion. 'Why is it latched from the inside?' She pressed the bell several times.

'Break the door,' Sandhya instructed John. 'Break it now.'

'But, madam, madam,' Das intervened patiently, 'Bablu is inside.

Maybe he is watching TV in our bedroom. Sometimes he does that. He must have latched it by mistake.'

'Break it now,' Sandhya told John, not looking at the Dases at all.

John decided to listen. Sandhya turned the key in the lock and kept waiting in readiness. In the tried and tested way of Hindi films, John moved away from the door and began to crash into it with as much force as he could muster. Gublu and his friends joined in immediately.

Mr Das and Mrs Das stood a few feet away from all this, their annoyance turning slowly into confusion as Bablu didn't come to the door despite so much noise.

After a few minutes, Ananda Bose, who had wandered upstairs hearing the commotion, joined John. Finally, the latch gave away.

Sandhya was the first inside.

The boy seemed asleep on his bed. From the door, you would not have guessed there was anything more to it than that. But if you stood at the foot of the narrow single bed, you would see the little white bottle that was upended beside him, striking against the blue bedspread. If you touched his forehead, you would draw back in fear at its unnatural coldness. And if you were the mother, who had entered the room in half-annoyance, only after the pushy strangers, you would know the upended bottle instantly. It was the one which contained pills that were consumed by your mother-in-law, who had come to visit during the pujas and only left this morning. Even as you cried out while the others, the strangers, checked his pulse and breathing, you tried to locate a loophole in the logic of what appeared. For it could not be so. It was your boy—he could not be dying.

SANDHYA

***From* Solstice.**
In the summer of 1975, I had the dream for the first time.
It was a glittering party, somewhere near the sea. Or perhaps

there was no sea but just the sound of waves, a consistent sound of waves. There was singing and dancing around me, all swish and style, hundreds of people. There was great merriment in the air. I could not hear the music though, only the sound of waves, but the dancing was to the tune of the unheard music. And then, suddenly, I saw that though I was dancing happily, my hair was on fire. I began to shout, but no sound emerged from my throat. There was no one around me any more, not the people, not the sea.

I woke up in severe cold sweat, shaking.

Our second record, Chelsea Chutney, *had just been released. It was a healthy success. The first, simply titled* Chutney, *was considered a hit in the alt-space. Though it did not sell too well, the reviews were good and it made us into some sort of youth icons. Female, coloured and very fashionably dressed—Meg often lent us clothes from The Sweet Shop. The more racist England behaved, the more fame was lumped on us. And, boy, did we enjoy it! The second record sold more, but the reviews were perhaps not quite as enthusiastic. The music scene was shifting perceptibly.*

I partied hard, travelled a lot, and worked overtime. I had now begun to produce songs for others, scoring a few moderate successes. I'd even got enough money from producing to buy myself a small flat in a fairly fashionable part of town.

But I had still not visited home.

Over that summer, as the foxgloves and bluebells and ox-eye daisies bloomed in abandon, the dream continued to recur. Sometimes the sea was clear and blue, sometimes it was a gigantic black mass. Sometimes the guests were familiar faces, sometimes they were strangers, sometimes their faces were blanked out. I ignored it, of course.

I continued to travel, party and produce. A Spanish song I produced went on become the Number 11 for a few weeks. We toured in Italy; after that, I managed to travel around a little, with a friend, before returning to London in September. On the last day of my Italian holiday, the dream recurred, a little altered but with great vividness. My hair was on fire, but my companion couldn't see it. He kept dancing with me.

With autumn, a wave of exhaustion hit me so hard that one morning I was simply unable to get out of bed. I cancelled my meetings and stayed home. A strange sense of hysteria had been pushing me all summer, one which I had deliberately avoided confronting. That day, I remember, I stayed in bed till noon. I had no appetite, but that was not strange since I seldom had a robust appetite. Nor did I have fixed times for eating.

A strange despair clung to my house, a grey veil. London can be severely depressing from autumn right through winter—the days short and miserable, the nights cold and long. A stale air permeated my flat. I was never there long enough to dust or cook or even air the rooms. But, in Indian fashion, I was very proud of the flat I owned. I'd bought it myself. A young, single, coloured woman—it had been almost unthinkable. I was proud of being a house-owner. One day my father would see it—he'd be proud too.

But that afternoon I was so exhausted that I could barely haul myself out of bed and make a cup of tea. My body ached, my head pounded and there was something the matter with my stomach—it was tightly drawn, like a ball of metal. Galvanizing the last vestiges of energy, I drew myself a hot bath.

That afternoon, in the bath, I discovered the lump in my armpit. I didn't know if it had sprung overnight. I hadn't observed it before. It was small, solid and painless.

I called Marie's GP and fixed an appointment for the same evening. I did not ask anyone to accompany me. The GP referred me to a specialist. The specialist ran a battery of tests and called me at the end of the week. There was bad news, he told me himself, very apologetically.

It was cancer. It had advanced to the third stage. I was not in the risk age group at all, that was what was surprising. I would have to undergo a mastectomy at the earliest.

I wept bitterly on my bed. I thrashed around on the mattress, tears running down my face, as though my heart would break. I was angry with a red-hot rage. I was so angry that I rushed into the kitchen and broke every single plate or glass I owned. Crystal, coffee mugs, even the expensive wineglasses. I was so angry that I pulled down the expensive silk curtains from the casement and rolled around in their folds. I broke the glass-topped table. I tore through a silk kimono. I was angry with my body for letting me down. I shouted into my pillow till my throat hurt. I was willing to strike a bargain: take away my voice, I will not sing a single note any more, but let me keep my beauty. Please, please let me keep my breast.

At some point, I fell asleep.

When I woke up I was dying of thirst. But all the cups and glasses had been smashed and glass bits were strewn all over the house. Outside, a sickly dawn was breaking. I cupped my palms below the tap and drank chilly water that scalded my throat.

I was twenty-three years old.

In the next four years, I had five surgeries, though after the loss of my left breast it had seemed to me that nothing *could hurt me any more. For months I would close my eyes when I changed my clothes. I removed mirrors from the bathroom. The shock to my femininity was profound. But my friends had rallied around me, telling me I should fight.*

Six months after the mastectomy, it seemed the cancer had metastasized; tumours seemed to have sprung up in several organs. But I trained myself not to feel anything. It was as though I had split into two people inhabiting roughly the same body: the me which was asleep; and the twin which did the everyday job of breathing and vomiting and eating and shitting, the twin who didn't feel anything. Not when my long dark hair fell after months of radiotherapy. Not when the other breast also had to be removed.

Three years later, after yet another battery of tests, as the twin sat exhausted in my doctor's chamber, Dr Sheila Gibson, a very young gynaecologist specializing in oncology and pain management, came in to speak to me gently. She had been assigned the difficult task of telling me and my twin that the team of doctors who were handling my case had run their gauntlet. There was nothing they could do any more.

I had known in my bones what she would say. I was tired of the fight. I had about two or three months to say my goodbyes. I was going to die.

I was twenty-seven years old.

BOOK 4
GATHERING

CHAPTER 14

14.1

Devi remained in her house, under the red canopy. Her children were next to her, in their silver-white ceremonial clothes. Not that any of them, except her favourite one perhaps—the one with his extreme devotion and his odd-shaped head—had made her entirely happy. But when they were all together, here, grouped around her, her other selves receded: warrior, slayer, lover, artist. She was the mother.

The mother-goddess remained alive all night, as idols of clay and water do, in swirling clouds of devotion and dust. But the night was terrible. The stars were remote. Tucked behind folds of clouds, planets turned. The wind that rose from the north lifted dead leaves and dirty paper-plates lying in the corner and bore the stench of loss. In the heat of shock and fear, the goddess remained abandoned for the time-being, forgotten by the crowds that had swelled around her in the morning. All except for the old woman with cropped hair who sat in front of her, in padmasana, in deep prayer.

The women lay next to their children at home, holding on to a foot or an arm, in fear. It was a strange primeval fear—it mirrored the mother's; yet, at its core, the seed in the fruit, was a smug shiny ball of relief. Stark, shameless relief. *They* had been spared. The men kept distant vigil with the father. The young felt guilty—but they did not cancel their plans; they escaped into the mad lights and sounds of the city.

All night, Death wandered over the terrain. Everyone heard its footsteps without knowing what it was. That rustle in the wind, that stray bark. Death brought its forbears, the spirits of howl, the brothers and sisters of lost souls.

Devi's face shone in the light of the single lamp the old woman had lit.

Durga's black eyes had been drawn this year by an ageing artist of Kumortuli whose wife had died, who loved his grandchild, who smoked bidis relentlessly to forget that he would never be remembered. He had painted such love and sorrow and regret into the eyes of Devi that she could not but choose to fight with the mother that night.

The mother whose heart was breaking; the mother who saw in every direction only signs of life: in every blade of grass, in each ant that scurried. The same texture of life that was ebbing from her heart as the life-force ebbed from her child's.

But the claims of Death were strong.

14.2

At dawn, a taxi drew up outside Nancy. A tall foreigner emerged from it and pulled out a bag. She wore a plain cotton salwar-kurta without a dupatta.

Sleepily rubbing his eyes, the guard left his stool in the little room that was the 'Security Office' and came to stand by the gate.

The cabbie had got a suitcase out of the boot and dragged it towards the guard. 'Nancy, toh?' The guard pointed silently to the board outside. 'Open the gate, bhai,' the driver now told the guard. 'Madam has just come from the international airport.'

The guard wanted to say in reply: 'You mind your own business, baba. Am I to open the gate for any Jodu-Modhu-Shyam?' But it was still the season of puja, and the lady was definitely a foreigner, a decent-looking lady foreigner, so he didn't want to be rude. But he didn't open the gate yet.

After several salaams—which meant he had been tipped

generously—the cabbie got into the car and drove off. The guard scowled. Some people had all the luck. Cabbies and restaurant waiters, for example. Just the tips people gave in this season were enough to run a household for a couple of months back in the village. If you were a luckless guard, all you had to show for the puja extravaganza was a measly bonus, free meals and loads of attitude from people coming and going all decked up, especially young chhokras and chhokris who were busy doing prem. The last evening had, at least, offered him a breaking-news-type story; he could not wait to return home and report the incident to everyone. What a terrible thing to happen on Nabami!

'Namaskar,' the lady said, smiling politely, from the other side of the gate. 'I would like to visit A-5.'

'Oh.' Everything fell into place with a click. 'Sandhya Madam?'

'Yes, exactly.' The lady nodded vigorously.

The guard opened the gate immediately and, in spite of protestations, began to pull the suitcase inside. He spoke in a Bengali peppered generously with English phrases. 'Madam, I can't leave my station since I'm alone. My colleague will come at seven-thirty, I shall send your suitcase then. Why to carry heavy suitcase? I will keep it safely here, no problem. There is no lift actually in any of the buildings here. Will be difficult for you to lift suitcase. A-5 is straight down, to the right. Last building. Beside the tree with red flowers.'

Dr Sheila paused a moment, thought this through and agreed. This is what happened in India. People were always offering to do things for one and would be genuinely disappointed if she did not heed their thoughtful offer. She'd been lugging this large suitcase through her entire American sojourn. Just as well. Clutching her black bag, Dr Sheila trotted in the direction pointed out by the guard.

It was five-thirty. A rosy glow bathed the eastern part of the sky; the rest of it was blue. The four-storey houses were uniformly festooned with strings of light. But now these were not lit, and the overall effect was a little depressing. As though the party were over. Or was it something else? While walking past the park, Dr Sheila paused. She decided to greet the goddess for a minute before going to Sandhya's. Which day of the puja was it today? The third day? Sheila had hoped to catch at least a couple of days of the legendary puja celebrations of Calcutta, but then she'd missed the connecting flight at Istanbul and everything had been hopelessly delayed. She was very curious about the goings-on at Nancy. Sandhya's brief mails had been increasingly filled with eccentric characters she seemed to be adopting left and right, leading Sheila to worry a little.

The Roman ruins of the pandal were deserted. The new rays of the sun fell on the idols and bathed them in orange light. Sheila folded her hands, chatted with the Devi for a bit and then turned to the concrete pathway that ran around the park.

But the overall atmosphere around the pandal—the bits and bobs lying around, toys, ice-cream cups, packets of chips—they all seemed to suggest that Sheila had perhaps missed the joyous part completely.

14.3

A deal of sorts was affected somewhere in the cosmos.

By noon, John Matthew and Mr Mukherjee returned from the hospital bearing good news, a sliver of hope. The boy, battling for life at National Medical College, where he had been transferred from the local nursing home in the middle of the night, was probably going to make it. He was not out of coma yet, and still on life support, but the vital signs had picked up.

It was Dashami. The fifth and final day.

At twilight, the redoubtable Mrs Abhaya Bose, formerly headmistress, Nellie Sengupta Girls' High School (MA, BT), mother to Dr Ananda Bose (philosopher and devoted pursuer of knowledge) and Mrs Aparna Mandal (social worker and devoted socialite), decided that perhaps it might be interesting if she accompanied the goddess on her return to Kailash this year.

The goddess had come by palanquin, but would be returning via the river.

At dusk, she passed away in her sleep. Bose was sitting on a chair next to her. The nurses had taken leave during the puja days, but Bose didn't mind sitting by his mother and reporting all that was happening in Bengal, the world and even in Nancy. He didn't mind giving her the bedpan or changing her clothes. On the rare occasions, that she replied to his reportage, it was usually a sharp retort. Mrs Abhaya Bose was not impressed by the doings of most people in Bengal, the world or Nancy.

Earlier that morning, Mrs Bose had said three things to her son: it is not too late; eat bananas every morning; your sister will need you more in the years to come, you will have to tolerate her. She had repeated the instruction about the bananas twice.

Through the open window—Mrs Bose had wanted the window left open today—the sounds from the pandal had drifted in. They would have drifted into the mosquito net, Bose thought. After news came from the hospital that Bablu, though still in ICU and on the ventilator, was probably out of danger, one by one people had returned to the pandal, guardedly exchanging news. The priest and his assistant had dared to increase their volume a decibel or so. Yet, everything remained muted. There was no question of an exaggerated sindoor khela; quietly women went up the steps to the goddess and applied vermilion on her forehead and at the parting of her hair. Then they heaped vermilion on her red feet. Thank you, Ma, for keeping *my* children safe, they each whispered, selfish relief swelling in their hearts.

When Ananda Bose realized that his mother had gone very still, he checked for her pulse several times. Nothing. The body was still warm, but all traces of pain had left the face.

Bose arose from the chair and kept his book aside. He went to the open window and looked at the pandal in front, where straggling lines of women, young and old, were patiently waiting for their turn to greet the goddess privately.

Before alerting Sandhya or telephoning the doctor, Bose decided wait for a few minutes. He observed himself and was a little surprised that above all he felt a strange sense of release. Profound grief would come, he knew, for his mother had been a large chunk of his life, solid like a rock. But now there was a still moment in the middle of it all as her lifeless body lay by the window, when, along with her soul, now freed into the light, it was as though Ananda too was lifted into the air, where he roamed for a few moments with the birds going home.

APU

27th October.
On Dashami night, as hundreds of thousands of noisy people bore their neighbourhood goddesses to the river for immersion, our neighbour Ananda Bose cremated his mother at the Keoratala burning ghat. It seems John M. and my father went to the burning ghat directly from the hospital where the Dases are camping out. Abeer, et al, accompanied him from Nancy, along with a few neighbours and relatives, which was a great relief, really, because AB looked very lost. I instructed Abeer to keep an eye on AB so he didn't get left behind at the shamshaan or get kidnapped by aghoris or something, but Abeer just looked at me like I was a dimwit. Feel terrible about AB. Have always been so short with him, snapping at him every time he's tried to be kind.

Anyway. What's done is done. Will just have to try to make it up to him now. Though, have no idea what to say to him. What do you tell somebody when the only person he has in the whole world dies? Is tough. Anything I say will sound phony. Have parents, grandmother, one useless brother. Even have the vague possibility of Chicago boy in my life. Come to think of it, have Sadia and Meera and now Sandhyaji. AB has annoying sister and simpering niece.

What a newsworthy puja this has been. Between hospital and burning ghat. I suppose madhouse next, if Meera's sister-in-law is to be believed. Which reminds me, tomorrow onwards, have to help Tara finish holiday homework!

Dr Sheila, who is Sandhyaji's oldest friend and the one who runs all those women's health workshops with her, arrived early Dashami morning. She was drinking tea with Mataji, praising the new international terminal (and hearing all about us, I suppose, for she seemed to know much about me when I joined them after breakfast). TM was still sleeping. Feel quite bad for her poor husband. She's just walked out of their flat, though now I know the reason and it's quite heartbreaking. But still. Is not end of world, is it? But then what would I know? John M., however, has thrown himself into colony life, what with back-to-back tragedies in Nancy. Is quite a handsome man, smouldering and serious. He looks at TM longingly all the time, I've noticed.

Dr Sheila is very tall, very blonde, very humorous. Quite a Calcutta-phile. I had no idea about half the places she was gushing about. Should get Calcutta guide, next time in College Street. Embarrassing how little one knows about own city. She's not stiff-upper-lip either, though that British accent is extremely cut-glass. (Not that, like some, I have predilection to foreigners automatically. That would be that Mandy's mother. One would think that having just lost her own mother she'd be more grief-stricken. But no. She was busy quizzing Dr Sheila about this and that.) Dr Sheila very disappointed to have missed pujas.

In the evening, had taken her to Roman ruins for sindoor khela. Even TM came with us. Sandhyaji stayed behind. But very soon AB's maid Madhobi began to wail so loudly and so bitterly that everybody downstairs in the park got scared and thought that it must be Mrs Das, back from the hospital, and the very worst had happened. It was later that John M. came down and told us the news about old Mrs Bose.

All I could do was inform my mother, who was bossing over the priest. She is one of those pillars-of-the-community types. Knows exactly what to do in case of births, deaths, illnesses and elopements. (When my cousin Tinni eloped, only my mother in the extended family was informed.) She immediately went to AB's flat and took over. While Sandhyaji prayed, Ma bathed the old lady and changed her clothes and cleaned her face and got her ready for the last rites. AB's sister and her entourage (including that silly Mandy) arrived after three hours. Insane traffic, apparently, thanks to all the famous award-winning Durga pujas on the way. Heaven forbid that somebody should need an ambulance during the pujas.

As it happens Sandhyaji also owns/has on lease the opposite flat on her floor. Now that Dr Sheila is here, was thinking that TM might have to go back home. Wish could have invited her over, but we have no space. Turned out, no need. Sandhyaji just unlocked the opposite flat and we carried Dr Sheila's stuff there. The drawing room is bare, except for a Turkish carpet, but the two bedrooms are discreetly—and very comfortably—furnished. I should ask Sandhyaji how come she has two flats here.

Ma and Mandy's mother cobbled together some food for the shamshaan yatris, as is tradition, and I decided to stay upstairs with Sandhyaji. (AJ would be staying over—as usual, and Deep and Rahul too, at our house. They were hanging around at Nancy and volunteered to go to the shamshaan ghat with Abeer and AJ.) But the shamshaan yatris returned to Nancy only at dawn. Am not sure what time I fell asleep on the carpet in Sandhyaji's flat. At the crack of dawn, the bell rang. I found myself under a duvet smelling of lavender. Before I could even stir, while my brain was still working through the cloud of sleep, Sandhyaji opened the door, as though she had been waiting. AB entered. Did not know what to say, so just dived in deeper under duvet and pretended was asleep. Don't think he noticed. After he began to speak, felt even worse for eavesdropping.

'Would you like some tea, Ananda?' Sandhyaji asked.

'No, madam. Thank you. I've just had tea after my bath. You see, I know you wake up early, so I took the liberty of dropping by. I needed to talk.' He walked vaguely to one of the settees and sat down. 'You see, madam, my father passed away fifteen years ago. I'd been much younger then. And I'd been away at the time. I was studying German philosophy those years and had won a fellowship for three months to Berlin. When I came back, he was already gone. My folks chose not to tell me.'

I was getting annoyed with AB, even as I pretended to sleep on the carpet. Anybody would. Why did he have to give so much background information? Fool.

'I never thought about his passing away very much. But today, madam, I am extremely overwrought. As a rational materialist, I used to believe that with the end of the body all ends. It took me many years to come to terms with this. That our time on earth is all we have. And yet, I just burnt to cinders what used to be my mother. This thought—that all ends with the body—cannot hold me any more. I wondered about the traditional views on this... What happens when we die?'

I had two very conflicting reactions to this. I wanted to batter the fool's head against a wall. I also wanted to pat him reassuringly on the head. He has a nice full head of hair, as it happens; good cushion against the battering. Why does he have to ask such questions?

Sandhyaji spoke. Softly. 'Even though I came close to dying, I did not cross over to the other side; so all I know about death is through the symbols and signs that wise men and women have left behind, scattered in ancient texts and in the stories we tell ourselves. These hints appear in every culture and every part of the world with astounding synchronicity. They say that when death comes naturally, at the appropriate time, the soul, like a whisper of light, leaves our body. As easily and gently as we step into a dream. They say that outside the confines of the body we can recognize ourselves as beings of light again. It is very disconcerting if it happens suddenly. Seeing the body lying there so still can be scary. Sometimes this fear brings the soul back into the body again. It is impossible for me to explain this, Ananda. Yogis taste this too during what is called Samadhi, but in their case they know how to return to the body at will. But very few people come back from it and remember the feeling. Just as a baby carries within itself the code that is activated after nine months, to push itself out of the mother's womb, to separate from the mother, the soul too knows how to leave when it's time. Ananda, when death comes naturally, when it is time for the old body to be cast aside like old clothes, then leaving behind the body and moving on is simplicity itself.'

And somehow, though I did not want to hear about death and what happens afterwards at all, the thought of the light and stepping into a dream does not seem scary. I tried to understand Sandhyaji's words, but they seemed to glide over me, all satiny and weightless, and slip outside my grip.

When I woke up, it was hot already and morning noises were streaming in from the balcony and the windows. Dr Sheila was sipping tea on the settee and reading a newspaper.

CHAPTER 15

15.1

'I would like to meet Mr Suresh Sahai.'

'Madam, you have to be a little specific. We have *only* 23,000 employees in this office,' the receptionist replied shortly. Her round face was perfectly made up. Her eyes were highlighted with blue-green eyeliner that matched her sari. Her hair, silky and hennaed generously, fell in little crimped waves on her shoulder. Apu was always in awe of women who could apply make-up so cleverly and whose hair never reacted to wind and dust and whose clothes always appeared crisp and freshly ironed, as though straight from a dry cleaner's. They were bound to have braved the Calcutta weather before stepping into this air-conditioned bubble. How did they do it?

'Sorry, sorry,' Apu apologized humbly. 'He's a tech lead in the London Transport Project.' She checked the battered business card Meera had given her once.

'Let me check.' The receptionist looked supremely bored. She punched something into the computer in front of her with her blue-green talons. (She painted her nails every night to match what she would wear the next day? Wow!) Apu instinctively drew her unmanicured hands with scuffed nails out of sight. She looked around. The office was a cliché: gleaming floors, shining stairs, a darkened glass façade through which one would not feel the existence of the sun outside or smell the air, a sitting area with leather-upholstered sofas and IT magazines, a powerful whiff of room freshener.

'It's a secure floor, you can't go up. Please speak to him.' The receptionist picked up the receiver of a sleek-looking phone and handed it to Apu.

Apu was taken aback. She had dialled the phone from the computer? One could do that? Oof. The world was getting divided into the tech-surprised (like her) and the tech-unsurprised (her brother) much too quickly. Disproportionate amount of power in the hands of the tech-unsurprised, of course. She spoke into the mouthpiece, a tad nervously, unsure of the response she might get, turning away from the receptionist as much as she could.

'Hello, Suresh Bhaiya?'

'This is Apu. Aparajita Mukherjee? Heehee, I know. Yes, yes, I'm downstairs in the lobby actually. I had just come to the neighbourhood with a friend and I remembered you worked here. Will you come to the CCD outside your office? We could have a cup of coffee.'

Assured that Suresh would be down in five minutes, Apu handed the phone back to the receptionist, smiling warmly. The receptionist merely bared her teeth for an instant before returning to her icy mask.

'I'm a smile slut,' Apu muttered, annoyed. 'I should not smile so much.'

15.2

'Apu doesn't smile enough in her photos,' Mrs Chhanda Mukherjee declared as she swished around her son's room, picking things up and swiftly returning them to their rightful places. Books, magazines, CD cases, balled-up socks. The ends of her green sari leapt behind her. To the sleepy eyes of the boys, the polka dots seemed to swim dizzily in the air.

Abeer, on the bed, and AJ, on the couch, had been woken up brusquely. They were still trying to cope with the bright midday sunlight that flooded in when Mrs Mukherjee pushed the curtains aside and threw the windows open. 'But still, there is that picture you took on Saptami evening, where Apu is wearing that pink sari? The picture with Sandhyaji? You have it on the computer, don't you? Or have you gone and lost it?'

'Of course I have it, Ma. It's saved on the hard disk. It can't get lost,' Abeer replied weakly. 'Why are you asking this now?'

AJ dragged himself up from the couch, excused himself and went to the bathroom.

'Because *The Lahiris* are coming tomorrow evening,' Mrs Mukherjee announced. Trying to ignore the sound of AJ peeing noisily, she sat on Abeer's bed and continued. 'Moni Di called me just now. Abhiroop's parents want to come formally and wish us Happy Bijoya. What that really means is that they want to meet our family, interact with us, see the house etc., etc. So they must be pretty keen to meet us, no? Moni Di has been pulling strings. Your father was so annoyed that I bought such an expensive dhakai sari for her for the pujas. But just see the dividends! I have to get cracking at once. Everything should be perfect—the food, the house, your manners.' Abeer rolled his eyes. 'And listen, Moni Di told me that Apu should not be introduced to them now. She is so clever, she has told them that Apu has gone to Puri with the children from the Blind School. Yes, yes, I did tell Moni Di that Apu volunteers at the Blind School. Don't look at me like that—since she does volunteer at the Blind School, I am perfectly at liberty to tell people. We will have to ask Apu to stay at Sandhyaji's tomorrow night.'

'Why?' AJ asked thickly. He had wandered out of the bathroom, brushing his teeth. Abeer's brown towel was on his shoulder, Abeer noticed, annoyed. AJ kept a toothbrush at Abeer's. He ought to keep a towel too.

'Because Apu is supposed to lose weight between now and February, no, when the boy visits. We can give her some more time that way. Parents and boy can meet her at the same time, what's the harm? The parents want to meet *us* now. Three months is a lot. Especially with Sandhyaji here in Nancy.'

'She's a yoga guru, Ma, not a gym instructor,' Abeer said. 'And certainly not a personal trainer.'

Mrs Mukherjee didn't seem to hear this. After Sandhyaji had 'saved' Bablu Das—and everybody was talking about this in a relentless loop of awe, admiration and fear—miracles were naturally expected of Sandhya. 'What I want the two of you to do now is this: get me copies made of Apu's best photos. Okay?'

'Fine, fine,' grumbled Abeer. There went the morning.

But AJ took the toothbrush out of his mouth excitedly. Foam dribbled. 'Bub, Aunty, be cab do mush more thad dad.' Realizing he wasn't making much sense, he dashed into the bathroom, rinsed his mouth and bounded out. 'But, Aunty, we can do much more than that. We can edit the photo to make Didi look slimmer. Like she will really look after three months. Simple.'

Abeer was aghast. 'AJ!'

But Mrs Mukherjee was intrigued. 'Really? That can be done?'

'Of course. Anything you want can be done, Aunty. We can make Didi look ten kilos slimmer. Easily. We can give her a different hairstyle. We can give her green eyes and brown hair. Whatever you like.'

'No, no, that much change is not necessary,' Mrs Mukherjee replied thoughtfully. 'Her eye colour is quite nice. Hair too. Just make her look slimmer, that's all. Highlight her good points if possible. Eyebrows and eyes. I mean... Do what you can, but be realistic—seven kilos slimmer is okay. No, five. She's so lazy. Nah, seven is okay. We can be a little optimistic. Sandhyaji is there.'

AJ had already switched on Abeer's desktop. Mrs Mukherjee hovered behind it uncertainly. Five or seven?

Abeer realized unhappily that the world had come to this: *he* was being called on by the universe to be the voice of reason. Crap. 'Ma. AJ. Please listen.' He tried to speak with equanimity. 'This is highly irregular, not to mention unethical—what you are thinking of doing. Didi is quite presentable as she is. Ma, please don't listen to AJ. He has no sense.'

'Oh-ho, I don't have any sense? How many sisters have you married off, Mr G? Haan? Aunty, you know how many cousins I have. My Indu Didi, Bindu Didi and Sindhu Didi—they all had arranged marriages. Believe me, Aunty, a little Photoshop is nothing. For Indu Didi we had to invent a whole college in Jaipur, from where she apparently did BA Honours in home science, with nutrition and economics pass courses. I even printed out some degrees from a shop in Chandni. They looked pretty impressive. And what harm in a little white lie?'

Mrs Mukherjee nodded eagerly.

Abeer buried his face in the pillow.

15.3

This was a bit of an awkward social situation for Suresh Sahai. He quickly scanned the problems that had been listed for the day. It was his job to ensure they were resolved in the next twenty-four hours. He gulped some water from a small green bottle on the side and almost instinctively pressed Windows plus L to lock the computer. He left his cubicle and motioned to the team's architect and his boss, Moidul, that he was taking a short break. Their team provided tech support to the British bus and tube services, and it was rush hour in London now. He couldn't just wander off without alerting someone. Moidul was spinning tall tales to a bunch of young developers who had joined recently (all but one were female, long-haired, early twenties). From inside his glass office, Moidul acknowledged Suresh with a wave.

Suresh walked past the rows of white consoles to the foyer. Most of his colleagues sported jaded, grumpy expressions and new clothes. Post-festivity blues were in the air. If only any of his colleagues knew of his problems, Suresh thought stonily, their 'long commute' and 'puja over' complaints would cease to bother them. But then these Calcuttans were a pampered lot. On this trip to Calcutta, his brother had unloaded some of the familial worries onto Suresh. Their uncles had sold off large chunks of agricultural land to the industrial mafia and had eaten up their share—not one paisa had come their way. Bhaisaab was planning to go to the courts. Just because Ramesh and Suresh were both professionals (as had been their father, the headmaster of a government school), the rest of the uncles, mostly farmers and their sons, petty businessmen and some—Suresh remembered with trepidation—gundas, were always trying to siphon off their hissa. This would be the third property litigation that would have to be funded by him from Calcutta. Given that Bhaisaab would do all the running around, he ought to shoulder the cost. In any case, his salary was far greater. The only problem that none of his relatives seemed to take into account was that living in a big city was also an expensive proposition. And as for the Civil Sessions—it was a black hole for money. But Bhaisaab too was justified in his decision. If they didn't take some steps, then this behaviour would continue unabated. Should his nephews not inherit even an acre each of the ancestral lands? Then there was Lovely. Lovely's return to her husband's house would mean sending lavish presents for the entire clan of her in-laws and, of course, for her.

And now this. Meera.

Meera. If only he knew better what went on in Meera's mind. But it was his fault. He had been a negligent husband he knew, far more familiar with her body than the contours of her soul. It made him feel very small. He got into the lift, scratching his chin.

Suresh knew Apu well enough, but he had never met her on his own. Whenever Apu came over, he would exchange a few pleasantries with her and then leave her to chat with Meera. What would he say to Apu? And why was she here?

Well, he could ask her about her PhD. He could also ask about young Bablu Das. That reminded him, he would have to drop into the hospital and then offer his condolences to Ananda Bose this evening.

Suresh had returned from Bangalore only last night. Lovely had gleefully filled him in on all the tragedies this morning. She had always been a ghoul, that one. The Bangalore trip had been exhausting. None of the Bengalis in his team had agreed to go to the weeklong all-India conference during the pujas, so he'd volunteered. It made him a hero in the department; besides, things at home were unbearable. That tiny house filled with so many women. Khichir-pichir-khichir-pichir all day. He'd been relieved to escape, though he'd felt a little guilty about leaving Meera behind.

But nothing—absolutely nothing—had prepared Suresh for last night.

He had reached home well past ten. His mother and Lovely and company had retired by then. Nalini had shifted the girls and herself to the study. The boys were in the drawing room. And Suresh was back in their bedroom, after almost a month. There was dust in the corners, cobwebs on the ceiling, a general sense of disarray everywhere. Meera was lying with her back to him, looking towards the wall.

His wife had not come to the door when he'd returned from the airport. She did not get up when he came in. She did not look at him. When he changed into his pyjamas and got into bed next to her, he touched her shoulder gently and asked what the matter was. It seemed she did not hear anything.

A cold chill had trickled down Suresh's spine. Silence had never been Meera's weapon. She was never patient enough to use the cold shoulder effectively. It was usually all storm and rain. 'Meera,' he'd called, slipping his hand around her waist and snuggling in beside her. She had remained cold, unmoved. Heavy like lead.

Suresh walked out of his office and into the cafe across the road.

'Suresh Bhaiya, this is Sandhyaji. She has moved into A-5.' Apu looked as embarrassed as Suresh was surprised.

He folded his hands and nodded briefly to the lady with the cropped hair and still eyes. He thought he had heard about Sandhya. From Lovely?

'Please forgive us,' Sandhya said, 'for interrupting you at work.'
'No, no, that's all right.'

'Cappuccino for you?' Apu asked and, without waiting for his answer, scarpered off to stand in the long queue. This was the only coffee shop in this block. Young people in Sector 5 were always in need of caffeine; the place was full and buzzing at all hours.

'Mr Sahai, I apologize in advance for interfering. I want to talk to you about Meera.'

Suresh could feel the flush that crept up his face. Did he want to talk about his wife to a complete stranger? Certainly not. What in Bhagwanji's name was Apu up to?

'You must be very surprised by what seems to have come over your wife suddenly. You are shocked perhaps?'

That was a no-brainer. Of course he was shocked. While playing with Chhoti this morning, as Bhabhiji made tea, he had spotted the scar on her hand. He had been nauseated. Nalini had crumpled and told him what she knew.

Meera's breakdown had been so rapid and so relentless that Nalini was stunned and did not know what to make of it. It seemed to be either madness or possession by a spirit. Sandhyaji had urged her to be patient, so she was. But she was thinking of consulting an old spirit-doctor back in her mother's village. The only problem was that the spirit-doctor did not have a mobile. Maaji and Lovely, having gallivanted during the pujas, were now holed up in Maaji's room, pretending they did not understand what was happening. They were both a little scared, now that Suresh had returned. Nalini was running the house and looking after the baby. Tara spent a lot of time with Apu and with her cousins. Meera had stopped talking completely. She did not even look at the children.

After she discovered the bite mark on Chhoti's hand, Nalini had stopped urging Meera to spend time with the children or even feed the baby. She herself had never been able to breastfeed (something Maaji Sahai had given her a very hard time about at the time) and so, after a brief discussion with Apu (who else?), she'd unilaterally decided to shift Chhoti to formula. For two days baby and aunt were locked in fierce battle over the matter, but finally baby was forced to yield.

Meera would get up only to go to the bathroom. She ate small meals sporadically. She did not change her clothes unless Nalini dragged her to the bathroom, left fresh clothes on the peg, filled the bucket with warm water and locked the door from outside until she heard the sound of water. She had subjected Meera to this yesterday; otherwise, she said in annoyance, Suresh wouldn't have been able to sleep next to her—there was a strange smell that emanated from her.

But it was the bite-mark which had flashed before Suresh's eyes all morning as he drove to work.

'Please believe me,' Sandhya continued, 'I know what has happened to her. It is nothing unnatural.'

Nothing unnatural?

Suresh Sahai was an eminently reasonable man. A patient man. A good man, even. Supported his extended family, silently shouldered extra work in office, refused to take any dowry despite his mother's injunctions. But how on earth was he supposed to accept that *this* lady, cropped hair and still eyes and white sari notwithstanding, knew what had happened to his wife? Did she know the Srivastavas of Barwadih in Jharkhand? Was she privy to a strain of insanity inherent in their genes? What else could possibly explain a mother biting a little flower-like child's petal-soft arm?

Suresh's face radiated his displeasure.

'Mr Sahai, have you heard of a condition called postpartum depression?'

Suresh was forced to nod his head sideways. No, he had not.

'Would you like to search for it on Google while your coffee comes?' Sandhya smiled gently. 'I'm sure you have one of those clever phones.'

Suresh whipped out his phone from his pocket. As a techie, there was one thing he held sacred: he deferred to Google; he *always* deferred to Google. He looked at the old lady again. It was annoying to be patronized by her. But then Apu was behind all this. Not that he disapproved of Apu like his mother did. Apu had been silently assisting Nalini through this tough phase, even as they all colluded to keep things from Maaji and that bitter-tongued Lovely. He waited for Google to flash on his phone screen.

'What did you say, madam?' he asked. 'Post what?'

'Postpartum depression,' Sandhya said. 'PPD in short.'

15.4

It was only after Bablu regained consciousness, after forty-eight hours of being on the ventilator, that Mrs Monalisa Das allowed herself to exhale. She saw him briefly—he was still drowsy and punctured with tubes, not ready to speak yet. She touched his forehead, now warm again, called her husband to give him the good news, then stepped outside the hospital.

Their neighbour Mr Qureishi (A-2) was a senior crime correspondent with a Bengali daily and it was he who had managed to get Bablu into this hospital. The neighbours had rallied around the family, dropping in religiously, though it was far away from Nancy and post-puja traffic in the city was insane. They offered all manner of support. But it was really Mr and Mrs De, and that Raja (real-estate broker, disappointer of Bor Da) who kept it all together. Raja and his father had dealt with the police (naturally, there would be the police—it was a 'suicide case' after all), sheltering Mrs Das from such unpleasantness.

Kumkum De was with Mrs Das as she finally left the hospital.

The last dregs of sunlight had cast on the city the sort of dusk that photographers in Calcutta yearn for. The traffic seemed enveloped in a soft surreal half-light shot through with pockets of orange. It transformed the mundane dust and filth and concrete into something meaningful and human, even haunting. For a moment Mrs Das was wrong-footed. It seemed all wrong. Nothing seemed to have altered in these last two days. But how was that even possible?

The city was right there in front of her. Ubiquitous. Nonchalant. The traffic screeched. Pedestrians rushed past the hospital building, in a great hurry so they don't catch any bug from the air. (Mrs Das knew the pinched hypochondriac look; at other times, she was likely to sport it herself as she would hurry along her boys). Kumkum De quickly bought two cups of tea from a kiosk outside the gate. She handed one earthen cup to Monalisa.

The hot, excessively sweet liquid burnt her throat and gave her an effective injection of energy. Mrs Das sat down heavily on one of the benches the chai-wallah had thoughtfully provided. Mrs De handed her another khuri. She drank that too.

Shock and fear. Fear and shock. These twin sentiments had literally run her body over the last two days, limiting all its usual functions to a bare minimum. As she sat on the bench, smack in the middle of the footpath, and drank her third cup of tea, she felt a giddy, hysterical rush shoot through her bloodstream and up to her head. It was relief. Her son had been spared. Excruciatingly exquisite relief. Mrs Das was not used to such a liberal dose of relief. In her case, it was always minor bursts of relief over small mercies: thank God Anwara came on time; thank heavens she packed in the boys' raincoats; thank goodness Bablu had studied those questions from the old exam papers. When this foreign hysterical relief coursed through her veins, Monalisa grabbed Mrs De's bony elbow urgently and said, 'Boudi, I am feeling very hungry.'

They found a small restaurant. There were five or six tables covered with tablecloths and laid out neatly. It was empty at this hour. A waiter came in and handed them laminated menu-cards. Monalisa began to turn the pages restlessly, but she could not focus on any of the words, they seemed to slide out of focus as soon as she tried to pin them down.

'Is there rice?' Monalisa asked the waiter. 'I am so hungry for rice, Boudi,' she explained to Mrs De.

The waiter shook his head. 'Madam, at this hour the lunch and dinner menus are not available. No rice. You have to pick snacks items.'

Monalisa's face fell.

'Bring us two coffees and pakoras. Whatever sort you have,' said Mrs De.

'I'm very hungry,' Monalisa repeated, 'I'm very hungry.' She looked blankly at the wall behind Mrs De. A print hung there, a waterfall amidst lush green dales. God, how many sorts of green had been crammed into that painting?

For the last couple of days Monalisa had no sense how time had gone by. There was a sense of extreme urgency inside government hospitals at all times, a prevailing smell of disinfectant and sickness, and the ICU was full of high-strung women. Shock and fear, fear and shock. The twin sentiments had swirled around her body, entering her and leaking out of her continuously. Where was Gublu? Monalisa panicked. Oh, at Kumkum's house, she remembered. He would be perfectly safe there.

The food came. Monalisa ate. Then she went to the bathroom. The hysteria subsided a little.

They found the city dark when they walked out of the restaurant. Evenings swooped in quickly these days. After Kali Puja, Monalisa thought, winter would be in the air. Calcutta winter. Mild, gentle, picnic-friendly.

They crossed a small makeshift temple under a tree. Monalisa kept walking, but twenty metres past, she stopped and rushed back. She folded her hands urgently in front of the assorted idols, though she could find no appropriate words. Her vocabulary seemed to have vanished from her skull. They found a cab. Mrs De would be taking Monalisa to her house for the night.

It was only when she neared Mrs De's house in the heart of north Calcutta, their old neighbourhood, where each house was known and each was filled with frenemies, that suddenly Monalisa felt a burning, itchy sensation spreading under her skin. All at once, relief receded and was replaced with something else. It was easy to pretend that her son, like several other patients in the ICU, had returned from the jaws of death after what was a fatal accident. But this was not true. It was not even remotely true.

As Mrs De rifled through her purse in the fluorescent light from the streetlamp to pay the cabbie, Mrs Das asked herself with words that suddenly seemed to have been returned to her as strangely as they had been taken away: had her son, the apple of her eye, the staff of her blind old age, her elder son…had he tried to kill himself? Had that really happened?

And she, the mother, the failed broken mother—for it was *her* failure, wasn't she supposed to keep them safe from everything including themselves—was she sitting in a taxi, breathing and calmly drinking water?

Apu

28th October.
On our way to Rajarhat, Sandhyaji joked in the taxi that this would be second time in recent present that she would sit down a hapless husband and lecture him. But what was probably cakewalk in case of John M. (think have tiny crush on him) is not going to be that easy in case of Suresh S. As I stood in the queue at CCD, I tried to read his face but could hardly see anything. Think am developing myopia. That's the one perfect-6 I had, but no, cosmos has to take that away from me also. Anyway.

When I returned with cappuccinos for Suresh S. and myself and green tea for Sandhyaji, I was afraid of the very worst. That we'd totally offended him. He seems a bit that type, you know, can't say boo to a goose but can get super-insulted if people try to interfere in his private matters. He was reading something on his phone. Funny. Sat down next to Sandhyaji quietly and began to spoon the sugar into coffee. Finally, Suresh S. looked up and I quickly gave him his coffee. For a lack of anything better to do, I'd spooned some sugar into it too.

He took a long sip. Then he said to Sandhyaji, 'So this is what she has? Postpartum depression?'

I don't want to seem mean. I simply think it is cute that he says the 's' like the 's' in station. Depre-sion.

Sandhyaji nodded.

'But have you seen the mark on Chhoti's hand?' His voice was heavy with pain. I felt guilty instantly. Being jokey and shallow at this juncture—wasn't I Meera's best (and only) friend?

'Yes,' Sandhyaji said, 'PPD can set in any time within a year of giving birth. Usually it happens at the time of birth and is mild. It's called 'baby blues'. But at its most severe, PPD can push a mother to harm the child or even herself. It is an extremely desperate cry for help. That is how you have to see it, Mr Sahai. We are lucky that nothing more severe has happened.'

Suresh S. exhaled. 'I should say thank you, I suppose. I feared things far worse.'

'My friend and colleague Dr Sheila is visiting me now. She's a gynaecologist. She does a lot of work in India. Indian midwives can be very good. Traditional childcare in India has many things to teach the world about sustainability and so on. But I must not digress. Dr Sheila was speaking to a gynaecologist friend of hers at AIIMS. She said that a week ago a woman in the hospital was suffering from such severe PPD that she attempted suicide.'

Suresh S.'s face blanched.

'This woman had had a baby after undergoing infertility treatment for eleven years. So you can imagine how desperate she had been for motherhood. I'm sure she loved the baby dearly. But depression is like that, Mr Sahai, it can capture anybody anytime. As for postpartum depression, the figures on this are slightly hazy since women often feel guilty talking honestly about problems that arise after childbirth. Motherhood is made out to be such an ennobling thing by society, these poor young mothers feel they cannot share these thoughts without being judged. Postpartum depression affects anything between ten to twenty-five per cent of women in the Western world. There are both physiological and psychological reasons behind this. In traditional societies there used to be many rituals around childbirth that also protected young mothers, did not force them to deal with all the scary changes on their own. In India women often go to their mother's house to have the baby, don't they? They stay on for a few months, where they have the support net that helps them regain their physical strength, helps balance out the time of immense vulnerability. Having a baby makes a woman very raw, literally open to all sorts of emotional highs and lows. In the past, it used to be assumed that sisters and sisters in law would pass on anecdotes on childrearing and gently initiate the young mother into this complex world. Pardon my asking, Suresh, but why didn't you send Meera home?'

'Madam, Meera's mother passed away a year after my eldest one was born. After that, Meera doesn't have a maika any more. Our flat is her home. After Tara was born, my mother-in-law stayed over for a couple of months in our house and helped Meera out. Those days we lived in a rented flat. But now there is nobody in her maika. Her brother and sister-in-law don't want to host her even for a week, let alone help her out during her confinement.'

'Sometimes it gets worse in an environment where the mother is made to feel incompetent or guilty,' Sandhyaji said gently. 'If there is some unhappiness about the gender of the child, for one.'

Suresh S. shut his eyes. 'It must be that. My mother hankers after boys. Like most Indian women.'

'Indian women and Chinese women, of course. But you'd be surprised, Suresh. Dr Sheila tells me that so many times in a delivery room, where she has been the obstetrician, the mother, a modern Western mother mind-you, apologized to her husband for having a baby girl.'

Oh dear. I hadn't known that. That is depressing. But if I do find someone to love me and if I can surmount this virginity, I am definitely having daughters. What is the big draw of having sons anyway? Consider Abeer. AJ.

'Madam, what would you recommend?' Suresh S. asked. 'Are there medicines for this?'

'There are anti-depressants. Dr Sheila can recommend a course. We ought to talk to Meera's usual gynaecologist. You must take an appointment. But the most important thing is to address the environment.' Sandhyaji's voice became kinder somehow. 'There is something else. Even today, if you are a student of medicine and have to suggest possible ways of treating several gynaecological conditions, including PPD, do you know what the first answer is supposed to be? TLC.'

'TLC?' Suresh S. and I asked simultaneously.

'Tender, loving care.'

Suresh S. bought us lunch at his office cafeteria (Sandhyaji ate two idlis and curd; I ate chicken curry and rice; Suresh S. ate veg thali.) Suresh S. discussed Meera situation with Sandhyaji in detail and seemed extremely committed to seeking solution. Has requested me to help him pick out suitable (expensive and garish) gifts for Lovely's clan. Best way to get rid of her. I like the task of spending someone else's money, though hate Lovely.

AB came over briefly in the evening. Dr Sheila and TM were out to meet some old Armenian lady and go to the Armenian Church.

AB seems to have changed a little. Does not gad about as much as he used to. He was wearing the traditional attire of Hindu mourning. White dhoti and chadar, unstitched clothes. He is quite broad-chested, though I didn't really want to notice. Had wrapped the chadar tightly around himself. Probably feels cold. Or is shy. Has strong arms. Sat on an asana that he is carrying around, also in keeping with rules. For a Commie, he seems to be following the dharmic rituals surrounding death pretty seriously. He was full of (boring philosophical) questions as usual. Following exchange ensued at the very end.

AB: 'I am a late starter in this field, madam, but I have begun to revise Sanskrit. I wish to read the Upanishads in the original. I will definitely attend your yoga sessions. I mean to read the Yoga Sutras in translation too.'

Sandhyaji: 'That is wonderful, Ananda. All in good time. Naturally, you are welcome to the yoga sessions. Apu is organizing everything. But you have to do something else that I recommend strongly. You cannot merely train your mind if you are indeed so keen to go deeper into Indian philosophy; though the temptation is strong, you cannot neglect your body. It will make you an incomplete scholar.'

AB: 'Yes, madam?' (Came forward eagerly. Probably cocked his ears to receive proffered wisdom, in manner of first boy in class.)

Sandhyaji: 'I have discovered a delightful park close by. Next to the lake behind the hospital. Do you know the one I'm talking about? It's very leafy and has a clear jogging track. I suggest you take up running.'

AB gulped.

Then she looked at me. 'Apu, don't think I recommend running to everybody. Not in the slightest. But I genuinely think it will be very good for you too. And it's always best to be part of a running group. You should join Ananda. You guys can decide what time would be best. Dawn is ideal. But then, something is better than nothing. If evening suits you more, so be it.'

My turn to gulp.

My fool of a mother has told Sandhyaji about that wretched Photoshop business regarding the Lahiris. I will murder AJ. The boys got copies made for my reference too, and dropped off one set at Sandhyaji's. The bastards.

Only thing: the digital picture of me seven kilos slimmer is extremely tempting.

But running with AB?

Kill. Me. Now.

CHAPTER 16

16.1

All night long, the intense burny sensation under the skin persisted, in Kumkum De's spare bedroom.

Now that the crisis had been averted, Mr and Mrs Das had become acutely aware of the well of sorrows this had opened up in their home. Between them lay the sleeping body of their younger son, as though floating in the chasm of guilt that stretched between the parents.

Mr Das had spent an hour last evening helping the authorities write up detailed notes. There was a senior doctor accompanied by a lady constable. He had reported the conversation faithfully to his wife.

How had the boy managed to find so many Alprazolam tablets?

Das had spoken clearly. They were his mother's pills, left behind after her visit. He could submit the prescription.

Why would your son attempt suicide, Mr Das?

He had tried to speak clearly about this too, but had found his voice cracking. His son had wanted to go on a holiday with his friends, but he was not allowed. His wife was very particular about studies. He did badly in maths in the last examination, so she got him a new teacher. A very famous teacher but he wanted to take classes during the holidays.

Even as he spoke, Das felt more and more bewildered. These were minor things, weren't they? The denied holiday, the fail marks in maths, the new teacher? How had the combination ballooned out of proportion so fatally? So quickly?

There were no signs before? Delinquent behaviour, perhaps? Or fights with the mother?

Numbly, Das had nodded his head. No. Nothing. Bablu was a very good boy.

In Kumkum De's dark spare bedroom, her head pounding, her husband's words sounding in her ears, Mrs Das decided what she would do first thing the next morning.

Sandhya was returning from her morning walk when she spotted Mrs Das entering the gates of Nancy. The proud Monalisa Das with that determined little chin and speedy walk was much the worse for wear. Her face looked haggard. Her hair had not been combed properly. She walked into Nancy with a heavy bag on her shoulder. She nodded at the guards but avoided speaking to them. When she spotted Sandhya, she hurried towards her.

'Mataji, I am very grateful for that day…' She could not finish. The memory of Nabami afternoon had that staggering effect on her, would probably continue to do so in the days and months to follow.

Sandhya took her by the crook of her arm and walked her towards A-5. 'Come and have some tea at my place.'

Glad to have not run into anybody else, however compassionate they might be, Monalisa walked with Sandhya. The only sort of people Monalisa was not averse to meeting now were women whose children had attempted suicide. None of the other smug mothers would do, however well they meant.

'I understand he is completely out of danger now, Monalisa?'

Monalisa nodded, wiping her eyes. 'I only came here now, Mataji, because I wanted to see you.' There was great urgency in Monalisa's voice. 'I have always prided myself on being a good mother. That is, in fact, my only identity. Where did I go wrong? I thought of myself as somebody who managed the lives of her children very well.' They had reached A-5, where hibiscus flowers were scattered on the grass. 'But look at me,' Monalisa grabbed one of Sandhya's palms. 'Look at me. What is worse than being a mother whose son attempts suicide?'

'Perhaps being a mother whose children died? Who thinks that somehow her own body is responsible for their death?'

They walked towards the flowers and sat down on the green bench under the hibiscus tree. Softly, Sandhya began to tell Monalisa Das the story of Treeza Matthew.

16.2

Apu and Sadia had bought dozens of books between them and were now huffing and puffing as they carried the heavy bags.

They had come to a meeting in Presidency College. A vague attempt had been made to organize lecturers on contract into a union of sorts, but both Apu and Sadia had found the proceedings unutterably pompous and funny. They had slipped out of the classroom soon enough and walked to College Square, where the pandal, a golden recreation of the Bahai Lotus Temple, was being dismantled. They lingered there for a while, among urchins and cranky old people and lovers, and then walked down College Street, eating ice cream and giggling. And, of course, buying books. They went into the lanes and by-lanes and haggled with shopkeepers and hawkers good-naturedly. Apu went on a novel-buying frenzy; Sadia picked out military history books for her husband and chick-lit for herself, to read on the long afternoons at the army mess in Srinagar. They were going away to join Ali for a few days. Then Sadia bought second-hand Enid Blytons for her children; and because in a joint family you couldn't just buy things for your own kids, she had to buy just as many for their cousins. But, at twenty rupees each, it was a steal.

'How I wish we could get permanent jobs in one of these north Calcutta colleges, Apu!' Sadia sighed. 'The second-hand bookstores in Gariahat or Golpark are just not as good as these. And not half as reasonable.'

'Easy for you to say, with your house barely fifteen minutes away.

Imagine how difficult it would be for me to get here from Nancy every day.'

'But you can get the metro now, Apu. Anyway, what does it matter? You're off to Chicago soon.'

Apu's cheeks reddened ever so slightly. She began digging into a gigantic pile of books kept on a bamboo mat under the colourful awning of the shop while Sadia wandered to a shop down the road that specialized in second-hand English literature reference books. Apu was paying the shopkeeper when she returned.

'You bought another book?' Sadia scolded. 'Will you have enough money to even go home?'

'But this is exactly what I was looking for, Sadia. And I'm carrying loads of cash. Didn't I tell you I've been delegated to buy presents for the Sahai superbitches? Suresh wants to give them all kinds of things and then send them packing.'

As Apu slid the book into one of the packets in her hand, Sadia caught the title and burst out laughing. 'You really do take Sandhyaji seriously, don't you?'

The book Apu had bought was called *Mastering the Art of Running*.

16.3

At Coffee House, they didn't find a single table downstairs; groaning, they carried their books upstairs to the little gallery that ringed the vibrant hall redolent with smoke and conversation. They managed to find a table there and settled down. Both of them knew that it would be at least a quarter of an hour before any of the extremely superior waiters would deign to come their way. Sadia called home to check on the kids while Apu busily stowed away their many bags and packets under the table. Someone vaguely familiar drifted in, looking around for a table.

In his white dhoti and the chadar wrapped around his torso, Ananda Bose cut a singular figure. By the time his eyes alighted on Apu, she had already realized they would have to invite him to join them and had even managed to signal Sadia with her eyes. Sadia promptly cut off her son with a perfunctory okay-bye-don't-fight-with-your-cousins and looked curiously as Ananda Bose approached them. Apu performed introductions; Ananda Bose took the asana out of his jhola, spread it neatly on the chair and then sat down on it.

'I am very sorry for your loss. Accept my deepest condolences, Mr Bose,' Sadia said.

Ananda Bose nodded graciously.

A sullen waiter arrived, and they ordered. Bose asked for only a cup of coffee. 'Since my mother was a believer, out of respect to her memory I am following all the rules,' he said. 'You seem to have bought many books?' he enquired politely.

'Oh, yes, loads,' said Sadia. 'We don't come to College Street often, so when we do we go out of control. You seem to have got a few too. Sorry, may I have a look?'

Sadia craned her neck cheekily and Ananda Bose, slightly unhappily, was compelled to remove his protective palms from atop his little pile. *What I Think about When I Think about Running*—Sadia read out the title, her face shining in glee.

'Murakami? Where did you get it?' Apu demanded. 'I have been looking for it all morning.'

Much later, months afterwards, Sadia would joke that it was *that* moment that the (former) colony bore, vague philosopher and now intense-and-brooding mourner Ananda Bose became Apu's friend. And, by extension, Sadia's. Apu would dispute this thesis, pointing out reasonably that though it sounded very apt—College Street and all—they only became friends later. That very day, though, when Bose accompanied her to New Market without the slightest hint of self-consciousness about his attire (full points for secure-ness, Apu had to admit) and helped her choose an array of garish presents for bitter-tongued Lovely. That was when they became friends.

16.4

'When are you coming home?' Dr Sheila asked her friend, proffering a cup of jasmine tea. They'd spent all afternoon discussing various official matters, going through the long list Sheila had brought with her. There had been such hectic activity all around ever since she'd arrived that they hadn't had any time for business.

Sandhya smiled. 'I feel at home here too, Sheila.'

'I know you do. I was worried about your excessive involvement in the lives of people here. It's different when people come to the ashram or attend one of the workshops—that's a voluntary acceptance of the teacher-student relationship. So I'd had misgivings. But I understand now. You've become a part of their lives, of the community. But we must also be practical. What are the Sens saying?'

'They will complete assessing everything and give us a figure only then. We will have to take it from there.'

Dr Sheila stood up and looked outside. The Roman ruins were intact, though the goddess had returned home. The pandal would only be dismantled after Lakshmi puja in a few days. The sun was slung low in the horizon. Children were running around in the park. It would be mid-morning at the Summertown ashram. Cold, clear day. She turned to face Sandhya. 'Are you serious about Calcutta?'

'Well, that is what he'd suggested. It's not an iron-clad clause, per se. Of course I cannot—and neither would I want to—transfer funds internationally.'

Dr Sheila concurred.

'But the more I think about it, the more I feel we *should* be serious about Calcutta. It's like the ending to my parallel life, Sheila. The one I never lived.'

'Hmm.' Sheila sat down next to Sandhya. 'That is that then, Mataji. I think I'll have to come back again in a few months to resolve matters.'

'Exactly. Until then, I think there is no need for me to rush around.'

'Oh, yes.' Dr Sheila smiled good-naturedly. 'You might as well run your halfway house here. Where is Treeza?'

'She is supposed to help plan a birthday party for her niece. John has taken her there.'

16.5

Though the pujas were officially over, lights still twinkled in Nancy. The decorators would come by to take them down in one or two days. Until then, by common consent, the orange-red-blue-green-pink toony bulbs were allowed to glitter on the building facades. At the entrance to Nancy, a small table had been set up with a photograph of Mrs Abhaya Bose. Rajanigandha sticks in a vase and incense in front. Apu had provided the 'In Memorium' text, mounted on a piece of thermocol next to the photo. She had written it out on a piece of chart paper in her good handwriting, acquiring the requisite details from Mandy's mother. Ananda Bose had been deeply touched, though he did not mention it to Apu.

Just as sometimes people lose their stammer after a profound shock, it seemed that his mother's passing had freed Ananda Bose from his ritual thanking of people. It was eerie. Some people, who'd made the most fun of his little eloquent speeches sprinkled with gratefulness, were disappointed these days when they failed to come. It was the end of an era.

The contingent of Lahiris, led by Moni Mashi, arrived exactly at seven. The Lahiris had suggested a casual teatime meeting, around five, but both Mrs Mukherjee and Moni Mashi would have nothing short of a sit-down dinner. The two had set up a command chain with military precision. As the car crossed Ruby Hospital, Moni Mashi gave Mrs Mukherjee a missed call. AJ frogmarched Abeer to the gates of Nancy, where they waited with appropriately welcoming expressions. AJ had been invited to stay back after his display of enthusiasm and dexterity in the matter of the photographs. Subsequently, he was appointed Mrs Mukherjee's chief aide de camp; she was not getting the desired level of support from either her son or her husband, neither of whom liked Moni, and neither of whom appreciated the Blind School children/Puri lie. It was AJ who had gone to Gariahat—accompanied by a surly Abeer—to get flowers, sweets and new doormats.

As soon as the black Honda City rolled around, the gates were opened with seamless coordination (AJ had gone over this with the guards) and Abeer and AJ smartly got the doors. Moni Mashi was riding shotgun in a peacock-blue kantha-stitch sari. She was the first to descend. The rest of the people were tightly squashed inside and took time to dismount and rearrange their finery. As Moni introduced the Lahiris (Chicago guy's father, mother, sister-in-law, nephew and niece) to Abeer, AJ showed Chicago guy's elder brother where to park.

The contingent walked through snatches of conversation, aromas of dinner and strains of TV serials that blew out from various flats. Abeer and Moni Mashi led the way. AJ brought up the rear; he had already ingratiated himself with the (prospective) sister-in-law by complimenting her children; he had also ingratiated himself with the children (aged six and three, he'd found out) by gifting them Dairy Milk Choco Shots. They ambled along to A-3. Abeer smirked inwardly at the thought that his mother had not red-carpeted the stairs to their flat. Perhaps she was saving that for the prospective groom's visit the next year. As they ascended the stairs, Abeer noted how AJ was chatting convivially with the (prospective) father-in-law about traffic and the state of roads. AJ spoke perfect idiomatic Bengali, without any trace of accent.

Mrs Mukherjee's small drawing room looked splendid. Under the pool of soothing yellow light cast by the chandelier on the ceiling (a modest chandelier, but it was Mrs Mukherjee's piece de resistance), the sofas looked plump and inviting, the curtains fell on the floor in rich satiny folds and the yellow roses on the dining table filled the room with cheer. The Mukherjees (Mr, Mrs and Mamoni) wore warm smiles and kept saying, 'Namaskar, come, come, sit, sit.'

The Lahiris, all said and done, were a friendly bunch. Old Mr Lahiri had been a WBCS officer. He had retired from the Secretariat five years ago. Now he and his wife liked to travel, though they couldn't bear to stay away too long from the grandchildren. They'd just returned from a cruise to Southeast Asia. His two sons were jewels, declared Mr Lahiri, even if he said so himself. The elder had stood ninth in Madhyamik and twenty-seventh in the Joint Entrance Exams. He was a surgeon. MBBS from NRS, no less, and MD from Chandigarh. His wife was an anaesthetist, also NRS, also brilliant, though now that the children demanded so much time, she had taken a break and wanted to go into teaching. The (prospective) sister-in-law seemed a happy sort (slightly big, slightly blunt features, fair but not a patch on the digitally re-mastered Apu, observed Mrs Mukherjee) and was quite free around the house, popping into the kitchen and chatting with Didi, wandering into the balcony and admiring the park.

Moni Mashi signalled something to Mrs Mukherjee with her eyes. Mrs Mukherjee, responding to the cue immediately, invited the ladies to sit in her bedroom and chat more intimately.

His younger son, continued Mr Lahiri, an earthy sort of pride radiating from his face, was an uncut jewel. He did not do all that well in school or at Shibpur, from where he did engineering. No records or anything. He was a cool guy, very relaxed, also into social work and stuff. But after he went to the US, there was no looking back. The American system was advanced; they didn't want rote learners, they appreciated true merit, out-of-the-box thinking. No politics as in Indian institutions. Look at Abhiroop now. He was doing a PhD at the University of Chicago, which was being paid for by Lockheed Martin, no less. Many laurels. All gathered on his own. Pure merit.

As he extolled Abhiroop's virtues and his connections with the topmost American aeronautics firms (the four horsemen of American imperialism—Boeing, Lockheed Martin, Northrop Grummon, Raytheon—though, naturally, the proud father was not familiar with the concept of American imperialism, nor would he have opposed it if he were), Mr Lahiri finished the last of the mini quiches Mrs

Mukherjee had baked. She'd served them with two kinds of fillings. One vegetarian, one non-vegetarian. Everything had been polished off already. 'Abhiroop will join one of these, though personally I feel it will be Lockheed Martin, given the liaisons he's already established. It's all about networking. And those Americans certainly respect talented Indians.' He looked Mr Mukherjee straight in the eyes. 'He is a brilliant chap, moshai, my younger son. Very tall too. My complexion but, not fair like his mother!'

Everybody laughed.

Old Mr Lahiri continued: 'Your daughter is an equally bright girl, I hear from Moni. Wonderful nature too. It will be a wonderful match.'

The women came out from Mrs Mukherjee's bedroom. The (prospective) sister-in-law asked for the recipe of the smoked salmon roulade Mrs Mukherjee had made.

'Arre, Nandini, it's extremely easy. The quiches are a bit tricky. Difficult to get the short-crust pastry right. Actually, I love reading recipe books and experimenting from them.' Truth was, Mrs Mukherjee was a huge fan of Nigella Lawson. 'Apu only bought me this book on world recipes, you know. She's always going to bookstores. Loves reading! That's where I learnt these recipes. And nowadays you get all ingredients everywhere. One doesn't have to go to New Market all the time. You're welcome to borrow the book if you like.'

Mrs Mukherjee did not spell out the price of smoked salmon, or that of cream cheese. AJ's heart had lurched when he'd picked them up for her.

Mrs Lahiri said to her daughter-in-law, 'If Apu cooks as well as her mother, Nandini, then I don't think we need to consult Babin at all. We might just as well set the date.'

'Or if she's as beautiful as her mother, then too,' old Mr Lahiri added gallantly.

The air in the room swelled with the promise of joy, good cheer, compliments well-meant if not quite politically correct, and, of course, the prospect of the dinner that would follow. Mrs Mukherjee had already set the bar pretty high with her homemade mocktails and starters and three different kinds of kebabs. People began talking all at once. The fathers discussed politics. Mamoni Mukherjee consulted the doctors about her knee. Mrs Lahiri, Mrs Mukherjee and Moni Mashi went inside again. And AJ showed magic tricks to the little ones.

Only Abeer slipped out of the melee to his room and looked wistfully out of the window, in the direction of A-5.

Apu

29th October.
Exhausted from all the action around me. As though there is constant buzzing in my ear.

Suresh S. has reclaimed his house. Maaji Sahai and Beti Chudail have been despatched to Nalini's house (poor Nalini, but she volunteered for the greater common good), along with bags full of gifts we bought: Twinkle Khanna-advertised white glittery phone for Chudail; blue, green and orange glittery saris for her three sisters-in-law; Raymond suit-length for Chudail's husband; train-set for Chudail's brat (AB was looking at train-set so fondly that will not be surprised if he goes back to the shop and buys one for himself); salwar suit for tribal maid; white leather bag for Chudail's mother-in-law.

Suresh S. has hired a full-time nanny to look after the children, for a few months at least, while Meera recovers. AB was helpful in this regard. His mother's nurse had been in search of employment and was, it seems, most happy to join the Sahais. Suresh S. has also taken leave from office. Two weeks. It is a first in his career. There was apparently a smattering of applause when he left for the day, he reported apologetically.

Dr Sheila examined Meera last evening and has started her on medication. She warned Suresh S. that it would take time—patience was a pre-requisite for the carers.

AB requested that we should commence running after his mother's shraddh. Was about to suggest so myself. Not because a few days here or there will make me less prone to embarrassing myself but because do not relish the idea of AB flailing around field in bloody dhoti and chadar. Note: he is not worried about running in dhoti and chadar; says cannot run in hawai chappals, which constitute current footwear. Is planning to buy Adidas running shoes. This time I did not cease and desist but demanded about his Communism.

He merely smiled.

Noticed he has a long dimple in his left cheek when he smiles. How had I not observed this before? Do not like dimples on men.

Sandhya

From Solstice.

When I returned to my flat in the cold November rain, cradling my death sentence close to my body, almost like a precious baby, yellow leaves dislodged in the wind fell around me like confetti. There was one significant thing that seemed to have been effected by Dr Sheila Gibson's pronouncement: my twin and I had merged into one body again.

Strange as it sounds, the principal feeling that crawled across my mind, the most overwhelming sense, was relief. Having dealt with the extreme uncertainty of cancer, its ebb and flow in my cells, the certainty of death was like balm on bitter wounds.

Memories of the evening are clearly etched in me. I had forgotten to leave the heating on in my bedroom, so the room was cold. I took a long hot bath. And then, oddly, I began to look for fresh bedclothes in the closet. Clean pillowcases and laundered sheets. For the first time in weeks, I made my bed carefully. By that time the room had warmed up somewhat. I got underneath the duvet and went to sleep.

I had a strange dream. I must have had several dreams that night, fading in and out of each other. (That's how it was usually; my sleep had been disturbed for years.) But this I remembered clearly. I was thirteen or fourteen years old and back on the island, in my school uniform. My mother and I stood at the bus-stop near my school. It was late evening and the place was deserted. My mother and I were both exhausted and we could not imagine walking back. Presently, a bus stopped in front of us. But the conductor insisted that only one of us could go. As it often happens in dream-logic, no one questioned this arbitrary instruction. I wanted my mother to go. But my mother urged me to take the bus. At home, my father and I waited and waited. My mother returned in the middle of the night, having walked the entire way home.

When I woke up, I had no idea what day or time it was.

In the evening, I got a call from Dr Sheila Gibson. I did not know her well at all, only that she was a bit of a radical gynaecologist. She had written a controversial book on the inherent wisdom of the female body, and exhorted medical practitioners to go beyond the clinical approach to a more holistic view of female health. I had heard all this vaguely, but given the immediate concerns of my own illness, I had never enquired further. Dr Sheila was not one of the main doctors assigned to my case. But it was kind of her to call.

She sounded very apologetic on the phone. It was only the other day she had told me the view of the team of doctors who had been treating me. She asked me if I would like to accompany her to a lecture organized by one of her colleagues. A Dr Bob Savarin, the only British doctor to date who had been accepted into an ayurvedic college in India and subsequently been awarded the highest degree. Before I could protest—and I had had enough of doctors, really—she clarified that it was not him she wanted me to meet but his guru. He was a siddha yogi, she told me.

I had been a singer in Swinging London, after all. I knew enough about gurus, whether siddha yogis or not, and was familiar with the fixation of a certain type of Britisher with such gurus. Was I particularly keen to meet this guru the next day? Not at all.

But Dr Sheila was trying very hard, and somehow that worked. She was so earnest and apologetic all at once. And she was a stranger.

There was something comforting about spending time with a stranger. I hadn't yet shared the news with my friends. I wasn't sure if I wanted to do anything with their dismay at my impending death. I knew that is what it would come to—I would have to comfort them.

I agreed to go.

I sat in a corner of the room on the carpet, near the door, ready to slip out. The room had been cleared of all furniture, though one could easily guess where each thing had been: the sofa, the coffee table, the chairs. I looked around, trying not to think of the meaningless things with which people fill up their homes. Whom should I leave my furniture to, I wondered. Meg? Or Nella? Dr Sheila had introduced me to our host out in the hall, though I had not lingered to chat. It seemed the gathering comprised a smattering of doctors, hippies and students. We all waited for the master to arrive.

He was about seventy years old, I'd been told. But when he came in, I thought he looked distinctly younger. He was dressed in white and was a small man, really, compact and glowing with a mix of good health and serenity. He smiled warmly, his eyes crinkling in pleasure, as he threaded his way through the crowd to the other end of the room, where his place had been earmarked with Indian-style bolsters. He sat in the middle, erect and alert. The room fell silent. He began to speak.

'I was asked to speak about healing today, for, it seems, there are several doctors and medical students among us this evening. My friend, the Jungian doctor Anthony Allina, says that at the University of California Medical School there used to be a standing joke. For every year in medical school, you need two to recover. And yet, Anthony says, this is an underestimation.

'Western medicine has progressed in leaps and bounds; it has plumbed deeper into physiology, histology, oncology, pathology— every other logy you can name—more than ever before. The man of medicine, the doctor, has become more and more scientific, more and more rational. He is a warrior against disease, focusing all his attention on trouble spots. This has, however, not been the traditional approach. In ayurveda, for instance, the emphasis is on healing. The thinking is

that when the body reverts to health, for health is the natural state, disease will vanish.

'The roots of all diseases are within us. Thus disease becomes an occasion for us to go deep within ourselves, to hear what the inner self is trying to say. Perhaps that is not something we want to hear because it doesn't agree with societal norms or simply our own illusions of what we think we ought to do or be or feel. To treat this, we must look beyond the symptoms to a more fundamental cause. You doctors will say, "But that is exactly what we do too."

'But here is what I am saying. The range of what the traditionalists call symptoms is broader. To be a little rhetorical, I shall say that cancer too is a symptom. The root of its cause is elsewhere.

'And naturally the causes would vary from one patient to another. To solve the puzzle that illness presents, each patient and each physician must undergo a unique journey deep within. If we eat more than what our body requires we will accumulate excess fat in the cells. But why do we overeat? What insecurity or pain are we trying to dull with food?

'To understand the individual's body and mind there are several general theories that would provide a frame of reference to the practitioner of ayurveda. One is, of course, the concept of prakriti: that every individual is a combination of vata, pitta and kapha properties. Most people have one or two of these humours in excess, which requires balancing. There is also the exceedingly sophisticated philosophy of dhatus that was articulated by Charaka. But I am not going to go into the nitty-gritties of these.

'I want, instead, to talk about the role of memory. The memory not only of our own actions but also ancestral memories. These are passed on to our bodies, coded in the language of biology. Healing will happen when we re-live and embrace these too, however painful the memories might be.

'The person who is ill must go deep within themselves and complete the assignment that illness provides. Nobody else can do it for them. Disease is not something to be waged war on. It is a signal from nature. It is a wake-up call. It is an opportunity.'

My mind latched on to those words hungrily.

Disease is not something to be waged war on. It is a signal from nature. It is a wake-up call. It is an opportunity.

Later on, after the talk, Dr Sheila introduced me to the master. She did not say anything about my illness, obviously, but pushed me towards him like a mother hoping to get a laggard child some special attention from the class teacher.

The old gentleman smiled long and deep. 'Why haven't you been singing?'

I was dumbfounded. Unless he was a chutney music aficionado—and the probability of that was dim—there was no way he could have known I was a singer. I hadn't sung in months.

'You will come out of this crisis,' he said, then, holding my hand briefly. 'Remember your guru. Sing.'

'I have no guru,' I mumbled.

'Why do I see the shadow of your guru in you, then? Ah, perhaps it is someone you don't think of as a guru.'

Winter brought blue-white snow. On an impulse, I decided to leave London. My doctors had given up; I, in turn, refused their offer of a drug-induced fog surrounding my last few days. That set me free. I decided to galvanize whatever little courage I could summon and do what the guru asked me: heed nature's wake-up call.

Nella had bought a traditional country house in the Cotswolds; she offered it to me. But what need had I for that large manor? I settled for the small cottage meant originally for the head gardener, deep inside the overgrown grounds. The next four months I remained in that cottage. My only visitors were Dr Sheila and Dr Savarin, who braved the cold every two weeks to bring me provisions: rice and dal was all I asked for, but they brought fruit and vegetables too. And medicines Bob would prepare himself, like a traditional ayurved. I had no faith in ayurveda then, but I had the medicines out of respect for him. From Bob I learnt that disease invades the body when the sense of being established within the self is destabilized. Ahamkara gives each cell in our body the identity of who it is—when ahamkara is wounded, one's own cells rebel and attack the body. All I could do was to meditate and reach deep within, in search of that self.

It was bitterly cold outside. In the fiery glow of the fire burning in the grate, I found myself praying, searching for my self. Now that time held no meaning for me, I was able to taste of its bittersweet sap. I found myself thinking of home, reflecting. The floodgates opened. I wept for hours, in the profound stillness of that room, death lurking in the corners. I confronted all the false selves I had collected over the years, each of which had pushed me a little further away from what I really was. I became a medium to the sorrows of my ancestors—right from their tumultuous journey to the new world from the old, to the tragedy of my talented father who neither found recognition from the world nor loyalty in his children. Their cumulative grief coursed through my veins, amplified by dreams and visions and long, dark silence. And then, after I was spent, I survived that storm to find a new centre within. My mother.

My barely literate mother, who never dreamt of escape. Who sang like a bird to the gods at her altar, and followed the seasons in her kitchen.

And the sense of profound loneliness I felt dimmed. After all these years, I became young and unformed again, like a mound of clay, and looked to the memories of my parents for guidance.

Spring came with such a promise of peace that I felt the end was nigh. And, yet, that was when the disease began to abate in my body.

After I returned to London, a severely diminished shell of a human, yet far stronger than I had ever felt, Dr Sheila herself ran all the tests to check if I was indeed cancer-free.

I was.

As soon as I was able, I travelled home and met my father. My mother, however, had passed away, as if shouldering a large chunk of my pain.

My mother. My first guru.

Mired in mystery, sorrow, freedom and spring, I found my calling. I became a renunciate, a sanyasini.

BOOK 5
Losing

CHAPTER 17

17.1

'I'm so sorry about your grandma,' Shabnam said to Mandy. 'Must be tough.'

'Well, it's most tough on my mamu, you know,' Mandy replied. 'He was closest to her. We are very worried about him. But I suppose he'll survive. It seems he's going to take up running.'

Mandy grinned, and immediately Shabnam realized why G had fallen for her. The girl had the most gorgeous smile; her front teeth were ever-so-slightly crooked and she had those sexy, pointy canines that were so much of a rage in Japan that women were apparently paying through their nose to get their teeth made crooked.

Mandy had never really hung out with the bunch. But an invite had been tendered to her for today on Abeer's insistence. The group's Bijoya get-together had been organized at Deep's house by popular vote. Deep's parents were divorced. He lived in a large apartment with his doctor mum, hippest among parents. Much food and fun had been had by all. Deep's mother had left for her clinic, which meant they had the entire house to themselves. They were to watch a movie later.

Abeer was regaling them with stories of AJ's expertise in matrimonial affairs (with special reference to Operation Lahiri); AJ, rather distracted, was hovering around the door, allowing G the pleasure of his stories; Shabnam was telling them about her holiday in Rajasthan, where her dad would hand everyone a neatly typed-out sheet each morning with the itinerary for the day. (Shabnam's dad was in the army and treated his family as a minor and rebellious faction of his unit.)

Afternoon waned. The shadows began to lengthen outside. Inside, the chatter dimmed and a lazy web was woven around their bodies, humming with electrical activity. Phones and tabs and laptops hummed in a modern-day version of companionable silence among friends. The only exception was Shriya's Kindle, which was as quiet as a book.

It was four—they'd almost finished the custard cake that was for dessert—when Molly arrived finally. AJ got the door. Molly looked fetching in a unique knotty dress made of multi-coloured gamchhas.

'Hello, my children,' Molly said. Waving away their greetings, she went straight to Abeer.

'G,' she demanded, flapping a file in his face, 'you know my course on feminism and performance studies?'

Abeer smirked. 'I didn't. But now I do.'

'Well, I need your help. I'm doing something on feminism and yoga. And dance. And the body. Can I speak to the *Autumn in the Ashram* lady, please, please, pretty please?'

'Well, hello, Molz!' Shriya interrupted. 'Do you want some lunch or not?'

'No, I'm fine,' Molly replied. 'Just dessert is okay.' AJ immediately handed her the large plate with what was left of the custard cake.

'G? Gee, Geee, Geeee!' Molly chanted.

'Well, okay, if you insist,' Abeer said. 'I'll have to ask my sister. She's her handler. But I guess it can be arranged.'

'Don't act pricey, G,' said AJ. 'I think there's a class or a talk or something tomorrow that Sandhyaji is holding. I'll find out for you, Molly—I'm more popular in their colony.'

'Oh, yes. AJ is the blue-eyed boy in Nancy,' Abeer drawled.

'Shut up, G,' Mandy said. 'Sandhyaji is extremely cool.'

'Wasn't she the one who alerted the boy-who-nearly-died's

parents?' Rahul asked, looking up from his phone. 'Like, after a vision? I wonder how one gets those visions. Is she Shakta? Then she definitely takes hallucinogens.'

'Yes, she was the one who alerted them,' Abeer said curtly, ignoring the rest of Rahul's comment. He broke off a bit from the custard cake. Molly slapped his hand away. 'The guy's come home now. He's on the mend. Poor chap. He's only in Class 9.'

'Molly, what movie did you get us?' Shabnam asked.

'*Friends with Benefits,*' Molly replied.

Everyone sniggered. AJ flushed a deep puce.

17.2

After Bablu returned home, Monalisa Das attempted to patch up the misshapen puzzles left of her routine—and her role—into a new beginning.

'My dear, you have to step back,' Sandhya said to her again. 'You are a wonderful mother in so many ways. But you *must* step back. You are an individual. It's because you have obliterated all other identities and simply focused on your boys that you are driving them on in this crazy way. Life is wonderful and complex all at once, Monalisa. Career is a small part of happiness. Encourage the boys to be kind and courageous. Everything else will follow.'

Monalisa fingered her chain unhappily. Kind and Courageous? Was that enough? Why was everyone always talking about killer instinct then? In the very next instant, she blanched. She seemed to have a lot of killer instinct herself. Had nearly killed her son, hadn't she?

Sandhya covered her hand with her own. 'Your motherhood is just one aspect of your life. I understand this obsessive kind of love, I really do. It is a natural human instinct. But we must fight against it. Love ought to be joyous and liberating. You must learn to enjoy your life fully—and life has so many aspects. What about your marriage? Your selfhood? I know, I know, you are a wonderful housewife. That is an important part of your identity. But I also sense that intense addictive streak in you about all household matters. Polish the counter. By all means, polish the counter, but polish it with a sense of awareness of the present. Don't polish it manically as you think of the maths tutor's problem sheet. Or something like that. You know?'

Monalisa laughed uncertainly. How did Sandhyaji know that? She sat at Sandhya's table, drinking a cup of tea and nibbling some delicious almond cookies Dr Sheila had baked.

Sandhya opened the window and drew her attention to the neem tree outside. 'Isn't it beautiful, Monalisa? I can sit here for hours, simply watching the leaves flutter lightly and the squirrels running up and down.'

Monalisa looked at the tree. In the fading light, the leaves were an orangey olive-green. The branches swayed gently in the breeze.

'You were right, Mataji. Bablu likes the idea of going to Rishikesh with John Matthew. He is very embarrassed about this whole episode. The counsellors had warned us that some children like to blackmail the parents after one suicide attempt. That we should be understanding but firm. But Bablu's reaction is very different. He is very apologetic, actually. He is also grateful that he will no longer have to go to Bor Da's tuition. The other students in the class are solving IIT entrance problems now! Can you believe it?' Her voice was a little wistful. Fourteen-year-olds solving calculus—there was something to admire there.

'Had you wanted to study further yourself, Monalisa?'

'Me? No, no, nothing like that. I mean...I had wanted to study nursing actually. One of my best friends studied nursing. She now works in Dubai. Huge salary. Huge. But my parents thought I'd be happier if I got married. They meant well.'

'Just as you think Bablu will be happier if he does engineering,' Sandhya said, kindly.

Monalisa thought about it. Unthinkingly, she stretched her arms and unwound her bun. Her hair fell across her back and the tightness she'd been feeling on her scalp dissolved. One by one, she lined up the hairpins on the table. 'I have also promised I will never ever take him to an astrologer.'

'Thank God for that!' Sandhya smiled.

'When we asked him about Rishikesh and John Matthew, his eyes lit up. He likes John a lot.'

'John is very cool, Monalisa, especially to a fourteen-year-old. He teaches English literature but is a black belt in karate. He can talk about girls with him.'

'Girls?' Monalisa was aghast.

Sandhya ignored her reaction and continued: 'And John has been very concerned. He has been to the hospital every day. He needs a break too. I think this is the only month in the year when he has time. After Kali puja, his tuitions will start again, three batches a day, right up to Christmas Day. Let them go for a couple of weeks. John is used to dealing with boys of Bablu's age.'

'That's true.' Monalisa poured herself another mug of hot water and freshened her tea. 'As an English teacher he is extremely famous in ICSE schools. Even people from the West Bengal board schools know him.'

'I have a job for you, Monalisa,' Sandhya said in response.

'Yes, madam?' Monalisa asked, alert.

They talked for an hour, until they were interrupted by Dr Sheila, who had finished packing and was hankering for tea.

'It's the Englishwoman in me, you see,' she laughed and promptly knocked down the electric kettle. 'And they say she's a superb surgeon,' Sandhya joked.

Dr Sheila was flying out tonight and, in the last hour, had already organized the trip for John and Bablu. They were to be allotted the room with the most picturesque view. They were to be plied with fruits, nuts and milk. ('The only sort of treats an ashram can offer, I'm afraid!') But they would not be compelled to eat only ashram food—Rishikesh had delightful restaurants specializing in all sorts of cuisine—and would be allowed to take library books back to their room. (Other ashramites had to read in the library.)

When Monalisa, much cheered up, was about to leave, Sandhya saw her to the door and said, 'One small thing. Every time you get tense about some maths marks or entrance exam or any of those things about the boys' future, close your eyes and remember the neem tree.'

Monalisa was confounded. 'That neem tree?' She gestured towards the window of the study.

'Exactly. Imagine that tall, beautiful neem tree and ask yourself this question: where is its mother?'

17.3

It was the day after all ceremonies of death had been duly performed.

It is said that the rituals around death are designed to be as they are—tedious and fussy—so that the chief mourners have something to absorb them through the days and nights that follow: cooking the very basic mourner-meal in one pot themselves; organizing the shraddh; distributing plain white cards that say 'Om Ganga' to invite people; buying the items the priest has listed. They keep them from the unbridled pull of grief.

Alongside the helpful Mrs Mukherjee, who knew all the rules, knew the priest, even knew the printer of said cards, and his own sister, who knew exactly how to push his buttons, Ananda Bose had carried out all these tasks dutifully. It was only after he scattered her ashes in the Hooghly (Mandy's father and brother and John Matthew had accompanied him) and had his head shaved—a sign that marked him out as man who had lost a parent—that he truly felt the force of his loss. It was an abiding presence.

The day after all the ceremonies had been concluded, he returned home from college at four. The city, white-hot for some strange reason, though it was November now and the weather ought to be mellow, had got on his nerves. When he unlocked the door to his flat, the rooms gaped at him, empty and suddenly small. How had a thin, dwindling old lady, her breath getting shorter and more urgent every day—how had her presence dominated this ordinary brick-and-mortar house so much that now that she was gone it was all meaningless and banal, downright ugly?

Ananda had sent Madhobi off to his sister's house. She had protested greatly. Who would cook for him? Do the chores? Ensure he ate even one meal? But he had said that he was thirty-six years old, and as a philosopher he should now put his money where his mouth was and do everything himself. Well, he had said that to himself. To Madhobi he had said, 'You will feel very lonely here all day. Now there is no nurse to fight with. Who knows, maybe your old mistress will come and haunt you.'

Madhobi, tickled by the joke, had shushed him and said, 'Now that you have followed all rituals, she won't.'

So, when Ananda Bose returned from college, feeling bitter and exhausted, there was neither Madhobi nor food.

He walked into the bathroom and stood under the shower with all his clothes on. The jet of water hit him like a torrent— unseasonably hot—and for a moment he was able to forget everything. The clothes stuck to his body, now heavy. One by one, he peeled them off and flung them into a bucket. He would wash them later.

He'd spoken to Sandhya several times after Dashami. She had told him how Rumi's followers used to celebrate the night of his demise as *urs*—the wedding night. The night of the union of the soul with the divine. She had given him a volume of Rumi's verses and one had particularly caught his attention:

> *On the day I die, when I'm being carried*
> *toward the grave, don't weep. Don't say,*
> *He's gone! He's gone. Death has nothing*
> *to do with going away. The sun sets and*
> *the moon sets, but they are not gone.*

Ananda's tears were washed away in the stream of water. It was only after he'd turned off the shower that he heard the doorbell. He hoped it hadn't been ringing for too long. The caterer was supposed to come and collect the rest of the payment. Damn! He'd forgotten to go to the ATM. Well, he'd write a cheque. He quickly wrapped the towel around his waist, pulled on a T-shirt that was hanging on a peg and, dripping water, went to open the door.

It was Aparajita.

Apu was stunned to see his shaven head—she had expected the usual Ananda Bose with his shock of hair and beard—glistening with water that he had not yet wiped off, little droplets dripping from his ears and eyebrows. His eyes were a little red. For a moment she didn't know him. But his AIR-news-reading voice was unmistakeable. It sounded embarrassed.

'Do come in, Aparajita,' he said, and disappeared inside hastily to find some clothes—and another towel.

Apu found her way inside and sat on the worn-out sofa. A few journals were piled on a table next to the sofa. *The Journal of Applied Ethics*. She fingered the spine tentatively.

Ananda Bose appeared finally, now in his usual pressed kurta and pyjama, a whiff of citrus-scented cologne emanating from his person. His face—without the shock of hair—drew attention to his features (distinguished) and his forehead (high). There was something vaguely intimate about his freshly bathed and clean-clean presence.

Apu began to burble wildly. 'Sorry to drop in just like that. But I saw you returning. I was at Sandhyaji's. I just wanted to check with you. Do you want to start running from tomorrow?'

After the initial burst of excitement (what with the books and the plans), in the buzz of activity surrounding the last week, running had slipped his mind. Now he grasped at it with gusto; this was exactly what he needed. It was not too late, his mother had said. If it weren't for the running, he might as well get a few cats and be done with it. 'Sure. I mean, I had sort of forgotten about it. But tomorrow I'll buy the shoes. And then we can start in the evening.'

'Right,' Apu said. 'I've checked out the park. It's actually extremely nice. And there seem to be hardly any people there. I mean,' she quickly added, 'it's deserted, so nobody will make fun of our running. Basically, my huffing and puffing. I get winded really easily.'

Ananda laughed.

'And I'm also here to communicate a dinner invitation to you for tonight. From Sandhyaji.'

'Oh, that's wonderful. I'm planning to learn cooking myself.'

'Cooking?'

Ananda began to tell her all about his harmony-in-household-chores project. Apu burst out laughing. The idea of Ananda Bose in the kitchen, a recipe book propped up on the counter, was hilarious. She said as much.

17.4

It was half-past seven. Meera and the girls were still sleeping, thank heavens. The nanny had been on leave yesterday and, amidst the supreme chaos, where he was virtually in charge of three kids, including his wife, Suresh had realized quickly that he would much rather have been debugging programs in office. Far, far easier.

But things were improving. Little by little. And it was Tara who had made the difference. She would do her homework or colouring, sitting next to her prostrate mother who still hardly spoke. Yesterday, he had entered their bedroom to find Tara lying next to Meera, playing songs on his phone; one earpiece was in Tara's ear, the other in Meera's. He'd smiled and retreated quietly. Into the utter anarchy of the house where he was still a novice.

17.5

'It's too early. I don't think I am ready yet.'

'Oh, no, you are.'

'I am not. You can't force me.'

'No, of course not. I am just trying to be gently persuasive. I am not asking *you* to do it. But *one* can benefit a great deal from this if one gives it a go.'

'How on earth do *you* know?'

'Okay, I'll come clean. I may come across as a vague and pacifist lecturer of philosophy—and I am—but once I spent three months perfecting my kusti in Benaras. They taught me a few things. Hindu push-ups and Hindu squats as these are called in the West, or plain and simple dand and uthak-baithak. Excellent exercises if one perseveres a little with them. At one time, I could do a hundred dands. At *one* time.'

'Okay, fine, you can teach me these next week.' Apu relented. Ananda Bose had done kusti in Benares? Well, well, well, wonders would never cease. 'Why did you go to Benares?'

Ananda Bose kept quiet for a while. Then he said, 'I was trying to impress a girl in BHU. So I went to stay at a friend's place. They lived in an old house with a hundred relatives, a few furlongs from Dashashwamedh Ghat.'

'Wow.' Apu smiled. 'So what happened to the girl?'

'She died,' he replied morosely.

'Really?' Apu was aghast.

Ananda Bose burst out laughing. 'No, I was joking. She married an NRI and lived happily ever after.'

17.6

'Why are you carrying all this cleaning equipment so early in the morning?'

'Good morning, Treeza. It seems John and Bablu are walking around a lot in Rishikesh. He sounded very happy. I didn't want to go back to A-1 after yoga, so I brought my basket.'

It was a lovely wicker basket. Others might have used it for picnics. Monalisa Das had packed her entire arsenal of multicoloured liquids, packets of wet wipes and brushes of various sizes neatly in it.

'Are you helping Mataji clean?'

'Oh, no. You and I will start cleaning your flat today. Don't worry, even if it takes a full week, no problem. I am fully available.'

17.7

'Bhaisaab? How are you?'

'Let me come in at least?'

'Of course, of course, please come. But why didn't you call? I'd have come to the station.'

'Arre, Suresh, why would I worry you? You know how late this Howrah-Hatia train can get. Luckily it was on time today. But how is Meera now?'

'Well, she's all right. But how did you know she was unwell?'

'Actually, last month she called me and sounded a little off. But what can I say? At the time the crop had got ruined, Suresh. The untimely rains in October. I asked her to call her Bhabhi and fix a time when she could come, perhaps in December. But she didn't call either of us again. Last week, your bade bhaisaab, what a gentleman, and Mataji came to visit us. They brought the finest rabri from Patna and such a lovely sari for your bhabhi. Mataji told us Meera was suffering from *depression*. She said that she was an old-fashioned woman and there was no *depresion* that couldn't be cured by a nice holiday at her maika. And she's right, Suresh.'

'I don't know, Bhaisaab. What she is suffering from is a condition called postpartum depression.'

'I know, I know, you're a modern man. But there would be no harm in a visit to the village, no? We've now built a nice two-room set with a bathroom. Western style. You are on leave too. Come to us.'

Suresh hemmed and hawed, not sure of what to say. At least here he had a support system. And Meera was improving bit by bit.

But the decision was made when he saw Meera standing in the doorway. After many, many days, Meera was heard giving a clear instruction. In a petulant voice, she told her daughter, 'Tara, tell your mamaji that I will not speak to him.'

Mamaji immediately told Tara, 'Tara Bitiya, tell your mummy I haven't come to speak to her. I have only come to deliver aam ka achaar from her sisters, hing ke paapad from her bhabhi and motichur ke laddu from the halwai whose son had wanted to marry her.'

Tara merely rubbed her sleepy eyes and ran across the hall to sit on her father's lap.

17.8

'Okay, I need some help from you guys.'

'What?'

'I am doing this performance-installation on feminism and yoga for my course. I've got some fabulous material from Sandhyaji. I'm choreographing it into a gorgeous yoga-dance thingy.'

'Impressed,' said Abeer, sounding anything but. 'What do you want us to do?'

'I want you to perform.'

'WTF?' Abeer said. 'Why us? Shouldn't it be done by women?'

'That is exactly the point. Women's health and feminism are not just female concerns. Trying to pigeonhole them as women's issues is part of the problem. So guys will be doing it. It's amazing, really, it is. Like, very fusion, very boho, but with solid basics. And you're surprisingly good at yoga, AJ.'

'We're in,' said AJ, deliberately avoiding Abeer's eye.

Oh crap, thought Abeer, now we'll be dancing in front of JU intellectuals, won't be able to show our faces in the 8B area ever.

17.9

Treeza's father, Will, had died young, leaving her mother, Dorothy, with their three daughters, a lifetime's lease on a flat in Kyd Street and a large collection of stamps. The girls had been twelve, eleven and three. First, Dorothy got the stamps inspected by an expert just to be certain there was no hidden legacy over there. Then she invested whatever money he'd left—it was not too small a sum; he'd been a chartered accountant—in post office accounts. The interest was small, but she left the capital untouched. Finally, she considered a career. She surveyed her skills and decided to back the one thing in which she'd always been better than others. She started a small business from home, baking specialty cakes. (Those days, baking was considered a skill, not an art.) At the time when local bakeries offered plain chocolate or vanilla or marble cakes with ordinary icing, and black forest was the height of luxury, Dorothy found fabulous and intricate recipes in old American and British magazines brought by foreign travellers and sold to second-hand bookstores in Mirza Ghalib Street. She wrote to friends far and wide to source ingredients. Each cake was a work of art. Long before novelty cakes had begun to appear in cooking programmes, Dorothy was creating life-like miniatures of zoos and aquarium cakes for children. Very soon, she developed a fantastic reputation among the glitterati of Calcutta. The business saw her girls through school and college.

Before he left for Rishikesh, John had gone to Dorothy. He had always been genuinely fond of Treeza's mother. Perhaps because his own mother had died years ago. Or maybe it was nothing sentimental at all—she was such a shining beacon of practicality, there was a great sense of comfort to be derived from her.

With earnestness, with charm, with love, John had bored away at all of Dorothy's objections, the months of despairing hurt caused by her youngest daughter's distance and silence. Dorothy would have to come stay in Nancy for the fortnight John was away—Treeza needed her.

Dorothy's heart had lurched, then finally given way. Treeze was her favourite child, the little porcelain doll she'd tried so hard to shelter from grief. So unsuited for the world. So exasperating.

'Mum, come to us. I am doing my best. I am praying to Mother Mary and Baby Jesus all the time—to bless us, to save our marriage,' John had pleaded. 'But Treeze needs *you*.'

'Your holy lady said this?'

'She did.'

'That's good. Tell her to keep that girl in control. Because I'm not taking any cheek. Didn't even invite me to the new house once!'

And so, Mrs Dorothy Alexander, entrepreneur, secretary of the Anglo-Indian Women's Association and editor of its cookbooks, pursuant of an independent school of practical philosophy, arrived at Nancy fully prepared to reprimand her daughter out of her depression, deal with a severely messy flat and disagree with the holy woman on most matters. Unfortunately, on all counts she was thwarted.

The moment she saw her daughter, with her puppy-dog eyes and her air of vulnerability, she teared up; within minutes, she was hugging Treeza tightly and promising the moon. The flat was so clean that it was uncanny and gave her goose-bumps. It was, all said, a lovely flat. Johnny had done well. Had Treeza's father been there, he'd have been so happy. Apparently, only the bedroom needed further work, and a few boxes from the old house were yet to be unpacked. As for Sandhya, she chatted about non-flour-based baking with Dorothy, treating her expertise with such reverence that the battle was won easy.

On Saturday, Sandhya's workshop at Nancy had been concluded. From the following week, Sandhya was to go into deep solitude for a month. The hall in the opposite apartment had been cleared entirely of furniture and would serve as a yoga and meditation room for whoever wanted to come. Apu was to organize the sessions. Three mornings a week, Sandhya would lead them in yoga and meditation; but otherwise she would not be leaving the apartment very often or taking visitors. They would practise at their own pace.

On Sunday, before Treeza moved back home with her mother, they had set about unpacking the boxes. Treeza had been enthusiastic all through Monalisa's marathon, chatting and laughing with her, as Monalisa taught her tricks about cleaning. She even jotted down the tips in a little notebook. But today she seemed tight and drawn again. But Sandhya knew the time of recuperative exile was up. Treeza would have to confront her own life again. 'Who can refuse to live her own life?' the poet Anna Akhmatova had said. Sandhya returned to this sentiment again and again.

Dorothy and Sandhya chatted lightly as they sorted through the closet. The clothes had all been dealt with: the ones that had not been handed over to Anwara for further distribution had been washed and ironed.

Treeza was looking through boxes of photographs. Suddenly, both Sandhya and Dorothy felt something faint—a shadow of a movement behind them perhaps, a flicker of the light—and turned. They found Treeza keeled over, weeping soundlessly, clutching a photograph.

Dorothy was the first to rush to her. 'Treezu darling, tell me what's the matter?'

But Treeza continued to weep silenty.

Sandhya picked up the photograph that had slipped from her clammy fist. It was an old photo (the date stamped on it indicated it was six years old) of John and her smiling into the camera. It seemed to have been clicked on someone's birthday. There were hands and feet in the background, a cake and twinkly lights. An ordinary picture. But Sandhya was able to sense something more.

She caressed Treeza's shoulders gently and prised her head from the floor onto her lap.

'Tell us, Treeza,' Sandhya asked gently, 'was there another baby you never talk about?'

She looked up immediately, her fragile face red and blotched. 'How did you know?'

'It's all right,' Sandhya said. 'You were young.'

Dorothy was confounded. 'Did you have another miscarriage, darling, that you haven't told anyone about? Why would you do that? It's not such a big deal. You should learn to talk about it. Aren't you a brave young woman of today? Instead you're behaving like a silly fossil!'

'That's because,' Treeza began to shout now, 'that's because it was not a miscarriage. I killed my baby. Our first baby—and I killed her! When that photo was clicked I was carrying. I didn't even talk to John. We were still newly married and so poor. This colleague told me people did it all the time, she took me to the clinic. That's why I left the job, Ma. That's why. You wanted to know, right? So I didn't have to see my accomplice in murder every day. People do it all the time, she said.'

'People do it all the time,' Sandhya said. Dorothy nodded.

'I just went to a doctor. So casually. And he gave me some pills. And it was over. Just like that. I didn't even feel too guilty about it then.' Treeza's shoulders began to shake. 'That's why I have these miscarriages. Idiopathic, the doctors say. No reason. But I know the reason. I am being punished. I sent my baby away, so now I will always be an incomplete mother. My body will refuse to cooperate.'

Dorothy moved away slightly, her body moving silently with her tears.

'Shush. It's going to be all right,' Sandhya said. 'It is. It will be all right. And I'm not saying this just to comfort you. I never do that. You know there is your baby in the universe. The one who you think you sent away? Silly girl, that baby is bound to you by shared karma. As you are to your mother. It's much, much more than accidental biology. There is so much shared karma that you will find your baby—or babies, most likely—in the course of your life. Your baby will find you. She might be physically born to you. Or you may find her through adoption. People see things in such a short-term way, they never understand this. There are very complex laws of love that govern the universe, my dear. One can never escape them.'

Whether or not Treeza processed all this was not clear; but she sat up and wiped her eyes, and reached a decision.

'I will have to tell John. If he can forgive me, then I can forgive myself.'

BOOK 6
SPRING

CHAPTER 18

18.1

Spring speaks to Calcutta with a forked tongue. In February, some days are delicious. Fragrant and mild and delicately breezy. On other days, the sun is blinding and intense. The oozy smell of summer wafts dangerously close to skin.

Today had been one of the mild days. By the time Apu reached the park, nearly a quarter of an hour late since her mother had insisted on writing down a grocery list for her (who did grocery shopping after running?), the sun had set and the air was piquant. She spotted Ananda Bose in the corner, doing his push-ups religiously. He had not reached the hundred mark yet; it had only been three months. But he did some forty already, and since they seemed to be, to Apu at least, the single most tortuous routine ever, devastating on the back, she could not help giving him some credit. Privately.

'Hi,' she called out brightly. 'Ninety-eight? Ninety-nine? One full hundred?'

Ananda would never count out loud. He did two more sets and finally stood up, his forehead muddy and neck glistening with sweat. 'Fifty. I'm getting to hundred before you do your thirtieth round for sure.'

'Don't be so smug,' Apu told him, adopting a rather smug tone herself. 'I'll be going for twenty rounds today, and thirty by the end of the month. Took you three months to get to fifty, no?'

It was a smallish park. So it afforded the runners great satisfaction in numbers.

The first couple of days in the course of their great fitness regimen, Apu had been mortified. She was highly self-conscious as she did her aerobic warm-up exercises before running. (Ananda Bose had demonstrated these to her and did them enthusiastically himself. She had somehow managed to suppress her giggles as he did jumping jacks with gravity.) She had continuously kept thinking if her new hyper-expensive running bra was doing its job properly and obsessed whether her bottom looked even worse while she jogged. She had bought two track pants which she paired with simple kurtis; so technically her butt, which could also be described as her cross, was well-covered. Even so, she felt silly and exposed. But in a day or two, as the yoga classes at dawn humbled them all, and Sandhya's talks infused her spirit with great lightness, Apu decided to free herself from these pointless considerations. It was about health, which was the natural state for the body to inhabit, not about vanity. Plus, she'd told herself, it was Ananda Bose. Not Hrithik Roshan. Or, for that matter, the Chicago boy. What did it matter if he saw her at her worst? He wouldn't judge her if she made a fool of herself. Sweaty and winded and crumpled in a heap while attempting a push-up. And it was not like he was so perfect on day one. He could barely do any of his famous Benarasi stunts; and after running the third round, he had appeared on the verge of exploding.

In three months, though, they had achieved a pattern. In the mornings, they did yoga at A-5. It had seemed exhausting the first three or four days, almost not worth the trouble. But there was something about doing yoga in the morning. If only you persevered with it—and they only did because of Sandhya—it would almost magically lead to the day becoming your friend. Not as though it were an annoying boss, out to exhaust the life out of you and make you run around endlessly as you tried to keep up with the clock. The day became a balanced, reasonable friend. After yoga, while rolling up their colourful yoga-mats, they would decide when they would meet in the park at dusk.

These days, both Apu and Ananda looked forward to returning home from their respective colleges, looked forward immensely to running. To be honest, they also looked forward to the conversation afterwards as they warmed down in the park, sipping their freshly squeezed unsweetened orange juice (courtesy Mrs Mukherjee). Then they would walk back to the colony at an excessively leisurely pace—well, naturally, they were tired. On Sundays, both would miss this greatly. So much that it was a bit weird. Both had independently Googled about this anxiety and breathed sighs of relief. It was common knowledge among amateurs that running was addictive. It sure was, they thought.

'So how was college today?' Apu asked. She had done her twenty rounds, with two short breaks in between, and was feeling pretty chuffed. Ananda was lying on the grass, unmindful of ants and other creepy-crawlies. Apu was picky about such things. She'd told him it could be dangerous, an insect might creep into his ear and climb up to his brain and, in short, kill him—he should at least bring the yoga mat along. But Ananda immediately said that he was recharging his energies directly from the earth. Batteries, perhaps he'd said, recharging his batteries. Sandhyaji had said something on these lines in one of her talks. That was one problem. He remembered everything, the bugger, and always gave a philosophical twist as and when it suited him.

'Same old, same old,' Ananda murmured. 'There was a meeting that went on for hours and hours. These professors hate having to stay back to invigilate external exams or stay with the principal in case there's a gherao or help students out with extra lessons—all of that is always left to me. But today they went on and on about the sort of changes that should be made in the teachers' room. Apparently, there is a new grant for this. There was much jubilation. And, immediately afterwards, much acrimony. The library is crying out for books, but, no, some money has to be diverted for the entertainment of teachers. The ladies wanted to section a part of the teacher's room into a private dressing room of sorts, with a dressing table, a first-aid kit and other bits and bobs. I wasn't listening. The men said that a flat-screen TV should be bought. I thought both were ridiculous ideas. But then it finally came down to me—deciding vote.'

'Which way did you vote?' Apu was curious.

'Dressing room. Always better to keep the ladies happy.' Apu rolled her eyes. 'Actually, it's because I will go insane if they blare cricket or news in the staff room, Apu. Or films. There is a limit to what even I can put up with.'

'Apparently.' Apu didn't know why she was feeling annoyed. 'So your female colleagues must have been happy then.'

Ananda stood up and dusted off the mud he could see. When he turned around, there were large brown splotches on his kurta. 'I hope so.' He smiled. 'One has to do what one has to do. I don't want them descending on me like a pack of wolves. They are very feisty, all of them.'

They started walking towards the little cluster of shops near Nancy, from which Mrs Mukherjee secured her provisions.

'I'm sure you do much to keep your female colleagues happy. Flash them your charming self or something?' Apu persisted.

Ananda laughed. 'I'm flattered that you think I *have* a charming self. I always thought you considered me very boring.'

Apu flushed at the truth. 'You've improved,' she said shortly. 'And all men are capable of being charming and flirty, I believe.'

Ananda looked at her in surprise.

'I'm appalled on behalf of women in general, victims of false flirtiness and un-meant charm...' Apu improvised, though she wasn't. Not really.

Ananda nodded. 'Ah, right. You're making a general point. I can't say I agree, though. I don't think all men have that talent. It is very rare, in fact. I, for instance, don't think I can be charming. I can be nice. I *am* nice. But girls don't seem to like that any more. Went out of fashion with Amol Palekar. Your brother and his friend PJ are nice guys. I don't suppose they're having any great luck with girls. Instead, consider the arm candy my niece flaunts. That pompous fop. I'm sure she finds him impossibly charming.'

Apu's sourness dissipated a little. 'AJ,' she said.

'Sorry?'

'AJ, not PJ. He's Aditya Jaiswal, AJ in short. Anyway, I'm sure the Benares girl found you charming. What was her name?'

Ananda fell silent. He was surprised that she even remembered the Benares girl. 'Malini,' he said. 'Her name was Malini.'

18.2

'How is it?'

'Oh-ho, now you wait, Boudi. Let me taste it first.'

'Fine, fine, take your time. I'm just curious.'

Treeza bit into the little pie; it melted in her mouth in a delicious medley of flavours. Homemade cottage cheese, spinach, salt, pepper, olive oil. These were the chief ingredients. Perhaps there were a few other herbs too? Monalisa never revealed all her tricks. Well, except to Treeza. And the best part was that they were baked, not fried. So utterly healthful.

'They're delicious!' Treeza reached for another.

Monalisa smiled happily and sat back in her chair. This had become their teatime ritual. Ever since Sandhya's food workshop, Monalisa Das spent a large amount of time tinkering with recipes. Trying to create healthy alternatives to her existing repertoire and inventing new kinds of snacks and main courses and desserts without flour or sugar. It was a challenge; and though it had never been officially extended to her, Monalisa Das had grabbed it with both hands. Her willing guinea pig—and, in many experiments, her sous chef—was Treeza.

In these three months, Treeze had gained, in addition to new friends, four kilos and a brand new husband.

When John returned home from Rishikesh in mid-November,

he found Treeze back at their flat. His mother-in-law, after making lots of goodies for them, had left. The house had been transformed. The boxes full of their Eliot Road stuff had finally been unpacked. The plastic chairs in the drawing room had been replaced by two settees (donated by Sandhya, he guessed correctly); a lovely wooden dining table with four chairs had been acquired from Dorothy's cluttered apartment; the divan had been shifted to the study; the new curtains in the window were from Russi's shop; there were flowers in a jug on the dining table. The house was shining. Treeza had been waiting by the door for him, blue ribbon in her hair.

John Matthew had been patient these many months. He had prayed earnestly, walking to his church every night before returning home and lighting three candles. (He always lit three candles: one for Bo, one each for him and Treeza, or his parents, or it could well be for the two lost babies. He never told himself exactly what the two candles represented). After Treeza had moved upstairs, John had begun to help out neighbours, practically seeking people out to help. He was sure one or two people had found this bordering on insanity. All the while, even as he chatted with Suresh Sahai about the IT industry and taught *The Tempest* to his Class 12s and walked around Ram Jhula and Laxman Jhula with young Bablu Das, there was one image he held on to. Treeza, standing by the door in her blue nightie, blue ribbon in her hair. Visualization, it was called. A meditation technique that Sandhya had taught him. She'd asked him to see clearly what it was he wanted most of all, never asking for details. It can be anything? he'd asked. Anything, she'd replied.

And yet, when it was right there in front of him, exactly as he'd wanted, John entered without looking at her twice. He kept his bags on the floor by the balcony. The house looked lovely. All the changes were appropriate. He felt so angry that he wanted to smash something. But whatever was smashable had already been smashed by her. She hadn't left a single glass for him to hurl. He felt even more furious and strode straight to the bedroom. It was as sparkling as the rest of the house and the bed was made with a bedsheet just like the one he had bought for Yasmeen. Russi, most likely. Without a word, he went into the bathroom.

When he came out, he felt slightly calmer. Treeza brought him tea in one of their old steel mugs from Eliot Road—just the way he liked, Darjeeling, without milk but with a spoonful of sugar—and a slice of cake. She bit her lip and hung around him as she used to on blue-ribbon days. He pulled one of the plastic chairs that had been placed by the wall with a small table in between, and sipped his tea and ate the cake. It was a trademark Dorothy tea cake. Treeze sat at the edge of the bed, dangling her legs. He noticed that she was wearing nail polish. Her feet, tiny in comparison to his Bata Size 10, and fair compared to his brown, had always been a bit of a turn-on for him.

John extended his large foot and rubbed her toe.

Treeza's cheeks coloured. 'Is Bablu much better now?' she asked.

John came and sat down next to her on the bed. 'I don't want to make small talk,' he said.

She blushed furiously now. It was as though they had been transported six years back; this was the sort of cheesy conversation they would have during the honeymoon they'd celebrated at home. Rila had sailed off with Jeff, leaving the house empty.

'I need to know certain things,' John said. 'Are you planning to go and live anywhere else in the near future?' When she made no answer, he added, 'Please let me know. Then I will sell this house and go back to Eliot Road.'

Immediately, Treeza's lips began to quiver. Tears glimmered in her eyes. There was only one thing John wanted to do. But he restrained himself and continued to be cruel.

'Tapworks right on time. Now, Treeza Matthew, I adore Sandhyaji. I like your mother. I am even prepared to like your new psycho best friend Monalisa Das—she's been giving me daily updates, by the way—but I am *not* going to have my wife go off to live with any of them. If you want to live with anybody else, be my guest. But then we will have to give up this house.'

In a broken way, Treeza got up from the bed and made to leave. Immediately, John grasped her hand and pulled her onto his lap. 'You're not going anywhere,' he ordered. She crumpled and clung to him.

'Listen to me, Treeza Matthew. I have no mother, no father. I have only you. Hear me carefully: I need you. I don't need some baby. I am so angry and so jealous of the way you have put this baby thing over everything else we have, over me, over our happiness.' He paused. 'I am so angry,' he said again, but he didn't sound so angry any more.

Her breath on his neck was hot and her cloud of hair tickled his face. He pulled her legs across his at right angles. He lifted her face and looked at it appraisingly. Softer now, he said, 'I will be extremely jealous when the baby comes along, let me tell you. You have to promise now that you'll always love me more. Otherwise, I'm not helping with Project Baby in any way.'

Treeza wiped her eyes and said, 'There is something I have to tell you.'

And she did. Sitting in his lap, engulfed by his arms, she told him all the details: how she'd found out, what the colleague had said, how easy it had been. He had been away for two weeks, accompanying the senior students on a school trip. She told him, and the earth did not quake, the walls did not dissolve and his body did not give away even a flicker of resentment. Instead, he held her closer.

'Darling, we have to forgive ourselves,' he said finally. 'I am afraid I would have agreed with your decision then, even if you told me. So there. I know you wanted to spare me the guilt. It's okay. We'll survive.'

Later, hours later, after she had fallen asleep in the crook of his arms, John shed a few tears for his lost children. He told them he was sorry he didn't get to know them better. He told them to come back if they liked. But he also set them free from their bedroom.

He claimed his bed.

18.3

It was a quarter past six when Monalisa decided to break up their little party. The tuition teacher had left and the boys were clamouring to watch TV; Mr Das would come soon; Treeza would go, pop into Sandhya's for a few minutes as she did every day, and consider dinner.

'Follow the rhythms of nature,' Sandhya had taught them. 'Follow the movement of the sun, rise and sleep with it. Follow the seasons and eat seasonal fruits and vegetables.' Treeza was scrupulously following the routine Sandhya had set her. Waking up at dawn; the walk and yoga (which she had begun to enjoy) early in the morning; regular warm hip baths; a concoction of soaked dates whizzed in the mixie every morning; a handful of nuts every day; three (mostly healthy) meals a day, though her mother would give them a cake every Sunday when they went to visit, and this she would savour through the week. Every Sunday, her mother asked if she was thinking of applying for a job. Other times she would have been annoyed. Now she would simply laugh and say, 'I know you can't retire, Mummy. So I retired instead. You can't grudge me that, now, can you?'

Monalisa Das had always prided herself on her hawk-like observation of details. So, on some mornings, when Treeza came to yoga with that particularly scrumptious, rosy bedroom glow, Monalisa would wag her fingers at her and raise her eyebrows accusingly. Eerily, she was always right. In the beginning, Treeza would blush. But now it had become yet another ritual in their friendship, and Treeza openly praised Monalisa's impeccable radar. She would tell Monalisa that they could have a burgeoning career in the detection business, specializing in adultery. Treeza would be the secretary, Monalisa could do the detection.

But little did Treeza know of the implications of her handsome John's ardour. Every morning the glow appeared, Monalisa would wonder about John Matthew's stamina. (After returning home at nine o'clock each day? Youth!) And this would set off a healthy chain reaction ending in Monalisa's bedroom. She would be less snappy, she would shower before bedtime and produce little treats for her husband. The boys were not allowed to keep late hours any more, anyway. Also, yoga had made her somewhat more bendy. Mr Das began to sport a glow of sorts. His bald head became shinier.

'So, I'll see you tomorrow morning then? At Sandhyaji's. I wonder what she's going to say.' Treeza said, jangling her key chain.

'Treeza,' Monalisa asked, 'are you free tomorrow afternoon?'

'Oh, no,' replied Treeza. 'I have to dash off to Delhi to meet the PM.' She flashed a smile. 'Of course I'm free. Unemployed and unemployable, says my mother.'

'I need you to come with me somewhere.'

18.4

The campus wore a festive look. Jashn 2013 was scheduled to begin in a day. Excitement was at fever pitch. The committee in charge of décor had done a fairly decent job. The head of décor walked around, clipboard in hand, checking every little detail. The head of food had delegated a bunch of eager first-years to buy all the ingredients—that is the deal they had struck in order to save money as well as provide top-quality fare. He sat in the canteen telling whoever was interested the packed lunch he had planned for each day for the students of the college and those who participated in the events. The finance guys obviously had no time to walk around or talk about food; they were holed up in a room on the second floor, poring over figures and loudly fielding hundreds of calls. There was much swearing in that room. It was all very important.

The music committee members, however, were walking around in little bunches with ashen faces, discussing something urgently.

If anybody asked why they were looking so sullen they would flash false smiles and evade giving a direct reply.

The core group was huddled inside the committee room with the doors closed. Mandy was talking on the phone. When she hung up they all looked at her eagerly. 'No,' she said. 'He can't do anything at such short notice.' She sat down heavily.

'I can't believe this,' Bobby Sen said. 'I just can't believe this.' The others nodded.

'There's still time,' Abeer said. 'We'll figure something out.'

'I hope you can,' Palash Palit lit a cigarette dispiritedly. 'Tomorrow we go live. I still can't imagine how something like this could happen. And that bastard has disappeared from the scene?' Abeer nodded. 'Chalo,' he said, 'We'll speak in a couple of hours, Abeer. AJ.'

Palit and Sen both picked up their bags and left.

Mandy looked devastated. Abeer went over to comfort her. Even now, there was a lurch in his stomach every time he saw her. AJ sat in the corner scribbling in a notebook. The others started filing out, carefully avoiding Mandy.

18.5

From the corridor, Sandhya surveyed the gathering. It was Saturday morning. Lazy and hot.

Dr Sheila was chattering away merrily with Ananda Bose. Possibly about her flight. She'd arrived yesterday after a great deal of trouble. Terrible snowfall in London and Paris had led to several hundred flights being cancelled; mayhem had ensued.

Meera Sahai was demonstrating asanas to Monalisa Das. Monalisa was taking notes. A great one, she was, for taking notes. Meera, who had started yoga with Sandhya only in December, had shown such natural promise that Sandhya had given her a great deal of one-on-one time. She was a natural. Meera had never learnt yoga. But all her childhood she had climbed many trees. Though she was not thin, she was extremely flexible and could easily do many asanas that people who had practised for months did not manage even now. Though depression meant that it was all the more difficult to find the motivation to learn and practise yoga, both Meera and Treeza had managed to persevere with it for the first few weeks, after which it became second nature.

John, Apu and Treeza were conversing in a little group. Apu threw her head back as she laughed.

Apu looked lovely. She wore a white flowing salwar-kurta and a printed silk dupatta. Her hair was untied and was being blown around by the fan. But it was not just the weight she'd lost—though six kilos in three months made a considerable difference; there was something else in her eyes. Something that looked like anticipation, but could well be another thing. Promise, perhaps. Sandhya smiled.

Her odd Calcutta family of eccentrics. Her halfway ashram. Amit would have been amused.

Abeer and AJ had dropped in earlier. Abeer had apologized profusely for not being able to stay on, but there was apparently a massive crisis brewing at their fest. They had wolfed down some refreshments and rushed out importantly. But their friend Molly, the one who had keenly discussed feminism with her, was due to come.

Eventually, Sandhya entered the drawing room which now doubled as the yoga hall every morning. Everyone scrambled onto the mats, looking at her eagerly. She sat at one end.

'Good morning,' Sandhya said. 'Thank you for coming. Dr Sheila and I wanted to share some news with you.

'You must have all wondered at some point what I was doing in Calcutta, in Nancy. I am ready to tell you now.

'Last September I received a somewhat mysterious letter from two solicitors in the city. Pranoy and Praful Sen. It seemed a legacy had been left in trust to me by an old friend. We had lost touch for over three-and-a-half decades. But he'd come across my books and learnt about the work I do. It was a considerable sum, though the Sens said that they could not tell me how much it was before assessing the estate. However, they suggested that I meet them while in India.

'That was when I came to Calcutta from Rishikesh. I met the solicitors and they were very helpful.

'My friend Amit had been an engineer; he headed companies, lectured and mentored senior managers. He never married; he made a lot of money; he lived very modestly. He left exactly half his estate to his nephew and niece; and the other half to the organization. However, his wishes were clear. The money had to be used in India, and preferably in Calcutta.

'The connection to Nancy is even more whimsical. It seems Bishwajit Nandy, the promoter of Nancy, was the son of Amit's old chauffeur. Since this was Bishwajit's first project, Amit ended up buying four of the flats here. He even furnished a couple of them, though he never put them on the market. And these ended up in the part of the estate that came to us. It seems Amit's nephew and niece, neither of whom live in Calcutta, are not interested in these flats at all.

'The legal process of getting the will probated is a long one. It was initiated when I first came down to the city. And the probate has now been obtained. The other parties were aware of the will and did not contest its terms. Dr Sheila and I want to figure out the details in the next few weeks, after which we shall set the money up in a trust and I shall then return to Oxford, to my other home. I am hoping that all of you, my family in the city, will be involved in this organization. All of you for moral support, and some of you as employees, I hope. Then we can begin work. I would like to talk to each of you in more detail in a day or two. And I would welcome all suggestions regarding what the organization we set up can do in and around Calcutta.'

For the first few moments after Sandhya paused, there was silence. Then there was a clamorous response.

'Orphanage,' said Monalisa. She saw herself immediately as a Florence Nightingale-ish character ministering to luckless kids.

Treeza nodded vigorously. She might adopt one of the kids. The darkest, tiniest, saddest one, whom perhaps nobody else would. Treeza and John would fill her life with love.

'Yoga school,' piped Meera. She saw herself in a white salwar suit, lecturing dumpy sari-wearing aunties on their posture. Eventually of course.

'A really bold, really radical women's organization that provides legal aid and protection to battered or abused women and engages in discursive analysis of feminism and yoga. And the body. And female sexuality.' This last was Molly. She had slipped in some time ago and sat with her files and notes at the back. Nobody was surprised any more. In her very first session, in her very first sentence, she had used the words vagina and lesbian, sending the genteel men into a flushed silence and the women into a paroxysm of giggles. If Meera was top student in yoga asanas, Molly was top in theory. Everybody was secretly thrilled by her clothes and missed her on days she couldn't come.

Sandhya smiled. This was exactly what she'd hoped might ensue.

CHAPTER 19

19.1

The fest was off to a flying start. In the afternoon, they got the news through several texts, one after the other. Abeer, AJ and Mandy were in the canteen at Deep's college. Deep, Rahul and Shabnam mirrored their expressions of grave tragedy.

'Mandy, yaar, how could Indian Ocean not have been booked at all?' Shabnam asked. 'I mean, *how?*'

Mandy sighed. 'Look, Rocky was dealing with them. He had some access to a very hotshot Delhi-based event management company. Not Kinjal, through whom we got the others. Someone else. These people had promised a few gigs to Rocky's band. You know how ten per cent is paid on signing, twenty-five per cent of the remainder three months ago and the rest twenty-four hours before they take the stage?'

'Standard practice,' Shriya said.

'Since I was the artist coordinator, I got the cheque made for the first ten per cent and gave it to Rocky. He forwarded it to the events person for Indian Ocean. The date was booked. Three months ago, I prepared the second cheque and gave it to him. He said he forwarded it to the events guy. No reason to worry. It seems this is when trouble started. Rocky's contact left the company and something happened to the cheque. Maybe he didn't deposit it deliberately. Or it got lost. Or maybe Rocky didn't forward it at all. You know he started his internship in December?'

They all nodded.

'He became very busy and didn't even have much time for us. I mean, I was hurt, but what could I do? A week ago I was alerted by someone from the finance team. They said that they'd been doing the final numbers. Though their calculations had been very tight, they found they had nearly a lakh in excess. They went through everything with a fine comb and discovered that our second cheque to Indian Ocean had not been encashed at all. I freaked out and called Rocky. He didn't take my calls all day. In the evening, I went over to his house. His mother behaved rather coldly. Apparently, he's going to Europe to complete the rest of his internship and will only come back to college to take his finals. He was not home. Even if he was at home, he didn't come to meet me. Employed his mother. And she neither knew anything about the fest nor wanted to.'

'Hah?' Everybody looked shocked. 'He didn't tell you himself?'

'Yeah. He sent me a Facebook message saying he was sorry for the "mix-up" over the band, but it was a "small matter". He had also "enjoyed our time together", but given that he was going to be abroad a lot we should not remain "exclusive" any more.'

'Right.' Shabnam stood up. 'Where is the fucker now? As long as he's in Indian territory, I'm going to get some of my army connections to kick his butt.'

'I cried my eyes out for two whole days. I knew the fest was screwed and I should have spoken earlier. But my heart was broken—is broken. Then I confided in Abeer and AJ.' She grasped Shabnam's hand and said, 'Let's save the fest, Shabnam Parveen. Then we'll set the army on him. My name is already in the mud with the music committee. If we can't do anything on Rock Night, it'll be an egg-in-the-face marathon for the rest of my college life.'

'Can't we get someone else?' Shriya asked.

'At such short notice? Kinjal has been on the case day and night. No chance in hell. Indian Ocean is touring abroad right now.' AJ was pragmatic. 'And we even checked with Kailash Kher and Sonu Nigam. Booked out.'

'You know, Sandhyaji told me to "think lateral" when I told her there was a problem. I didn't tell her what problem.'

'Lateral, lateral,' murmured Rahul. 'See, you obviously can't get a sidey band for Rock Night. Not after Rashid Khan and Bhoomi. You have to give it a twist. So lateral is about right.'

'Oh God.' Abeer groaned. 'I can't think any more. I am going to get some tea.'

'We have a class,' said Deep. 'We'll be back in an hour. You guys continue to brainstorm.' They trooped out.

Mandy rested her head on the table. She had no hopes left. Just deserts, she thought mournfully. She had been flying too high; now she was five feet below rock bottom and all the girls who had hated her guts and her iPhone and her dad's car with the bloody red light would have a field day. Shit. Why had Rocky turned out this way? The suave, charming Rocky, who could make her toes curl by simply uttering a few words on the phone, who had kissed her lips and licked her chin and praised her long legs?

Abeer brought back three cups of tea and a newspaper. He tried to distract himself by actually reading it.

AJ wandered off to the counter and returned with a samosa. He broke it in half and offered one part to Mandy. The canteen whirred with the doings of the medical students; some read gigantic books with grotesque drawings, some spoke on the phone, most chatted noisily. Several smoked.

Suddenly, Abeer threw the newspaper down and rapped the table in great excitement. All activity in the canteen ceased for a moment. Everyone looked up and then returned to their business. Only Mandy and AJ looked at him. There was not much hope in their eyes. Mandy had huge dark circles underneath hers.

'I think I know what we can do. An idea is taking form in my head. AJ, call Molly this instant. Even if she has a class with the ghost of Shakespeare, she should forget about it and come here right now.'

19.2

When Monalisa and Treeza reached the school and paid off the fees at the counter, the school-gate moms had just begun to get into their stride. It was half past twelve. They were talking loudly, swapping old question papers, exchanging notes about tuition teachers and ladies' tailors in their respective neighbourhoods.

'These are the women who terrify you?' Treeza asked, surprised. They were middle-aged women with tired lines on their faces and dowdy clothes. All of them looked pinched and stressed. 'They spend the whole day here? Waiting for their sons?'

Monalisa nodded solemnly. 'They make me really nervous about the boys' futures.'

'I can tell you what is in their boys' futures. Horrible fights between these mothers and whoever they have the misfortune to marry.'

'Don't say misfortune, Treeza. Many of these boys are brilliant.'

'Brilliant-shmilliant.' said Treeza. 'They must be as boring as their mothers! Use your radar, na. Tell me who has got some bedroom action in the recent past.'

Monalisa looked at them critically. 'None, I'm sorry to say.'

They giggled like schoolgirls.

Mrs Ghoshal, boss of the school-gate moms, happened to glance their way. 'Ei, Monalisa na? How are you?' She came to them immediately. 'Was there any problem with Bablu? He was absent from school for three weeks or so? Must have missed a lot of stuff.'

'Yes, Mrs Ghoshal, he was very unwell. After that we sent him on a holiday to recuperate,' Monalisa said. 'He's much better now, thank you,' she added pointedly.

'Oh,' said Mrs Ghoshal. 'I hear you have put him in Baraha Bagchi's tuition. My God, that is like cracking the IIT! How did you get him in?'

'He did join, Boudi, but he's left Bor Da's tuition now.'

'Left it? Permanently left it? After getting in? *Why?*' Mrs Ghoshal was flabbergasted.

'Too much pressure, Boudi. Maths is not his strong point anyway.'

'Baba, you're very casual about these things toh, Monalisa? I wish I could be like you.'

'It's not so hard, Mrs Ghoshal,' Monalisa said, feeling a sudden real tug in her heart. Mrs Ghoshal was a short dumpy woman who wore printed saris with mismatched blouses and carried a huge bag. She brought breakfast for herself and her son, lunch, and then a snack. Her husband worked at the post office. 'It is important to let go of our children. Do you see that banyan tree?' Luckily the gigantic banyan tree was right where they stood. 'Now tell me: where is its mother?'

Confused and irritated, Mrs Ghoshal muttered something under her breath and walked off.

19.3

By the time she was into her tenth round, Apu would feel very, very angry. Everything would annoy her. The heat, the park, the pathway, her shoes, her uncomfortably sweaty kurti. It was only after she hit the fifteenth round that she began to relax again, and run fast and free to complete the cycle. And when she did, it was a great high.

Today was no exception. She came to her favourite bench under the gulmohar tree and drank some water. Ananda was lying on the grass. He'd finished his rounds quicker than her. He got up and sat next to her. 'It's only five o'clock. We can still make it,' he said.

Apu groaned. She didn't feel like dressing up at all. Abeer, AJ and Mandy had invited them to the fest with great fanfare. Special passes and all. Today was the world-famous Eastern Night.

'It's Rashid Khan,' Ananda continued. 'It would be well worth it. Plus, they've put in so much effort…'

'Fine, fine,' said Apu with ill grace. 'But it'll take me time to get ready. Apparently, all the women wear saris on Eastern Night.'

'Oh?' said Ananda, a little taken aback. 'Sure. Take your time.'

An hour later, Apu came downstairs. Ananda Bose was waiting in a taxi. Apu was wearing the light pink chiffon with little silver sequins studded far apart (the same one that she had been wearing in the digitally re-mastered version of herself) and a pair of meenakari jhumkas borrowed from Meera. Her hair was left loose on her shoulders and she wore the slightest hint of kajal and a very light pink lip gloss. She looked so natural and lovely that Ananda Bose turned his face away for a second. Then he looked at her and smiled. She didn't see. Her brows were furrowed in concentration. She took every step towards the taxi carefully, as though afraid of a landmine in the way. She held up her sari with her right hand and Ananda saw she was wearing a pair of pretty pink slippers with high heels.

It was only when she was safely inside the taxi and the driver shut the door carefully that Apu looked at Ananda and smiled that warm, utterly unselfconscious smile. She made a bit of an apologetic gesture, scrunching her nose up. 'Sorry,' she mouthed.

Suddenly, Ananda felt a very strange sensation in his stomach. A swirly feeling. What had he had for lunch, he tried to ask himself. But he got distracted again at the sight of Apu busily arranging her pallu. He blushed and looked away.

After a few minutes, the sense of awkwardness dissolved. They chatted about what Sandhyaji had said. Its vast and wonderful possibilities.

Then, out of the blue, Apu asked him, 'Why did you come back from America after one year, Ananda? I'd meant to ask.'

'I never went with the idea of settling there, Apu. I went on a fellowship for young lecturers for a year. And I understood again how much of a misfit I am. I spent all my adult life deeply embedded in Western philosophy, only to find I did not like the West.'

He laughed. Apu merely smiled politely. He saw she expected her to continue.

'And now I'm so glad I didn't. I do not like the idea of America, you know. Its exaggerated sense of its own worth, its talk of democracy while constantly waging war and destabilizing other nations, its self-righteousness, its arrogance. Anyway, don't let me rant. Weren't you saying I had improved from my previous boring self?'

Apu's phone rang. It was Abeer. 'Hi, Didi. Are you guys on the way?'

'Yes. We are.'

'Right, so, everything is on track. But because of the crisis I am not going to be there. AJ can…'

'That's fine,' said Apu. 'Ananda and I can take care of ourselves. We have the passes. You go save the world.'

'So there's no need for AJ to be there either? That's great. Thanks!'

'We're almost there, I think,' Ananda said. 'Isn't that the road to their college?'

19.4

When the show got over at eight-thirty, there was not a taxi in sight. Apu and Ananda had to walk.

'It was a wonderful show, wasn't it?' Apu said. 'My favourite song is, of course, "Aoge Jab Tum, Saajna". I'm so glad he sang it twice.'

'Well, you begged him to, didn't you? Shouting from the first row like a schoolgirl.' Ananda was amused.

None of Abeer's gang had been there, and it was all for the better. Apu could slip into her own youth—as did, she suspected, Ananda.

Within ten minutes of walking, Apu handed her purse to Ananda, struggling with her heels and her sari. 'See, this is why I don't believe in fashion,' she said, annoyed. The saving grace was that at least the weather was spectacular. Clear skies studded with stars, a proper spring breeze.

At the crossing, they came to one of those little buildings which housed several shops. It was brightly lit. Apu said they'd have to take a break. Her feet were killing her. Ananda said those were his sentiments exactly, and asked her to wait for a moment. He disappeared inside. Then he came out after a few minutes with a mysterious package.

Apu was sitting on one of the benches in front, resting her feet. She had taken off those heels and was rubbing her feet. They were such pretty shoes, she reflected mournfully, but so uncomfortable.

Ananda walked up to her and said, 'Try these instead.'

He placed before her, on the ground, two pink chappals.

Apu was startled.

'It's nothing,' Ananda clarified quickly. 'A school friend of mine owns a shoe shop in this complex.'

Apu felt a swoop inside her chest. 'Thank you,' she said, slipping her feet into the chappals. 'These are most comfortable.'

They reached home around nine-thirty. They'd found a taxi only near the bridge.

'I had such a great time, Apu,' Ananda said as they reached A-3. It seemed as though he wanted to say more, thank her profusely like he would have in the past—but he didn't. He just waved.

'I had a wonderful time too. See you tomorrow.'

Apu lingered until the taxi backed up, and then went straight and right to A-5. Slowly she climbed the stairs, thinking of the evening again. The songs, the walk, the ease of it all.

As she rang the bell, that curious feeling continued to swirl inside her, a light spring breeze that carried the scent of flowers.

Mrs Mukherjee opened the door wearing a radiant smile.

The moment Apu entered the doorway and got rid of her purse, her mother began to talk. She didn't even notice that Apu was carrying her shoes in a packet in her hand and wearing new pink chappals. 'Apu, Moni Mashi called,' she reported excitedly, 'Abhiroop is in town. He's returned to India earlier than expected. He wants to meet you. At the soonest.'

19.5

'I would like it very much if you come with me, Apu,' Sandhya said. 'We could talk in the car.'

'Certainly, Mataji,' Apu replied. 'Let me just text my mother. Shall we be back by noon?'

'I should think so. It's only half-eight now anyway.'

'She's got some beauty parlour lady to come at one. Wants to spit-polish me before I meet the guy this evening.'

'Ah! The Chicago groom is here. Is the family going to come over then?'

'Oh, no,' Apu said. 'He wants to take me to dinner alone. At the ITC.'

'That's rather fancy.' Sandhya smiled.

Apu nodded weakly and followed Sandhya to the car. She had no idea why she was feeling so sick. In the last three months, her recurrent nightmare had been meeting the Chicago boy and family but without having lost any weight. And then Moni Mashi concocting a wild and improbable story about how she had gained seven kilos after the pujas to help physically challenged children by buying cakes they'd baked or something. At least that was not happening. She had actually—miracle of miracles—lost six kilos. Seven, perhaps. She hadn't taken her weight since Monday last. And yet, she felt hardly any excitement about this dinner date. It was as though there was a ball of lead suspended in her stomach.

It was a gorgeous house that Sandhya took Apu to. A large mansion with a pillared portico in front. The caretaker led them through a slightly cavernous hallway with paintings on the walls to the interior of the house. A large square courtyard stood in the middle, surrounded on all sides by a red veranda. Rooms opened onto the veranda, though the house was clearly unoccupied. The caretaker took them upstairs to a study. The room had chessboard flooring and bookshelves on all sides, filled with classics. At one end of the room was a large table with a stand lamp on one side. At the other end were a carpet and several sofas. That is where Sandhya and Apu made themselves comfortable. The caretaker would not take no for an answer and went to get them tea.

'Whose house is this?' Apu finally broke the silence.

Sandhya had been absorbed in thought. 'This is Amit Ray's house, Apu.'

'Of course,' Apu said, things falling into place. 'The décor is a lot like your drawing room in Nancy.'

'That's right.' Sandhya smiled. 'That's exactly what I thought when I came here the first time. I've been here once or twice now.'

Apu nodded.

'I had just turned twenty-three when I met him. He was studying at Imperial College. Doing a doctorate on something extremely obscure. Our band was performing at the Central London Polytechnic. He'd been invited by a friend. He came up and spoke to me after the show, thinking I was from India. I told him I was an East Indian. He promptly invited me for dinner. Until then, I had never dated an Indian. One or two white guys, several black guys. But the Indians I met those days were too goody-goody for me. Not Amit, though. He said he'd been named after an iconic character in a Bengali novel, so he had a sort of duty to be romantic.'

'The hero of Tagore's *Shesher Kobita* is called Amit Ray,' Apu supplied.

The caretaker arrived with a tea tray. He poured two cups, asked about milk and sugar, then shut the door behind him discreetly and left.

Sandhya said, 'We were engaged in three weeks.'

'Wow! That was impulsive.'

'It was a very impulsive time, my dear.' Sandhya's eyes twinkled. 'We were inseparable. We went on a trip to Venice, where we decided in St Mark's Square that we would marry as soon as we could. He found me a Murano glass engagement ring. He would bring me to Calcutta. He loved the city. Talked about its spirit all the time. He'd described this house to me in detail. At that time, it was full of people. Now it's just the nephew and niece who no longer live here. After we perfected the plans, and went over them again and again, tinkering with details here or there, I returned to London for the time-being. I was just achieving some success as a producer, so I couldn't be away too long. He would return to Calcutta via Calais and speak to his parents. He insisted that after he returned to England we must go and meet my parents. The thought of home always filled me with trepidation. But with him I was willing to admit that it might not be such a bad thing. For one, my father had always wanted to build ties with India. For another, Amit was not only a very handsome man but also had all the sort of degrees that my father had wanted me to get. He would approve of him, whether or not he approved of what I'd become. It was the happiest summer of my life, Apu. In spite of those nightmares I would have regularly, it was a heavenly summer. Brittle and evanescent, but heavenly.'

'You were diagnosed after you returned?'

'Ten days after I returned.'

'You didn't tell him?'

'No. I wrote him a letter breaking off our ties. I was young and vain, Apu. I could not trust our love enough to think it would survive the loss of a breast. I never told him the truth.' Sandhya smiled sadly.

'His father died. He stayed on in India. I never replied to his letters. He even called several times, though it was prohibitively expensive. I had become very bitter then, Apu. I did not want his sympathy. I wanted him to always have the memory of our perfect summer. The only people whose company I could tolerate were other cancer patients. I was stupid and shallow and cruel.'

'How did he find you afterwards?'

'This I learnt later. From one of the letters left in custody of the lawyers. While on a holiday to the US, he found one of my books.'

'He never married?'

'He never married.'

Apu sighed. It was a sad story. It made her feel positively wretched now. It was not as though she didn't trust Sandhyaji one hundred per cent—she did—but why did Sandhyaji have to tell her this? This was exactly the sort of story she did not want to hear.

CHAPTER 20

20.1

'On the upside, we have the funds. Bus, T-shirts, portable stereophonic music system and speakers, network support, we can easily manage all this.' AJ sounded upbeat.

'On the downside, we barely have any time.' Mandy sounded exhausted.

'Since it's a do-or-die mission, we will have to divide the work,' Abeer said. 'AJ, Palit and Sen are waiting for instructions. Take care of the business end.'

'Done,' said AJ.

'Mandy, have you got the names of the juniors with you?'

'Yes,' she replied. 'I've got 300 names here.'

'I'll get another 200,' Molly replied, 'Easily.'

'Right. So why don't you two and Shriya go to college and sort this out? You have till tomorrow afternoon to fine-tune the details.'

'Let's go in my car,' said Mandy. 'It's outside.'

They left quickly. There was much to be done.

'Deep and Rahul, you're on social network strategy.' Abeer instructed.

'On it,' they chimed.

'Now, Shabnam Parveen, let's go and tackle the lieutenant general.'

20.2

'One Billion Rising?'

'Exactly, sir,' said Abeer.

'Hmm,' replied Lieutenant General Mahmood, GOC, Bengal Area. 'Baburam, please get us some cake.'

'That means it's looking good,' Shabnam whispered to Abeer.

'Sit down, Mr Mukherjee,' said Lt Gen. Mahmood.

Abeer had made a dynamic presentation on his laptop. He knew it would not be possible to convince the Lt. Gen. otherwise. He sat down at the edge of the sofa.

'It cannot be denied that it is a fabulous idea Abba,' said his eldest daughter, Sahar Anjum, who was a feisty political correspondent (married to an investigative journalist) in Delhi and visiting her father for a few days. 'It's actually a spectacular idea,' she said.

'Have I denied it's a good idea? Have I said that it's not an important issue?' said the Lt. Gen. gravely. 'It's just that all good ideas cannot be implemented. Tell me, Mr Mukherjee, realistically, how on earth can I set such a precedent? Take my advice: do it in your college.'

Baburam brought cake. Abeer took a slice and bit into it morosely. It tasted a bit weird.

'Oh, come on, Abba! What impact will it create on a wider scale if it is just performed in a college?' The Lt. Gen.'s youngest, Mehr Mounira, now jumped into the fray. 'I mean, think about it. If this happens, it'll be in keeping with the ethics of the army anyway. The army will look cool.'

'The army *is* cool,' said the Lt. Gen.

His daughters rolled their eyes.

'It can always get cooler, Abba, think about it,' purred Mehr, perching on one arm of her father's chair. She was the baby of the family. She had been only three when the Lt. Gen. lost his wife. He could hardly ever say no to her.

'Let me put it starkly, Abba. One in three women on the planet will be raped or beaten in her lifetime. You have three daughters. What does it mean?'

That did it.

'Okay, okay, that's enough. Now get out of here, all three of you, always emotionally blackmailing me... Do you understand how much paperwork this is going to be, Mr Mukherjee?' The Lt. Gen. sighed. 'Why aren't you eating the cake? I baked it this morning. It's a healthy cake: gur instead of sugar and applesauce instead of butter.'

Immediately, Abeer crammed the slice into his mouth.

20.3

'Hello, Tara, this is Charlie. Charlie, Tara.'

The two five-year-olds considered each other gravely.

'Hi,' said Charlie. 'I was playing a computer game. You want to play?'

'Sure,' said Tara. 'But I always win.'

Charlie looked her up and down and said, 'I always win too.'

They went into John's study. Soon, much shouting was heard. John popped out from the study for a moment, said hi to Meera and went right back in. He closed the door.

'Your nephew is very cute, Treeza,' Meera said. 'Will he stay for a few days?'

'Oh, no. We'll go and drop him tonight. He's just spending the day with us.'

Treeza took the baby from Meera's lap and tickled her under the chin. Chhoti gurgled with pleasure. 'So, I hear Lalita Pawar is back. How is she reacting to your yoga lessons?'

Meera burst out laughing. 'Lalita Pawar! You're so funny, Treeza. I must tell Nalini Bhabhi this name.' She giggled some more. 'Well, actually, she is fine with it. It's just that I'm having to teach her too.'

'Really?'

'Yes. So, every evening, she and I sit facing each other. And I get to lecture.'

'We won, we won, we won,' the kids shrieked and rushed out of the study.

The adults left them to their devices and basked in the mellow glow of the afternoon.

20.4

Mr Mukherjee manoeuvred his Maruti 800 adeptly through the endless rivers of traffic that flowed along the Eastern Metropolitan Bypass. How Apu wished she'd been going to the trade fair instead. She would look at stuff and eat fish fries. Shit, she was fantasizing about food again. That had completely stopped these last three months. She must be really stressed. Why couldn't it be an informal chat in a coffee shop in lieu of this five-star affair? Mrs Mukherjee was babbling so foolishly in her excitement that Apu had refused to speak to her for the entire duration of the journey; that meant she was stuck in her own thoughts. That bloody ball of lead in her stomach was getting heavier and heavier. Maybe he'll reject me, she thought, and then we'll be done with it.

The parents dropped her off in front of the hotel at exactly twenty past seven, promising to pick her up whenever she wanted. 'Of course,' said Apu's mother hurriedly, as Apu shut the door on her side and rearranged her sari pallu, 'if he wants to drop you home, then just go with him. Text us, and we'll come home by ourselves. And do invite him to our house along with his family when they return from Kerala. Okay?'

As she walked into the lobby, Apu could hear Sandhya's voice in her head: 'Straighten your spine!' She drew herself up to her full height. Her hair, which had been shampooed and beautifully blow-dried by the parlour lady, cascaded down her back in abandon. The lady had asked her if she wanted her hair straightened, but she didn't—she liked the curly mass.

Other than taking her along to the tailor to order her blouse, Mrs Mukherjee had acted completely independently on the matter of Apu's outfit. The sari was a sheer black tissue number with a thin gold border on both sides. It had cost a bomb. But then Mrs Mukherjee knew a good investment when she saw one. 'Even your daughter can wear it, Apu, it's one of those classic saris,' she'd said, fondly fastening a black-and-dull-gold choker around her throat. Great, so now she had progressed from dreaming about force-feeding her son-in-law on jamai shashthi to bouncing grandchildren on her lap—talk about pressure on a girl—Apu had thought.

There was still some time. Apu went into the ladies' room and freshened her lipstick. She looked at herself in the mirror and smiled tentatively. For a second, the ball of lead vanished from her stomach. It was really the blouse that made this such a remarkable ensemble. It was a black, silken, cleverly cut item with a little air-hostess collar and sleeves that were short but so delicately flared that the arms which emerged from them looked slimmer than they were. Maybe *I'll* reject him, Apu told herself, trying to galvanize what courage swirled inside.

'Aparajita?' the guy enquired when Apu walked into the dimly lit restaurant.

'Hello,' Apu said, smiling politely. 'You must be Abhiroop.'

Abhiroop was not as tall as Moni Mashi had claimed; he was only a couple of inches taller than Apu. He wore a powder-blue shirt with trousers and had one of those closely cropped corporate hi-flier hairstyles. Expensive-looking rimless glasses. An ordinary face with an ordinary forehead, Apu decided. That was fine, wasn't it? In any case, who knew the comparative worth of an extraordinary nose and an extraordinary forehead against an extraordinary CV?

'Please come,' he said expansively. 'This way.'

Abhiroop had an American twang. He led the way, bobbing importantly on his feet. They were surprisingly small feet, Apu noticed as she reached their table. In very highly polished black shoes. Apu realized with a sinking feeling that she had slipped into a terrible cliché from somewhere. She thought about the food. She would order something neat and eat it tidily, though naturally she couldn't stuff her face. Why was it that one always came to fancy eateries with people in front of whom one couldn't eat properly? Now, if she'd come with AB, they'd have really made good use of that buffet displayed so temptingly at the far end.

'It's very nice to meet you finally,' Abhiroop Lahiri said when they'd seated themselves in a corner. 'You are more beautiful in person actually,' he said.

Apu smiled and was about to thank him, but Abhiroop Lahiri had already moved on from there.

'Gawd, it feels good to be in Calcutta.' He looked around appreciatively.

How was this five-star hotel Calcutta, Apu thought, and then checked herself. She ought not to be catty.

'Have you been to the book fair?' she asked him conversationally. She had thought up the question on the way.

He passed on the menu to her. As Apu perused it, he said, 'Book fair, eh? Nah! I can't bear so much dust any longer. I have this allergy. You see, the place where I live, Evanston, the air there is so fresh, so pollution-free that now I can't stay on in India for anything more than three weeks.' He made a mock sheepish grimace. 'In any case, books on my subject and my interest area are not available in India. No point, really. Do you need any help with that?' he gestured to the menu. 'I make it a point to come here as often as I can when I'm in Calcutta. I think you might like the dum pukht kakori. Shall I order that for you? And a glass of red wine?'

'Umm, sure, that sounds fine,' Apu said, though she'd have preferred fish. 'But I'd like white wine please.'

Lahiri summoned the young waiter to their table imperiously and said, 'One Scotch on the rocks for me. A glass of red wine for the lady.'

'White wine,' Apu corrected.

'Right, sawrry, a glass of white wine for the lady. Aur dum pukht kakori, yaar.'

Abhiroop Lahiri was quite the talker. In fact, Apu thought, some women might have even found him charming, in a brash, cocky sort of way. As for what she thought of him—she hadn't let herself get to that just yet. She just relaxed and tried to let the wine and the dim lights and lavish décor weave a spell around her. The food was delicious. And the good thing was that he didn't expect her to talk much. He was sort of demystifying himself for her benefit. It was all right, really. How on earth could she make up her mind unless she knew enough about him? She tried to listen, though sometimes the conversation at the next table got extremely interesting and she got a little distracted. (It was an emotional debate between pati, patni and woh.) But on the whole, she got the exquisite beauty of Lake Michigan, the charms of Evanston, its good healthcare system, its superior transport system and the fact that it had a pretty strong network of likeminded Bengalis who got together every other Saturday and cooked up a storm and enjoyed adda that went on till the wee hours of the morning.

However, by the time the main course came along—biriyani and murg khuskh parda ('A sort of a Mughlai chicken pot pie. Do you know what a pot pie is?')—the ménage à trois had left, both women in tears, and Abhiroop Lahiri was talking about his work.

'What I do directly saves lives. For instance, our programs improved the efficacy of the guided bombs by several factors. These were used by the US Air Force in Libya. That way collateral damage was literally reduced to a minimum.'

'Libya?' asked Apu, looking up from her plate.

'Ya,' said Lahiri. 'The war actually demonstrated the critical importance of the work we do, you see. We got a huge grant after that.'

'Right,' said Apu, returning to her food. The rice seemed to stick in her throat. She sipped water from her glass.

'Currently I'm working on a project called Prong Global Strike. It's a program that is being developed so the US military can hit time-centred targets anywhere in the world in less than an hour. You can imagine how this will benefit the war on terror, right?'

'I can imagine,' Apu said weakly, pushing the plate away.

'If we had this kind of technology before, Aparajita, 9/11 need never have happened. It seems in 1998, Osama bin Laden had been tracked down and Tomahawks been despatched to deal with him. But those took three-and-a-half hours to get there—by then Osama had left... You're not eating, Aparajita?'

'I'm full,' she said. 'The food was fantastic.'

'I'm glad you enjoyed,' Lahiri said. 'Very glad. I wanted to bring you some place special, you know. Where we could talk in peace. So, tell me about your work,' he said.

'I'm a botanist.'

'Hmm. I understand you are a fantastic cook?'

'Oh, no,' said Apu. 'That's my mother.'

'Right, right. Would you like dessert?'

'No.' Apu was firm. 'I'm absolutely full. But you help yourself.'

'No, no dessert for me today. It's my cousin's birthday, so a whole gang of us will go and surprise her at midnight. She lives in Hind Motors. It'll take us a couple of hours to get there. Traffic in the city is getting from bad to worse, don't you think? Every time I come, I wonder how people live here. Anyway, how are you going home? I would have dropped you off if it weren't for this.'

'Don't worry,' said Apu. 'I've made my arrangements.'

'Let's all meet after we're back from Kerala?'

'Sure. Thanks again, Abhiroop. Dinner was delicious.'

Abhiroop Lahiri left, after promising to meet up soon. Apu wandered off to the lobby and dialled Sadia's number. She was in Kashmir again for Valentine's Day, sans kids. Oof, just when she was needed the most!

20.5

Dr Sheila entered the room and saw that Sandhya was alone.

'What did he say?'

'He agreed. He was actually very happy, Sheila.'

'See, I'd told you.'

'But it'll be a while before he can quit his school. And he cannot leave his private students in the lurch either. So ironing it all out will take time. But, in principle, he agrees.'

'So the first and most important thing has been achieved then: the Prakriti Foundation has acquired its chief executive. John Matthew.'

'We couldn't have done better, Sheila, could we?'

'No chance,' said Dr Sheila. 'So, Mary Poppins, are you ready to return now?'

'I think so.' Sandhya smiled. 'I have finally come to terms with Calcutta.'

CHAPTER 21

21.1

By seven o'clock, there were some thousand-odd students gathered in the grounds of the institute. 'Is Indian Ocean performing?' Aniruddha Chaki of St Xaviers asked Simarpreet Kaur of IIT KGP. 'No, I don't think so,' she said. 'But it's apparently a promising band.'

'Is it Miles, then?' T. K. Chitra of Basanti Debi College asked Prateek Mehta from Bhawanipore Education Society. Prateek Mehta, who was busy tweeting, merely shrugged. He had no idea.

The grounds were surrounded by the steel-and-glass buildings on three sides. Gigantic swatches of pink satin had been draped artistically on the building facades. They glimmered in the evening light, billowed in the breeze.

'Why is there no sign of the band, man?' Akira Mitra of IIM-C nudged Rincy George of Scottish Church. 'It's weird.' Rincy agreed.

The students of the institute were pretty tight-lipped. Many of them had no idea what was going on.

The crowd swelled and became restive. Why were there no chairs, the young people wondered.

Suddenly, there was a commotion. Everybody began to point in one direction, towards the middle of the grounds, where the crowd was the thickest. Standing on a gigantic speaker, a girl was dancing wildly. There was the ambient noise all around. Chattering, tittering, laughter. People moved back. Many of them began recording this utter strangeness on their mobiles.

All of a sudden, there was music. The girl jumped off the speaker into the clearing the crowd had created for her. Her movements became orderly and choreographed. Another girl came and joined her. Then a boy. The three danced in perfect co-ordination. Simple, clean steps. The music was rousing. In half a minute, there was a chant that was being sung to the tune.

> *Claim the night!*
> *Claim the night!*
> *One billion rising*
> *to claim the night!*

In front of people's eyes, three became six, six became thirty and thirty became ninety. It was uncanny. Aniruddha Chaki of St Xaviers suddenly found Simarpreet Kaur rushing to join the group.

The music gave way to great cacophony: shouting, shrieking, crying, pleading. The dancers cowered and crawled on all fours. Then they raised posters in their hands, called for an end to violence against women.

The rousing bars of *Rang De Basanti* changed the tenor abruptly. Hundred became 500. Girls and boys dancing for freedom.

At a quivering high, the music ended and cries of 'Claim the night!' rent the air.

Mandakini Mandal took the stage and spoke clearly into the microphone. 'Thank you, everyone, for being a part of this unique flash mob. Today is 14th February. The day of the pink revolution. All around the globe, men and women are flash-mobbing together to end violence against women. Tonight, on behalf of women everywhere, we shall claim the night. Listen to me, please. History is in the making. And all of you are part of this moment when we students shall take this outside. We have made all the arrangements.'

There was a massive surge towards Mandy's makeshift stage—and

Abeer felt a little worried for a moment—but it seemed everybody was eager to hear what was being said.

21.2

In the meantime, two people were sitting in the leafy park near Nancy. They had taken a break from the exercise routine. At seven-thirty, however, Apu had texted Ananda saying that she was going for a walk anyway, would he like to come? He had joined her, and they'd walked to the park together. Now they sat morosely on their regular bench.

'Congratulations,' said Ananda thickly. 'I wish you and Shri Lahiri a very happy life together.' His tone suggested that he wished them a painful pus-ridden time in a Christian hell.

'What rubbish are you talking?' Apu asked, annoyed beyond all measure.

'You know what I am talking about. Your engagement.'

'And who has given you that good news?'

'Your mother. I met her in the market this morning.' Ananda had spent the day moping in bed. If only he hadn't been maintaining all the bloody rules of a Hindu mourner (more correctly, rational materialist mourner of Hindu parent), he would have finished a bottle of whisky by now. 'You could have told me yourself. I thought we were friends.'

This statement angered Apu even more. Friends. Really? Why was she wasting her time? Maybe she should just say yes to Lahiri. But the thought of that pompous prat making love to her in a prim apartment in the dust-free, pollution-free, roads-paved-with gold town of Evanston or whatever, after which he would rush to design a micro-chip that would do effective selection of American bombing targets in the Middle East while she cooked some of her mother's recipes, was nauseating. The very thought of a lifetime with Abhiroop Lahiri made her skin prickle.

'I *would* have told you if there had been anything to tell. I am *not* engaged.'

'You mean not *yet* engaged.'

'Not that it is any of your business, but I may not be engaged ever.'

'To Shri Lahiri or anyone at all?'

Apu stopped herself from jumping on him and rubbing his head in the mud where he did his bloody push-ups and recharged his batteries. 'Stop calling him *Shri* Lahiri!' she yelled.

'You are really not engaged, Apu?' Ananda asked, his AIR voice all deep and meaningful suddenly.

'No.' Apu sighed.

'In that case, there are no moral compunctions about my asking you this. Would you consider being engaged to *me*?'

Apu's instinct to pound him to paste became stronger. 'Why on earth would I consider that?' she demanded.

Ananda's face fell.

'Have you bothered to tell me that you love me and can't live without me—or anything of the sort?'

'But I do, Apu!' Ananda said. 'I have loved you for a long time, I think. But I am old, I am not a scientist in Chicago, I wasn't sure what your parents would think of me, I never took you to a five-star hotel for dinner.'

'Well,' said Apu. 'At least you bought me pink chappals.'

There was something in her voice that made Ananda pick her hand up from the bench. It was soft and warm and she had lovely long fingers. 'On the slender off-chance that your mother did not have the correct information and you had, indeed, rejected Chicago Lahiri, I brought you this.' From his pocket, Ananda took out his handkerchief. Inside its folds was a little velvet bag. He pushed it into Apu's palm.

Intrigued, Apu opened the little velvet string tying it together.

'My grandfather made it for my grandmother after she passed her BA examinations. I thought you might like it,' Ananda said humbly.

It was an exquisite pendant. An oval miniature—an actual

miniature in the Kangra style—set in a gold frame. It showed a beautiful, long-haired girl reading a book under a tree.

'He was an artist, you see. I would have liked to get you one with a picture of a long-haired girl doing jumping jacks, but Chicago Lahiri hurried my move.'

By now, Ananda's breath was on Apu's shoulder, and somehow or the other she found she was in his arms.

'Wait, wait, I have one question,' Apu said, breaking away. 'You don't love that Benaras Malini any more, right?'

Ananda said, his voice husky, 'I know you are a very educated girl with many degrees and all that. But when you ask such silly questions, I must shut you up.'

He kissed her softly.

Then he kissed her some more.

And then, finally, he kissed her so that she felt she was the first woman in the world who had felt such intense beauty and pain and happiness all at once.

Then Apu's phone beeped.

They broke apart guiltily, and scrabbled around for her phone. It was lying on the grass. There was a cryptic text from Abeer: 'Success. See you and AB da at the end.'

21.3

In fifteen minutes, the Kolkata flash mob was trending wildly on social media. Videos were posted on Youtube. Twitter was abuzz. Facebook began to track its purported 'outward movement' from the campus into the city.

At eight-thirty, the flash mob performed at the 8B bus-stop in Jadavpur. At nine-thirty, as wild rumours circulated on the web, it was observed in Park Street, where friends, lovers and those in between were celebrating Valentine's Day. At ten-thirty, the flash mob took Howrah Station. The numbers of placard-bearing supporters who marked the performance space with their body was increasing rapidly. The numbers of performers too had grown in leaps and bounds. It seemed there were several talented dancers around, perfectly capable of learning the steps from Youtube and debuting directly on stage.

By eleven o'clock, the press in Kolkata was covering it as breaking news. The symbolic cry of women claiming the night was being hailed by all. The students, however, keeping to the classic style of flash mobs, were vanishing immediately after their performance. But at every location, they left their placards.

At eleven-thirty, the police commissioner had to get out of bed, put on his uniform and summon his driver. At eleven-forty, he received a phone call from the chief minister.

21.4

At eleven-fifty, when the spontaneous gathering of young people and old people (and everyone in between) near Victoria Memorial had reached worrying proportions, Lt. Gen. Mahmood, father of three daughters, all of whom were in that cauldron of drama, received a call from the commissioner.

'I expect you know about the 10,000 people who are milling about Victoria, Naseer,' said the commissioner. 'Do you know something I don't? Where are your people?'

'As it happens, Samar, the event has our clearance. But I suggest you don't worry. I have it covered.'

'Remind me, Lt. Gen. Mahmood,' said the commissioner to his tennis buddy, 'to kick your butt when I see you next.'

The people who were waiting expectantly for something to happen, including the newly engaged Aparajita Mukherjee and Ananda Bose, suddenly heard a chopper flying overhead.

'Shit, shit, shit,' said Prantik Sarkar, 'they're setting the army on us.'

'Can the state actually *do* such a thing?' a belligerent Sahar Anjum shouted to her sisters. 'They're students, for God's sake.' And then she remembered that in this case it was her father who had sent the helicopters. As per plan.

One by one, female officers of the Parachute Regiment posted in Bengal shimmied down the ropes. 'One billion rising!' shouted the crowd. 'Women reclaim the night!' While the officers spread out into the grounds, two marched towards the gates and opened them. The giant human hotbed entered, jostling and pushing, as one body. The women army officers stood marking the area which had been cleared for the flash mob. Placard-bearers joined them and made the boundary thicker.

After a few minutes, a girl stood on a wooden chest and began to dance in silence. An electric frisson shuddered through the crowd. Then, when the music started, she jumped off and danced in the middle to choreographed steps. She was joined by another girl, and then a boy. The crowd chanted alongside:

> *Claim the night!*
> *Claim the night!*
> *One billion rising*
> *to claim the night!*

Three became six, six became thirty, thirty became ninety, and ninety was multiplied by first ten, and then hundred. The full moon shone on them as they danced.

Molly and AJ were in that crowd, dancing.

'You move well,' said Molly to AJ.

AJ blushed. 'So do you,' he managed to say. He was grateful to Molly for that—if she hadn't cast them in the JU project, he'd never have learnt dancing.

'You remember that movie? *Friends with Benefits*?' Molly asked. AJ nodded, trying hard to keep up with his gyrating partner. 'So...' said Molly. 'Do you want to be? Friends with benefits?'

AJ stumbled, crashed into someone else, was pushed back genially. 'Uh. Umm. No,' he managed to mumble.

Molly was stunned. This was not the answer she had expected. Not at all. Not after these many months of watching AJ watch her.

'I, uh...' AJ's voice trailed off. Laughing, dancing, chattering people brushed past them. After a moment or two, AJ spoke again, his voice firm. 'It's not just benefits I want from you, Molly.'

It was Molly's turn to blush.

At the other end of the cordon, in the shadow of huge boom-box speakers that spilt intoxicating rhythms into the grounds of Victoria, Abeer Mukherjee and Mandakini Mandal danced. The trees were silver in the moonlight. The grass was soft and dewy under their bare feet.

'Thank you,' mouthed Mandy.

Abeer waved away her thanks with a smile. It was nothing. He could have done much, much more for her.

ACKNOWLEDGEMENTS

I had often heard writers claim that so-and-so character floated into their room and demanded to be written about—I always thought it was a bit of a stretch. But I was writing about our travels through India on an extreme budget when Monalisa Das interrupted. And not happy with merely forcing me to engage with her sons and the patron ghosts of mathematics, she brought the entire cast of Nancy clamouring in. I still do not know what happened, but somewhere down the line this book emerged.

The Weight Loss Club would not have been written without the following.

Bri. Maya Tiwari, whose book *The Path of Practice* (Motilal Banarassidas, 2002) I encountered in 2007, and to which I return to again and again, dipping into its wisdom and soaking in the sense of calm, unalloyed strength it evokes. Though I have never met Maya Tiwari—and neither can I claim to have gone deep into the path of practice myself—she is a teacher to me. Thus Brahmacharini Sandhya is a fictional tribute to her (though, obviously, in a very flawed and limited way) and is inspired by her life and teachings in the hope that others might derive the comfort I have received from her philosophies.

Dr Robert Svoboda's *Prakriti* (Motilal Banarassidas, 2010) and Dr Christiane Northrup's *Women's Bodies, Women's Wisdom* (Hachette, 2008)—two outstanding books that provide a deep understanding of healing from within; since Dr Svoboda and

Dr Northrup both began their careers as hard-core practitioners of Western medicine, their books set out the terms of a comparative framework with a great deal of insight.

B. K. S. Iyengar's classic *Light on the Yoga Sutras of Patanjali* (Thorsons, 2002).

Prof. H. S. Shivaprakash, my teacher, who is both a scholarly mystic and a mystical scholar, and his soon-to-be-published spiritual memoirs, *Everyday Yogi* (HarperCollins India, forthcoming), from which, particularly, I have learnt about messages from the cosmos that come coded in our dreams.

Various family members who were badgered for information. In proportional order of hours that they suffered badgering: Sukumar Jha, my father-in-law, whose years in London corresponded to Sandhya's early years, and who was often forced to recall King's Street, Carnaby Street or Tilbury Docks in great detail at odd hours; Mummy, who is quite the repository of information on shraddh and Durga puja rituals; my brand new sister-in-law, Dr Saumya Srivastav, gynaecologist, for being always available to incessant stalking and her excellent anecdotes on women's health; her husband, Dr Tirthajit Maitra, who supplied all details of Alprazolam poisoning and its consequences, after ensuring that it was not I who was experimenting with said drug; Manaspratim Mitra, who helped research the workings of IT companies; Amrita Mukherjee, army wife, for badgering on my behalf her husband, my brother-in-law the Colonel, for exact information on army hierarchies—presumptions on the relaxation of army protocol are, of course, my own; Indrayudh Banerjee, who acquired the 'Dr' before his name even as the book was being written, for not only information on medical matters but also on organizing fests in Calcutta; Subit Chakraborty, who supplied fascinating maths problems for said fest, though the event was finally scrapped.

Arati Rai Chaudhuri, who has courageously battled cancer twice and shared her experiences with such humour and good spirit.

Dipanjan Rai Chaudhuri, for this and that.

ACKNOWLEDGEMENTS

Gitanjali Chatterjee, first reader, best friend and co-seeker in the healing project. She indulged my severe moods and the odd hours I kept in the final fifteen days in Gorakhpur, when the characters of Nancy decided to resolve their lives somewhat.

Eugenia Bleta, who often generously provided both food and food-for-thought in Paris, where much of this book was written.

The few people in whose presence I can always feel grown-up, extremely responsible and un-vague, whose love is sightless and unjudging (in chronological order of their worldly years): Meenakshi and Saksham Jha, Juhi Banerjee, Joey Mukherjee, Nayantara and Abhishek Chatterjee.

My parents, Nilanjan and Manidipa Roy, my father-in-law Sukumar Jha, and my uncle, Susnato Roy, who have mastered the art of stepping back to allow us to lead eccentric lives—it is a great gift.

Our gigantic, exciting clan of loving family and tolerant friends (you know who you are), who will obviously have to buy the book.

My editor, Pradipta Sarkar, owner of the original knotty gamchha dress—who, come to think of it, probably sent Monalisa Das to my room in the first place. Don't ask how. She has her wicked bag of tricks.

And, naturally, Saurav Jha. The reason I can flaunt (a few) geeky defence titbits. The reason I write.

Made in the USA
Monee, IL
03 May 2026

49438837R00177